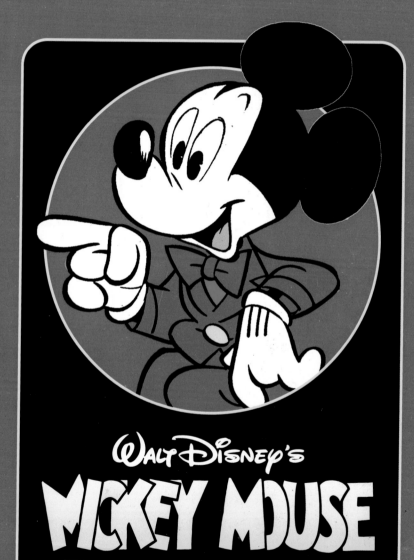

Walt Disney's

MICKEY MOUSE

The Mysterious Crystal Ball

The Mysterious Crystal Ball
Writer: Carl Fallberg
Artist & Letterer: Paul Murry
Colorist: Digikore Studios with Travis and Nicole Seitler

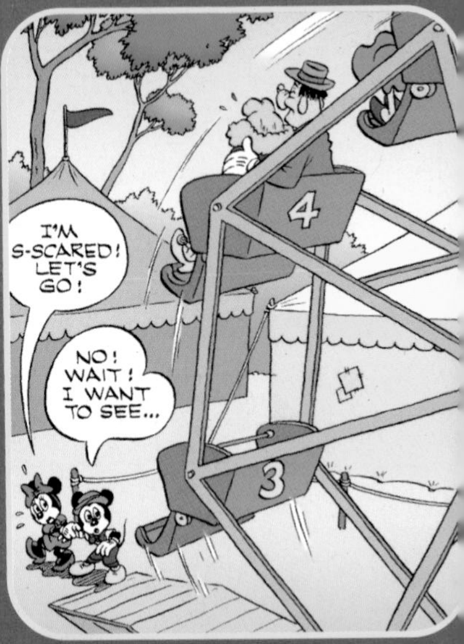
I'M S-SCARED! LET'S GO!
NO! WAIT! I WANT TO SEE...
4
3

Introducing Ellsworth
Writer: Bill Walsh
Artist & Letterer: Manuel Gonzales
Colorist: Digikore Studios

Polly Coddled
Writer: Bill Walsh
Artist & Letterer: Manuel Gonzales
Colorist: Digikore Studios

The Great Escape
Writer: Bill Walsh
Artist & Letterer: Manuel Gonzales
Colorist: Digikore Studios

The Lost Explorers' Trail
Writer: Andrea "Casty" Castellan
Artist: Giorgio Cavazzano
Colorist: Disney Italia with Tom B. Long
Letterer: Tom B. Long
Translation and Dialogue: Jonathan H. Gray

What's Cookin'?
Writer: Bill Walsh
Artist & Letterer: Manuel Gonzales
Colorist: Digikore Studios

Special thanks to Curt Baker, Julie Dorris, Manny Mederos, Beatrice Osman, Roberto Santillo, Camilla Vedove, Stefano Ambrosio, Carlotta Quattrocolo, and Thomas Jensen.

ISBN: 978-1-63140-445-0

18 17 16 15 1 2 3

IDW®
www.IDWPUBLISHING.com
IDW founded by Ted Adams, Alex Garner, Kris Oprisko, and Robbie Robbins

Ted Adams, CEO & Publisher
Greg Goldstein, President & COO
Robbie Robbins, EVP/Sr. Graphic Artist
Chris Ryall, Chief Creative Officer/Editor-in-Chief
Matthew Ruzicka, CPA, Chief Financial Officer
Alan Payne, VP of Sales
Dirk Wood, VP of Marketing
Lorelei Bunjes, VP of Digital Services
Jeff Webber, VP of Digital Publishing & Business Development

Facebook: **facebook.com/idwpublishing**
Twitter: **@idwpublishing**
YouTube: **youtube.com/idwpublishing**
Tumblr: **tumblr.idwpublishing.com**
Instagram: **instagram.com/idwpublishing**

Originally published as MICKEY MOUSE issues #1–3 (Legacy #310–312).

Reform and Void
Writer: Colette Bezio
Artist & Letterer: Rick Hoover
Colorist: Digikore Studios

Mynah Madness
Writer: Bill Walsh
Artist & Letterer: Manuel Gonzales
Colorist: Digikore Studios

The Sound-Blot Plot
Writer: Bruno Enna
Artist: Giorgio Cavazzano
Inker: Sandro Zemolin
Colorist: Disney Italia with Tom B. Long
Letterer: Tom B. Long
Translation: David Gerstein
Dialogue: Joe Torcivia

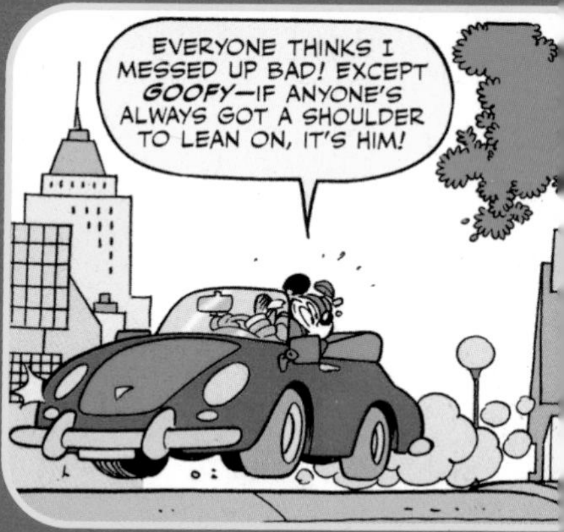
EVERYONE THINKS I MESSED UP BAD! EXCEPT GOOFY—IF ANYONE'S ALWAYS GOT A SHOULDER TO LEAN ON, IT'S HIM!

The W'angler
Writer, Artist, & Letterer: Wilfred Haughton
Colorist: Digikore Studios

Caws and Effect
Writer: Don R. Christensen
Artist & Letterer: Paul Murry
Colorist: Digikore Studios

The Lawnatic
Writer, Artist, & Letterer: Wilfred Haughton
Colorist: Digikore Studios

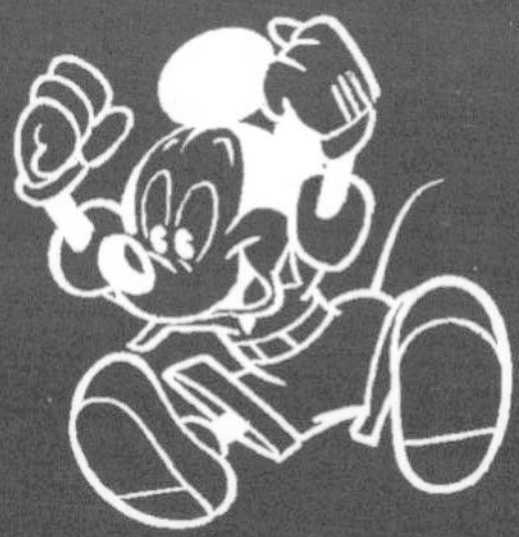

Series Editor: Sarah Gaydos
Archival Editor: David Gerstein

Cover Artists: Jonathan Gray (Pencils)
& Jonathan Griffiths (Inks)
Cover Colorist: Thom Pratt
Collection Editors: Justin Eisinger
& Alonzo Simon
Collection Designer: Clyde Grapa

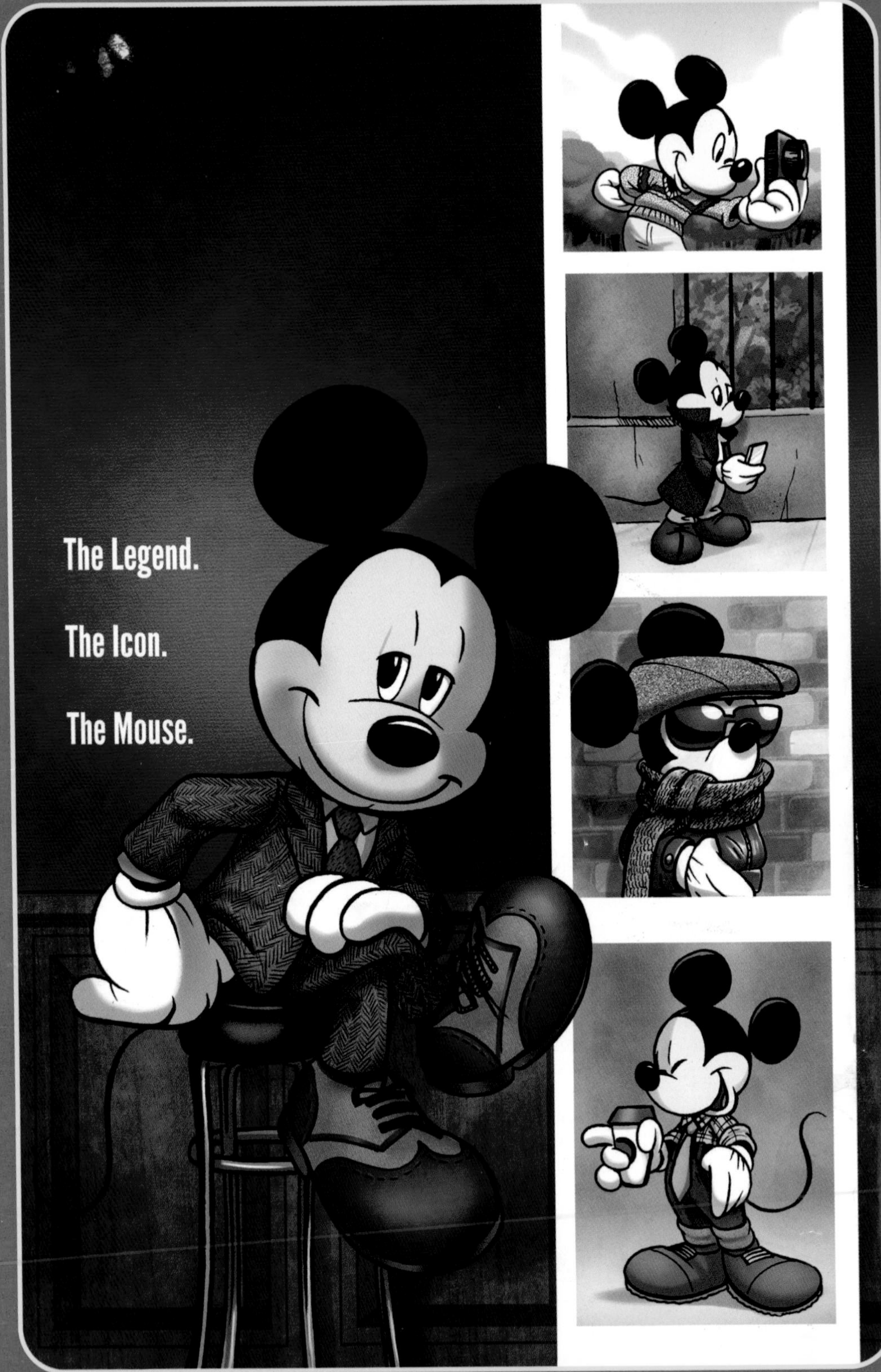
The Legend.
The Icon.
The Mouse.

Art by Amy Mebberson

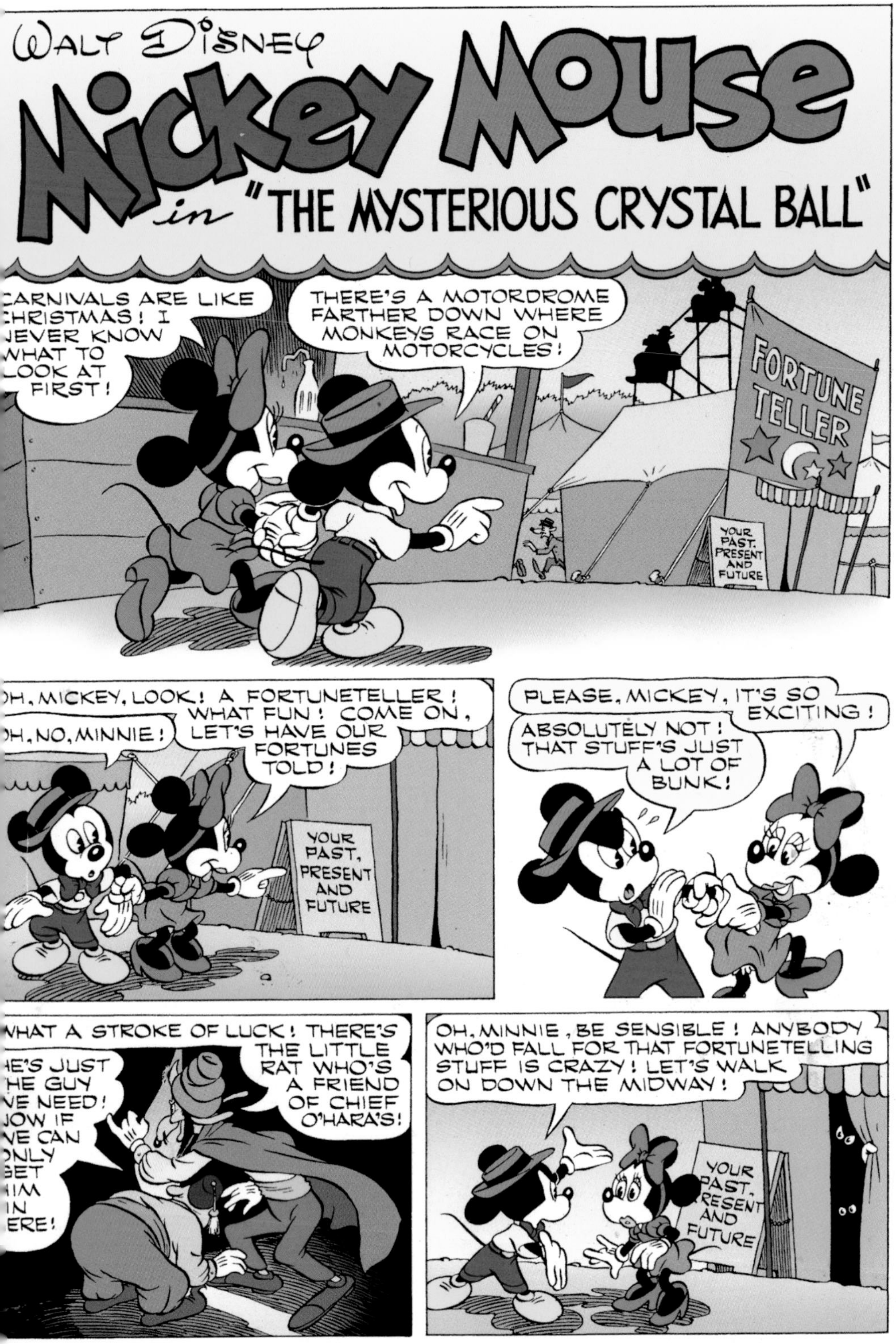
WALT DISNEY
Mickey Mouse
in "THE MYSTERIOUS CRYSTAL BALL"
CARNIVALS ARE LIKE CHRISTMAS! I NEVER KNOW WHAT TO LOOK AT FIRST!
THERE'S A MOTORDROME FARTHER DOWN WHERE MONKEYS RACE ON MOTORCYCLES!
FORTUNE TELLER
YOUR PAST, PRESENT AND FUTURE
OH, MICKEY, LOOK! A FORTUNETELLER! WHAT FUN! COME ON, LET'S HAVE OUR FORTUNES TOLD!
OH, NO, MINNIE!
YOUR PAST, PRESENT AND FUTURE
PLEASE, MICKEY, IT'S SO EXCITING!
ABSOLUTELY NOT! THAT STUFF'S JUST A LOT OF BUNK!
WHAT A STROKE OF LUCK! THERE'S THE LITTLE RAT WHO'S A FRIEND OF CHIEF O'HARA'S!
HE'S JUST THE GUY WE NEED! NOW IF WE CAN ONLY GET HIM IN HERE!
OH, MINNIE, BE SENSIBLE! ANYBODY WHO'D FALL FOR THAT FORTUNETELLING STUFF IS CRAZY! LET'S WALK ON DOWN THE MIDWAY!
YOUR PAST, PRESENT AND FUTURE

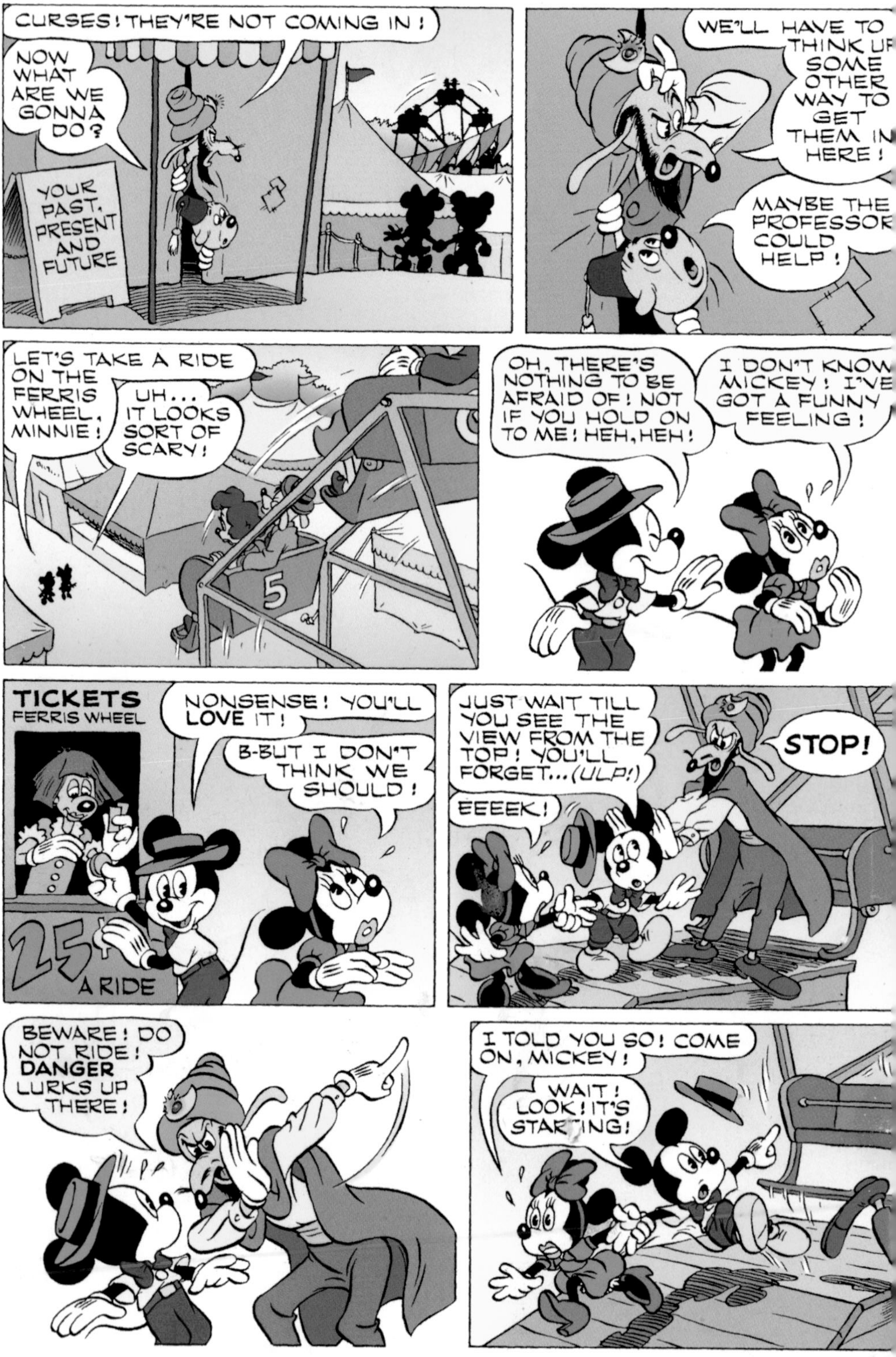
CURSES! THEY'RE NOT COMING IN!
NOW WHAT ARE WE GONNA DO?
YOUR PAST, PRESENT AND FUTURE
WE'LL HAVE TO THINK UP SOME OTHER WAY TO GET THEM IN HERE!
MAYBE THE PROFESSOR COULD HELP!
LET'S TAKE A RIDE ON THE FERRIS WHEEL, MINNIE!
UH... IT LOOKS SORT OF SCARY!
5
OH, THERE'S NOTHING TO BE AFRAID OF! NOT IF YOU HOLD ON TO ME! HEH, HEH!
I DON'T KNOW MICKEY! I'VE GOT A FUNNY FEELING!
TICKETS FERRIS WHEEL
25¢ A RIDE
NONSENSE! YOU'LL LOVE IT!
B-BUT I DON'T THINK WE SHOULD!
JUST WAIT TILL YOU SEE THE VIEW FROM THE TOP! YOU'LL FORGET...(ULP!)
STOP!
EEEEK!
BEWARE! DO NOT RIDE! DANGER LURKS UP THERE!
I TOLD YOU SO! COME ON, MICKEY!
WAIT! LOOK! IT'S STARTING!

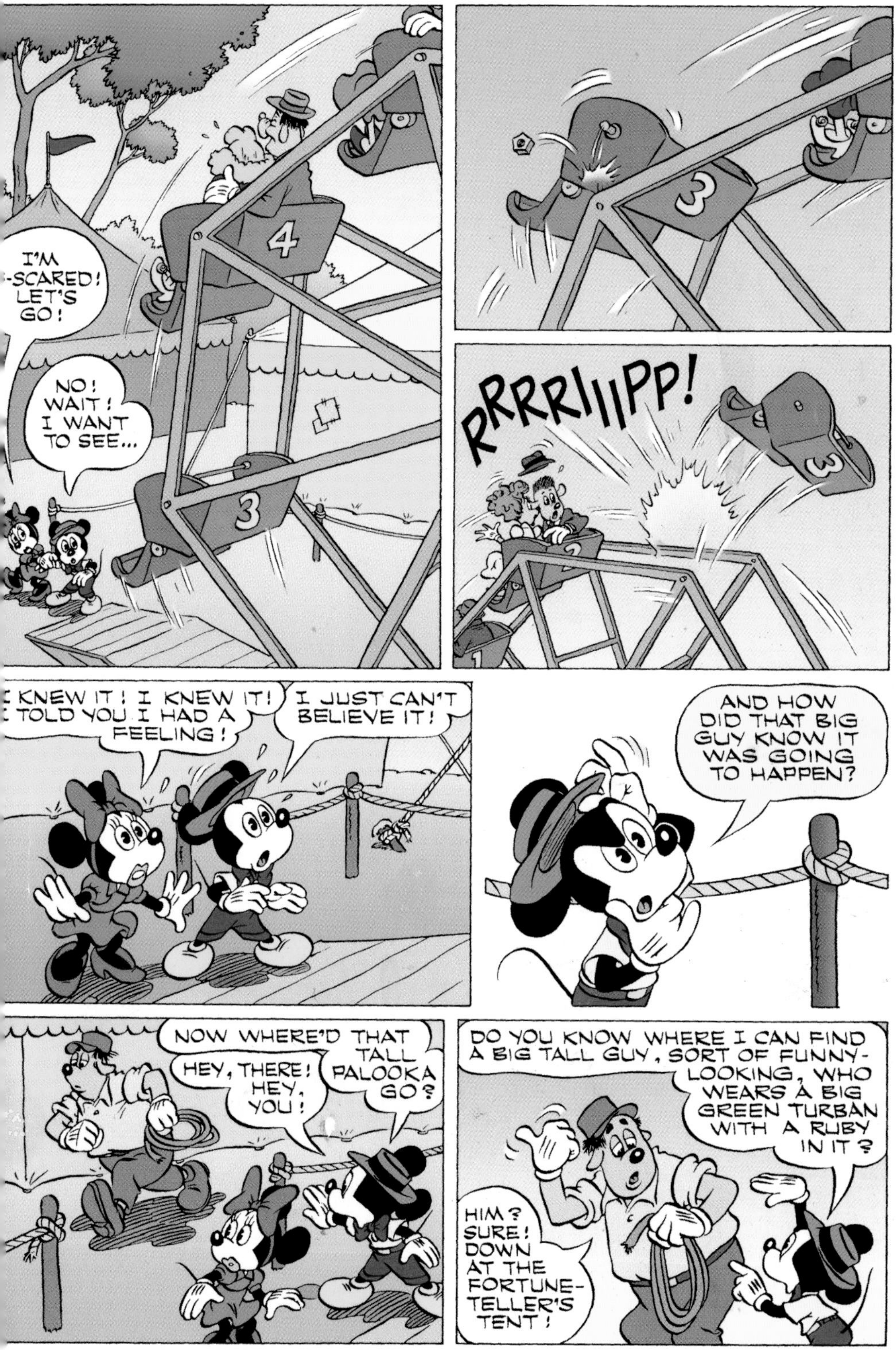

I'M -SCARED! LET'S GO!
NO! WAIT! I WANT TO SEE...
RRRRIIIPP!
KNEW IT! I KNEW IT! TOLD YOU I HAD A FEELING!
I JUST CAN'T BELIEVE IT!
AND HOW DID THAT BIG GUY KNOW IT WAS GOING TO HAPPEN?
NOW WHERE'D THAT TALL PALOOKA GO?
HEY, THERE! HEY, YOU!
DO YOU KNOW WHERE I CAN FIND A BIG TALL GUY, SORT OF FUNNY-LOOKING, WHO WEARS A BIG GREEN TURBAN WITH A RUBY IN IT?
HIM? SURE! DOWN AT THE FORTUNE-TELLER'S TENT!

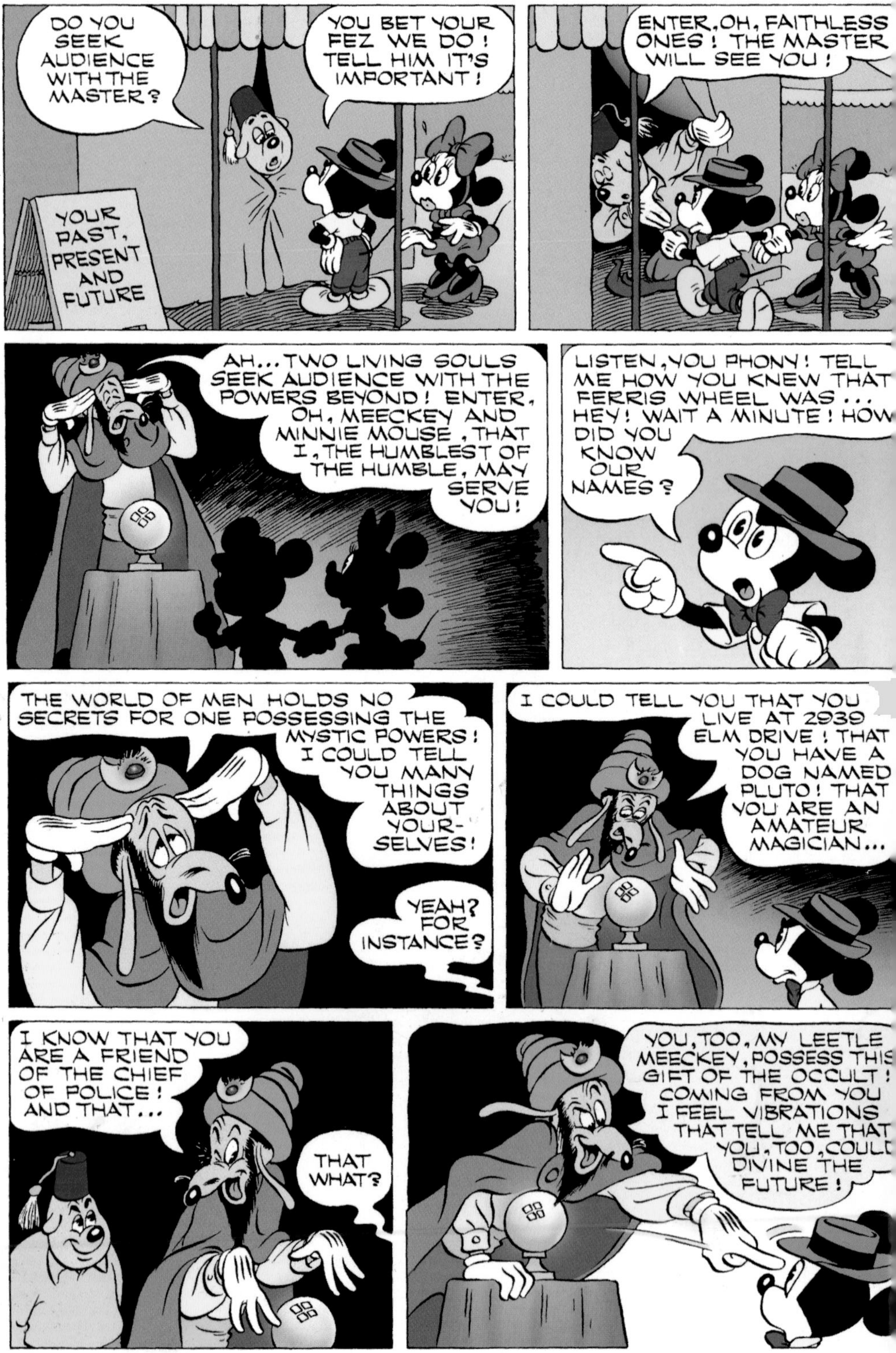
DO YOU SEEK AUDIENCE WITH THE MASTER?
YOU BET YOUR FEZ WE DO! TELL HIM IT'S IMPORTANT!
YOUR PAST, PRESENT AND FUTURE
ENTER, OH, FAITHLESS ONES! THE MASTER WILL SEE YOU!
AH... TWO LIVING SOULS SEEK AUDIENCE WITH THE POWERS BEYOND! ENTER, OH, MEECKEY AND MINNIE MOUSE, THAT I, THE HUMBLEST OF THE HUMBLE, MAY SERVE YOU!
LISTEN, YOU PHONY! TELL ME HOW YOU KNEW THAT FERRIS WHEEL WAS... HEY! WAIT A MINUTE! HOW DID YOU KNOW OUR NAMES?
THE WORLD OF MEN HOLDS NO SECRETS FOR ONE POSSESSING THE MYSTIC POWERS! I COULD TELL YOU MANY THINGS ABOUT YOURSELVES!
YEAH? FOR INSTANCE?
I COULD TELL YOU THAT YOU LIVE AT 2939 ELM DRIVE! THAT YOU HAVE A DOG NAMED PLUTO! THAT YOU ARE AN AMATEUR MAGICIAN...
I KNOW THAT YOU ARE A FRIEND OF THE CHIEF OF POLICE! AND THAT...
THAT WHAT?
YOU, TOO, MY LEETLE MEECKEY, POSSESS THIS GIFT OF THE OCCULT! COMING FROM YOU I FEEL VIBRATIONS THAT TELL ME THAT YOU, TOO, COULD DIVINE THE FUTURE!

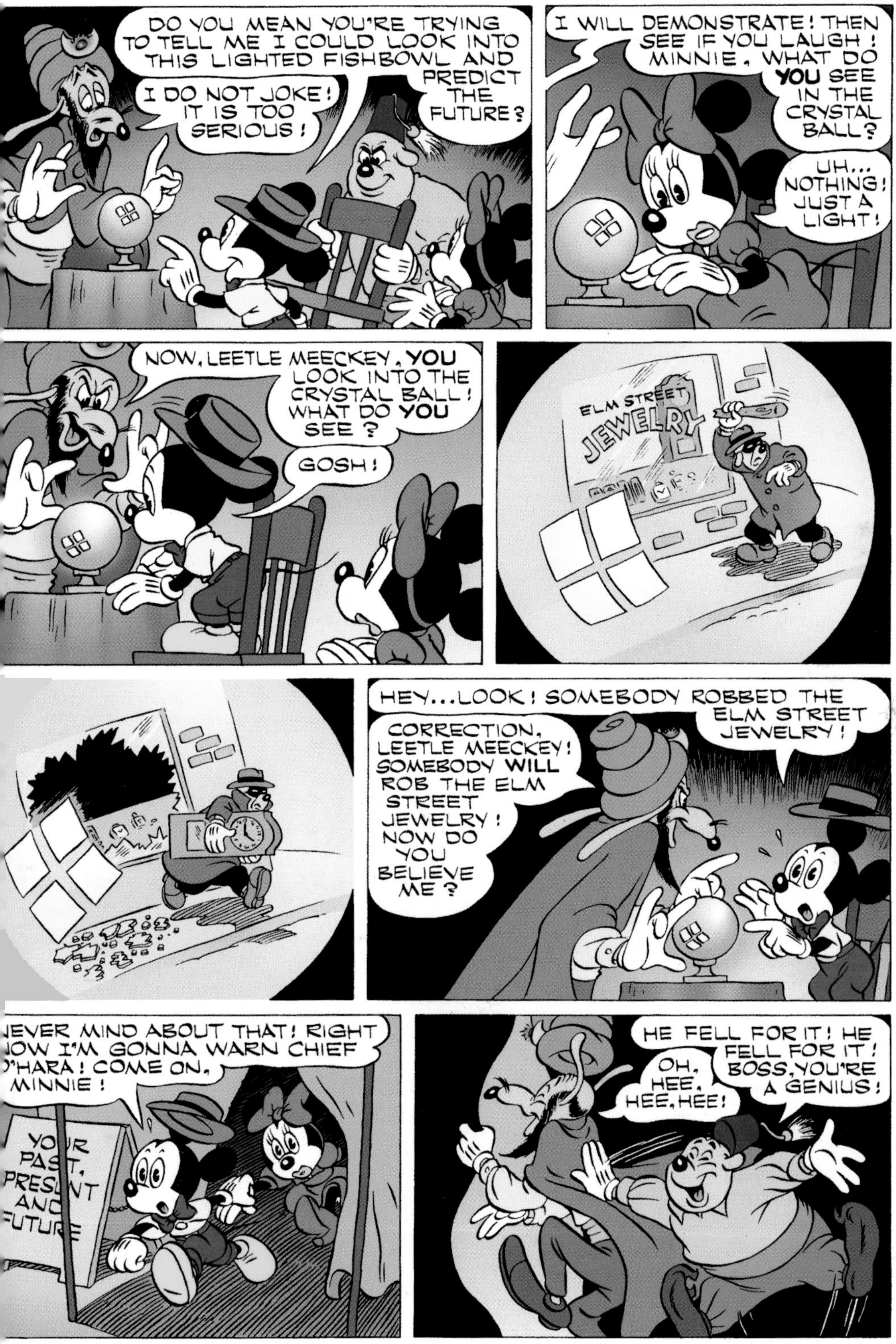
DO YOU MEAN YOU'RE TRYING TO TELL ME I COULD LOOK INTO THIS LIGHTED FISHBOWL AND PREDICT THE FUTURE?
I DO NOT JOKE! IT IS TOO SERIOUS!
I WILL DEMONSTRATE! THEN SEE IF YOU LAUGH! MINNIE, WHAT DO YOU SEE IN THE CRYSTAL BALL?
UH... NOTHING! JUST A LIGHT!
NOW, LEETLE MEECKEY, YOU LOOK INTO THE CRYSTAL BALL! WHAT DO YOU SEE?
GOSH!
ELM STREET
JEWELRY
HEY...LOOK! SOMEBODY ROBBED THE ELM STREET JEWELRY!
CORRECTION, LEETLE MEECKEY! SOMEBODY WILL ROB THE ELM STREET JEWELRY! NOW DO YOU BELIEVE ME?
NEVER MIND ABOUT THAT! RIGHT NOW I'M GONNA WARN CHIEF O'HARA! COME ON, MINNIE!
YOUR PAST, PRESENT AND FUTURE
HE FELL FOR IT! HE FELL FOR IT! BOSS, YOU'RE A GENIUS!
OH, HEE, HEE, HEE!

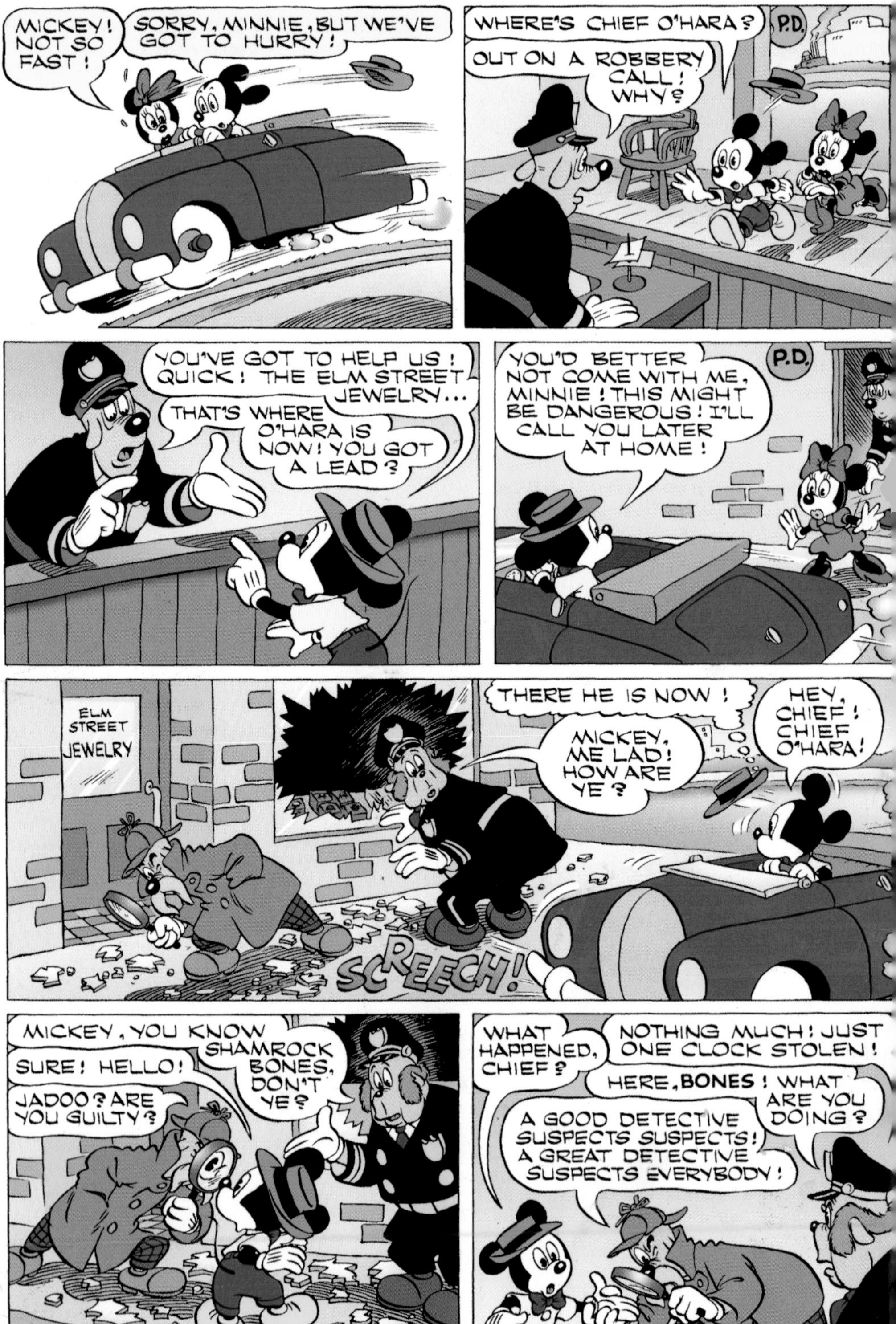
MICKEY! NOT SO FAST!
SORRY, MINNIE, BUT WE'VE GOT TO HURRY!
WHERE'S CHIEF O'HARA?
P.D.
OUT ON A ROBBERY CALL! WHY?
YOU'VE GOT TO HELP US! QUICK! THE ELM STREET JEWELRY...
THAT'S WHERE O'HARA IS NOW! YOU GOT A LEAD?
YOU'D BETTER NOT COME WITH ME, MINNIE! THIS MIGHT BE DANGEROUS! I'LL CALL YOU LATER AT HOME!
P.D.
ELM STREET JEWELRY
THERE HE IS NOW!
HEY, CHIEF! CHIEF O'HARA!
MICKEY, ME LAD! HOW ARE YE?
SCREECH!
MICKEY, YOU KNOW SHAMROCK BONES, DON'T YE?
SURE! HELLO!
JADOO? ARE YOU GUILTY?
WHAT HAPPENED, CHIEF?
NOTHING MUCH! JUST ONE CLOCK STOLEN!
HERE, BONES! WHAT ARE YOU DOING?
A GOOD DETECTIVE SUSPECTS SUSPECTS! A GREAT DETECTIVE SUSPECTS EVERYBODY!

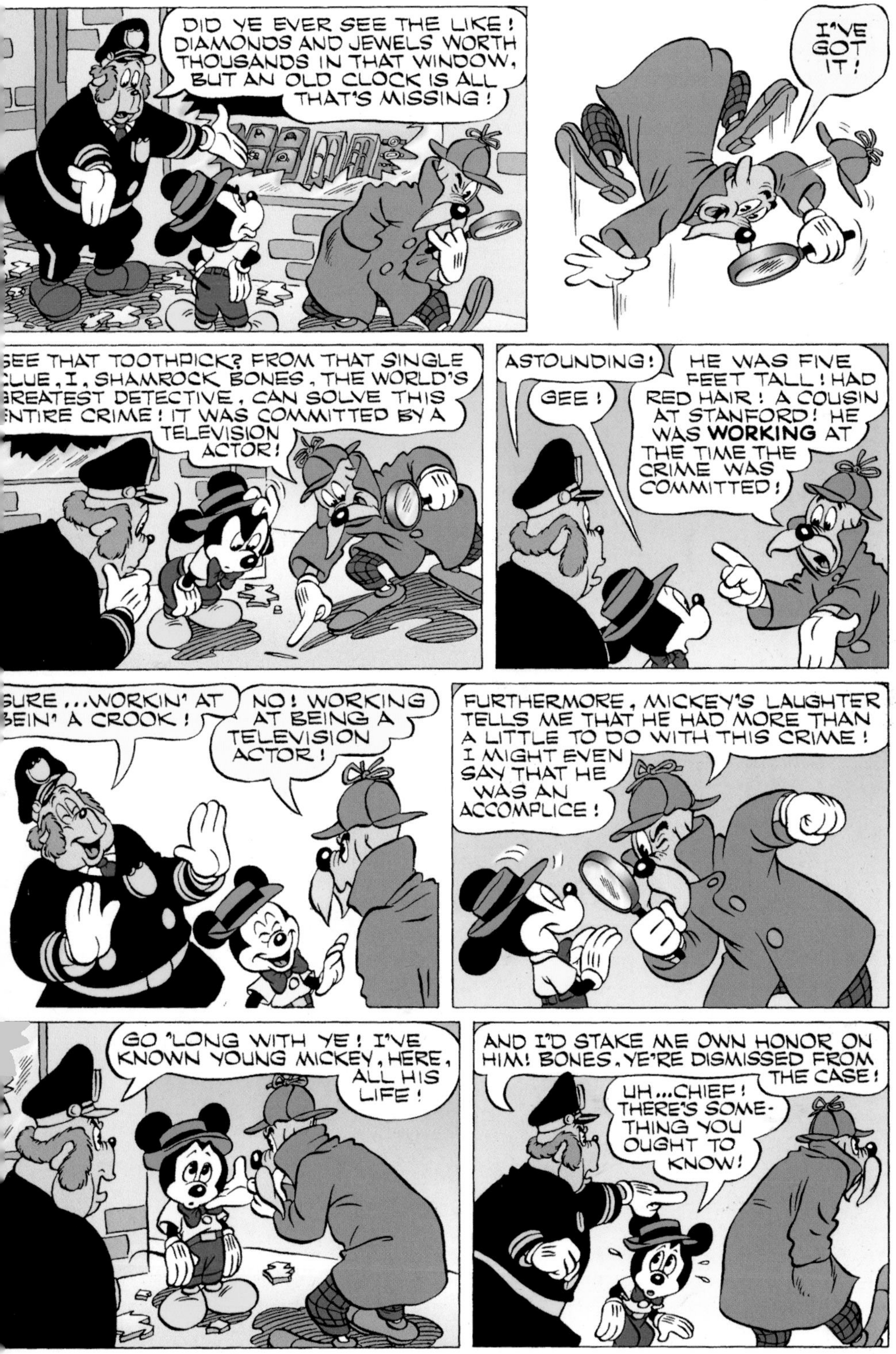
DID YE EVER SEE THE LIKE! DIAMONDS AND JEWELS WORTH THOUSANDS IN THAT WINDOW, BUT AN OLD CLOCK IS ALL THAT'S MISSING!
I'VE GOT IT!
SEE THAT TOOTHPICK? FROM THAT SINGLE CLUE, I, SHAMROCK BONES, THE WORLD'S GREATEST DETECTIVE, CAN SOLVE THIS ENTIRE CRIME! IT WAS COMMITTED BY A TELEVISION ACTOR!
ASTOUNDING!
GEE!
HE WAS FIVE FEET TALL! HAD RED HAIR! A COUSIN AT STANFORD! HE WAS WORKING AT THE TIME THE CRIME WAS COMMITTED!
SURE...WORKIN' AT BEIN' A CROOK!
NO! WORKING AT BEING A TELEVISION ACTOR!
FURTHERMORE, MICKEY'S LAUGHTER TELLS ME THAT HE HAD MORE THAN A LITTLE TO DO WITH THIS CRIME! I MIGHT EVEN SAY THAT HE WAS AN ACCOMPLICE!
GO 'LONG WITH YE! I'VE KNOWN YOUNG MICKEY, HERE, ALL HIS LIFE!
AND I'D STAKE ME OWN HONOR ON HIM! BONES, YE'RE DISMISSED FROM THE CASE!
UH...CHIEF! THERE'S SOMETHING YOU OUGHT TO KNOW!

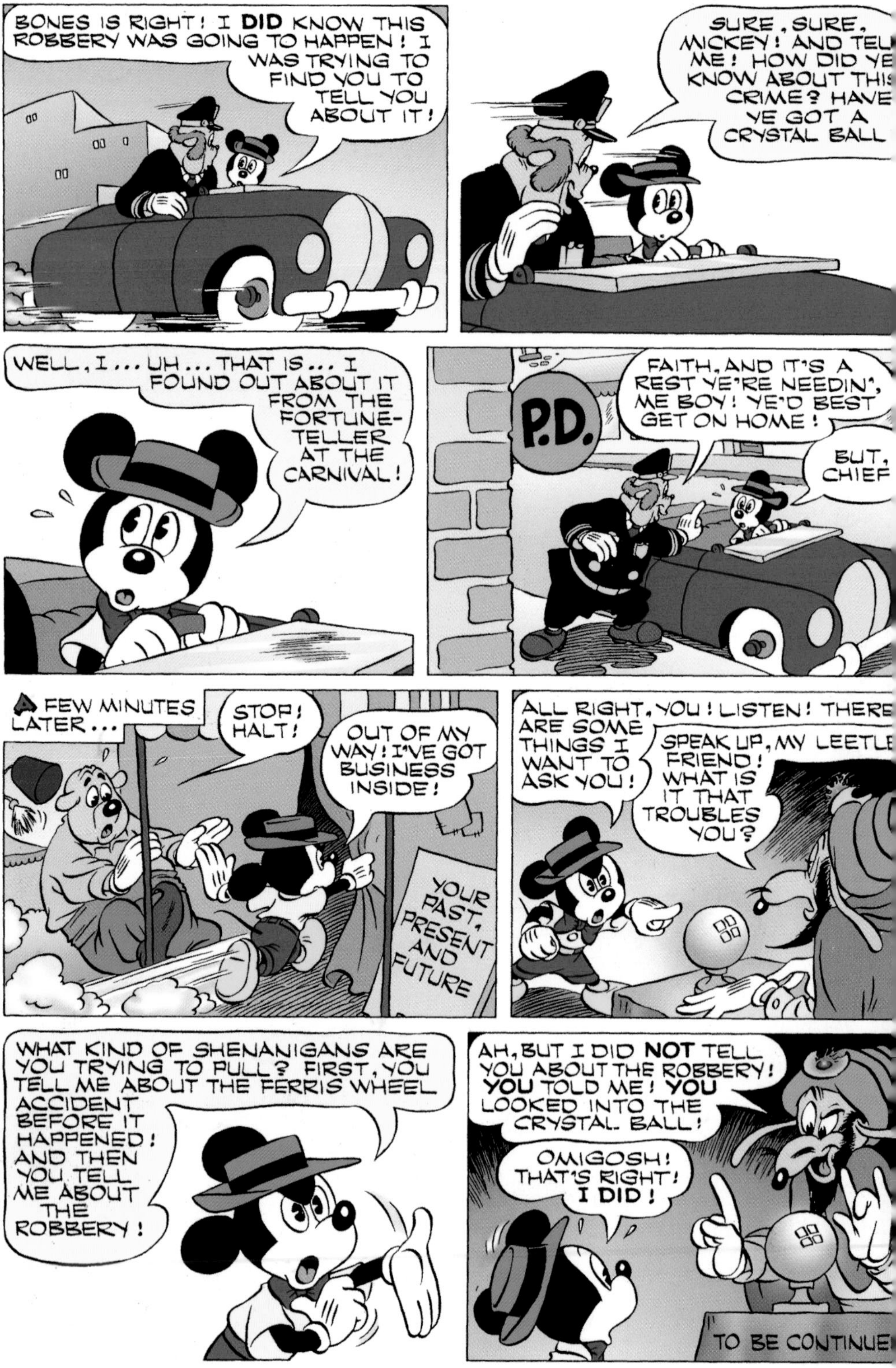
BONES IS RIGHT! I DID KNOW THIS ROBBERY WAS GOING TO HAPPEN! I WAS TRYING TO FIND YOU TO TELL YOU ABOUT IT!
SURE, SURE, MICKEY! AND TEL ME! HOW DID YE KNOW ABOUT THI CRIME? HAVE YE GOT A CRYSTAL BALL
WELL, I ... UH ... THAT IS ... I FOUND OUT ABOUT IT FROM THE FORTUNE-TELLER AT THE CARNIVAL!
P.D.
FAITH, AND IT'S A REST YE'RE NEEDIN', ME BOY! YE'D BEST GET ON HOME!
BUT, CHIEF
A FEW MINUTES LATER...
STOP! HALT!
OUT OF MY WAY! I'VE GOT BUSINESS INSIDE!
YOUR PAST, PRESENT AND FUTURE
ALL RIGHT, YOU! LISTEN! THERE ARE SOME THINGS I WANT TO ASK YOU!
SPEAK UP, MY LEETL FRIEND! WHAT IS IT THAT TROUBLES YOU?
WHAT KIND OF SHENANIGANS ARE YOU TRYING TO PULL? FIRST, YOU TELL ME ABOUT THE FERRIS WHEEL ACCIDENT BEFORE IT HAPPENED! AND THEN YOU TELL ME ABOUT THE ROBBERY!
AH, BUT I DID NOT TELL YOU ABOUT THE ROBBERY! YOU TOLD ME! YOU LOOKED INTO THE CRYSTAL BALL!
OMIGOSH! THAT'S RIGHT! I DID!
TO BE CONTINUE

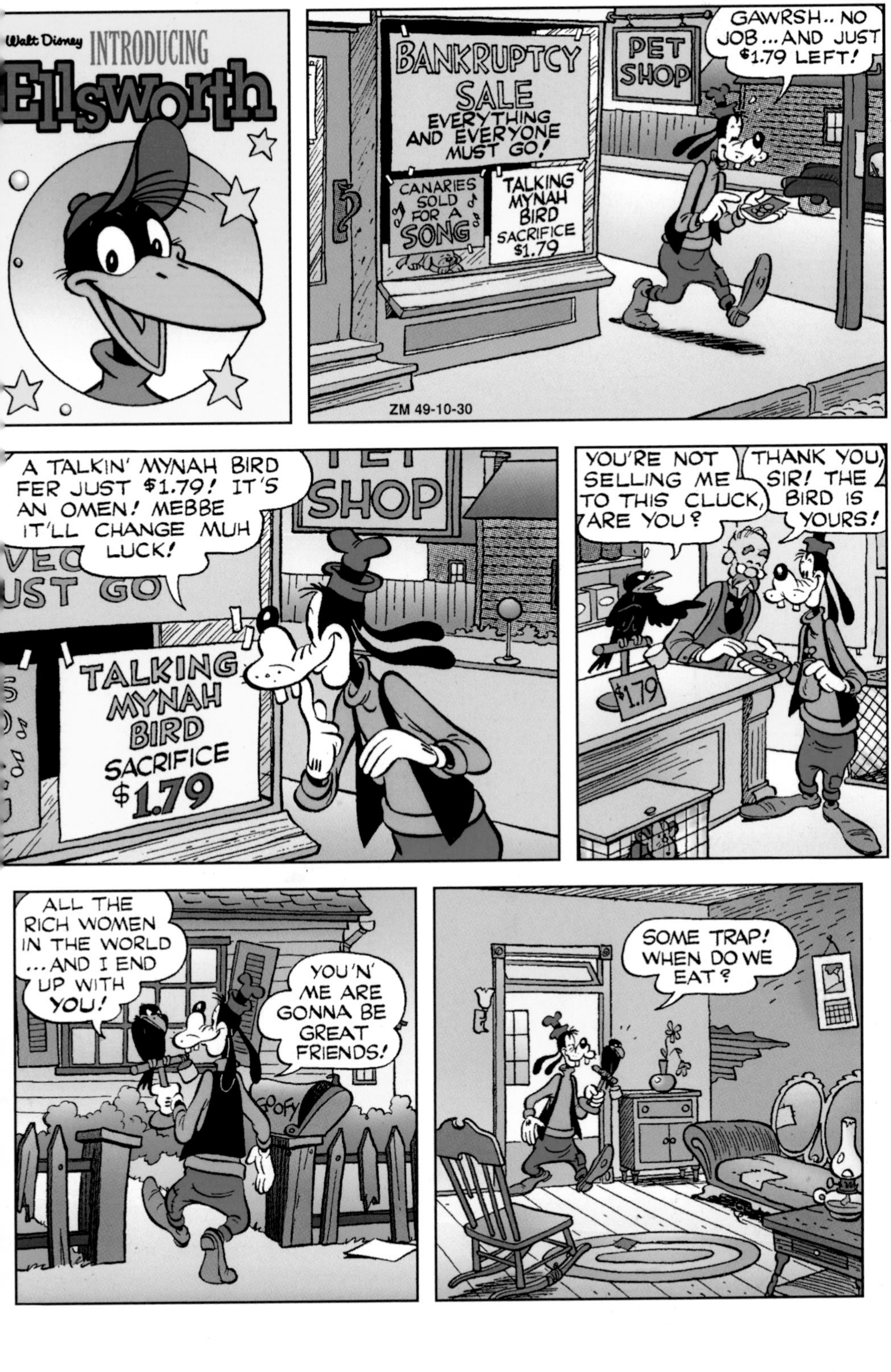
Walt Disney INTRODUCING
Ellsworth
BANKRUPTCY SALE EVERYTHING AND EVERYONE MUST GO!
CANARIES SOLD FOR A SONG
TALKING MYNAH BIRD SACRIFICE $1.79
PET SHOP
GAWRSH.. NO JOB... AND JUST $1.79 LEFT!
ZM 49-10-30
A TALKIN' MYNAH BIRD FER JUST $1.79! IT'S AN OMEN! MEBBE IT'LL CHANGE MUH LUCK!
SHOP
TALKING MYNAH BIRD SACRIFICE $1.79
YOU'RE NOT SELLING ME TO THIS CLUCK, ARE YOU?
THANK YOU, SIR! THE BIRD IS YOURS!
$1.79
ALL THE RICH WOMEN IN THE WORLD ...AND I END UP WITH YOU!
YOU'N' ME ARE GONNA BE GREAT FRIENDS!
GOOFY
SOME TRAP! WHEN DO WE EAT?

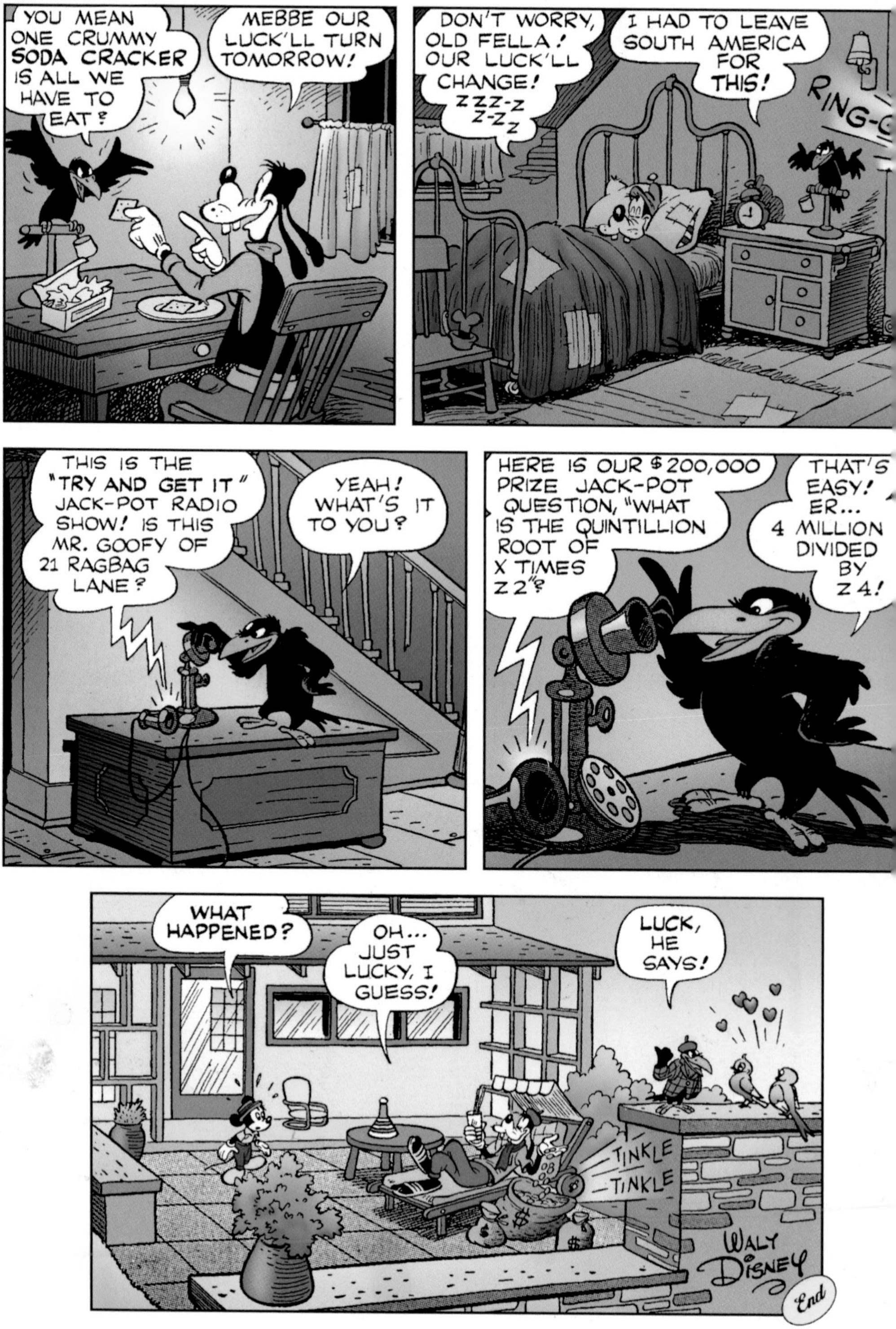
YOU MEAN ONE CRUMMY SODA CRACKER IS ALL WE HAVE TO EAT?
MEBBE OUR LUCK'LL TURN TOMORROW!
DON'T WORRY, OLD FELLA! OUR LUCK'LL CHANGE! ZZZ-Z Z-ZZ
I HAD TO LEAVE SOUTH AMERICA FOR THIS!
RING-G
THIS IS THE "TRY AND GET IT" JACK-POT RADIO SHOW! IS THIS MR. GOOFY OF 21 RAGBAG LANE?
YEAH! WHAT'S IT TO YOU?
HERE IS OUR $200,000 PRIZE JACK-POT QUESTION, "WHAT IS THE QUINTILLION ROOT OF X TIMES Z 2"?
THAT'S EASY! ER... 4 MILLION DIVIDED BY Z 4!
WHAT HAPPENED?
OH... JUST LUCKY, I GUESS!
LUCK, HE SAYS!
TINKLE TINKLE
WALT DISNEY
End

WALT DISNEY MICKEY MOUSE in "THE MYSTERIOUS CRYSTAL BALL"

MICKEY WOULD NOT BELIEVE IT WHEN THE FORTUNETELLER AT THE CARNIVAL TOLD HIM HE WAS CLAIRVOYANT. YET THE ROBBERY THAT MICKEY SAW IN THE CRYSTAL BALL REALLY HAPPENED! AND LIKE THE POLICE, MICKEY IS BAFFLED...

BUT SUCH A THING IS IMPOSSIBLE! IT MUST HAVE BEEN A COINCIDENCE!

NO, LEETLE MEECKEY! LET ME EXPLAIN!

BEING ABLE TO FORETELL THE FUTURE IS A STRANGE AND WONDERFUL GIFT! FEW PEOPLE HAVE IT! EVEN FEWER UNDERSTAND IT!

YET YOU AND I, AND OTHERS WHO POSSESS THIS GIFT, HAVE PERCEPTIONS FAR MORE SENSITIVE THAN THOSE OF ORDINARY PEOPLE!

IT'S LIKE CATS BEING ABLE TO SEE IN THE DARK...

"OR A DOG BEING ABLE TO HEAR SOUNDS THAT PEOPLE CANNOT HEAR!"

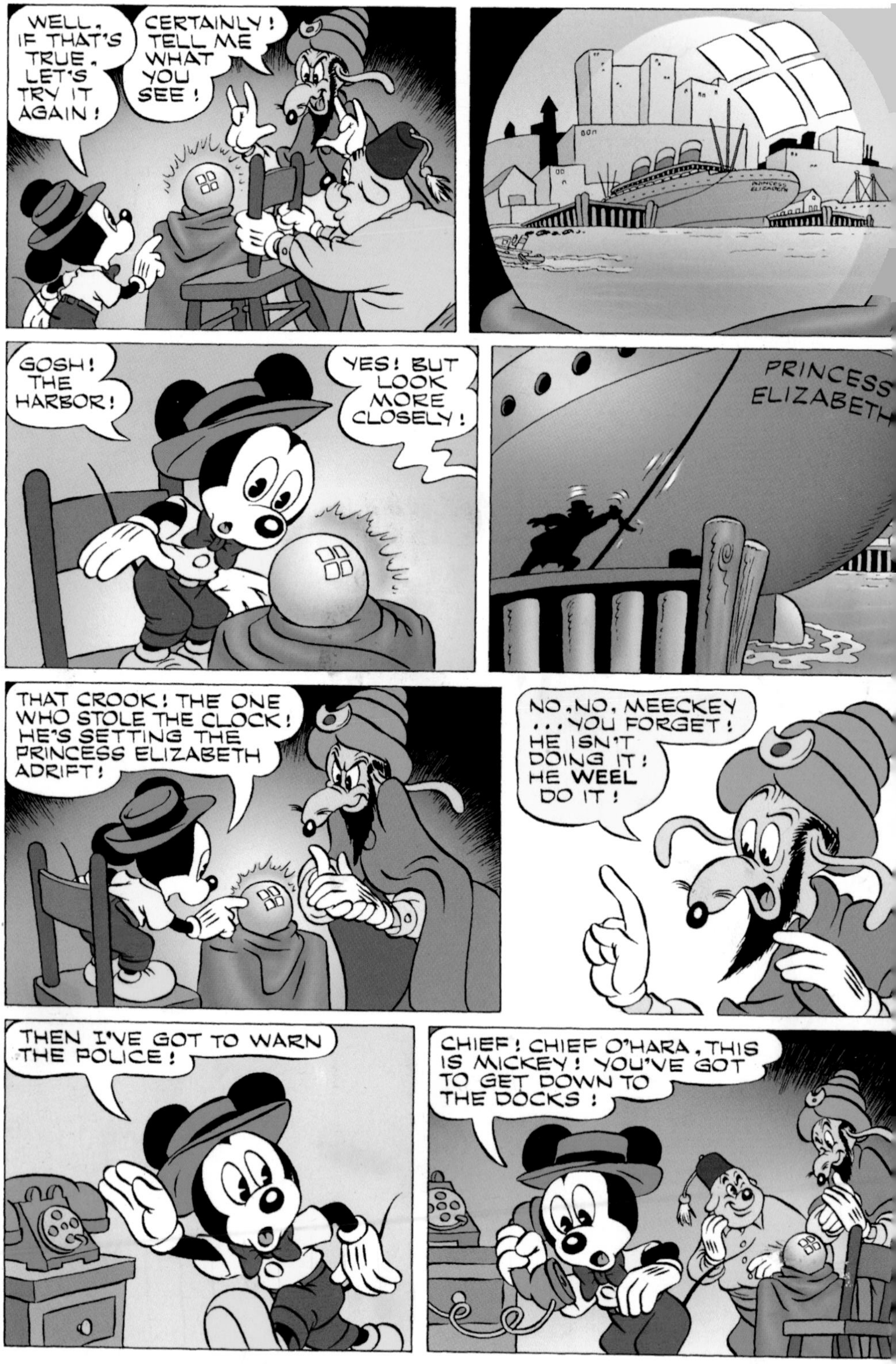
WELL, IF THAT'S TRUE, LET'S TRY IT AGAIN!
CERTAINLY! TELL ME WHAT YOU SEE!
PRINCESS ELIZABETH
GOSH! THE HARBOR!
YES! BUT LOOK MORE CLOSELY!
PRINCESS ELIZABETH
THAT CROOK! THE ONE WHO STOLE THE CLOCK! HE'S SETTING THE PRINCESS ELIZABETH ADRIFT!
NO, NO, MEECKEY ... YOU FORGET! HE ISN'T DOING IT! HE WEEL DO IT!
THEN I'VE GOT TO WARN THE POLICE!
CHIEF! CHIEF O'HARA, THIS IS MICKEY! YOU'VE GOT TO GET DOWN TO THE DOCKS!

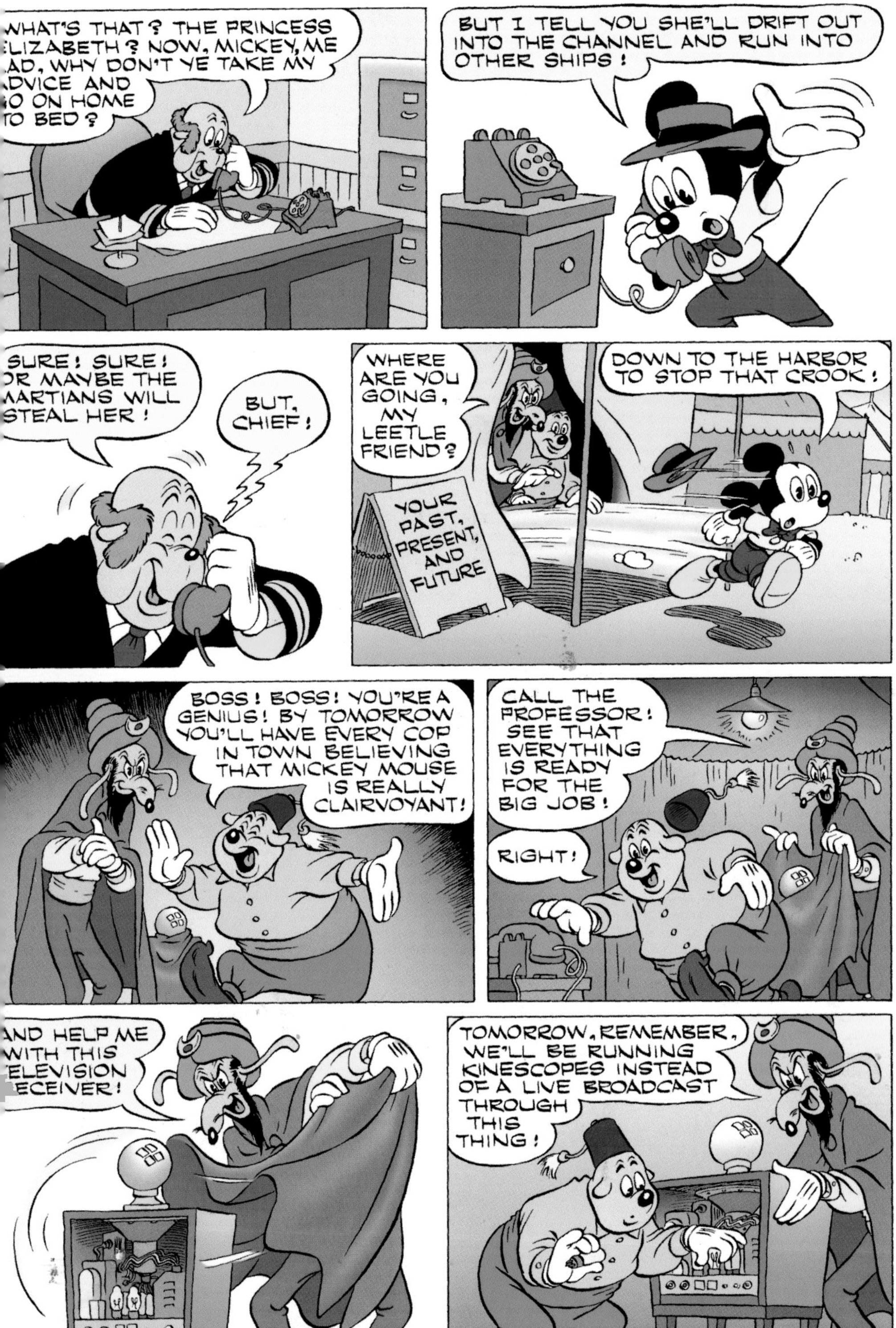
WHAT'S THAT? THE PRINCESS ELIZABETH? NOW, MICKEY, ME LAD, WHY DON'T YE TAKE MY ADVICE AND GO ON HOME TO BED?
BUT I TELL YOU SHE'LL DRIFT OUT INTO THE CHANNEL AND RUN INTO OTHER SHIPS!
SURE! SURE! OR MAYBE THE MARTIANS WILL STEAL HER!
BUT, CHIEF!
WHERE ARE YOU GOING, MY LEETLE FRIEND?
DOWN TO THE HARBOR TO STOP THAT CROOK!
YOUR PAST, PRESENT, AND FUTURE
BOSS! BOSS! YOU'RE A GENIUS! BY TOMORROW YOU'LL HAVE EVERY COP IN TOWN BELIEVING THAT MICKEY MOUSE IS REALLY CLAIRVOYANT!
CALL THE PROFESSOR! SEE THAT EVERYTHING IS READY FOR THE BIG JOB!
RIGHT!
AND HELP ME WITH THIS TELEVISION RECEIVER!
TOMORROW, REMEMBER, WE'LL BE RUNNING KINESCOPES INSTEAD OF A LIVE BROADCAST THROUGH THIS THING!

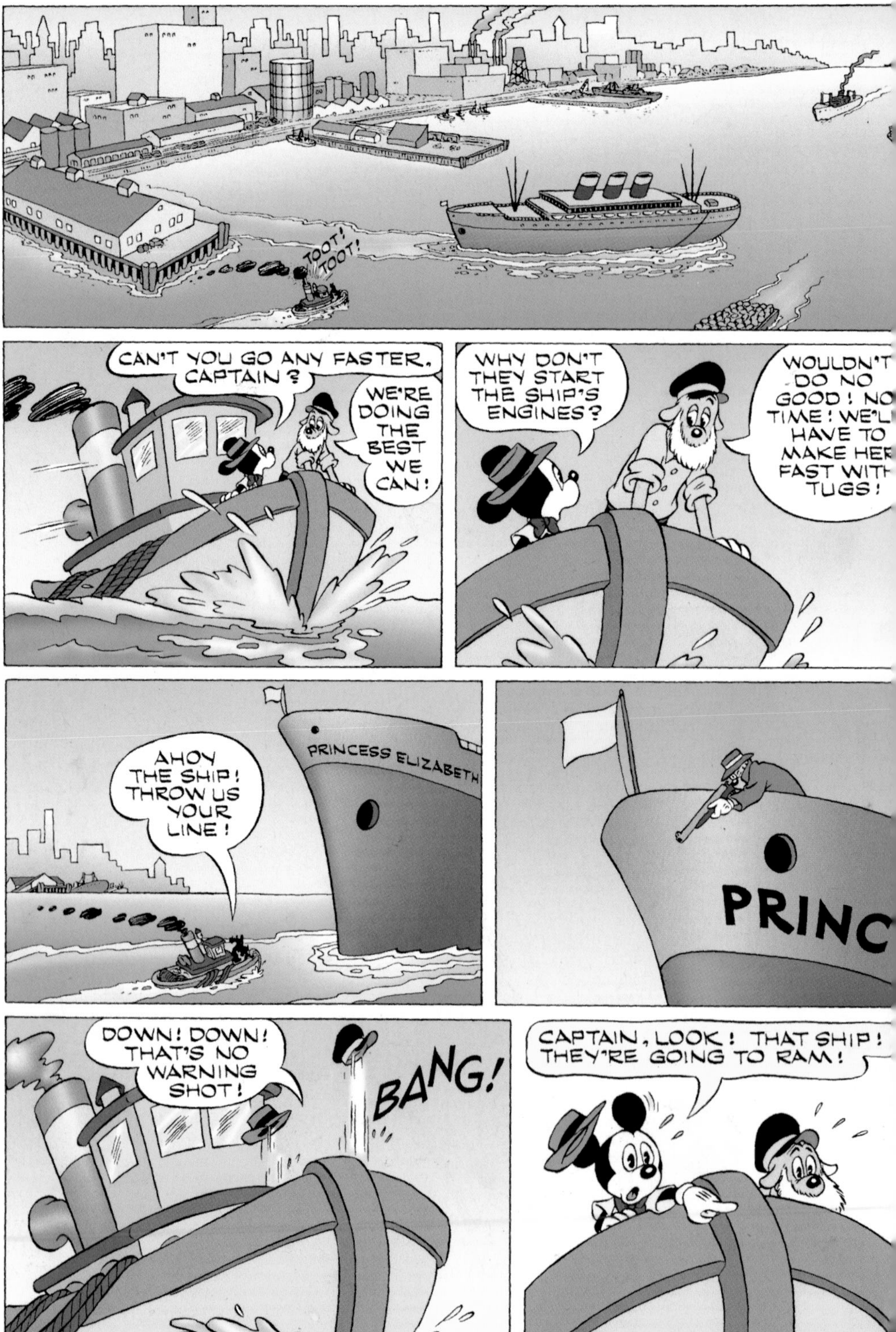
TOOT! TOOT!
CAN'T YOU GO ANY FASTER, CAPTAIN?
WE'RE DOING THE BEST WE CAN!
WHY DON'T THEY START THE SHIP'S ENGINES?
WOULDN'T DO NO GOOD! NO TIME! WE'LL HAVE TO MAKE HER FAST WITH TUGS!
PRINCESS ELIZABETH
AHOY THE SHIP! THROW US YOUR LINE!
PRINC
DOWN! DOWN! THAT'S NO WARNING SHOT!
BANG!
CAPTAIN, LOOK! THAT SHIP! THEY'RE GOING TO RAM!

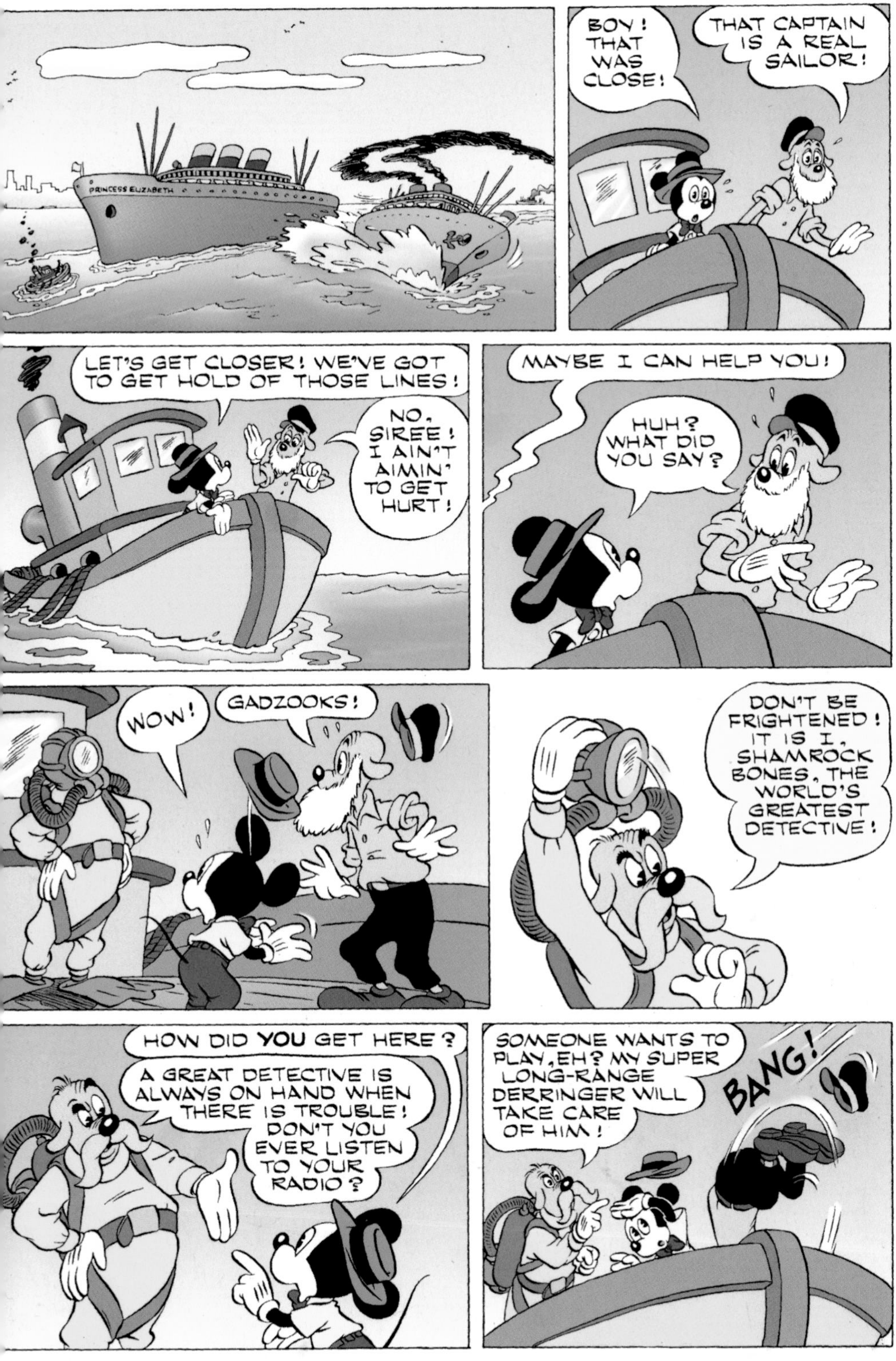
PRINCESS ELIZABETH
BOY! THAT WAS CLOSE!
THAT CAPTAIN IS A REAL SAILOR!
LET'S GET CLOSER! WE'VE GOT TO GET HOLD OF THOSE LINES!
NO, SIREE! I AIN'T AIMIN' TO GET HURT!
MAYBE I CAN HELP YOU!
HUH? WHAT DID YOU SAY?
WOW!
GADZOOKS!
DON'T BE FRIGHTENED! IT IS I, SHAMROCK BONES, THE WORLD'S GREATEST DETECTIVE!
HOW DID YOU GET HERE?
A GREAT DETECTIVE IS ALWAYS ON HAND WHEN THERE IS TROUBLE! DON'T YOU EVER LISTEN TO YOUR RADIO?
SOMEONE WANTS TO PLAY, EH? MY SUPER LONG-RANGE DERRINGER WILL TAKE CARE OF HIM!
BANG!

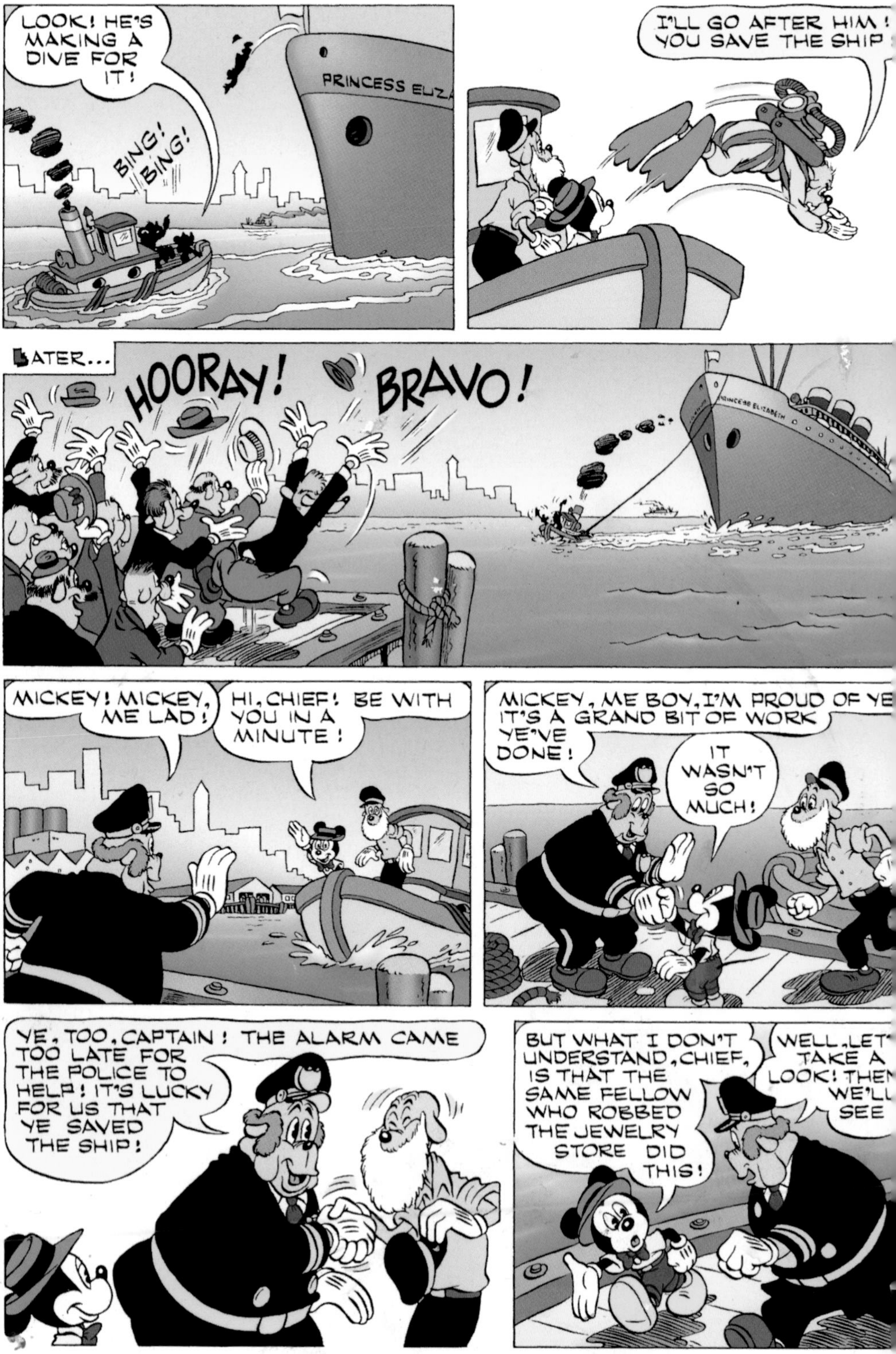

LOOK! HE'S MAKING A DIVE FOR IT!
BING! BING!
PRINCESS ELIZA
I'LL GO AFTER HIM! YOU SAVE THE SHIP
LATER...
HOORAY!
BRAVO!
MICKEY! MICKEY, ME LAD!
HI, CHIEF! BE WITH YOU IN A MINUTE!
MICKEY, ME BOY, I'M PROUD OF YE
IT'S A GRAND BIT OF WORK YE'VE DONE!
IT WASN'T SO MUCH!
YE, TOO, CAPTAIN! THE ALARM CAME TOO LATE FOR THE POLICE TO HELP! IT'S LUCKY FOR US THAT YE SAVED THE SHIP!
BUT WHAT I DON'T UNDERSTAND, CHIEF, IS THAT THE SAME FELLOW WHO ROBBED THE JEWELRY STORE DID THIS!
WELL, LET' TAKE A LOOK! THEN WE'LL SEE

HERE'S BONES! MAYBE HE CAN HELP US!

OUT ON THAT TUG HE SAVED OUR NECKS!

THAT BOUNDER GOT AWAY! BUT WHAT DO YOU THINK OF THIS?

A PIECE OF ROPE! THE ONE THE ROBBER CUT!

THIS CASE IS ELEMENTARY! IN FACT, EXCEPT FOR APPREHENDING THE CULPRIT, IT'S AS GOOD AS SOLVED!

THIS CRIME WAS COMMITTED BY THE SAME **WORKING** TELEVISION ACTOR WHO ROBBED THE JEWELRY STORE! HE HAS A MOLE ON HIS LEFT CHEEK!

BEJABBERS!

HOW DOES HE DO IT?

WE'LL ROUND UP EVERY TELEVISION ACTOR IN THE CITY! WE'LL HAVE A LINE-UP!

NOT PRACTICAL! DON'T DO ANYTHING TILL AFTER I'VE MADE THE ROUNDS OF THE TELEVISION STUDIOS!

RIGHT!

BUT TELL ME ONE THING, MICKEY, ME LAD! HOW DID YOU KNOW IN ADVANCE THAT THIS TERRIBLE THING WAS GOING TO HAPPEN?

THE CRYSTAL BALL! I DON'T BELIEVE IN IT EXACTLY! BUT THREE TIMES TODAY IT PREDICTED DISASTER! FIRST THE FERRIS WHEEL, THEN THE ROBBERY, THEN THIS!

THEN MAYBE WE'D BETTER HAVE A LOOK AT THIS MYSTERIOUS CRYSTAL BALL!

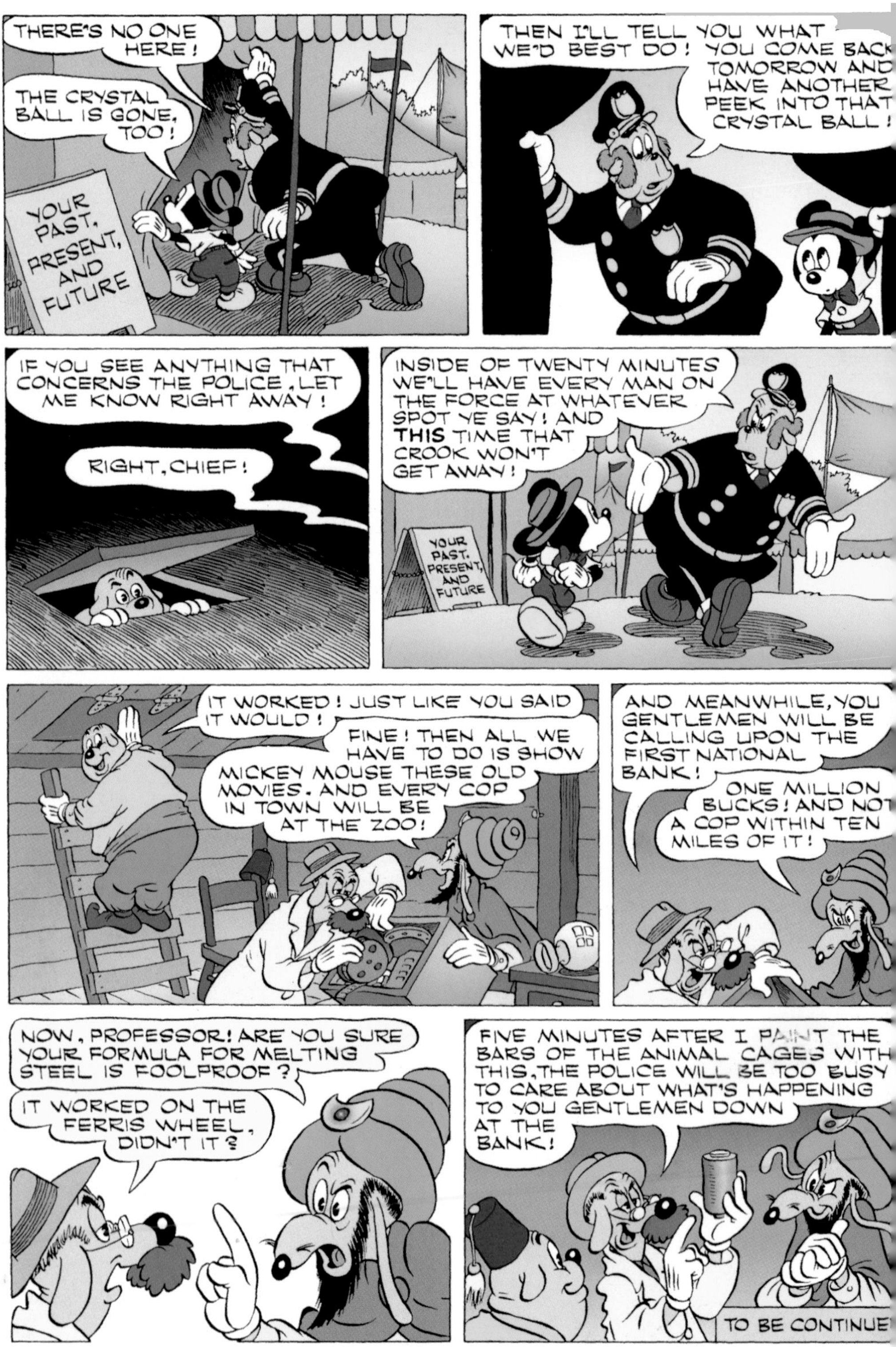

THERE'S NO ONE HERE!
THE CRYSTAL BALL IS GONE, TOO!
YOUR PAST, PRESENT, AND FUTURE
THEN I'LL TELL YOU WHAT WE'D BEST DO! YOU COME BACK TOMORROW AND HAVE ANOTHER PEEK INTO THAT CRYSTAL BALL!
IF YOU SEE ANYTHING THAT CONCERNS THE POLICE, LET ME KNOW RIGHT AWAY!
RIGHT, CHIEF!
INSIDE OF TWENTY MINUTES WE'LL HAVE EVERY MAN ON THE FORCE AT WHATEVER SPOT YE SAY! AND **THIS** TIME THAT CROOK WON'T GET AWAY!
YOUR PAST, PRESENT, AND FUTURE
IT WORKED! JUST LIKE YOU SAID IT WOULD!
FINE! THEN ALL WE HAVE TO DO IS SHOW MICKEY MOUSE THESE OLD MOVIES. AND EVERY COP IN TOWN WILL BE AT THE ZOO!
AND MEANWHILE, YOU GENTLEMEN WILL BE CALLING UPON THE FIRST NATIONAL BANK!
ONE MILLION BUCKS! AND NOT A COP WITHIN TEN MILES OF IT!
NOW, PROFESSOR! ARE YOU SURE YOUR FORMULA FOR MELTING STEEL IS FOOLPROOF?
IT WORKED ON THE FERRIS WHEEL, DIDN'T IT?
FIVE MINUTES AFTER I PAINT THE BARS OF THE ANIMAL CAGES WITH THIS, THE POLICE WILL BE TOO BUSY TO CARE ABOUT WHAT'S HAPPENING TO YOU GENTLEMEN DOWN AT THE BANK!
TO BE CONTINUED

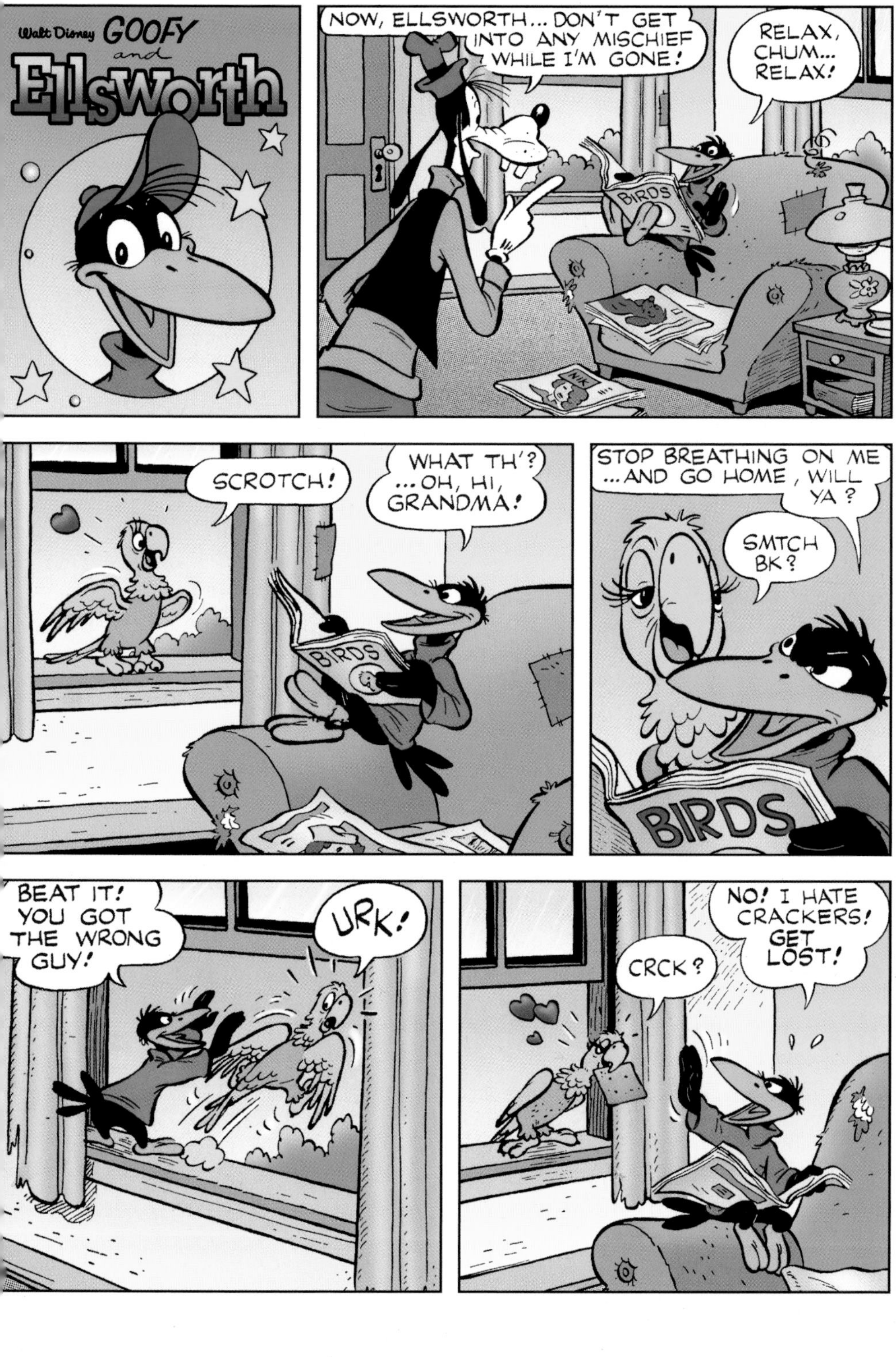
Walt Disney GOOFY and Ellsworth
NOW, ELLSWORTH... DON'T GET INTO ANY MISCHIEF WHILE I'M GONE!
RELAX, CHUM... RELAX!
BIRDS
SCROTCH!
WHAT TH'? ...OH, HI, GRANDMA!
BIRDS
STOP BREATHING ON ME ...AND GO HOME, WILL YA?
SMTCH BK?
BIRDS
BEAT IT! YOU GOT THE WRONG GUY!
URK!
CRCK?
NO! I HATE CRACKERS! GET LOST!

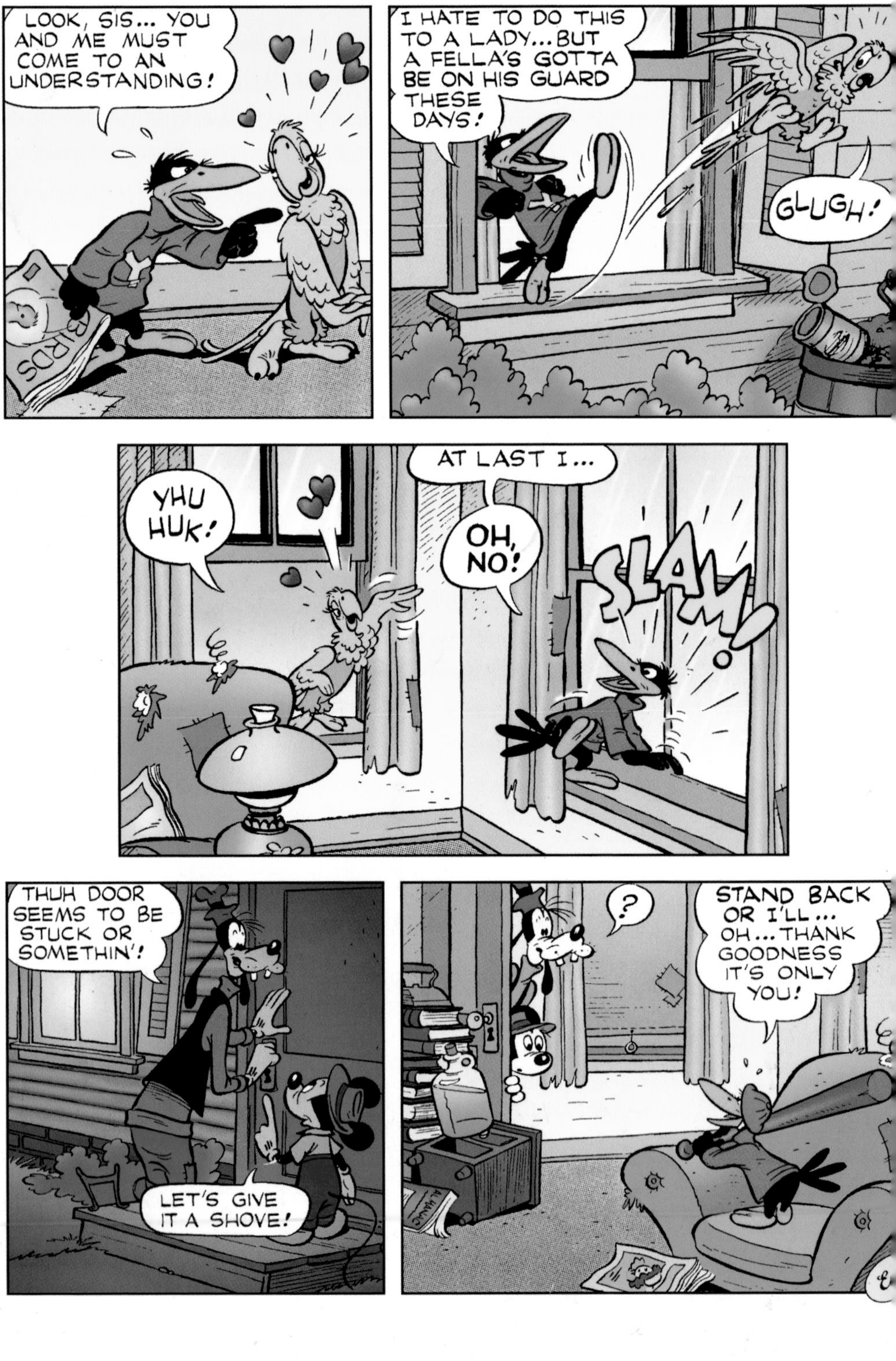

LOOK, SIS... YOU AND ME MUST COME TO AN UNDERSTANDING!
BIRDS
I HATE TO DO THIS TO A LADY... BUT A FELLA'S GOTTA BE ON HIS GUARD THESE DAYS!
GLUGH!
YHU HUK!
AT LAST I...
OH, NO!
SLAM!
THUH DOOR SEEMS TO BE STUCK OR SOMETHIN'!
LET'S GIVE IT A SHOVE!
?
STAND BACK OR I'LL... OH... THANK GOODNESS IT'S ONLY YOU!

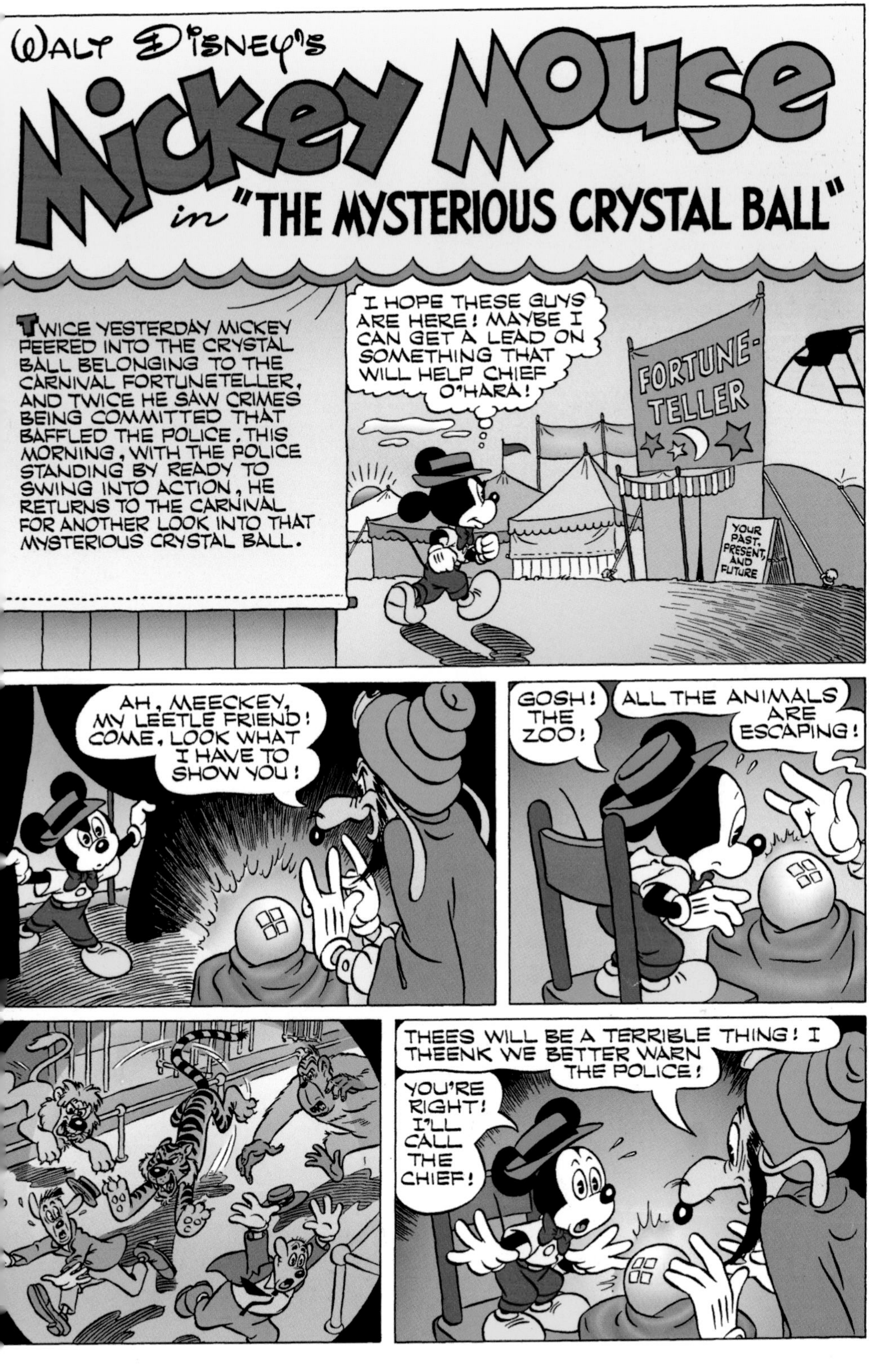

WALT DISNEY'S
MICKEY MOUSE
in "THE MYSTERIOUS CRYSTAL BALL"
TWICE YESTERDAY MICKEY PEERED INTO THE CRYSTAL BALL BELONGING TO THE CARNIVAL FORTUNETELLER, AND TWICE HE SAW CRIMES BEING COMMITTED THAT BAFFLED THE POLICE. THIS MORNING, WITH THE POLICE STANDING BY READY TO SWING INTO ACTION, HE RETURNS TO THE CARNIVAL FOR ANOTHER LOOK INTO THAT MYSTERIOUS CRYSTAL BALL.
I HOPE THESE GUYS ARE HERE! MAYBE I CAN GET A LEAD ON SOMETHING THAT WILL HELP CHIEF O'HARA!
FORTUNE-TELLER
YOUR PAST, PRESENT, AND FUTURE
AH, MEECKEY, MY LEETLE FRIEND! COME, LOOK WHAT I HAVE TO SHOW YOU!
GOSH! THE ZOO!
ALL THE ANIMALS ARE ESCAPING!
THEES WILL BE A TERRIBLE THING! I THEENK WE BETTER WARN THE POLICE!
YOU'RE RIGHT! I'LL CALL THE CHIEF!

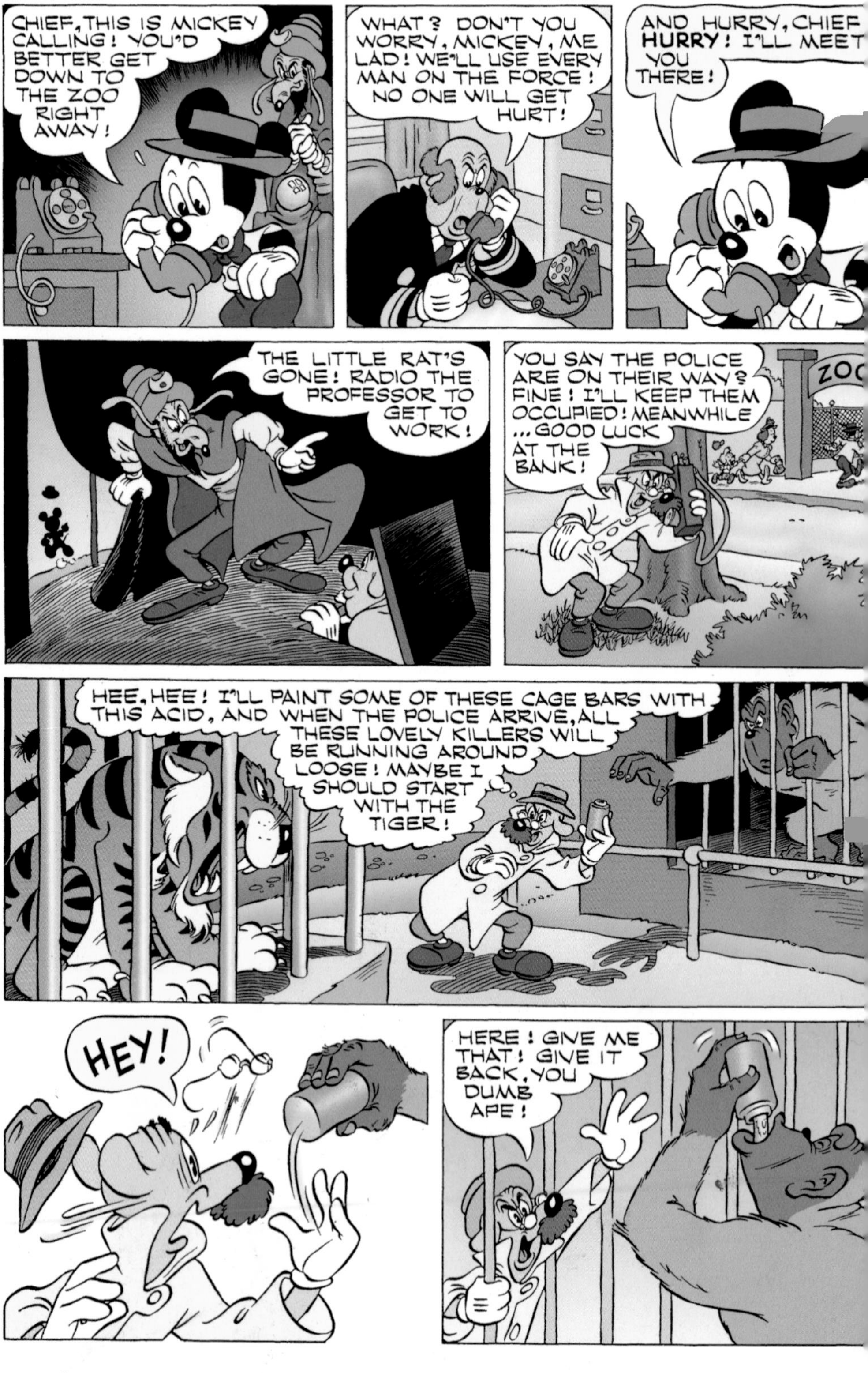
CHIEF, THIS IS MICKEY CALLING! YOU'D BETTER GET DOWN TO THE ZOO RIGHT AWAY!
WHAT? DON'T YOU WORRY, MICKEY, ME LAD! WE'LL USE EVERY MAN ON THE FORCE! NO ONE WILL GET HURT!
AND HURRY, CHIEF **HURRY**! I'LL MEET YOU THERE!
THE LITTLE RAT'S GONE! RADIO THE PROFESSOR TO GET TO WORK!
YOU SAY THE POLICE ARE ON THEIR WAY? FINE! I'LL KEEP THEM OCCUPIED! MEANWHILE ...GOOD LUCK AT THE BANK!
ZOO
HEE, HEE! I'LL PAINT SOME OF THESE CAGE BARS WITH THIS ACID, AND WHEN THE POLICE ARRIVE, ALL THESE LOVELY KILLERS WILL BE RUNNING AROUND LOOSE! MAYBE I SHOULD START WITH THE TIGER!
HEY!
HERE! GIVE ME THAT! GIVE IT BACK, YOU DUMB APE!

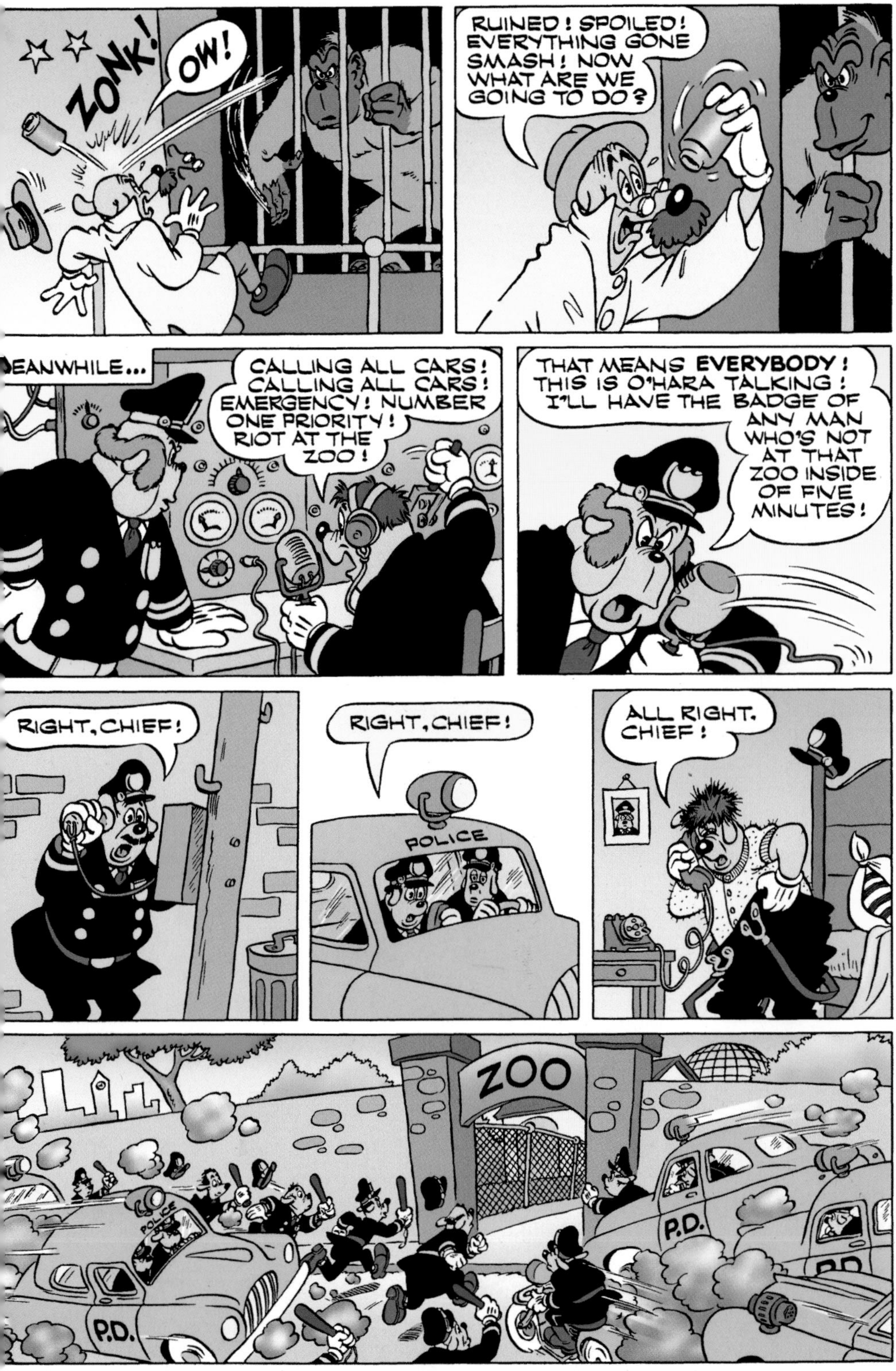
ZONK!
OW!
RUINED! SPOILED! EVERYTHING GONE SMASH! NOW WHAT ARE WE GOING TO DO?
MEANWHILE...
CALLING ALL CARS! CALLING ALL CARS! EMERGENCY! NUMBER ONE PRIORITY! RIOT AT THE ZOO!
THAT MEANS EVERYBODY! THIS IS O'HARA TALKING! I'LL HAVE THE BADGE OF ANY MAN WHO'S NOT AT THAT ZOO INSIDE OF FIVE MINUTES!
RIGHT, CHIEF!
RIGHT, CHIEF!
POLICE
ALL RIGHT. CHIEF!
ZOO
POLICE
P.D.
P.D.
P.D.

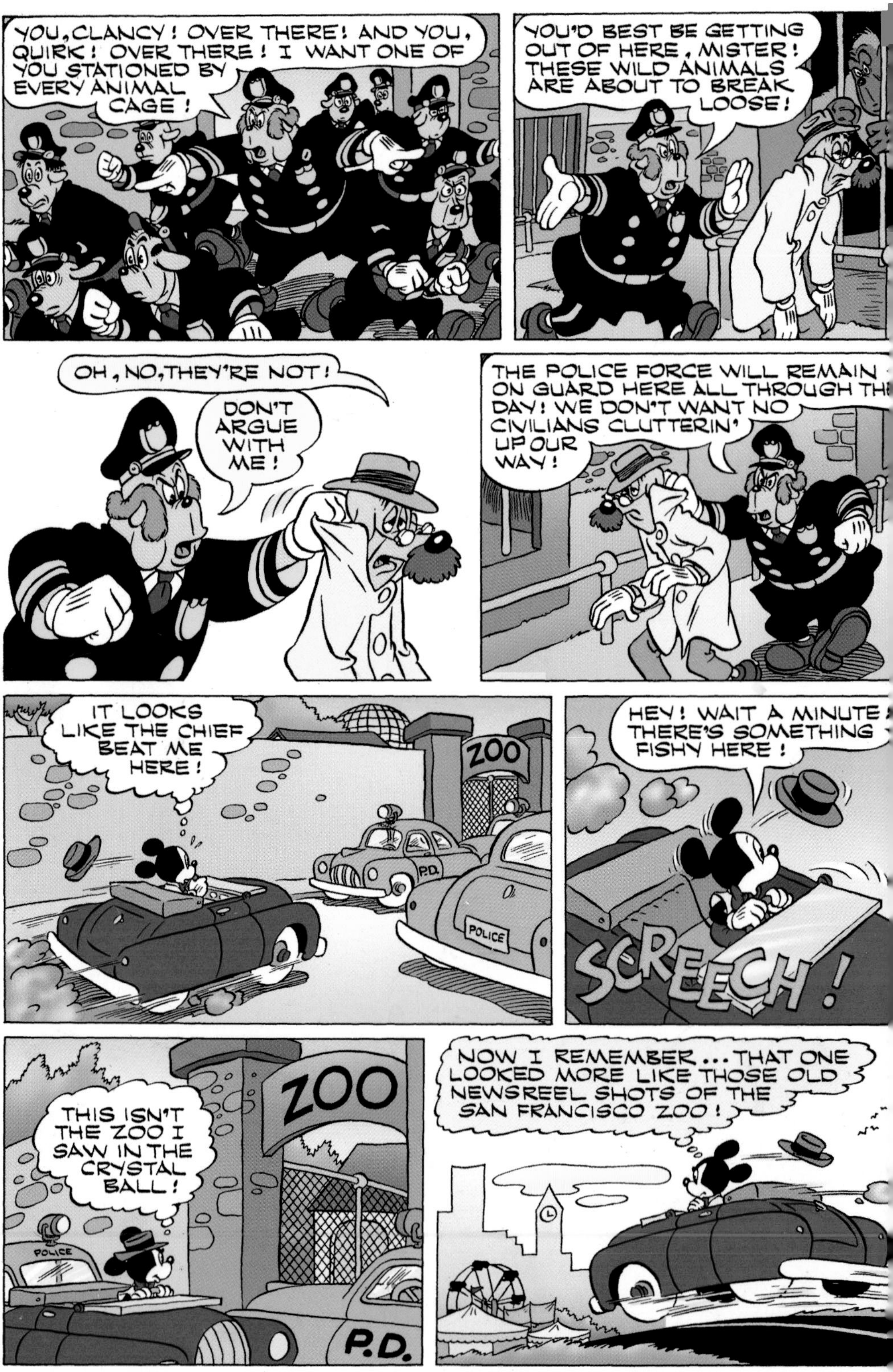
YOU, CLANCY! OVER THERE! AND YOU, QUIRK! OVER THERE! I WANT ONE OF YOU STATIONED BY EVERY ANIMAL CAGE!
YOU'D BEST BE GETTING OUT OF HERE, MISTER! THESE WILD ANIMALS ARE ABOUT TO BREAK LOOSE!
OH, NO, THEY'RE NOT!
DON'T ARGUE WITH ME!
THE POLICE FORCE WILL REMAIN ON GUARD HERE ALL THROUGH THE DAY! WE DON'T WANT NO CIVILIANS CLUTTERIN' UP OUR WAY!
IT LOOKS LIKE THE CHIEF BEAT ME HERE!
ZOO
P.D.
POLICE
HEY! WAIT A MINUTE! THERE'S SOMETHING FISHY HERE!
SCREECH!
THIS ISN'T THE ZOO I SAW IN THE CRYSTAL BALL!
ZOO
POLICE
P.D.
NOW I REMEMBER... THAT ONE LOOKED MORE LIKE THOSE OLD NEWSREEL SHOTS OF THE SAN FRANCISCO ZOO!

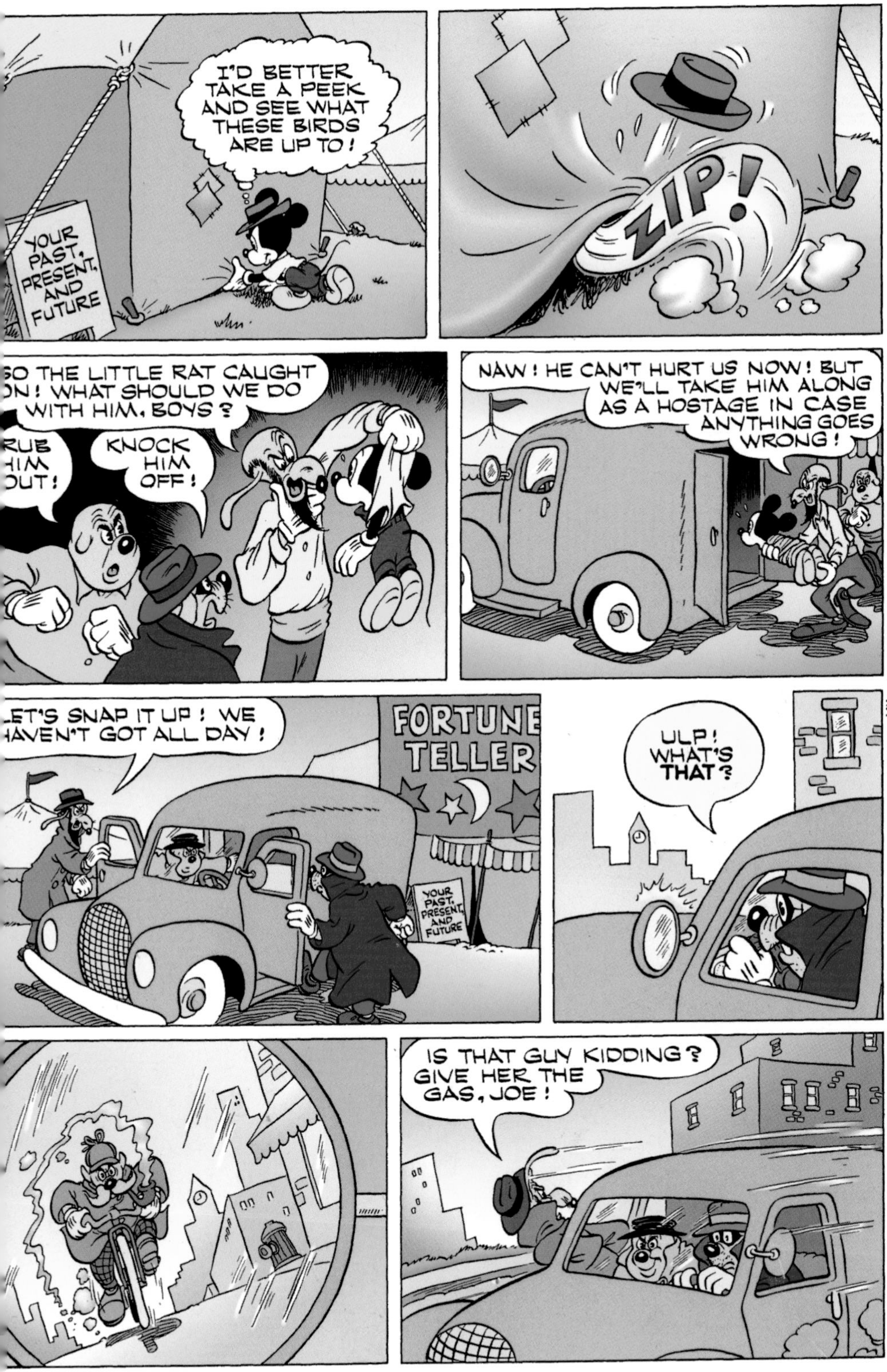
I'D BETTER TAKE A PEEK AND SEE WHAT THESE BIRDS ARE UP TO!
YOUR PAST, PRESENT, AND FUTURE
ZIP!
SO THE LITTLE RAT CAUGHT ON! WHAT SHOULD WE DO WITH HIM, BOYS?
RUB HIM OUT!
KNOCK HIM OFF!
NAW! HE CAN'T HURT US NOW! BUT WE'LL TAKE HIM ALONG AS A HOSTAGE IN CASE ANYTHING GOES WRONG!
LET'S SNAP IT UP! WE HAVEN'T GOT ALL DAY!
FORTUNE TELLER
YOUR PAST, PRESENT, AND FUTURE
ULP! WHAT'S THAT?
IS THAT GUY KIDDING? GIVE HER THE GAS, JOE!

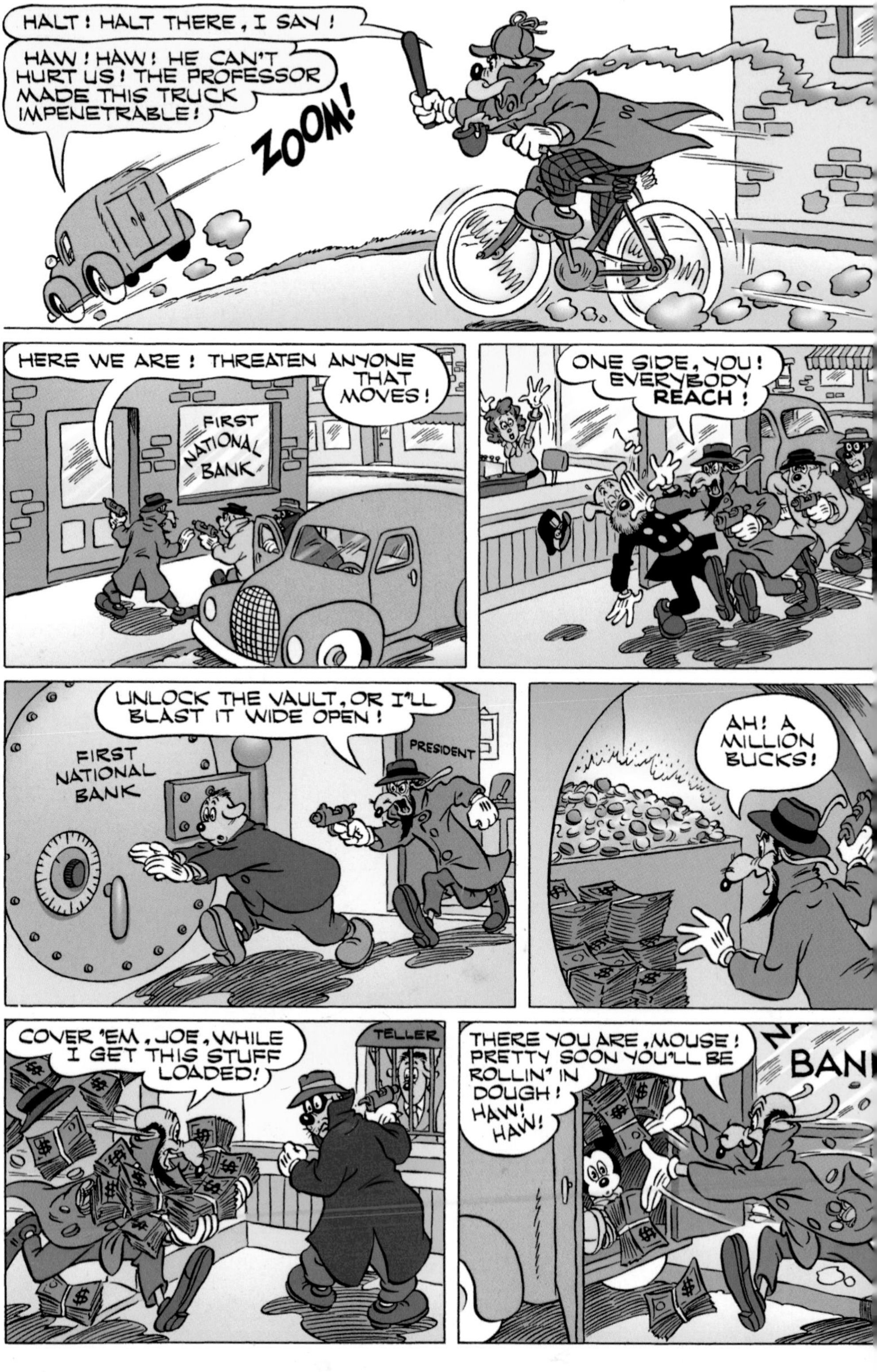
HALT! HALT THERE, I SAY!
HAW! HAW! HE CAN'T HURT US! THE PROFESSOR MADE THIS TRUCK IMPENETRABLE!
ZOOM!
HERE WE ARE! THREATEN ANYONE THAT MOVES!
FIRST NATIONAL BANK
ONE SIDE, YOU! EVERYBODY REACH!
UNLOCK THE VAULT, OR I'LL BLAST IT WIDE OPEN!
FIRST NATIONAL BANK
PRESIDENT
AH! A MILLION BUCKS!
COVER 'EM, JOE, WHILE I GET THIS STUFF LOADED!
TELLER
THERE YOU ARE, MOUSE! PRETTY SOON YOU'LL BE ROLLIN' IN DOUGH! HAW! HAW!

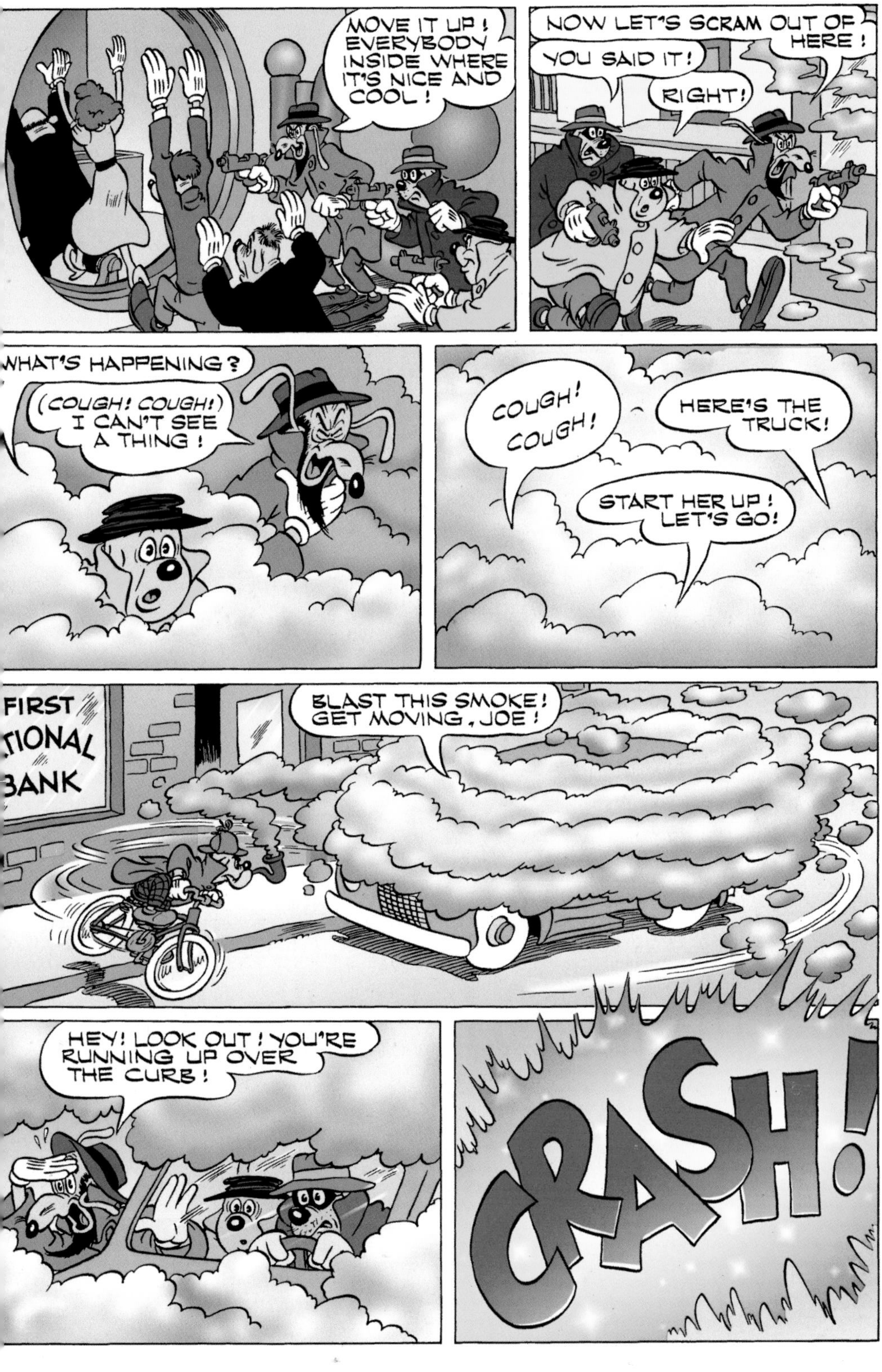
MOVE IT UP! EVERYBODY INSIDE WHERE IT'S NICE AND COOL!
NOW LET'S SCRAM OUT OF HERE!
YOU SAID IT!
RIGHT!
WHAT'S HAPPENING?
(COUGH! COUGH!) I CAN'T SEE A THING!
COUGH! COUGH!
HERE'S THE TRUCK!
START HER UP! LET'S GO!
FIRST
TIONAL
BANK
BLAST THIS SMOKE! GET MOVING, JOE!
HEY! LOOK OUT! YOU'RE RUNNING UP OVER THE CURB!
CRASH!

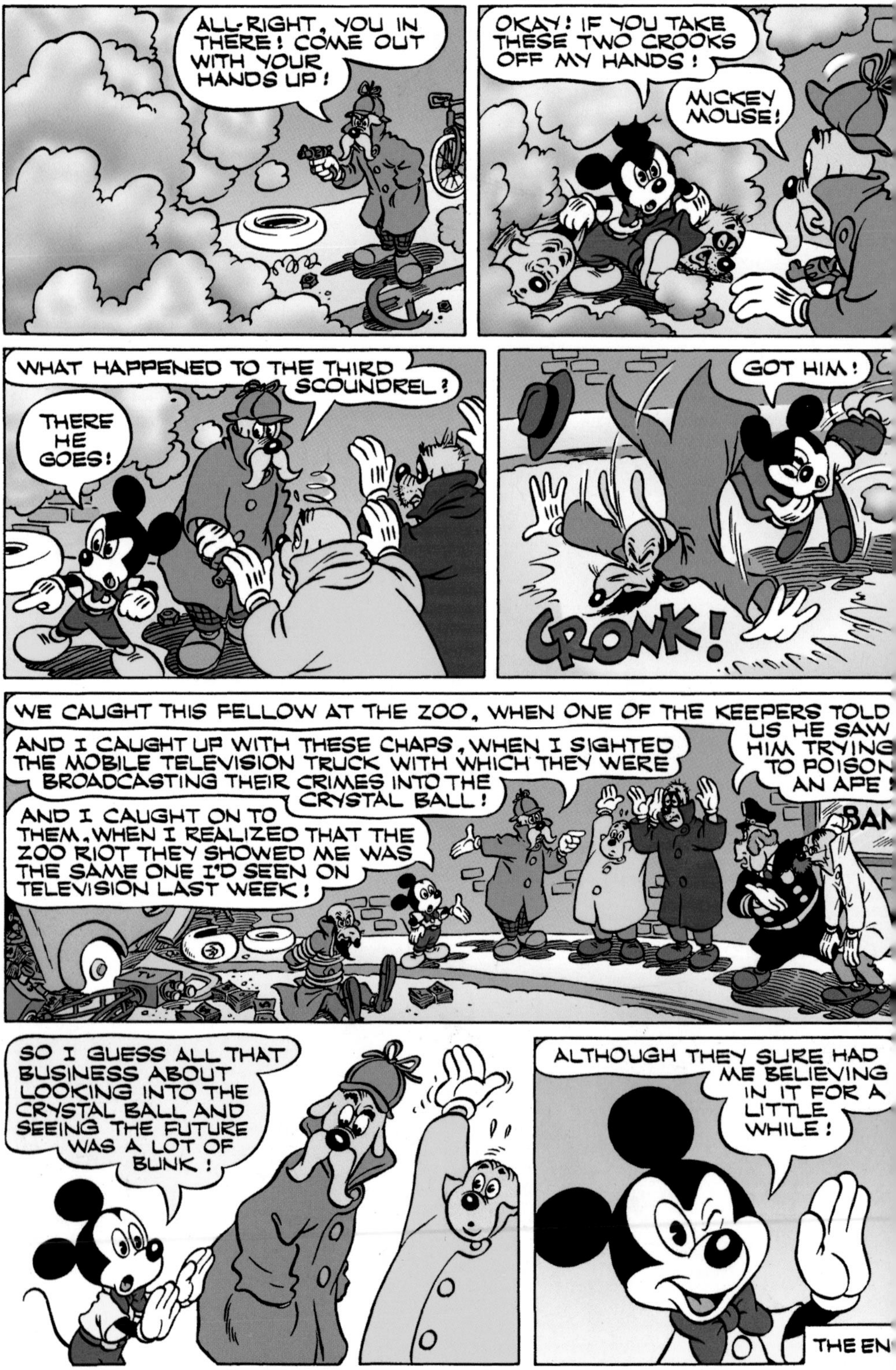
ALL-RIGHT, YOU IN THERE! COME OUT WITH YOUR HANDS UP!
OKAY! IF YOU TAKE THESE TWO CROOKS OFF MY HANDS!
MICKEY MOUSE!
WHAT HAPPENED TO THE THIRD SCOUNDREL?
THERE HE GOES!
GOT HIM!
CRONK!
WE CAUGHT THIS FELLOW AT THE ZOO, WHEN ONE OF THE KEEPERS TOLD US HE SAW HIM TRYING TO POISON AN APE!
AND I CAUGHT UP WITH THESE CHAPS, WHEN I SIGHTED THE MOBILE TELEVISION TRUCK WITH WHICH THEY WERE BROADCASTING THEIR CRIMES INTO THE CRYSTAL BALL!
AND I CAUGHT ON TO THEM, WHEN I REALIZED THAT THE ZOO RIOT THEY SHOWED ME WAS THE SAME ONE I'D SEEN ON TELEVISION LAST WEEK!
TV
SO I GUESS ALL THAT BUSINESS ABOUT LOOKING INTO THE CRYSTAL BALL AND SEEING THE FUTURE WAS A LOT OF BUNK!
ALTHOUGH THEY SURE HAD ME BELIEVING IN IT FOR A LITTLE WHILE!
THE EN

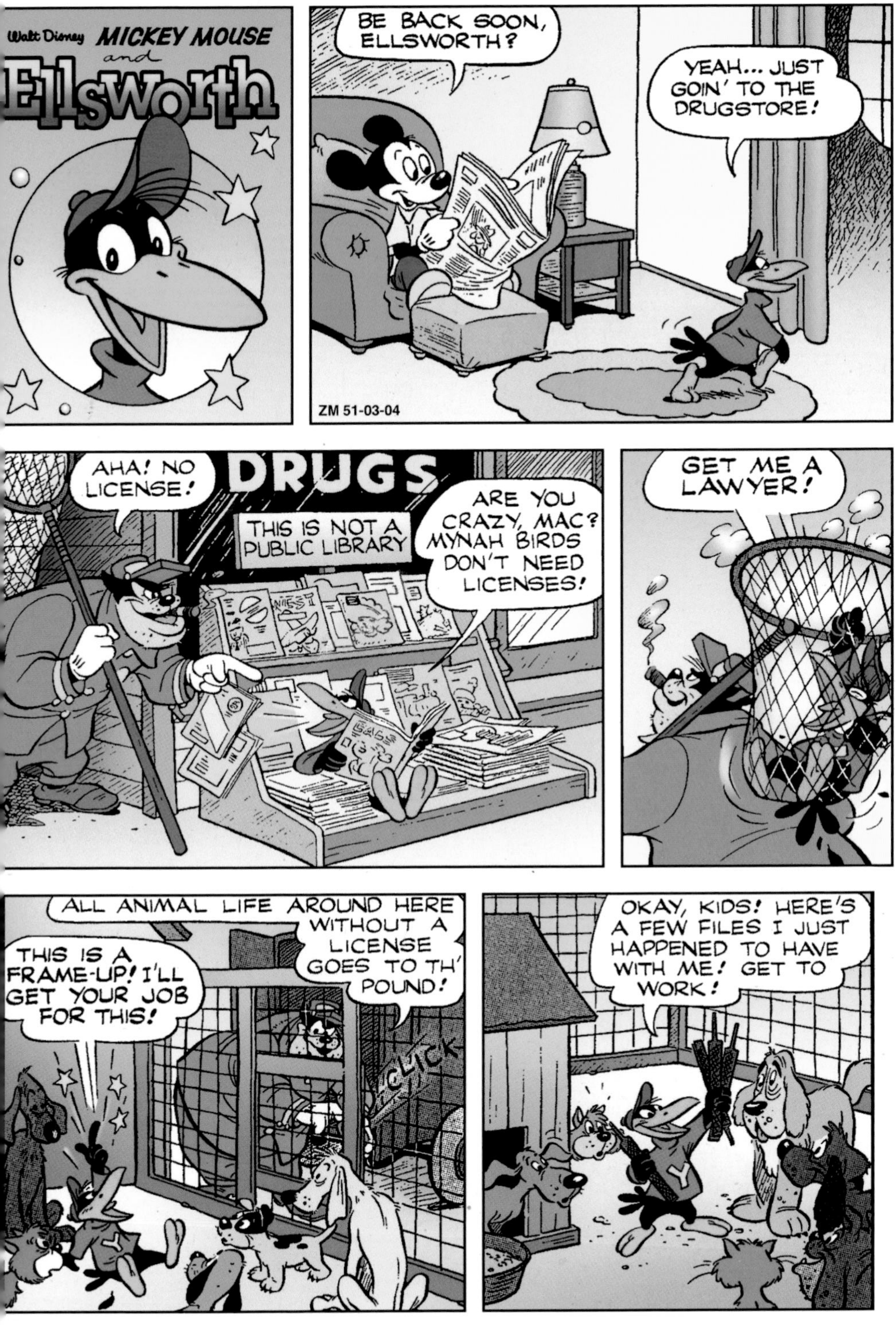
Walt Disney MICKEY MOUSE and Ellsworth
BE BACK SOON, ELLSWORTH?
YEAH... JUST GOIN' TO THE DRUGSTORE!
ZM 51-03-04
DRUGS
AHA! NO LICENSE!
THIS IS NOT A PUBLIC LIBRARY
ARE YOU CRAZY, MAC? MYNAH BIRDS DON'T NEED LICENSES!
GET ME A LAWYER!
ALL ANIMAL LIFE AROUND HERE WITHOUT A LICENSE GOES TO TH' POUND!
THIS IS A FRAME-UP! I'LL GET YOUR JOB FOR THIS!
CLICK
OKAY, KIDS! HERE'S A FEW FILES I JUST HAPPENED TO HAVE WITH ME! GET TO WORK!

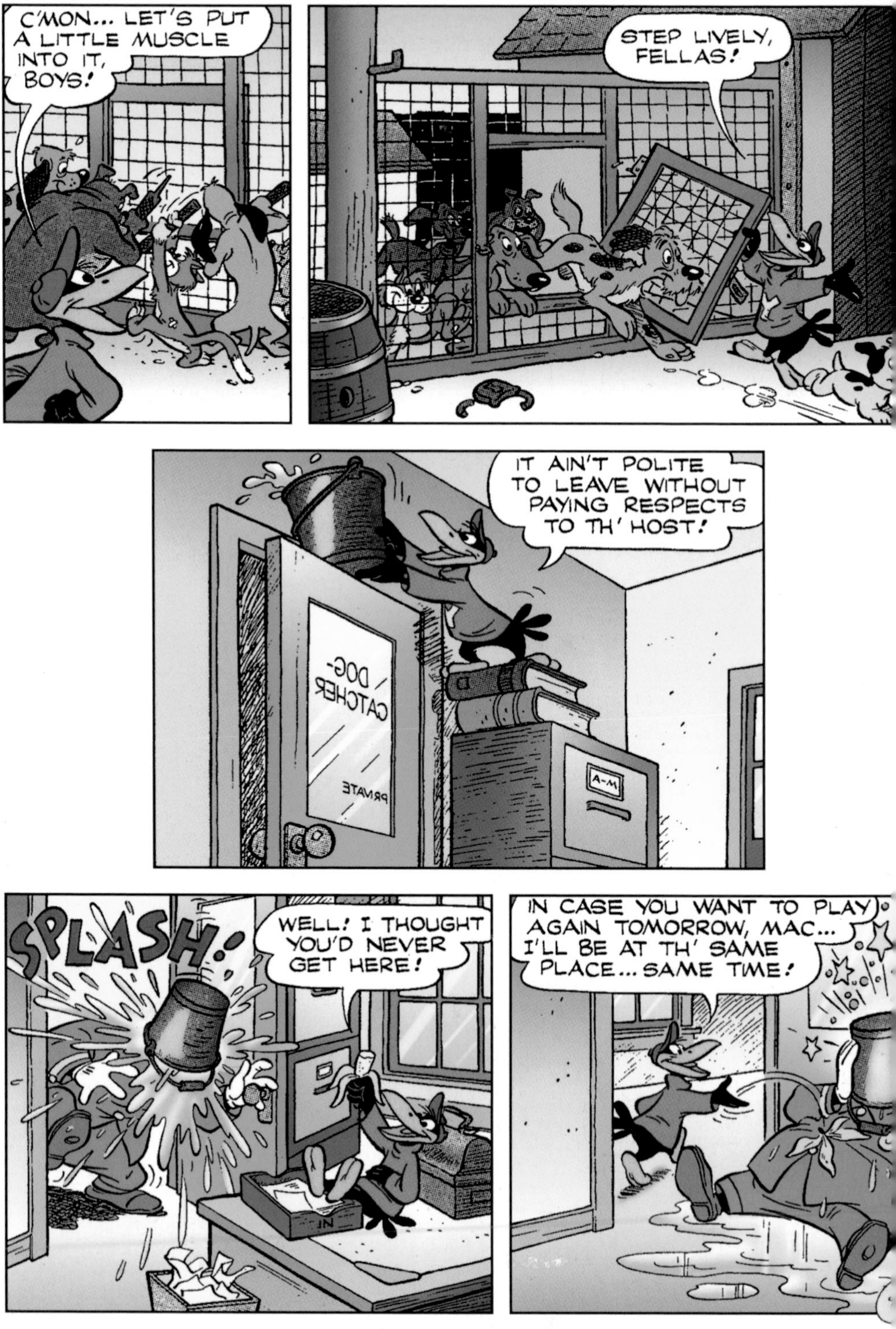
C'MON... LET'S PUT A LITTLE MUSCLE INTO IT, BOYS!
STEP LIVELY, FELLAS!
IT AIN'T POLITE TO LEAVE WITHOUT PAYING RESPECTS TO TH' HOST!
DOG-CATCHER
PRIVATE
A-M
SPLASH!
WELL! I THOUGHT YOU'D NEVER GET HERE!
IN
IN CASE YOU WANT TO PLAY AGAIN TOMORROW, MAC... I'LL BE AT TH' SAME PLACE... SAME TIME!

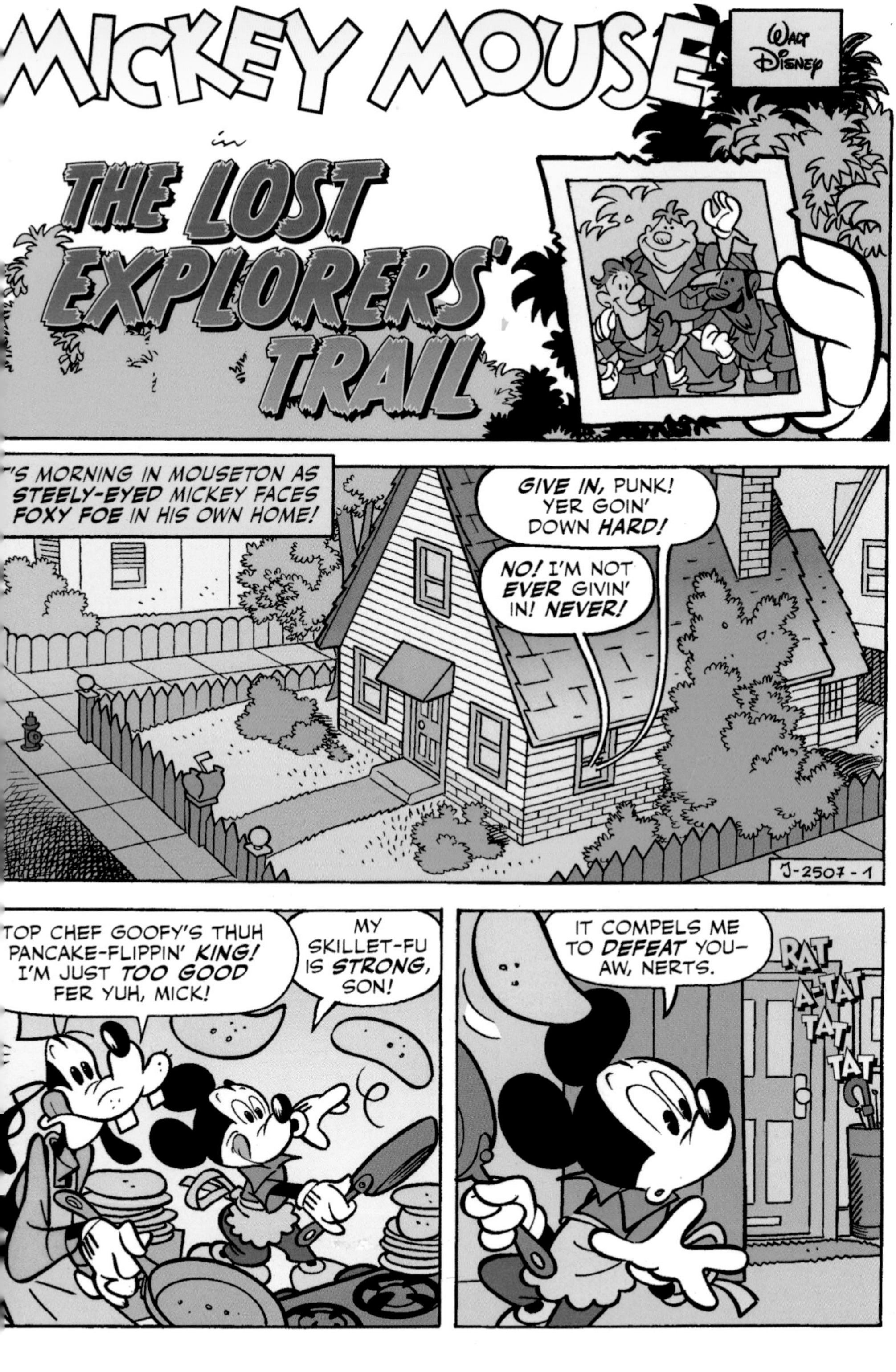

MICKEY MOUSE
WALT DISNEY
in
THE LOST EXPLORERS' TRAIL
'S MORNING IN MOUSETON AS STEELY-EYED MICKEY FACES FOXY FOE IN HIS OWN HOME!
GIVE IN, PUNK! YER GOIN' DOWN HARD!
NO! I'M NOT EVER GIVIN' IN! NEVER!
J-2507-1
TOP CHEF GOOFY'S THUH PANCAKE-FLIPPIN' KING! I'M JUST TOO GOOD FER YUH, MICK!
MY SKILLET-FU IS STRONG, SON!
IT COMPELS ME TO DEFEAT YOU— AW, NERTS.
RAT A-TAT TAT TAT

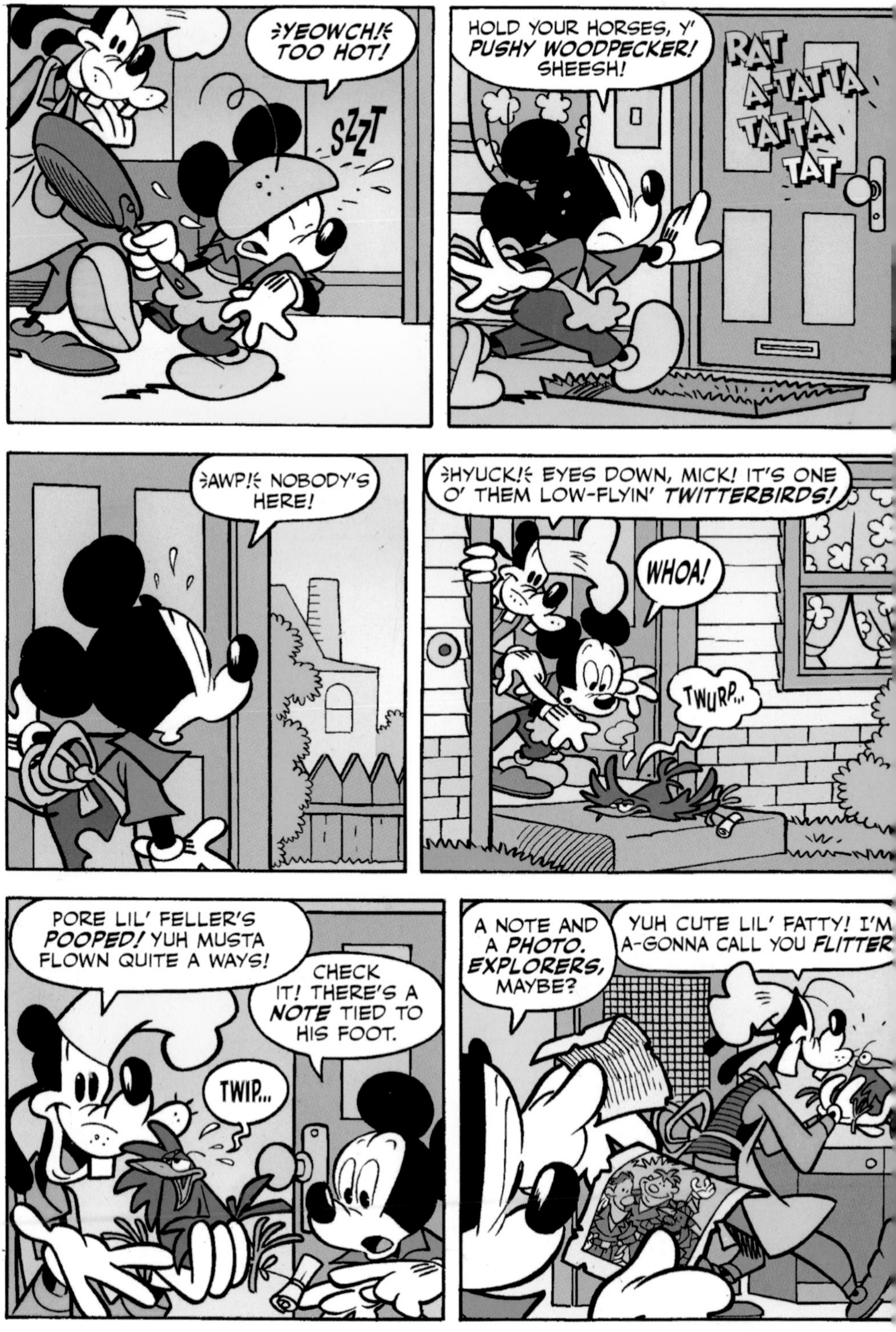

YEOWCH! TOO HOT!
SZZT
HOLD YOUR HORSES, Y' PUSHY WOODPECKER! SHEESH!
RAT A-TATTA TATTA TAT
AWP! NOBODY'S HERE!
HYUCK! EYES DOWN, MICK! IT'S ONE O' THEM LOW-FLYIN' TWITTERBIRDS!
WHOA!
TWURP...
PORE LIL' FELLER'S POOPED! YUH MUSTA FLOWN QUITE A WAYS!
CHECK IT! THERE'S A NOTE TIED TO HIS FOOT.
TWIP...
A NOTE AND A PHOTO. EXPLORERS, MAYBE?
YUH CUTE LIL' FATTY! I'M A-GONNA CALL YOU FLITTER

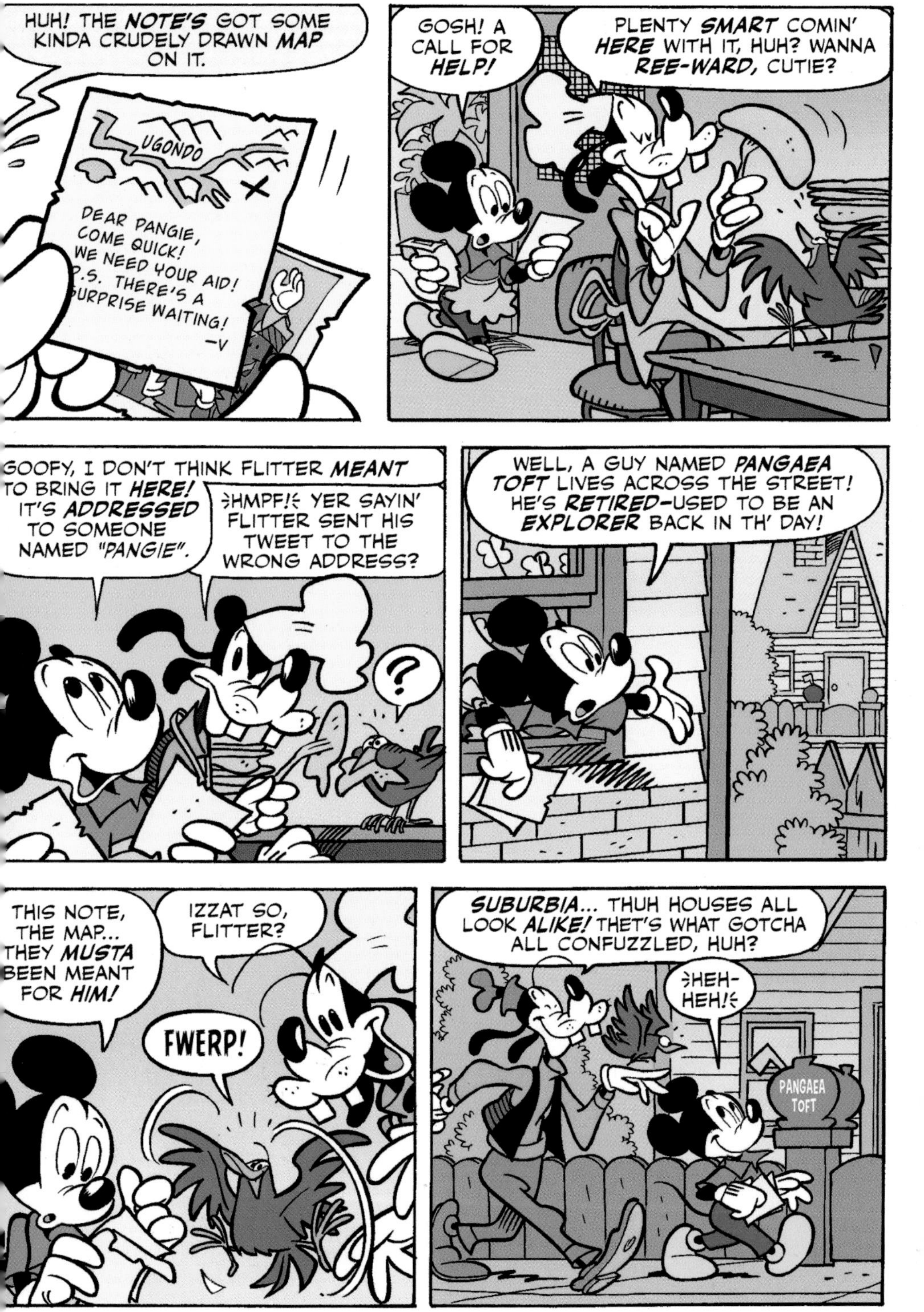

HUH! THE NOTE'S GOT SOME KINDA CRUDELY DRAWN MAP ON IT.
UGONDO
DEAR PANGIE,
COME QUICK!
WE NEED YOUR AID!
P.S. THERE'S A SURPRISE WAITING!
—V
GOSH! A CALL FOR HELP!
PLENTY SMART COMIN' HERE WITH IT, HUH? WANNA REE-WARD, CUTIE?
GOOFY, I DON'T THINK FLITTER MEANT TO BRING IT HERE! IT'S ADDRESSED TO SOMEONE NAMED "PANGIE".
HMPF! YER SAYIN' FLITTER SENT HIS TWEET TO THE WRONG ADDRESS?
?
WELL, A GUY NAMED PANGAEA TOFT LIVES ACROSS THE STREET! HE'S RETIRED—USED TO BE AN EXPLORER BACK IN TH' DAY!
THIS NOTE, THE MAP... THEY MUSTA BEEN MEANT FOR HIM!
IZZAT SO, FLITTER?
FWERP!
SUBURBIA... THUH HOUSES ALL LOOK ALIKE! THET'S WHAT GOTCHA ALL CONFUZZLED, HUH?
HEH-HEH!
PANGAEA TOFT

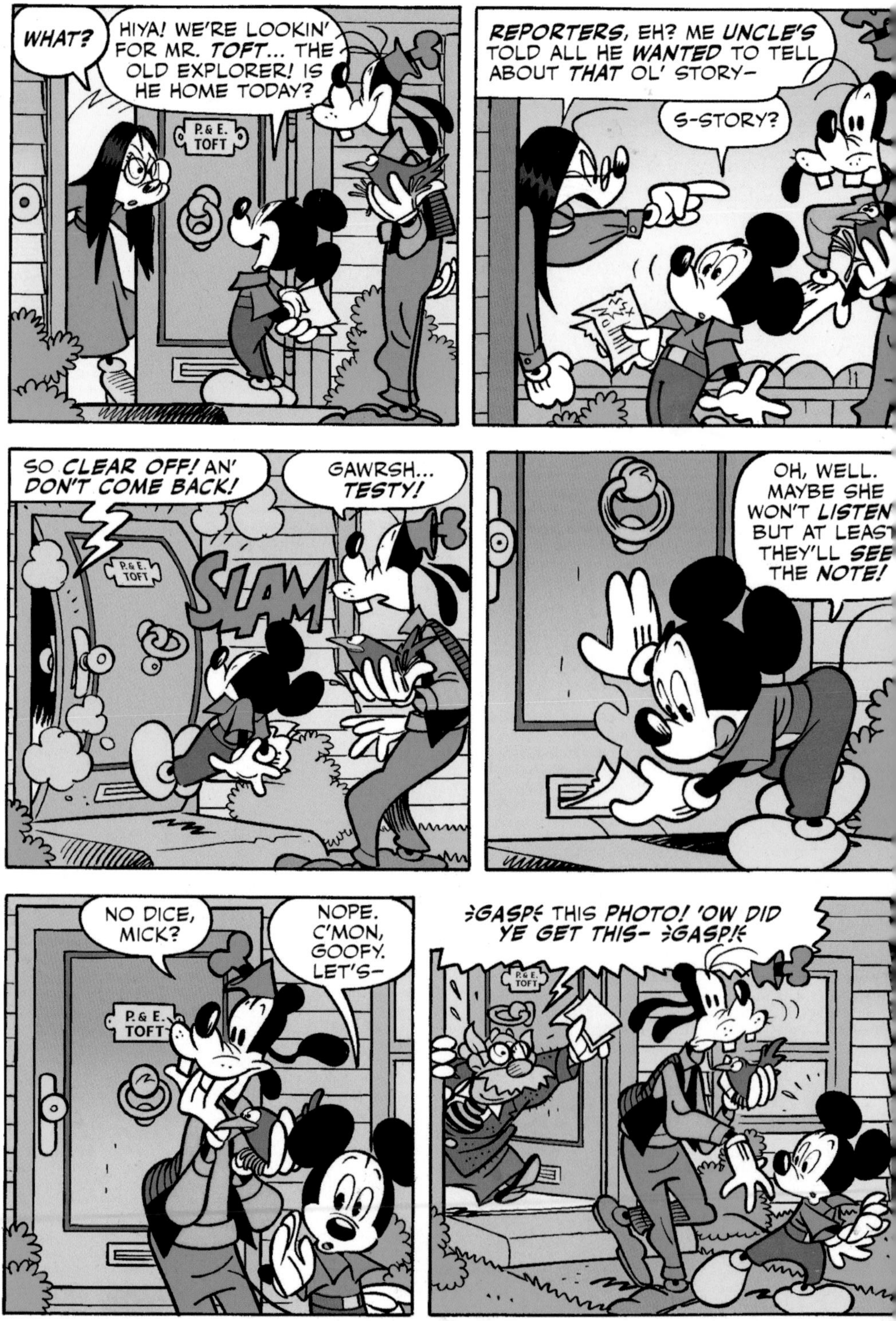

WHAT?
HIYA! WE'RE LOOKIN' FOR MR. TOFT... THE OLD EXPLORER! IS HE HOME TODAY?
P. & E. TOFT
REPORTERS, EH? ME UNCLE'S TOLD ALL HE WANTED TO TELL ABOUT THAT OL' STORY–
S-STORY?
SO CLEAR OFF! AN' DON'T COME BACK!
GAWRSH... TESTY!
SLAM
OH, WELL. MAYBE SHE WON'T LISTEN BUT AT LEAST THEY'LL SEE THE NOTE!
NO DICE, MICK?
NOPE. C'MON, GOOFY. LET'S–
GASP THIS PHOTO! 'OW DID YE GET THIS– GASP!

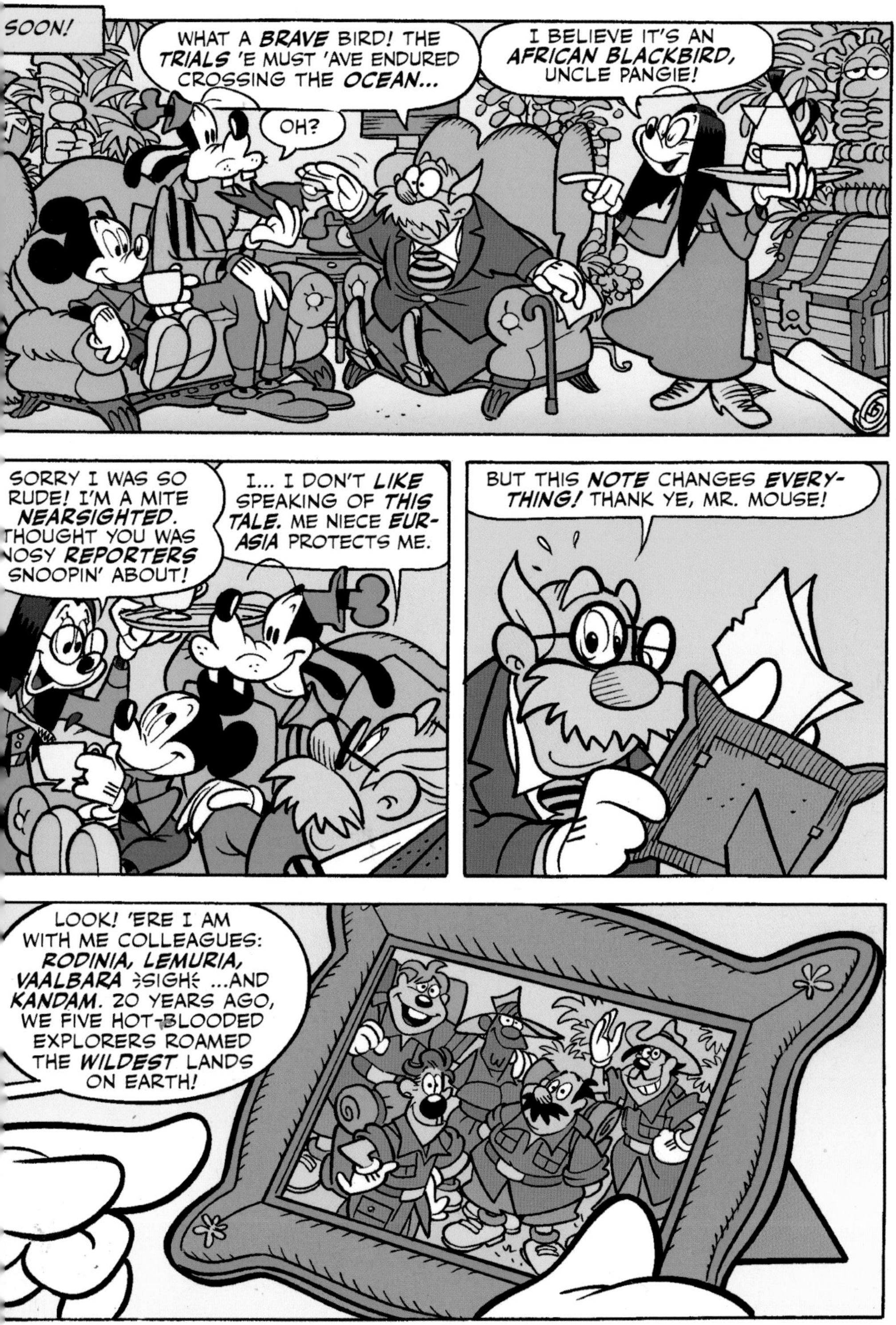
SOON!
WHAT A BRAVE BIRD! THE TRIALS 'E MUST 'AVE ENDURED CROSSING THE OCEAN...
OH?
I BELIEVE IT'S AN AFRICAN BLACKBIRD, UNCLE PANGIE!
SORRY I WAS SO RUDE! I'M A MITE NEARSIGHTED. THOUGHT YOU WAS NOSY REPORTERS SNOOPIN' ABOUT!
I... I DON'T LIKE SPEAKING OF THIS TALE. ME NIECE EURASIA PROTECTS ME.
BUT THIS NOTE CHANGES EVERYTHING! THANK YE, MR. MOUSE!
LOOK! 'ERE I AM WITH ME COLLEAGUES: RODINIA, LEMURIA, VAALBARA ⟩SIGH⟨ ...AND KANDAM. 20 YEARS AGO, WE FIVE HOT-BLOODED EXPLORERS ROAMED THE WILDEST LANDS ON EARTH!

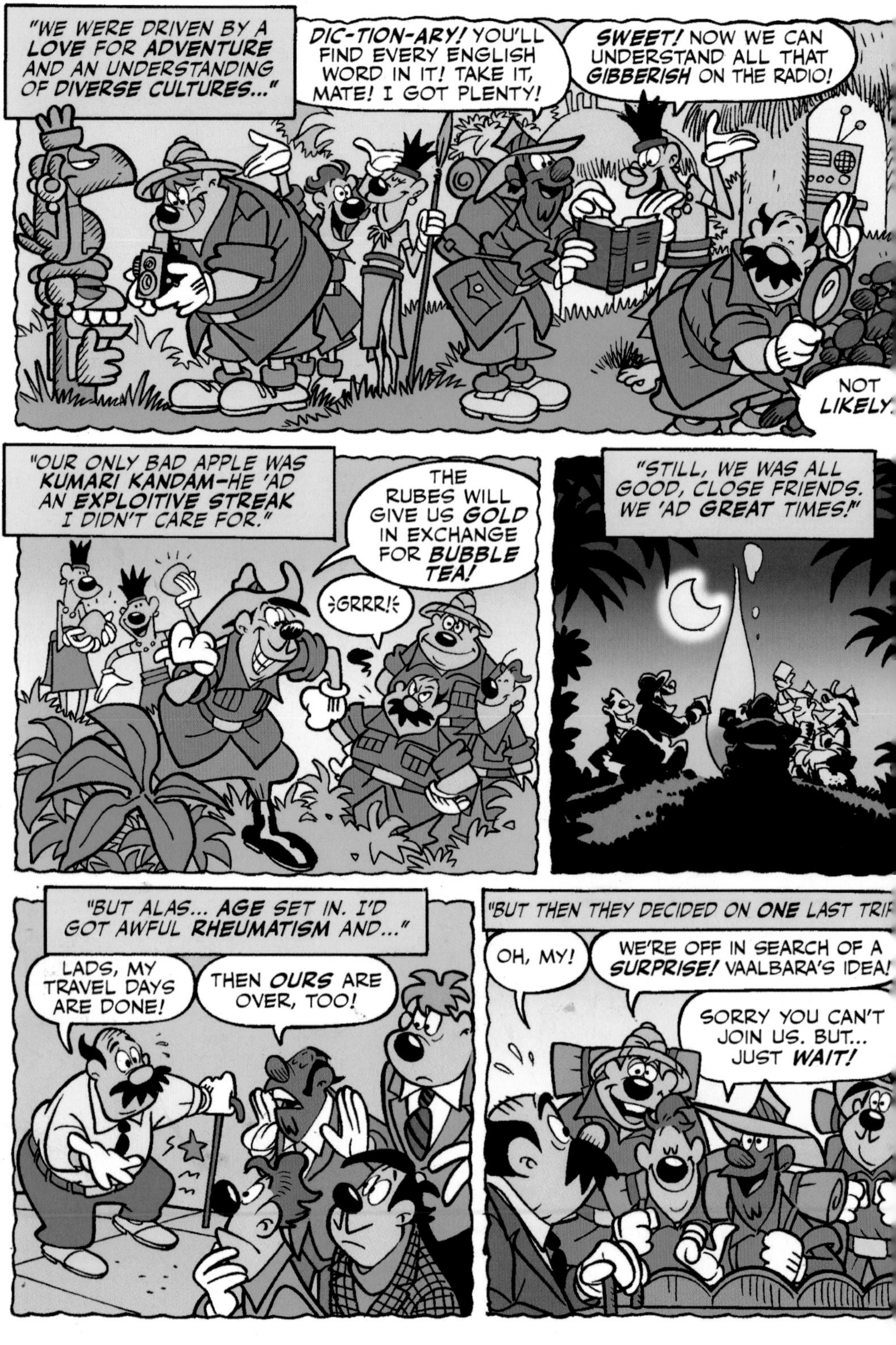
"WE WERE DRIVEN BY A LOVE FOR ADVENTURE AND AN UNDERSTANDING OF DIVERSE CULTURES..."
DIC-TION-ARY! YOU'LL FIND EVERY ENGLISH WORD IN IT! TAKE IT, MATE! I GOT PLENTY!
SWEET! NOW WE CAN UNDERSTAND ALL THAT GIBBERISH ON THE RADIO!
NOT LIKELY.
"OUR ONLY BAD APPLE WAS KUMARI KANDAM—HE 'AD AN EXPLOITIVE STREAK I DIDN'T CARE FOR."
THE RUBES WILL GIVE US GOLD IN EXCHANGE FOR BUBBLE TEA!
GRRR!
"STILL, WE WAS ALL GOOD, CLOSE FRIENDS. WE 'AD GREAT TIMES!"
"BUT ALAS... AGE SET IN. I'D GOT AWFUL RHEUMATISM AND..."
LADS, MY TRAVEL DAYS ARE DONE!
THEN OURS ARE OVER, TOO!
"BUT THEN THEY DECIDED ON ONE LAST TRIP
OH, MY!
WE'RE OFF IN SEARCH OF A SURPRISE! VAALBARA'S IDEA!
SORRY YOU CAN'T JOIN US. BUT... JUST WAIT!

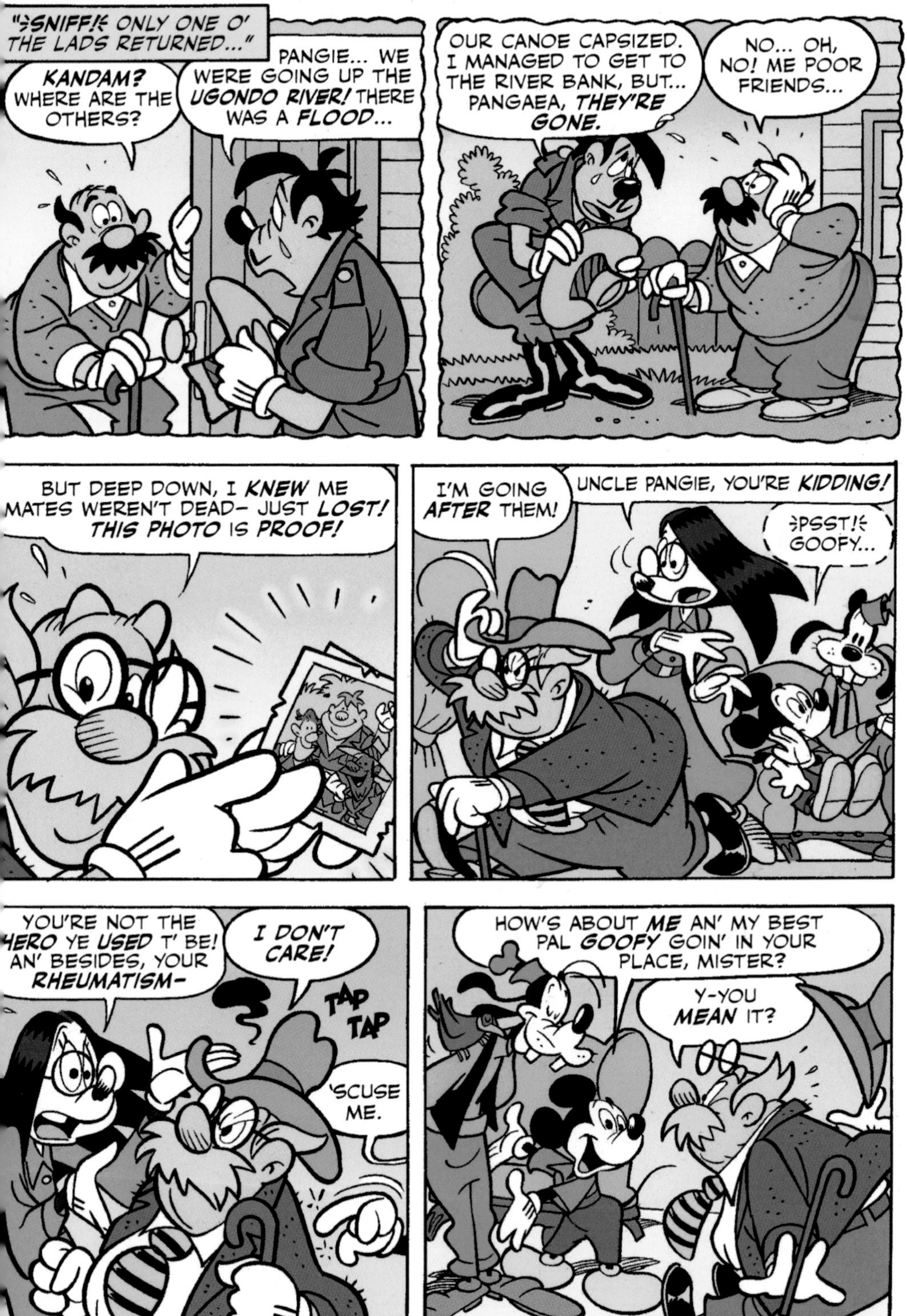
"*SNIFF!* ONLY ONE O' THE LADS RETURNED..."
KANDAM? WHERE ARE THE OTHERS?
PANGIE... WE WERE GOING UP THE UGONDO RIVER! THERE WAS A FLOOD...
OUR CANOE CAPSIZED. I MANAGED TO GET TO THE RIVER BANK, BUT... PANGAEA, THEY'RE GONE.
NO... OH, NO! ME POOR FRIENDS...
BUT DEEP DOWN, I KNEW ME MATES WEREN'T DEAD– JUST LOST! THIS PHOTO IS PROOF!
I'M GOING AFTER THEM!
UNCLE PANGIE, YOU'RE KIDDING!
PSST! GOOFY...
YOU'RE NOT THE HERO YE USED T' BE! AN' BESIDES, YOUR RHEUMATISM–
I DON'T CARE!
TAP TAP
'SCUSE ME.
HOW'S ABOUT ME AN' MY BEST PAL GOOFY GOIN' IN YOUR PLACE, MISTER?
Y-YOU MEAN IT?

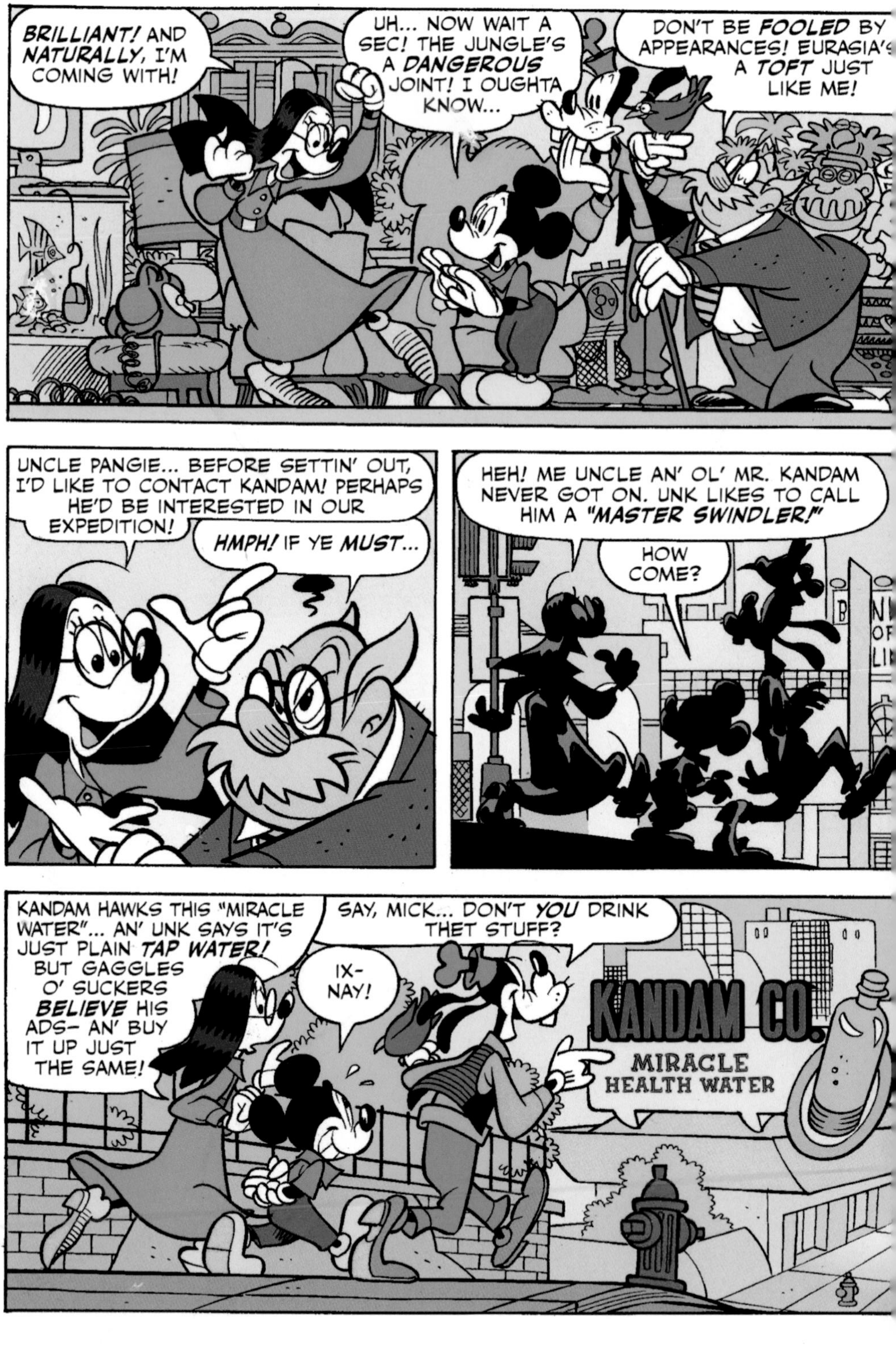
BRILLIANT! AND NATURALLY, I'M COMING WITH!
UH... NOW WAIT A SEC! THE JUNGLE'S A DANGEROUS JOINT! I OUGHTA KNOW...
DON'T BE FOOLED BY APPEARANCES! EURASIA'S A TOFT JUST LIKE ME!
UNCLE PANGIE... BEFORE SETTIN' OUT, I'D LIKE TO CONTACT KANDAM! PERHAPS HE'D BE INTERESTED IN OUR EXPEDITION!
HMPH! IF YE MUST...
HEH! ME UNCLE AN' OL' MR. KANDAM NEVER GOT ON. UNK LIKES TO CALL HIM A "MASTER SWINDLER!"
HOW COME?
KANDAM HAWKS THIS "MIRACLE WATER"... AN' UNK SAYS IT'S JUST PLAIN TAP WATER! BUT GAGGLES O' SUCKERS BELIEVE HIS ADS– AN' BUY IT UP JUST THE SAME!
SAY, MICK... DON'T YOU DRINK THET STUFF?
IX-NAY!
KANDAM CO.
MIRACLE HEALTH WATER

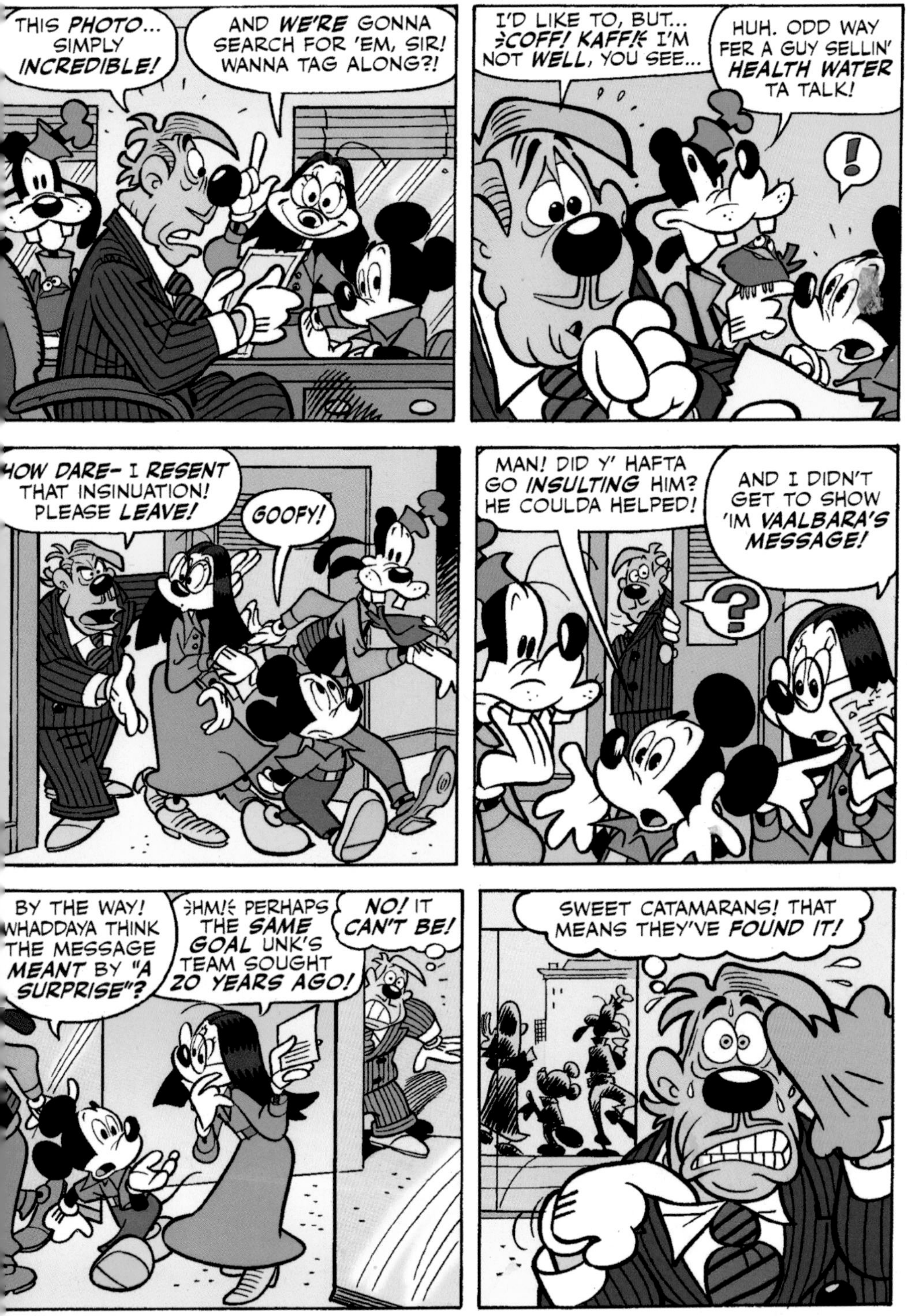
THIS PHOTO... SIMPLY INCREDIBLE!
AND WE'RE GONNA SEARCH FOR 'EM, SIR! WANNA TAG ALONG?!
I'D LIKE TO, BUT... COFF! KAFF! I'M NOT WELL, YOU SEE...
HUH. ODD WAY FER A GUY SELLIN' HEALTH WATER TA TALK!
!
HOW DARE- I RESENT THAT INSINUATION! PLEASE LEAVE!
GOOFY!
MAN! DID Y' HAFTA GO INSULTING HIM? HE COULDA HELPED!
AND I DIDN'T GET TO SHOW 'IM VAALBARA'S MESSAGE!
?
BY THE WAY! WHADDAYA THINK THE MESSAGE MEANT BY "A SURPRISE"?
HM! PERHAPS THE SAME GOAL UNK'S TEAM SOUGHT 20 YEARS AGO!
NO! IT CAN'T BE!
SWEET CATAMARANS! THAT MEANS THEY'VE FOUND IT!

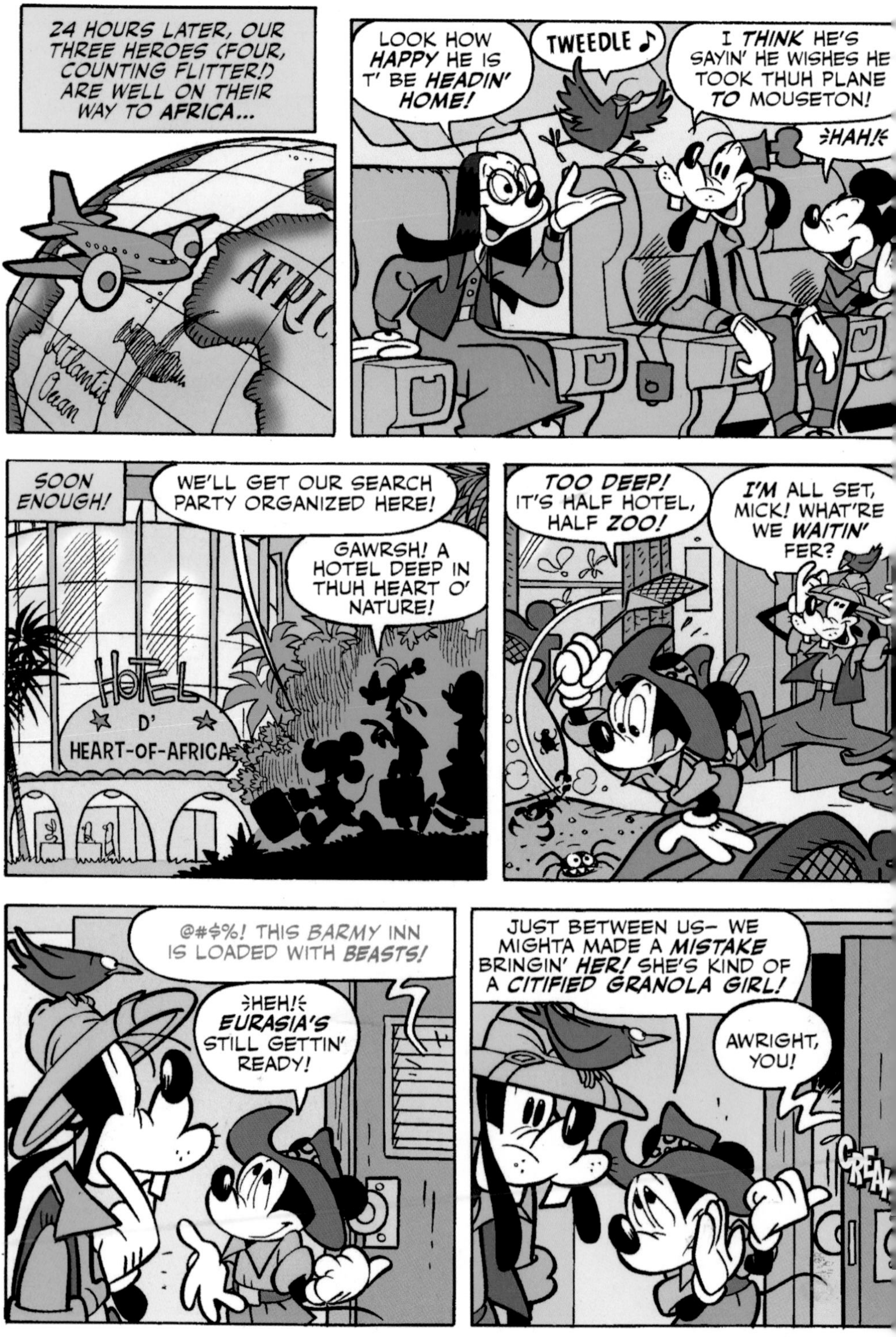
24 HOURS LATER, OUR THREE HEROES (FOUR, COUNTING FLITTER!) ARE WELL ON THEIR WAY TO AFRICA...
AFRIC
Atlantic Ocean
LOOK HOW HAPPY HE IS T' BE HEADIN' HOME!
TWEEDLE ♪
I THINK HE'S SAYIN' HE WISHES HE TOOK THUH PLANE TO MOUSETON!
HAH!
SOON ENOUGH!
WE'LL GET OUR SEARCH PARTY ORGANIZED HERE!
GAWRSH! A HOTEL DEEP IN THUH HEART O' NATURE!
HOTEL D' HEART-OF-AFRICA
TOO DEEP! IT'S HALF HOTEL, HALF ZOO!
I'M ALL SET, MICK! WHAT'RE WE WAITIN' FER?
@#$%! THIS BARMY INN IS LOADED WITH BEASTS!
HEH! EURASIA'S STILL GETTIN' READY!
JUST BETWEEN US— WE MIGHTA MADE A MISTAKE BRINGIN' HER! SHE'S KIND OF A CITIFIED GRANOLA GIRL!
AWRIGHT, YOU!
CREAK

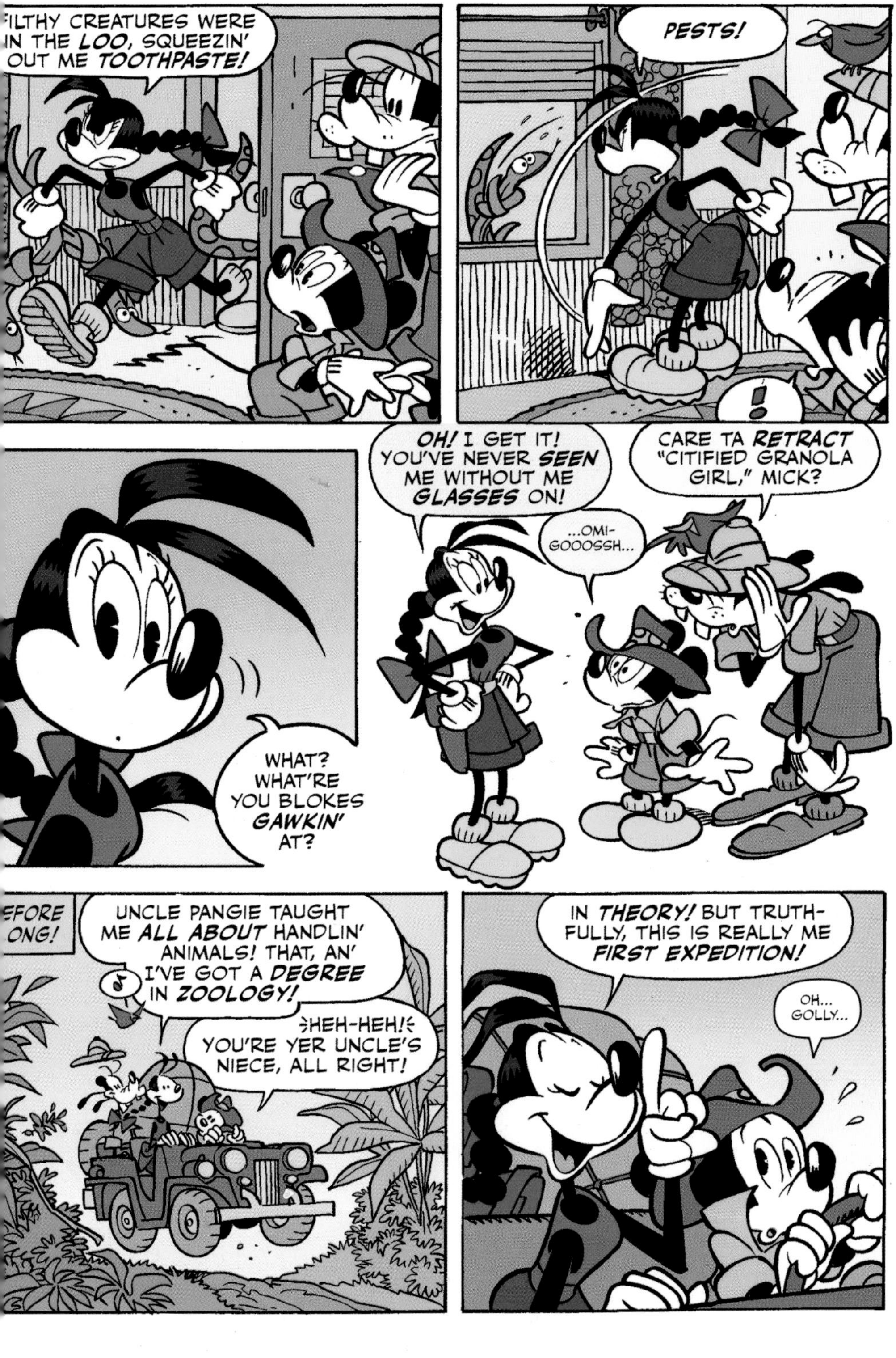

FILTHY CREATURES WERE IN THE LOO, SQUEEZIN' OUT ME TOOTHPASTE!
PESTS!
!
WHAT? WHAT'RE YOU BLOKES GAWKIN' AT?
OH! I GET IT! YOU'VE NEVER SEEN ME WITHOUT ME GLASSES ON!
...OMI-GOOOSSH...
CARE TA RETRACT "CITIFIED GRANOLA GIRL," MICK?
EFORE ONG!
UNCLE PANGIE TAUGHT ME ALL ABOUT HANDLIN' ANIMALS! THAT, AN' I'VE GOT A DEGREE IN ZOOLOGY!
HEH-HEH! YOU'RE YER UNCLE'S NIECE, ALL RIGHT!
IN THEORY! BUT TRUTH-FULLY, THIS IS REALLY ME FIRST EXPEDITION!
OH... GOLLY...

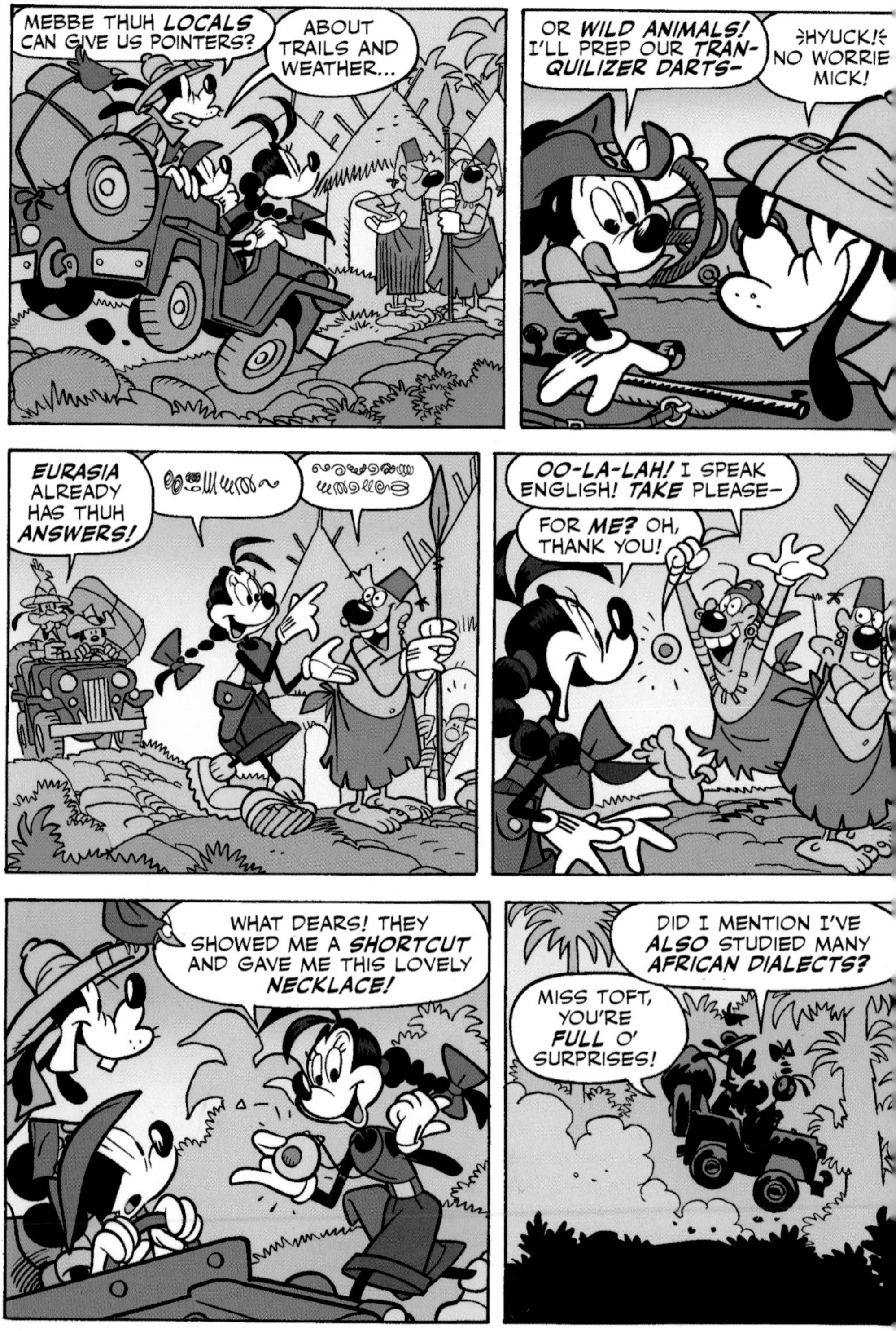
MEBBE THUH LOCALS CAN GIVE US POINTERS?
ABOUT TRAILS AND WEATHER...
OR WILD ANIMALS! I'LL PREP OUR TRANQUILIZER DARTS-
HYUCK! NO WORRIE MICK!
EURASIA ALREADY HAS THUH ANSWERS!
OO-LA-LAH! I SPEAK ENGLISH! TAKE PLEASE-
FOR ME? OH, THANK YOU!
WHAT DEARS! THEY SHOWED ME A SHORTCUT AND GAVE ME THIS LOVELY NECKLACE!
DID I MENTION I'VE ALSO STUDIED MANY AFRICAN DIALECTS?
MISS TOFT, YOU'RE FULL O' SURPRISES!

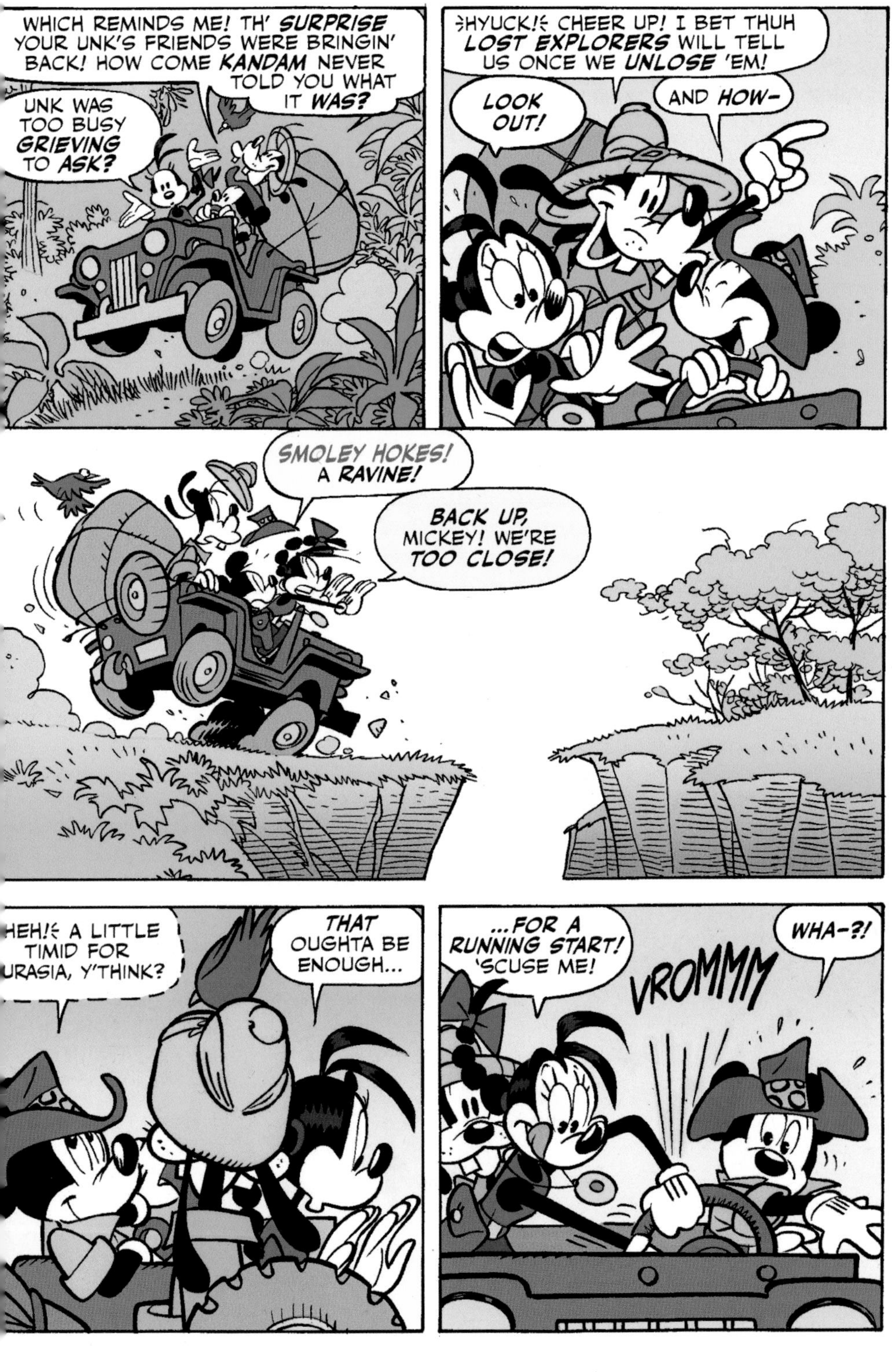
WHICH REMINDS ME! TH' SURPRISE YOUR UNK'S FRIENDS WERE BRINGIN' BACK! HOW COME KANDAM NEVER TOLD YOU WHAT IT WAS?
UNK WAS TOO BUSY GRIEVING TO ASK?
HYUCK! CHEER UP! I BET THUH LOST EXPLORERS WILL TELL US ONCE WE UNLOSE 'EM!
LOOK OUT!
AND HOW-
SMOLEY HOKES! A RAVINE!
BACK UP, MICKEY! WE'RE TOO CLOSE!
HEH! A LITTLE TIMID FOR URASIA, Y'THINK?
THAT OUGHTA BE ENOUGH...
...FOR A RUNNING START! 'SCUSE ME!
VROMMM
WHA-?!

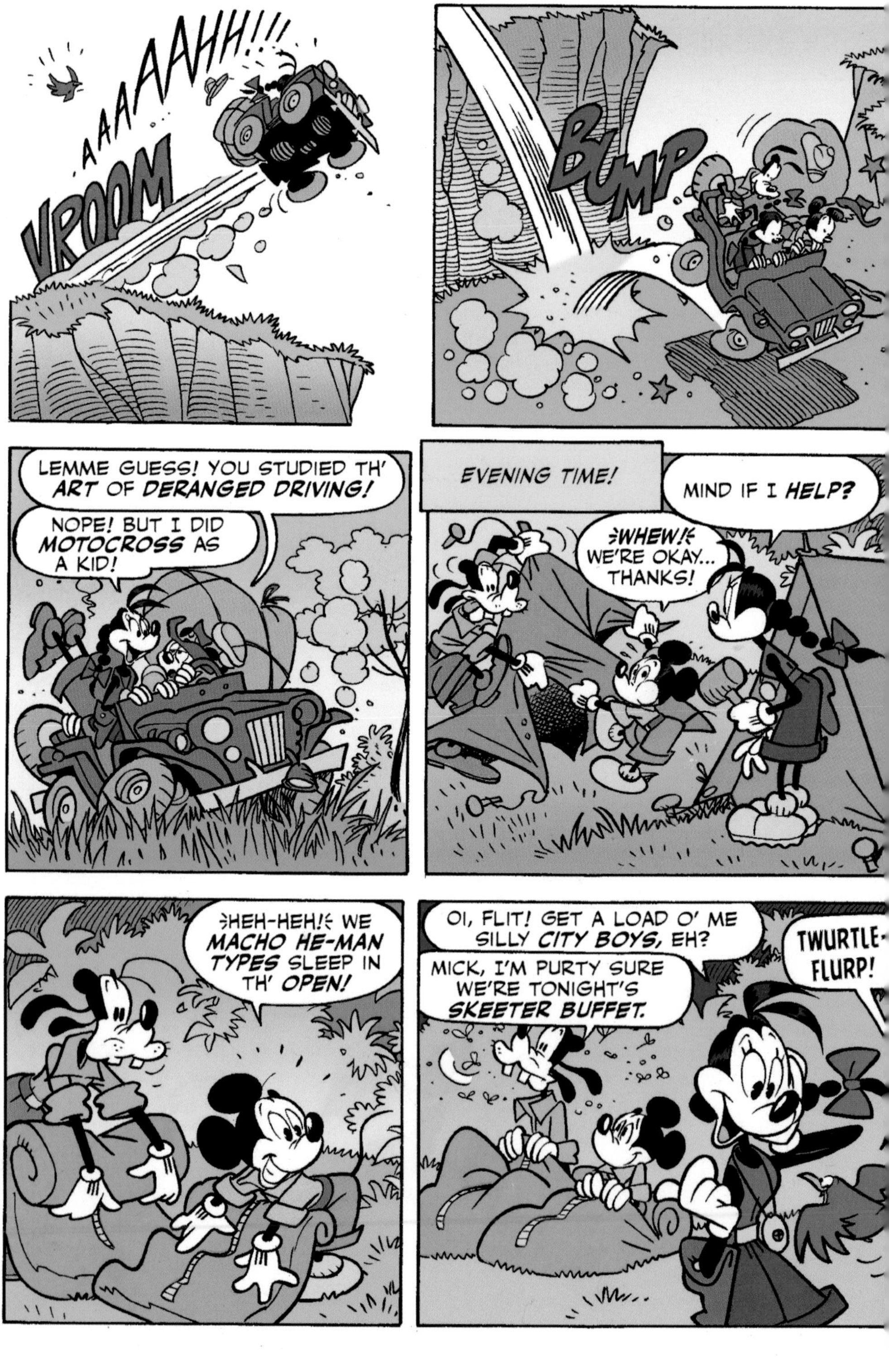
AAAAAAHH!!!
VROOM
BUMP
LEMME GUESS! YOU STUDIED TH' ART OF DERANGED DRIVING!
NOPE! BUT I DID MOTOCROSS AS A KID!
EVENING TIME!
MIND IF I HELP?
WHEW! WE'RE OKAY... THANKS!
HEH-HEH! WE MACHO HE-MAN TYPES SLEEP IN TH' OPEN!
OI, FLIT! GET A LOAD O' ME SILLY CITY BOYS, EH?
MICK, I'M PURTY SURE WE'RE TONIGHT'S SKEETER BUFFET.
TWURTLE-FLURP!

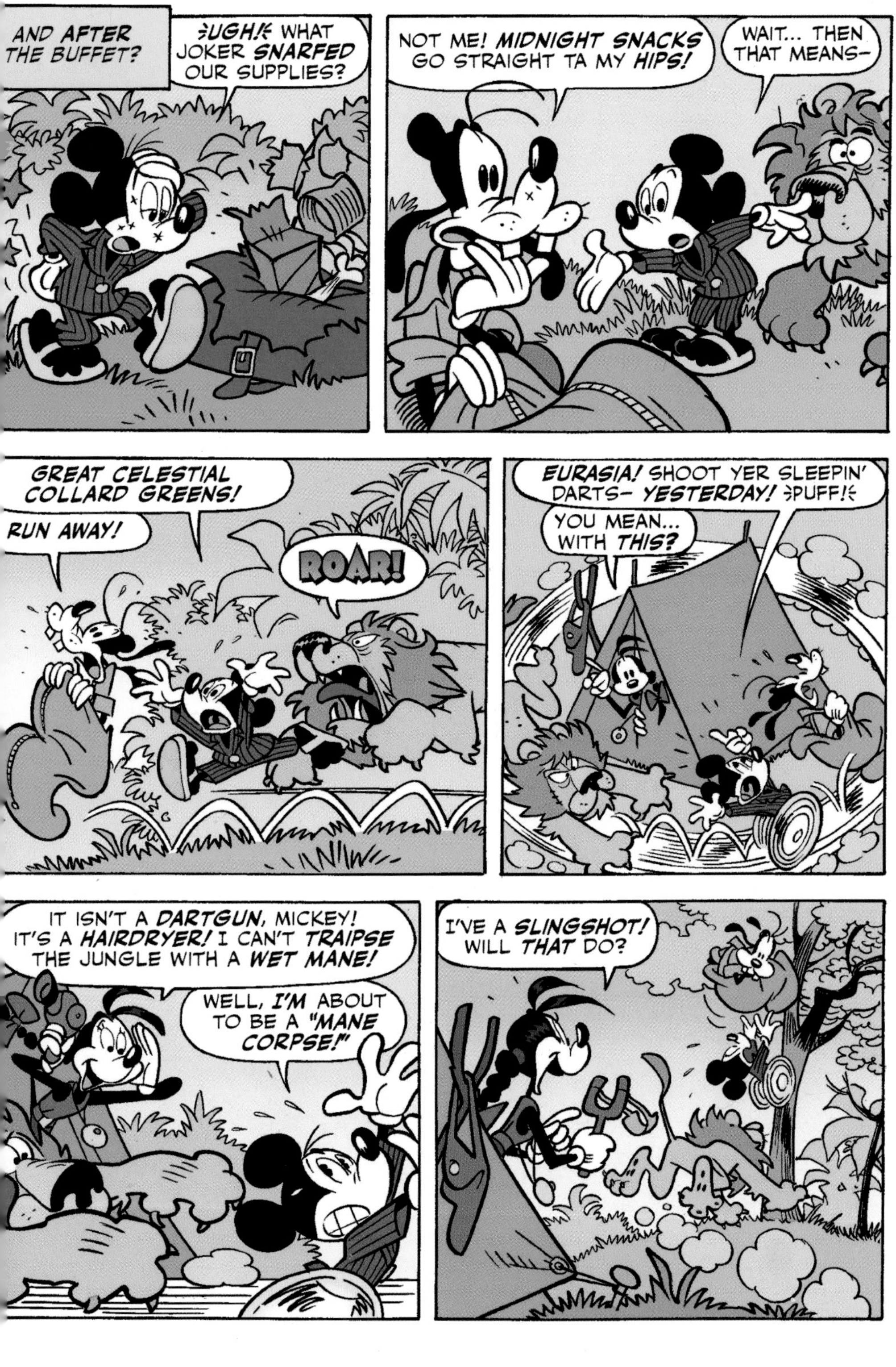

AND AFTER THE BUFFET?
UGH! WHAT JOKER SNARFED OUR SUPPLIES?
NOT ME! MIDNIGHT SNACKS GO STRAIGHT TA MY HIPS!
WAIT... THEN THAT MEANS–
GREAT CELESTIAL COLLARD GREENS!
RUN AWAY!
ROAR!
EURASIA! SHOOT YER SLEEPIN' DARTS– YESTERDAY! PUFF!
YOU MEAN... WITH THIS?
IT ISN'T A DARTGUN, MICKEY! IT'S A HAIRDRYER! I CAN'T TRAIPSE THE JUNGLE WITH A WET MANE!
WELL, I'M ABOUT TO BE A "MANE CORPSE!"
I'VE A SLINGSHOT! WILL THAT DO?

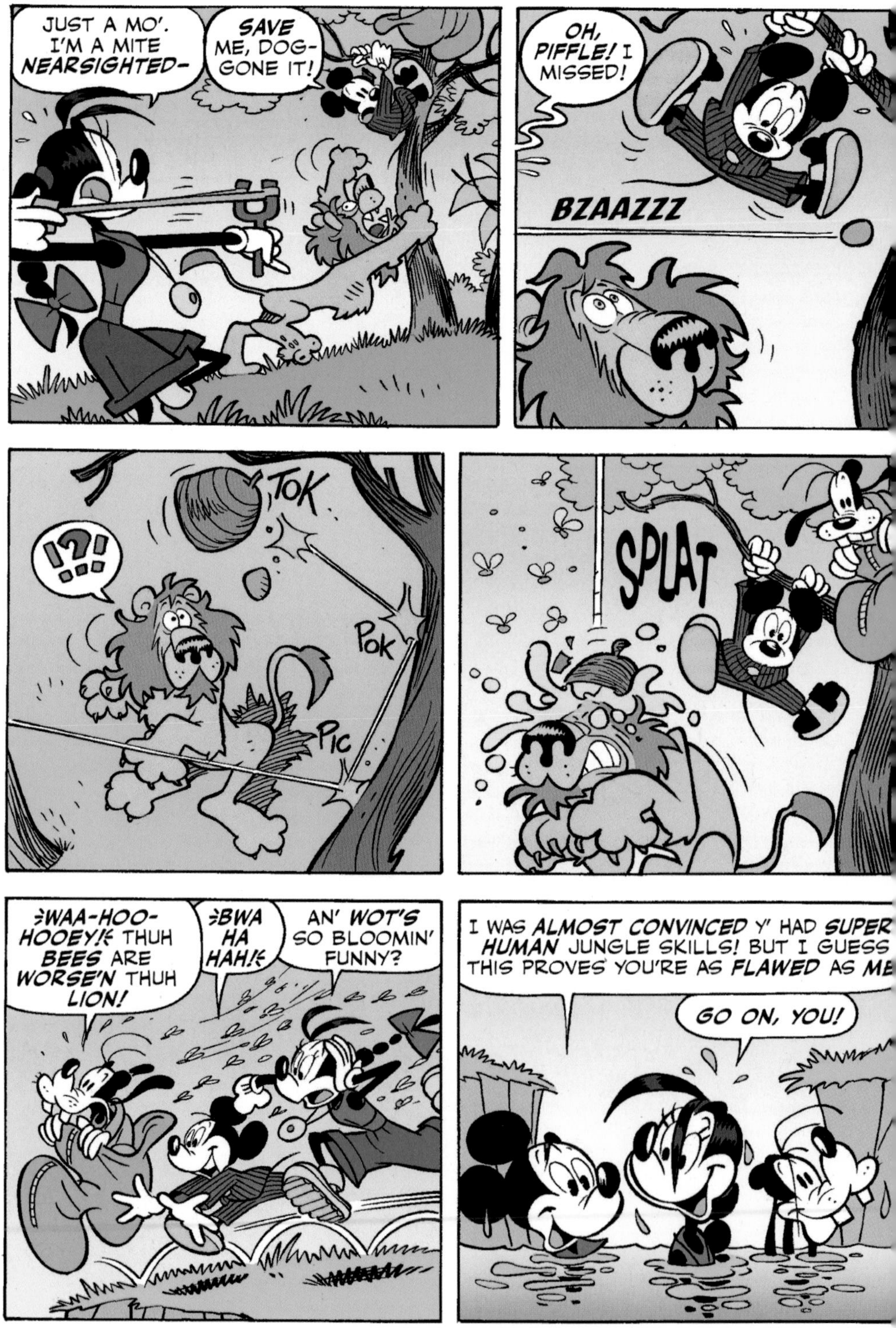
JUST A MO'. I'M A MITE NEARSIGHTED–
SAVE ME, DOG-GONE IT!
OH, PIFFLE! I MISSED!
BZAAZZZ
TOK
!?!
POK
PIC
SPLAT
WAA-HOO-HOOEY! THUH BEES ARE WORSE'N THUH LION!
BWA HA HAH!
AN' WOT'S SO BLOOMIN' FUNNY?
I WAS ALMOST CONVINCED Y' HAD SUPER HUMAN JUNGLE SKILLS! BUT I GUESS THIS PROVES YOU'RE AS FLAWED AS ME
GO ON, YOU!

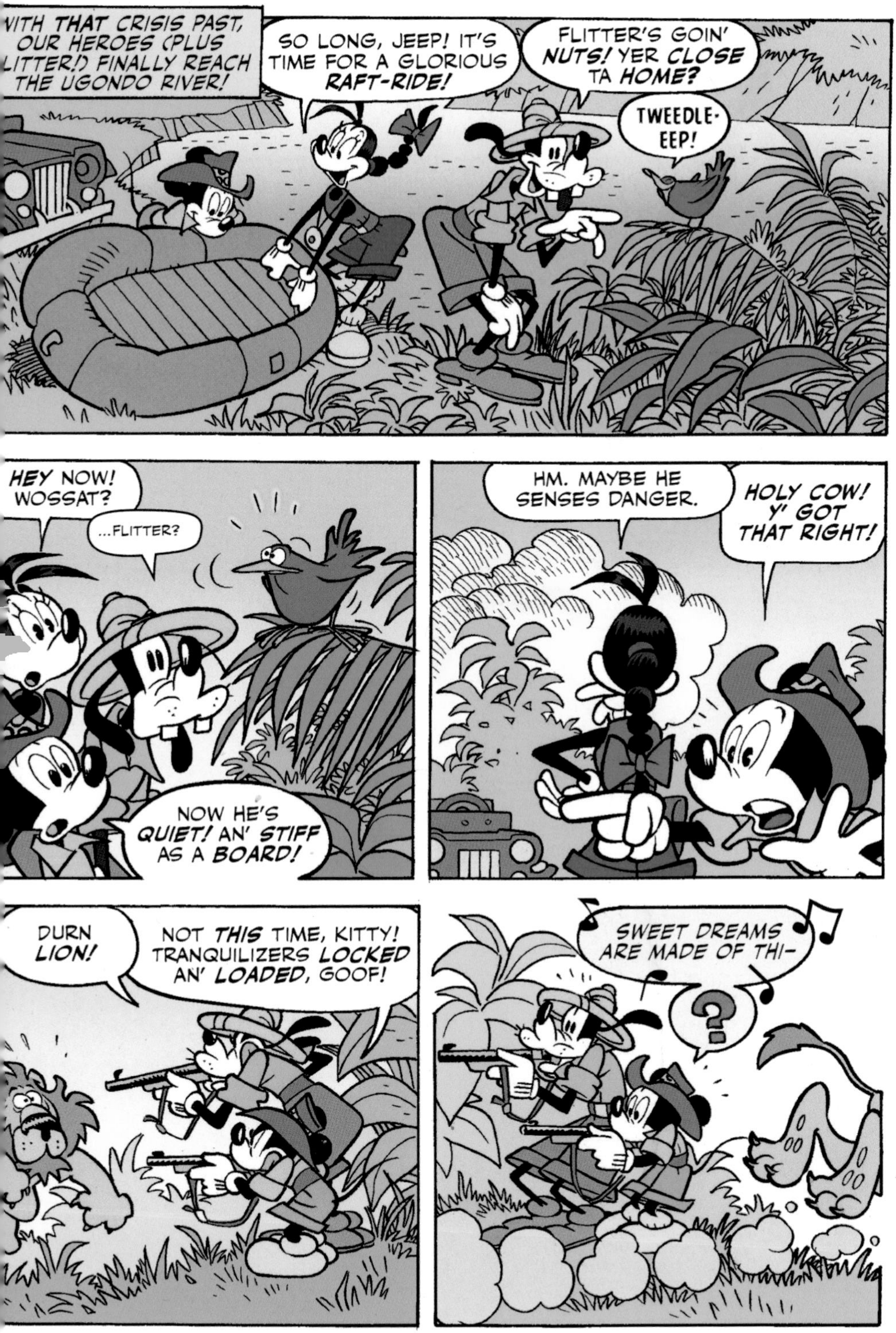
WITH THAT CRISIS PAST, OUR HEROES (PLUS FLITTER!) FINALLY REACH THE UGONDO RIVER!
SO LONG, JEEP! IT'S TIME FOR A GLORIOUS RAFT-RIDE!
FLITTER'S GOIN' NUTS! YER CLOSE TA HOME?
TWEEDLE-EEP!
HEY NOW! WOSSAT?
...FLITTER?
NOW HE'S QUIET! AN' STIFF AS A BOARD!
HM. MAYBE HE SENSES DANGER.
HOLY COW! Y' GOT THAT RIGHT!
DURN LION!
NOT THIS TIME, KITTY! TRANQUILIZERS LOCKED AN' LOADED, GOOF!
SWEET DREAMS ARE MADE OF THI–
?

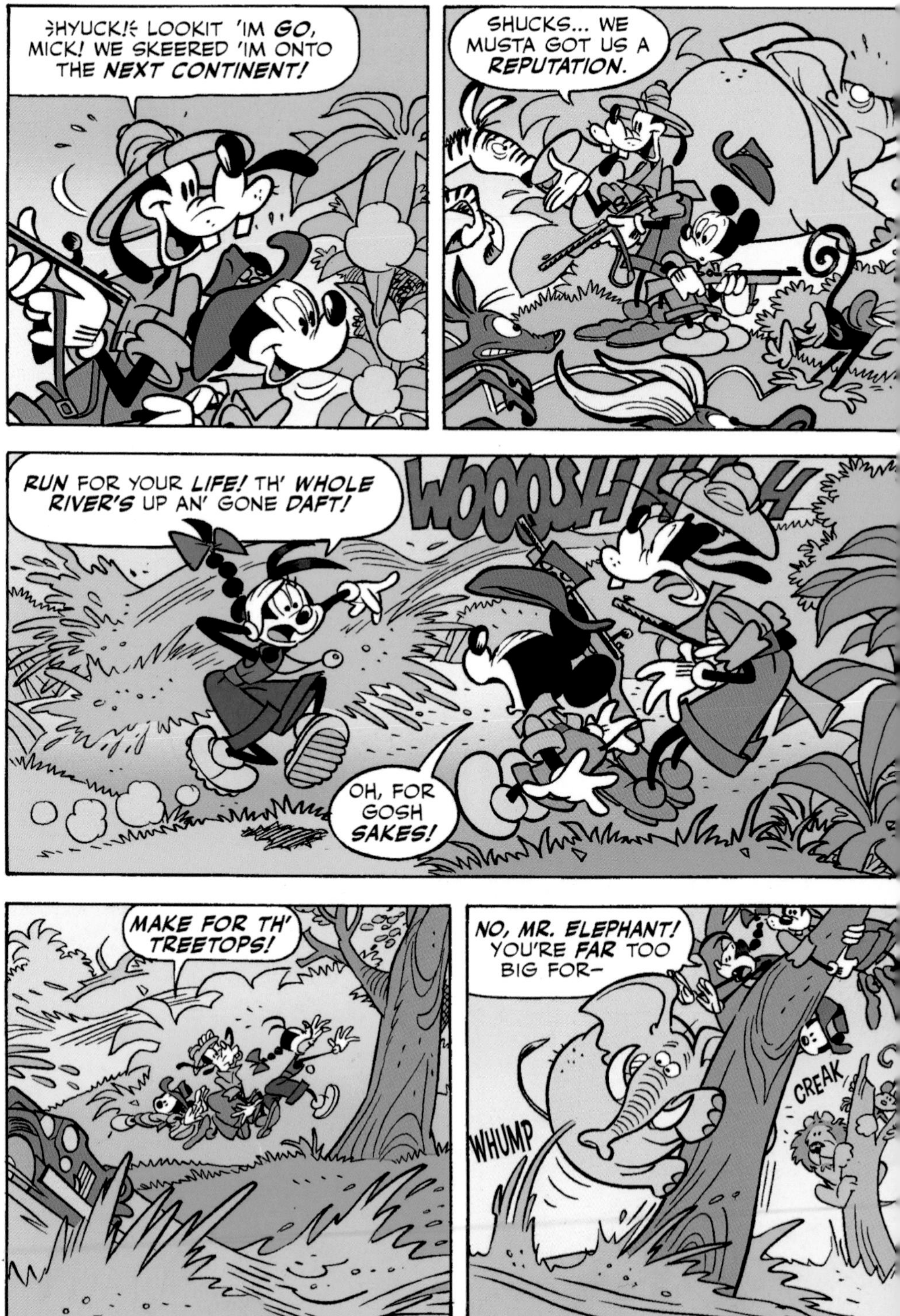

HYUCK! LOOKIT 'IM GO, MICK! WE SKEERED 'IM ONTO THE NEXT CONTINENT!
SHUCKS... WE MUSTA GOT US A REPUTATION.
RUN FOR YOUR LIFE! TH' WHOLE RIVER'S UP AN' GONE DAFT!
WOOOSH
OH, FOR GOSH SAKES!
MAKE FOR TH' TREETOPS!
NO, MR. ELEPHANT! YOU'RE FAR TOO BIG FOR–
WHUMP
CREAK

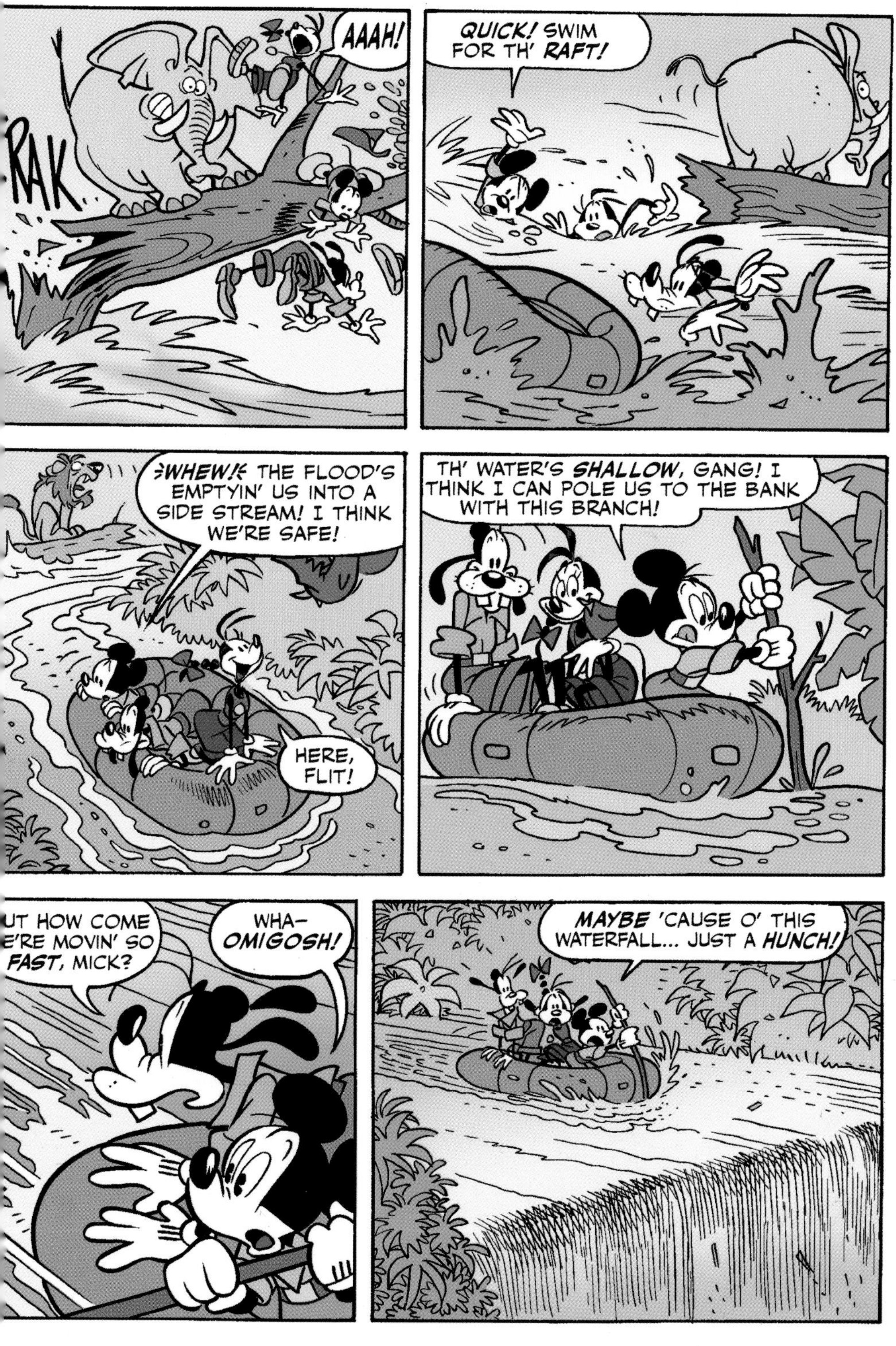
AAAH!
RAK
QUICK! SWIM FOR TH' RAFT!
WHEW! THE FLOOD'S EMPTYIN' US INTO A SIDE STREAM! I THINK WE'RE SAFE!
HERE, FLIT!
TH' WATER'S SHALLOW, GANG! I THINK I CAN POLE US TO THE BANK WITH THIS BRANCH!
UT HOW COME E'RE MOVIN' SO FAST, MICK?
WHA— OMIGOSH!
MAYBE 'CAUSE O' THIS WATERFALL... JUST A HUNCH!

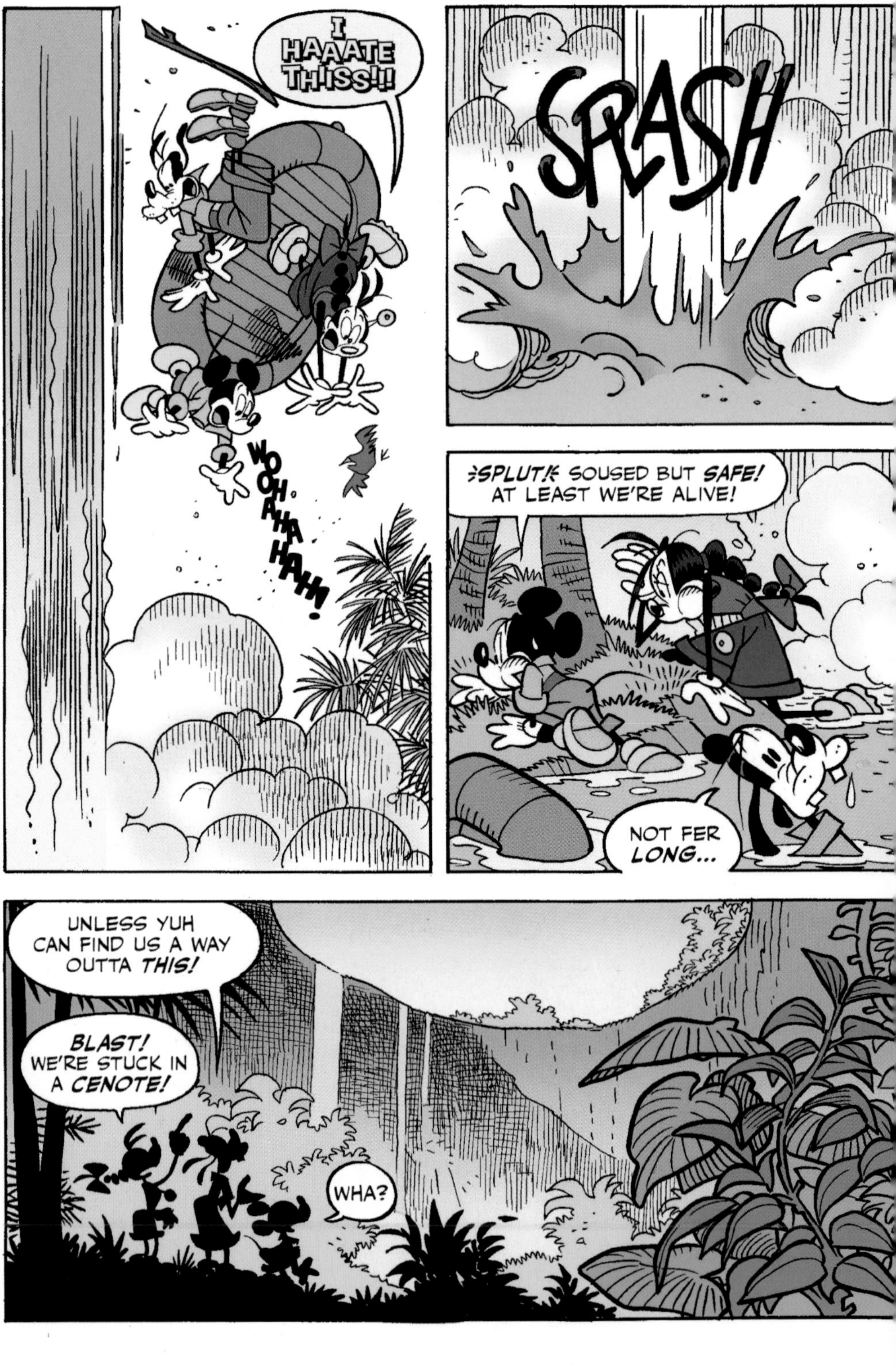
I HAAATE THISS!!!
WOOOH AHAHA HAHH!
SPLASH
SPLUT! SOUSED BUT SAFE! AT LEAST WE'RE ALIVE!
NOT FER LONG...
UNLESS YUH CAN FIND US A WAY OUTTA THIS!
BLAST! WE'RE STUCK IN A CENOTE!
WHA?

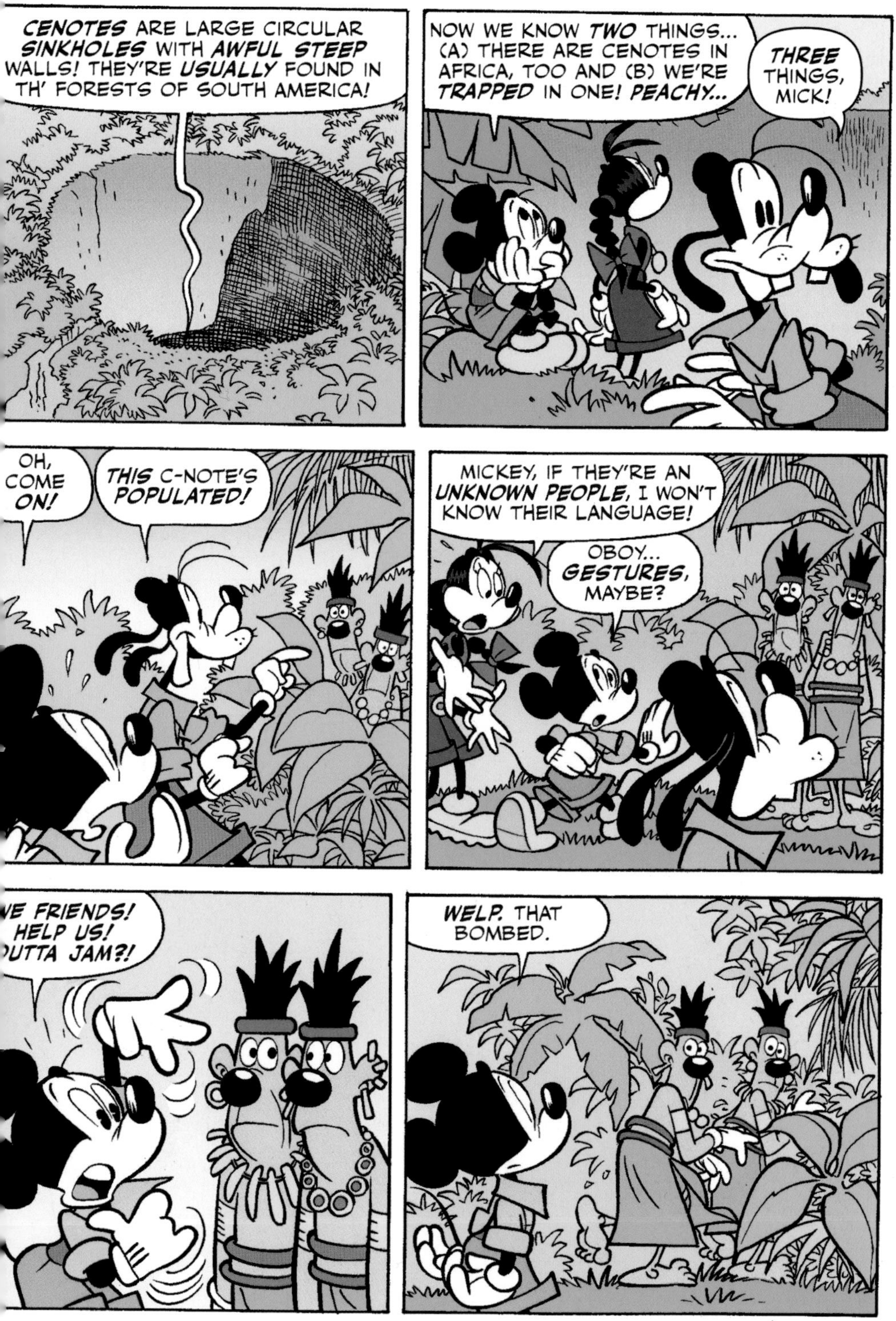
CENOTES ARE LARGE CIRCULAR SINKHOLES WITH AWFUL STEEP WALLS! THEY'RE USUALLY FOUND IN TH' FORESTS OF SOUTH AMERICA!
NOW WE KNOW TWO THINGS... (A) THERE ARE CENOTES IN AFRICA, TOO AND (B) WE'RE TRAPPED IN ONE! PEACHY...
THREE THINGS, MICK!
OH, COME ON!
THIS C-NOTE'S POPULATED!
MICKEY, IF THEY'RE AN UNKNOWN PEOPLE, I WON'T KNOW THEIR LANGUAGE!
OBOY... GESTURES, MAYBE?
E FRIENDS! HELP US! UTTA JAM?!
WELP. THAT BOMBED.

NO, WAIT! THEY'RE... *RETURNING?*

LOOK, MAC! ON BEHALF OF THE *QUATLOO TRIBE,* OUR *LANGUAGE* CLASS IS *FILLED!* BUT IF WE GIVE YOU THIS *DICTIONARY,* WILL IT KEEP YOU FROM *BLITHERING* LIKE A *GRAMMARLESS NINNY?*

MERRIAM-WEBFOOT

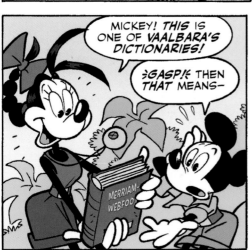

MICKEY! *THIS* IS ONE OF *VAALBARA'S DICTIONARIES!*

≥GASP!≤ THEN *THAT* MEANS—

MERRIAM-WEBFOO

EURASIA?

LITTLE EURASIA!?

I CAN'T BELIEVE MY *EYES...*

IT'S *PANGIE'S NIECE!* COME TO *RESCUE* US!

TOO-RA-LOO!

TH—THE *LOST* EXPLORERS!

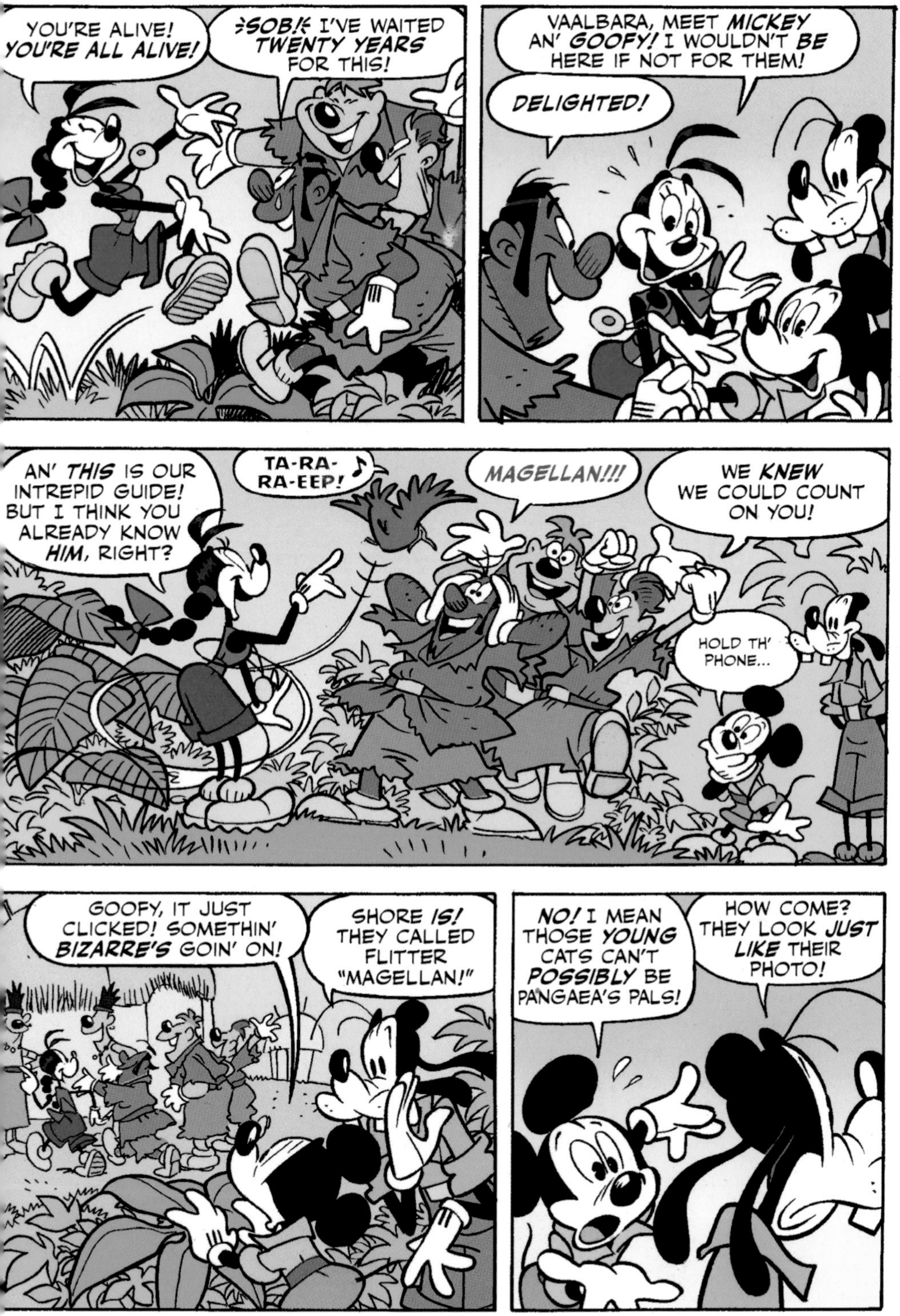
YOU'RE ALIVE! YOU'RE ALL ALIVE!
SOB! I'VE WAITED TWENTY YEARS FOR THIS!
VAALBARA, MEET MICKEY AN' GOOFY! I WOULDN'T BE HERE IF NOT FOR THEM!
DELIGHTED!
AN' THIS IS OUR INTREPID GUIDE! BUT I THINK YOU ALREADY KNOW HIM, RIGHT?
TA-RA-RA-EEP! ♪
MAGELLAN!!!
WE KNEW WE COULD COUNT ON YOU!
HOLD TH' PHONE...
GOOFY, IT JUST CLICKED! SOMETHIN' BIZARRE'S GOIN' ON!
SHORE IS! THEY CALLED FLITTER "MAGELLAN!"
NO! I MEAN THOSE YOUNG CATS CAN'T POSSIBLY BE PANGAEA'S PALS!
HOW COME? THEY LOOK JUST LIKE THEIR PHOTO!

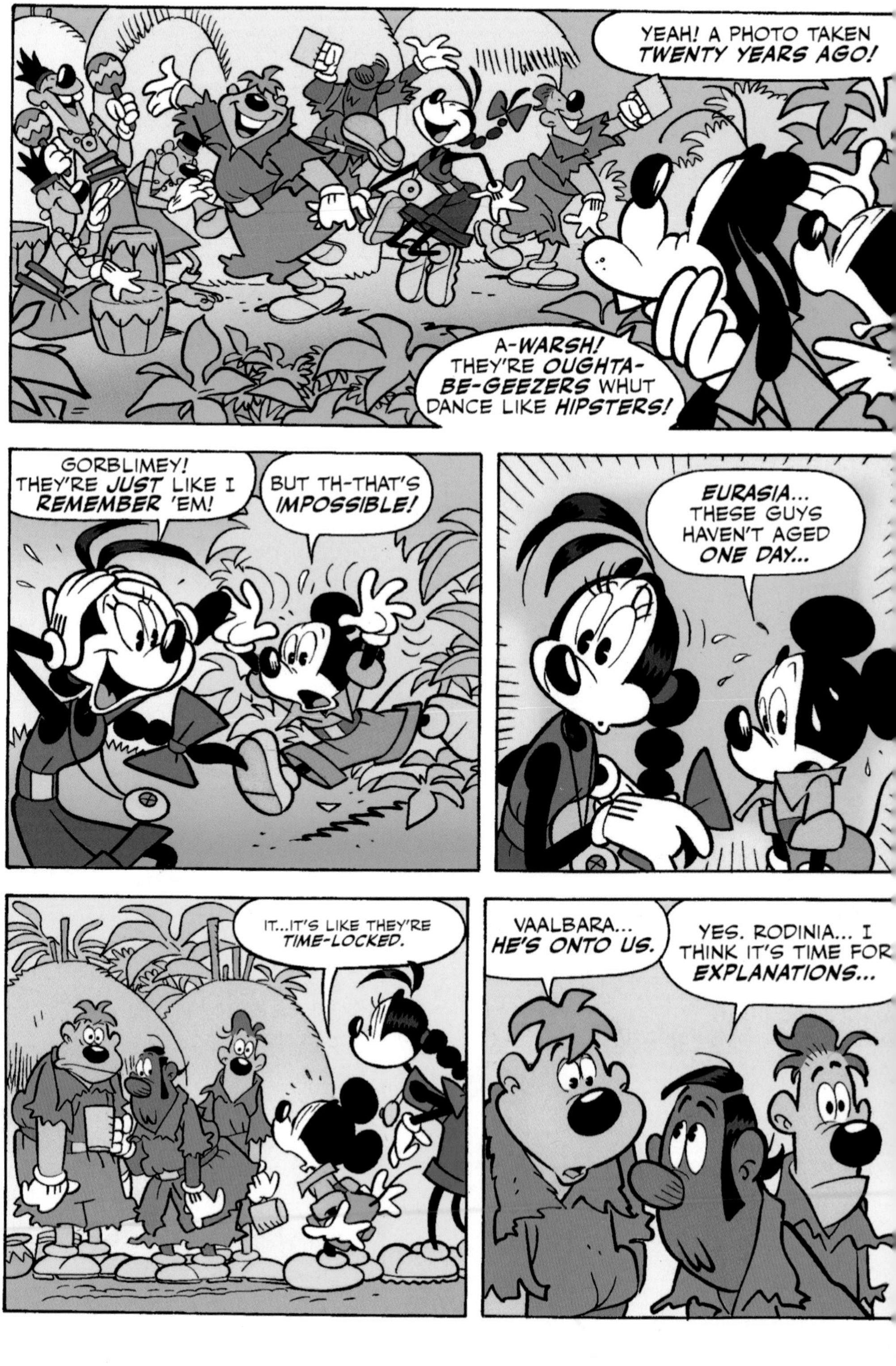
YEAH! A PHOTO TAKEN TWENTY YEARS AGO!
A-WARSH! THEY'RE OUGHTA-BE-GEEZERS WHUT DANCE LIKE HIPSTERS!
GORBLIMEY! THEY'RE JUST LIKE I REMEMBER 'EM!
BUT TH-THAT'S IMPOSSIBLE!
EURASIA... THESE GUYS HAVEN'T AGED ONE DAY...
IT...IT'S LIKE THEY'RE TIME-LOCKED.
VAALBARA... HE'S ONTO US.
YES. RODINIA... I THINK IT'S TIME FOR EXPLANATIONS...

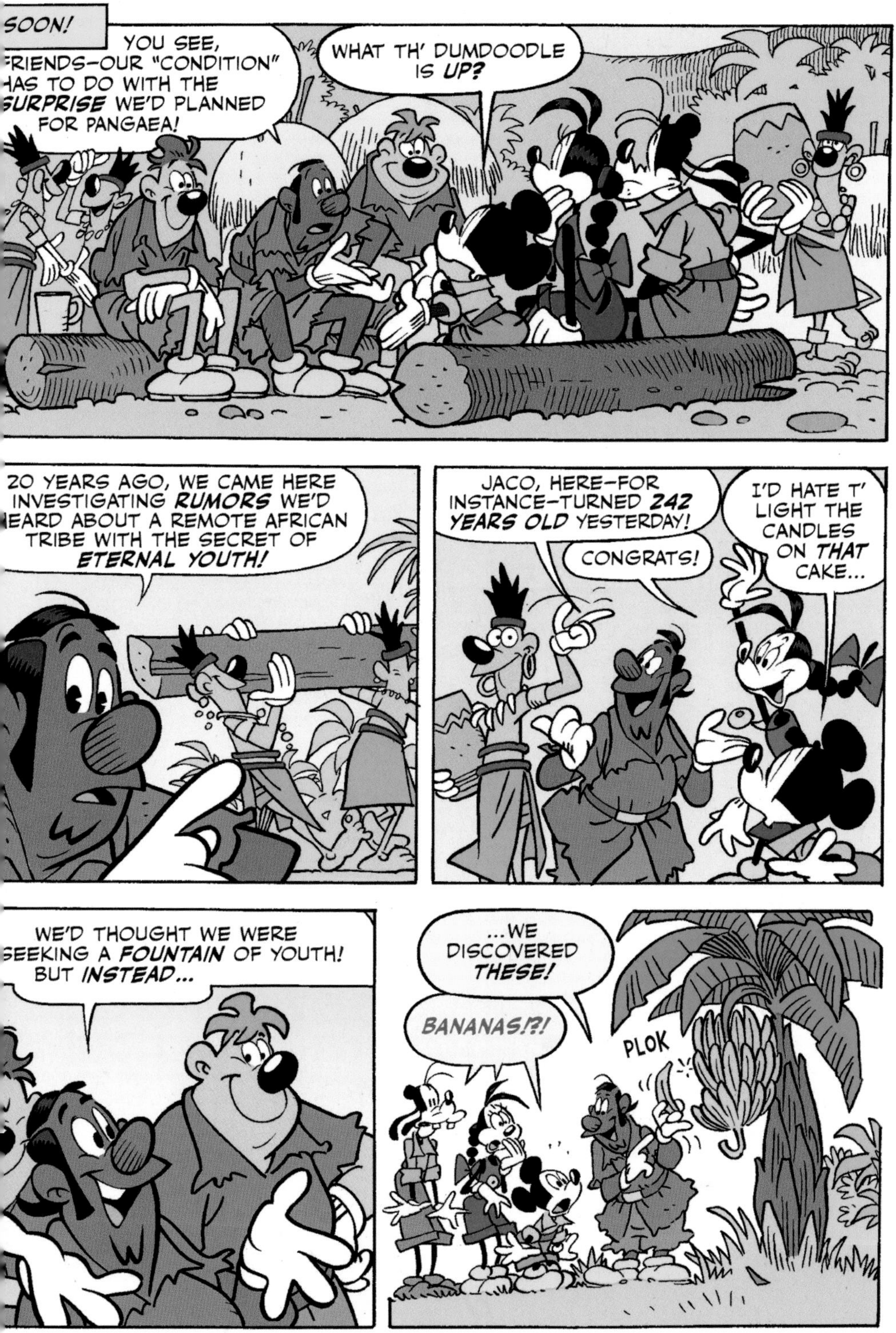
SOON!
YOU SEE, FRIENDS—OUR "CONDITION" HAS TO DO WITH THE SURPRISE WE'D PLANNED FOR PANGAEA!
WHAT TH' DUMDOODLE IS UP?
20 YEARS AGO, WE CAME HERE INVESTIGATING RUMORS WE'D HEARD ABOUT A REMOTE AFRICAN TRIBE WITH THE SECRET OF ETERNAL YOUTH!
JACO, HERE—FOR INSTANCE—TURNED 242 YEARS OLD YESTERDAY!
CONGRATS!
I'D HATE T' LIGHT THE CANDLES ON THAT CAKE...
WE'D THOUGHT WE WERE SEEKING A FOUNTAIN OF YOUTH! BUT INSTEAD...
...WE DISCOVERED THESE!
BANANAS!?!
PLOK

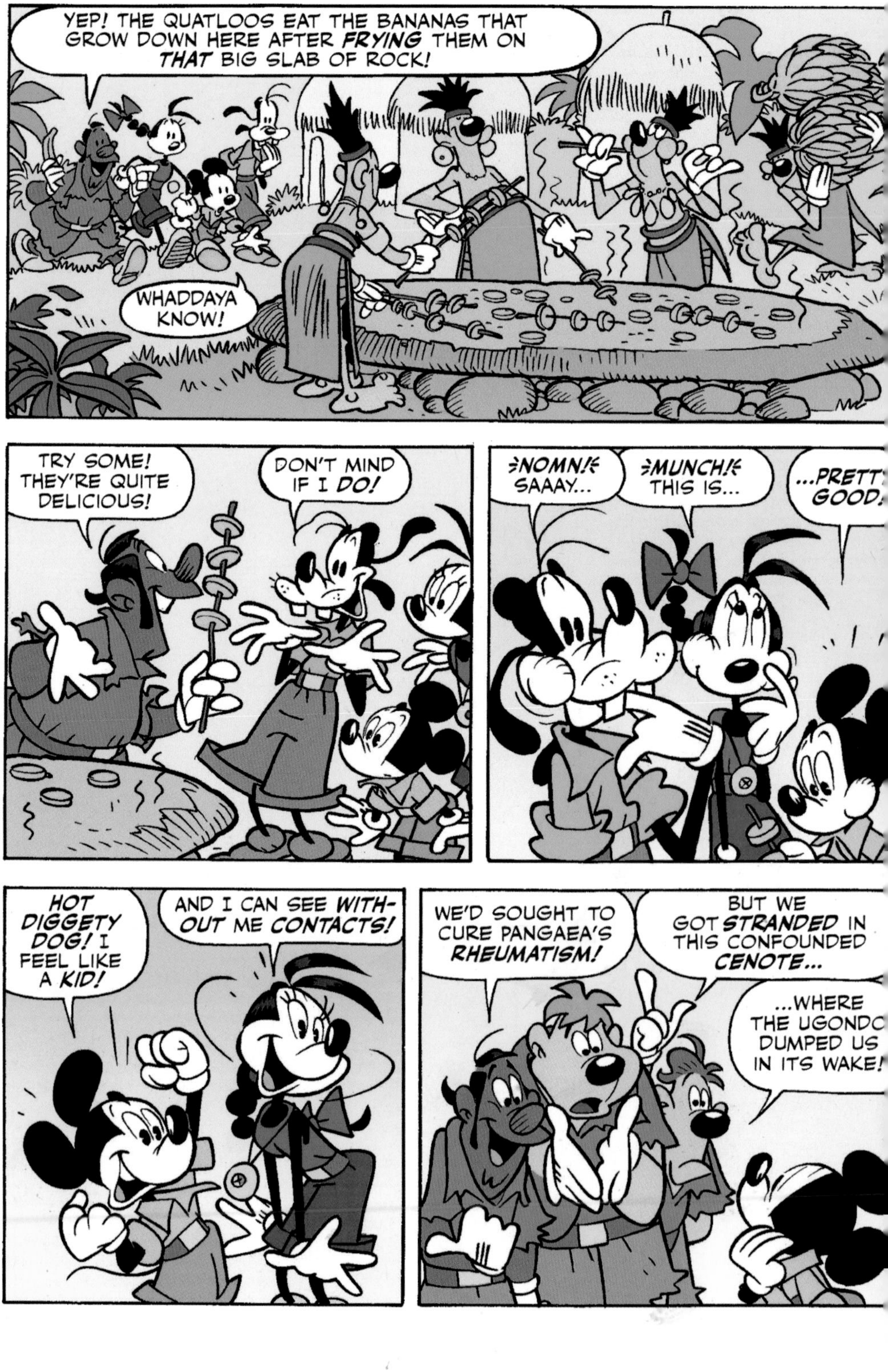

YEP! THE QUATLOOS EAT THE BANANAS THAT GROW DOWN HERE AFTER *FRYING* THEM ON *THAT* BIG SLAB OF ROCK!
WHADDAYA KNOW!
TRY SOME! THEY'RE QUITE DELICIOUS!
DON'T MIND IF I *DO!*
NOMN! SAAAY...
MUNCH! THIS IS...
...PRETT GOOD.
HOT DIGGETY DOG! I FEEL LIKE A *KID!*
AND I CAN SEE *WITH-OUT* ME *CONTACTS!*
WE'D SOUGHT TO CURE PANGAEA'S *RHEUMATISM!*
BUT WE GOT *STRANDED* IN THIS CONFOUNDED *CENOTE...*
...WHERE THE UGONDO DUMPED US IN ITS WAKE!

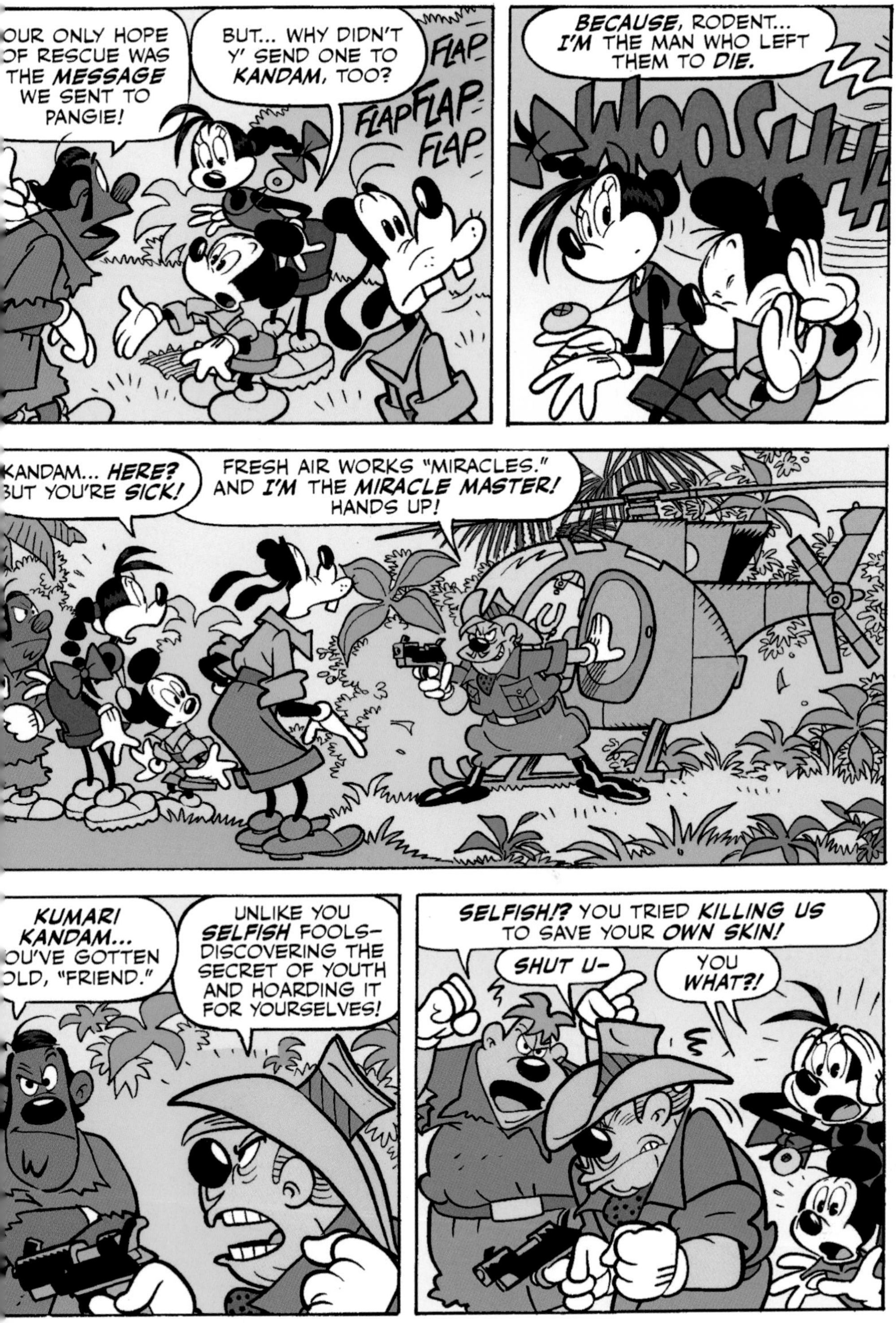

OUR ONLY HOPE OF RESCUE WAS THE *MESSAGE* WE SENT TO PANGIE!
BUT... WHY DIDN'T Y' SEND ONE TO *KANDAM*, TOO?
FLAP FLAP FLAP FLAP FLAP
BECAUSE, RODENT... *I'M* THE MAN WHO LEFT THEM TO *DIE*.
WOOSHH
KANDAM... *HERE?* BUT YOU'RE *SICK!*
FRESH AIR WORKS "MIRACLES." AND *I'M* THE *MIRACLE MASTER!* HANDS UP!
KUMARI KANDAM... YOU'VE GOTTEN OLD, "FRIEND."
UNLIKE YOU *SELFISH* FOOLS– DISCOVERING THE SECRET OF YOUTH AND HOARDING IT FOR YOURSELVES!
SELFISH!? YOU TRIED *KILLING US* TO SAVE YOUR *OWN SKIN!*
SHUT U–
YOU *WHAT?!*

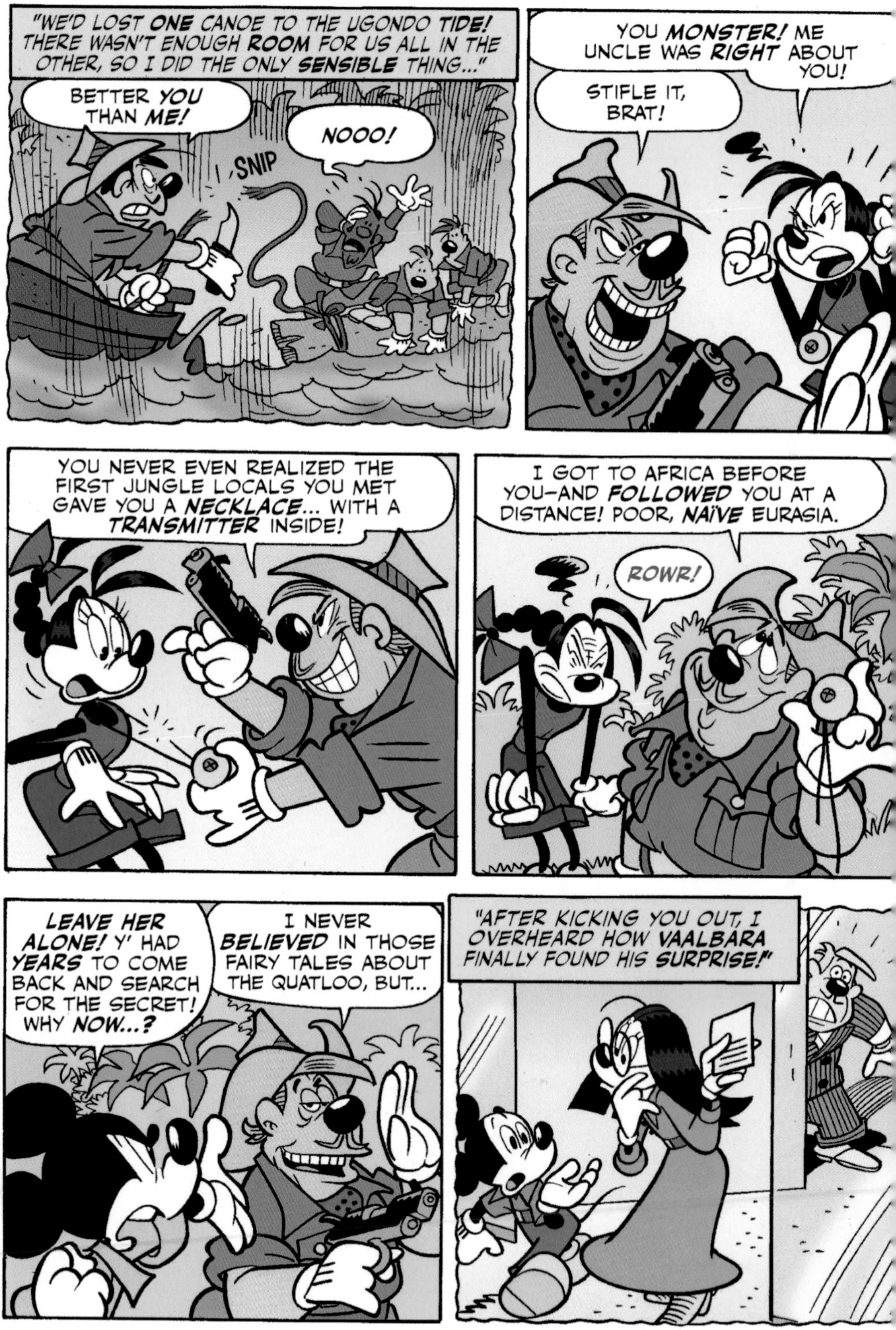
"WE'D LOST ONE CANOE TO THE UGONDO TIDE! THERE WASN'T ENOUGH ROOM FOR US ALL IN THE OTHER, SO I DID THE ONLY SENSIBLE THING..."
BETTER YOU THAN ME!
SNIP
NOOO!
YOU MONSTER! ME UNCLE WAS RIGHT ABOUT YOU!
STIFLE IT, BRAT!
YOU NEVER EVEN REALIZED THE FIRST JUNGLE LOCALS YOU MET GAVE YOU A NECKLACE... WITH A TRANSMITTER INSIDE!
I GOT TO AFRICA BEFORE YOU—AND FOLLOWED YOU AT A DISTANCE! POOR, NAÏVE EURASIA.
ROWR!
LEAVE HER ALONE! Y' HAD YEARS TO COME BACK AND SEARCH FOR THE SECRET! WHY NOW...?
I NEVER BELIEVED IN THOSE FAIRY TALES ABOUT THE QUATLOO, BUT...
"AFTER KICKING YOU OUT, I OVERHEARD HOW VAALBARA FINALLY FOUND HIS SURPRISE!"

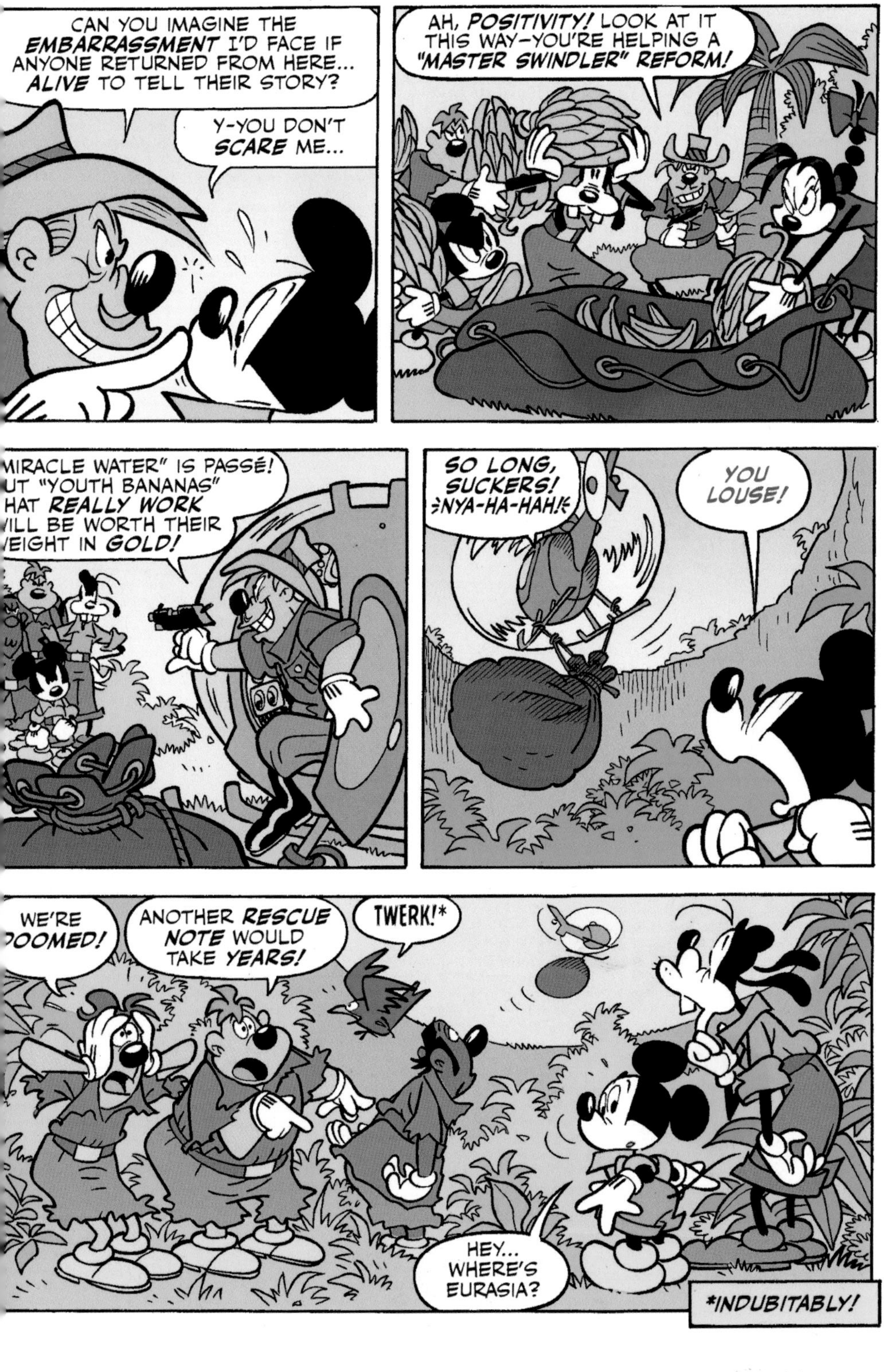

CAN YOU IMAGINE THE EMBARRASSMENT I'D FACE IF ANYONE RETURNED FROM HERE... ALIVE TO TELL THEIR STORY?
Y-YOU DON'T SCARE ME...
AH, POSITIVITY! LOOK AT IT THIS WAY—YOU'RE HELPING A "MASTER SWINDLER" REFORM!
MIRACLE WATER" IS PASSÉ! UT "YOUTH BANANAS" HAT REALLY WORK VILL BE WORTH THEIR VEIGHT IN GOLD!
SO LONG, SUCKERS! NYA-HA-HAH!
YOU LOUSE!
WE'RE DOOMED!
ANOTHER RESCUE NOTE WOULD TAKE YEARS!
TWERK!*
HEY... WHERE'S EURASIA?
*INDUBITABLY!

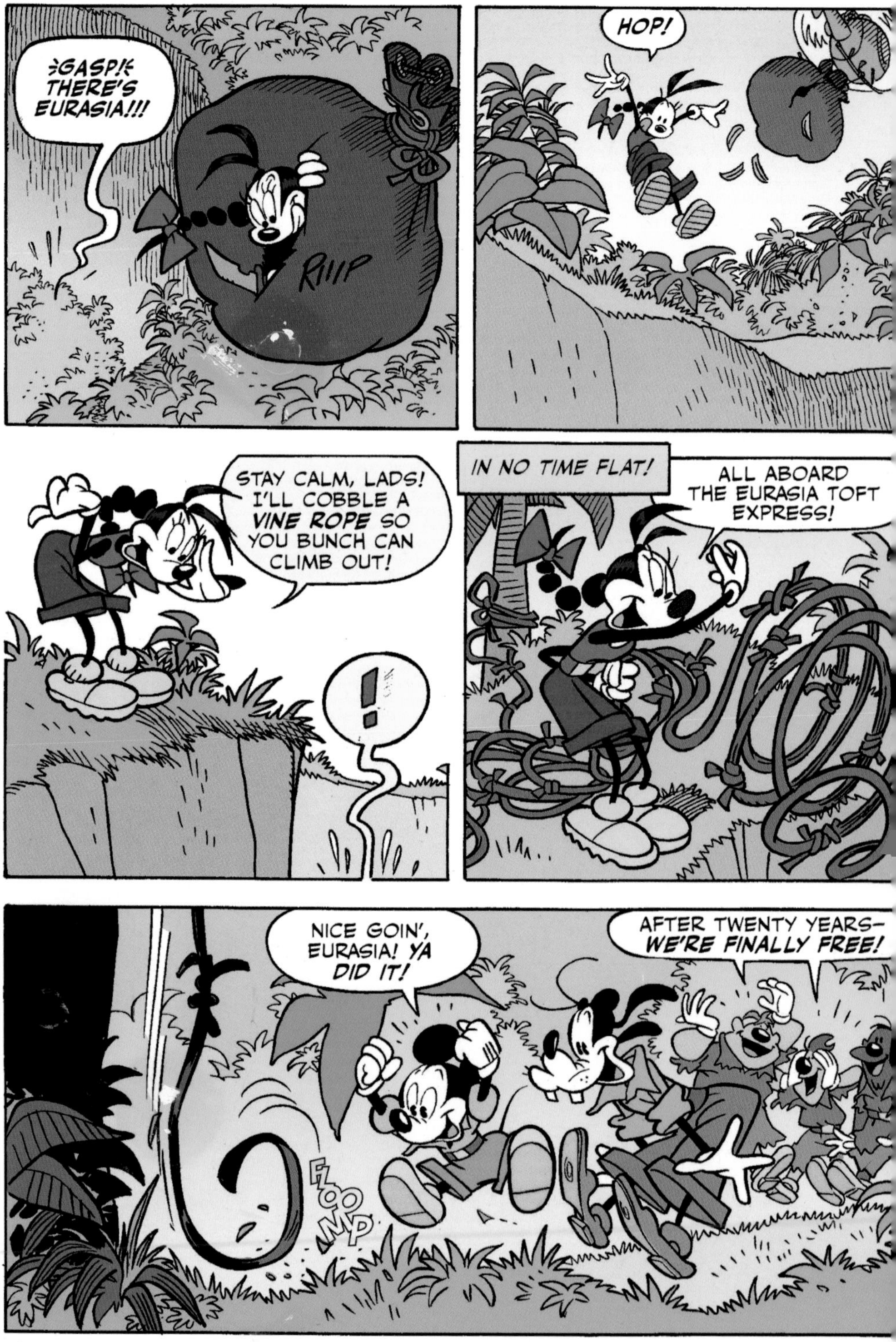

GASP! THERE'S EURASIA!!!
RIIIP
HOP!
STAY CALM, LADS! I'LL COBBLE A VINE ROPE SO YOU BUNCH CAN CLIMB OUT!
!
IN NO TIME FLAT!
ALL ABOARD THE EURASIA TOFT EXPRESS!
NICE GOIN', EURASIA! YA DID IT!
AFTER TWENTY YEARS— WE'RE FINALLY FREE!
FLOOMP

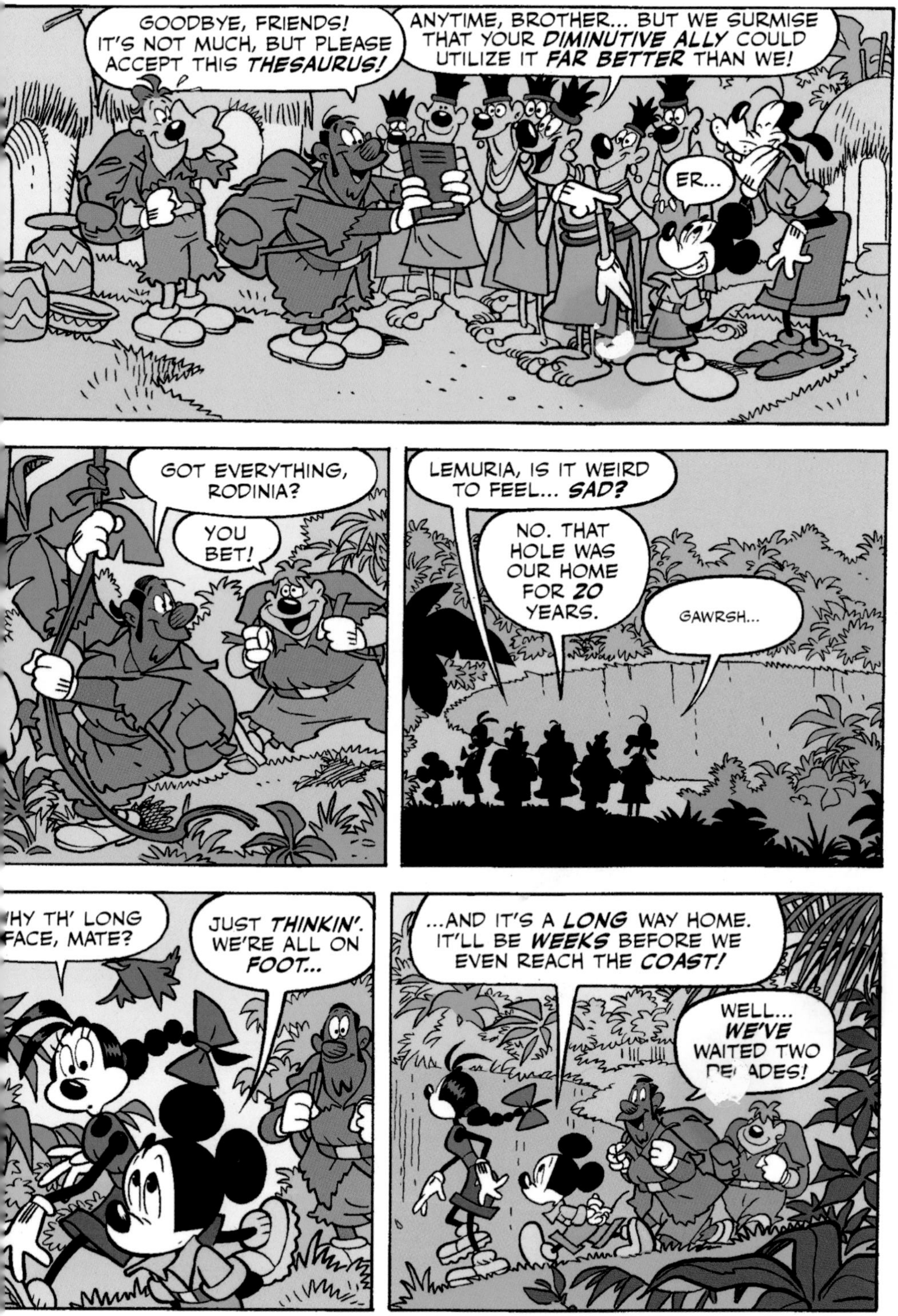

GOODBYE, FRIENDS! IT'S NOT MUCH, BUT PLEASE ACCEPT THIS *THESAURUS!*
ANYTIME, BROTHER... BUT WE SURMISE THAT YOUR *DIMINUTIVE ALLY* COULD UTILIZE IT *FAR BETTER* THAN WE!
ER...
GOT EVERYTHING, RODINIA?
YOU BET!
LEMURIA, IS IT WEIRD TO FEEL... *SAD?*
NO. THAT HOLE WAS OUR HOME FOR *20* YEARS.
GAWRSH...
HY TH' LONG FACE, MATE?
JUST *THINKIN'*. WE'RE ALL ON *FOOT...*
...AND IT'S A *LONG* WAY HOME. IT'LL BE *WEEKS* BEFORE WE EVEN REACH THE *COAST!*
WELL... *WE'VE* WAITED TWO DECADES!

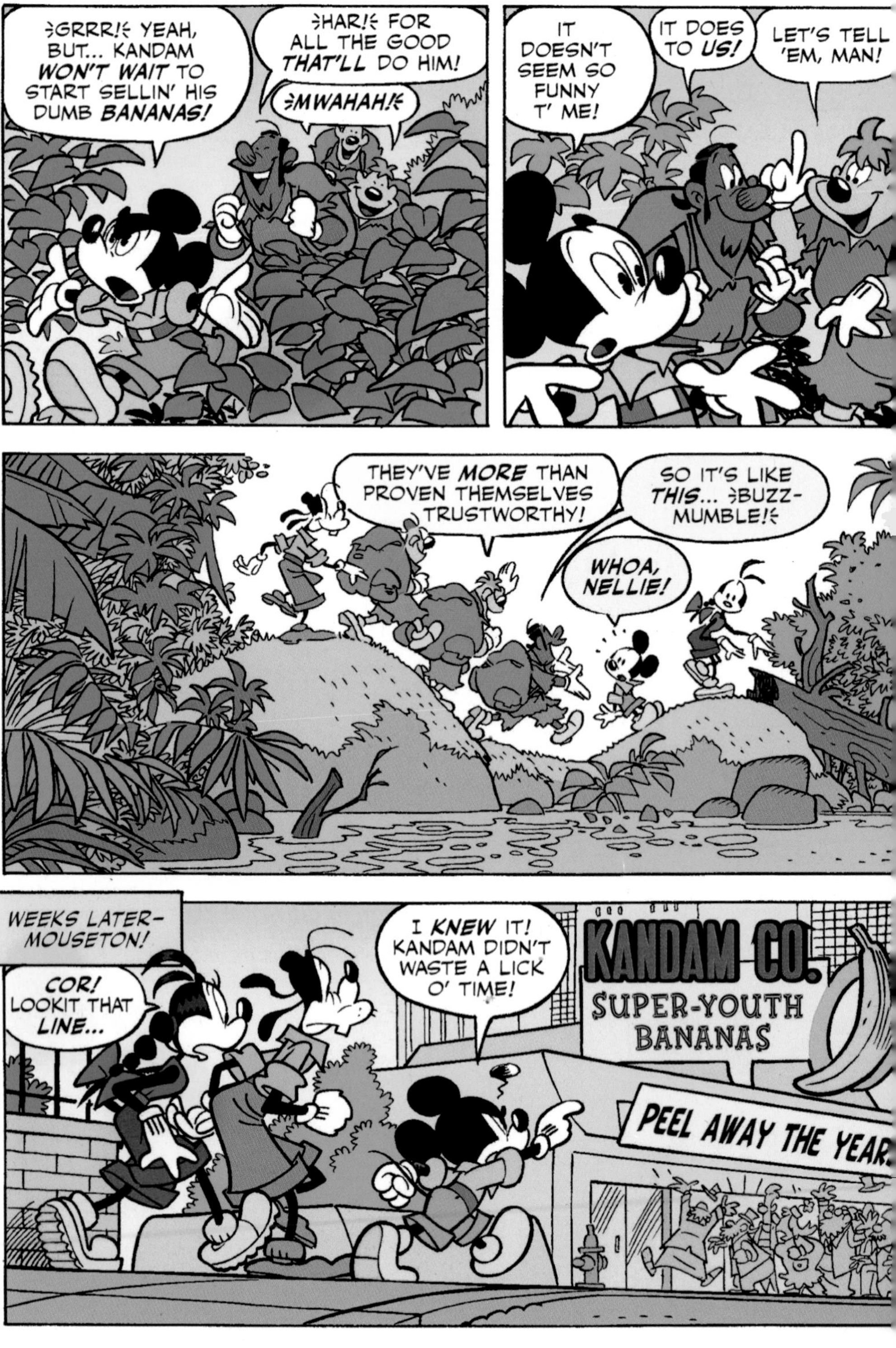

ƎGRRR!Ɛ YEAH, BUT... KANDAM WON'T WAIT TO START SELLIN' HIS DUMB BANANAS!
ƎHAR!Ɛ FOR ALL THE GOOD THAT'LL DO HIM!
ƎMWAHAH!Ɛ
IT DOESN'T SEEM SO FUNNY T' ME!
IT DOES TO US!
LET'S TELL 'EM, MAN!
THEY'VE MORE THAN PROVEN THEMSELVES TRUSTWORTHY!
SO IT'S LIKE THIS... ƎBUZZ-MUMBLE!Ɛ
WHOA, NELLIE!
WEEKS LATER–MOUSETON!
COR! LOOKIT THAT LINE...
I KNEW IT! KANDAM DIDN'T WASTE A LICK O' TIME!
KANDAM CO.
SUPER-YOUTH BANANAS
PEEL AWAY THE YEAR

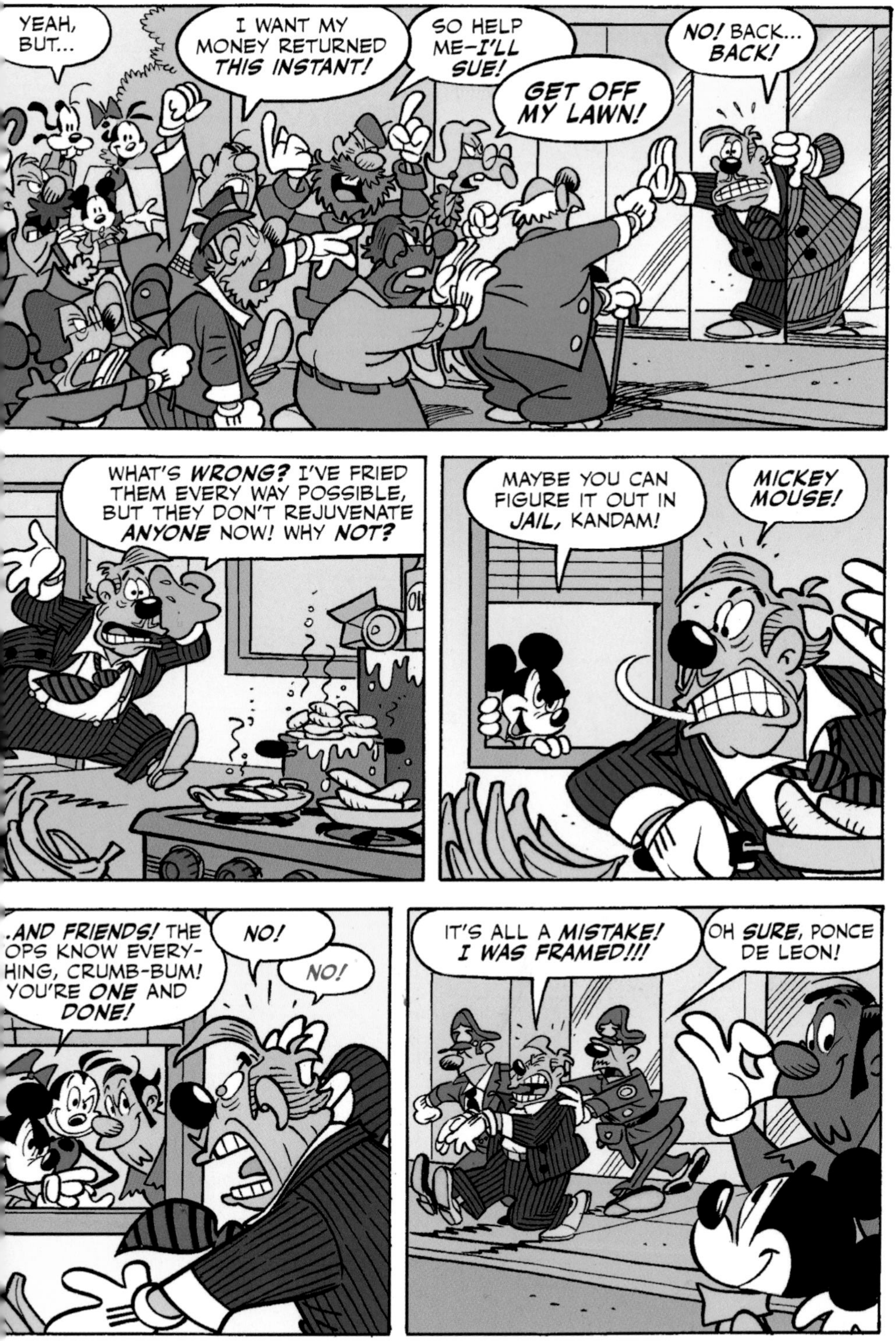
YEAH, BUT...
I WANT MY MONEY RETURNED THIS INSTANT!
SO HELP ME—I'LL SUE!
GET OFF MY LAWN!
NO! BACK... BACK!
WHAT'S WRONG? I'VE FRIED THEM EVERY WAY POSSIBLE, BUT THEY DON'T REJUVENATE ANYONE NOW! WHY NOT?
MAYBE YOU CAN FIGURE IT OUT IN JAIL, KANDAM!
MICKEY MOUSE!
.AND FRIENDS! THE OPS KNOW EVERY-HING, CRUMB-BUM! YOU'RE ONE AND DONE!
NO!
NO!
IT'S ALL A MISTAKE! I WAS FRAMED!!!
OH SURE, PONCE DE LEON!

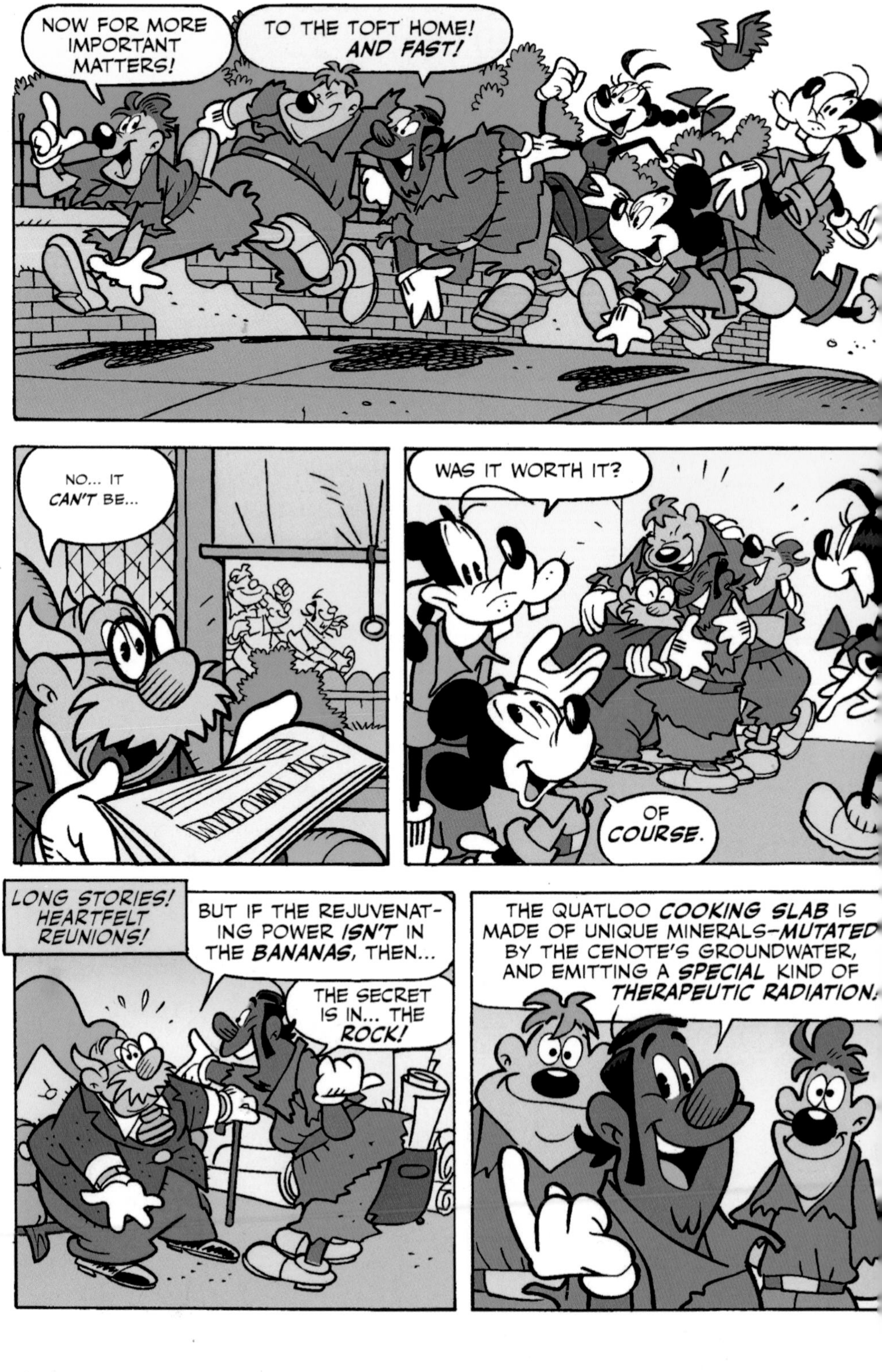

NOW FOR MORE IMPORTANT MATTERS!
TO THE TOFT HOME! AND FAST!
NO... IT CAN'T BE...
WAS IT WORTH IT?
OF COURSE.
LONG STORIES! HEARTFELT REUNIONS!
BUT IF THE REJUVENATING POWER ISN'T IN THE BANANAS, THEN...
THE SECRET IS IN... THE ROCK!
THE QUATLOO COOKING SLAB IS MADE OF UNIQUE MINERALS–MUTATED BY THE CENOTE'S GROUNDWATER, AND EMITTING A SPECIAL KIND OF THERAPEUTIC RADIATION.

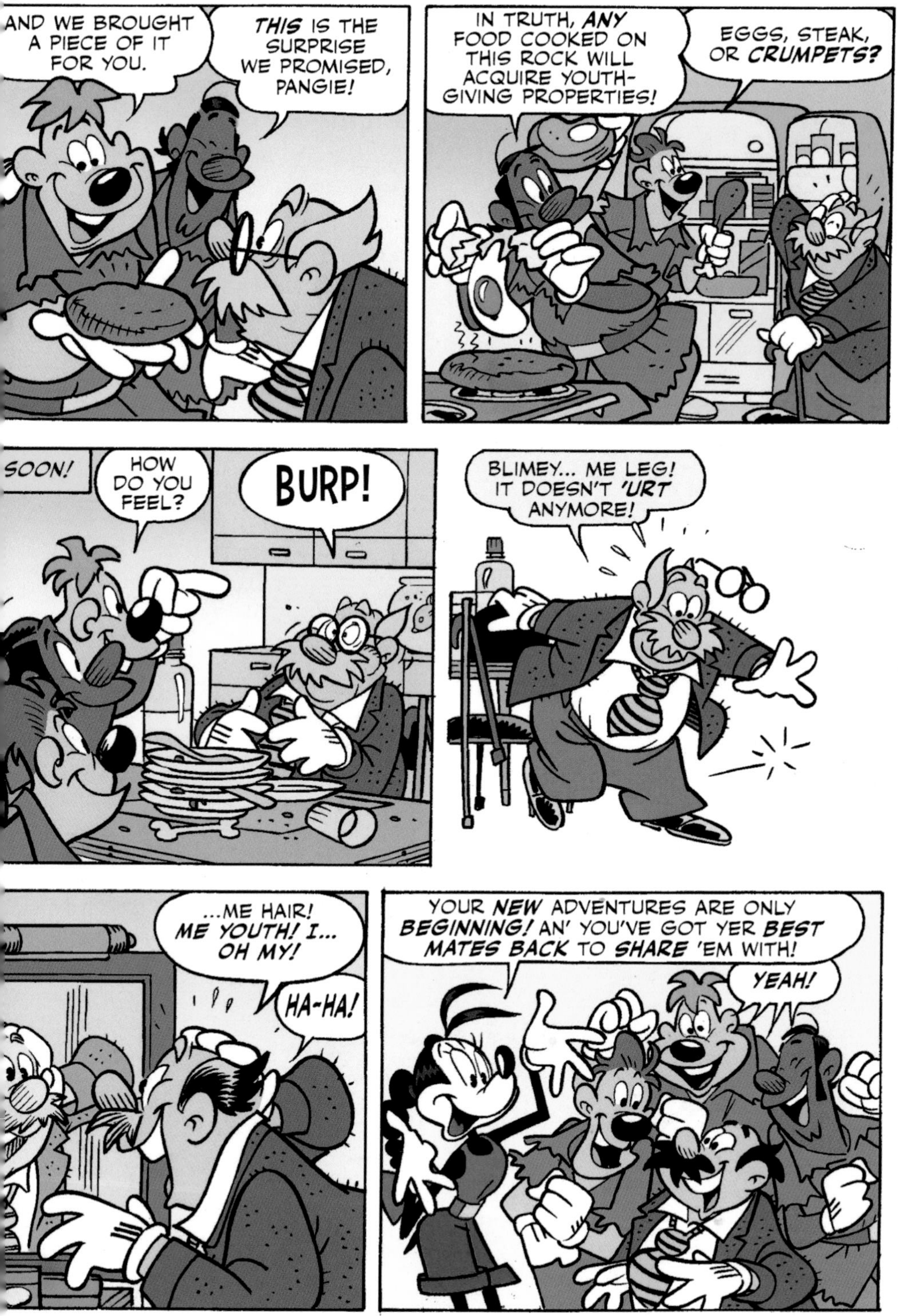
AND WE BROUGHT A PIECE OF IT FOR YOU.
THIS IS THE SURPRISE WE PROMISED, PANGIE!
IN TRUTH, ANY FOOD COOKED ON THIS ROCK WILL ACQUIRE YOUTH-GIVING PROPERTIES!
EGGS, STEAK, OR CRUMPETS?
SOON!
HOW DO YOU FEEL?
BURP!
BLIMEY... ME LEG! IT DOESN'T 'URT ANYMORE!
...ME HAIR! ME YOUTH! I... OH MY!
HA-HA!
YOUR NEW ADVENTURES ARE ONLY BEGINNING! AN' YOU'VE GOT YER BEST MATES BACK TO SHARE 'EM WITH!
YEAH!

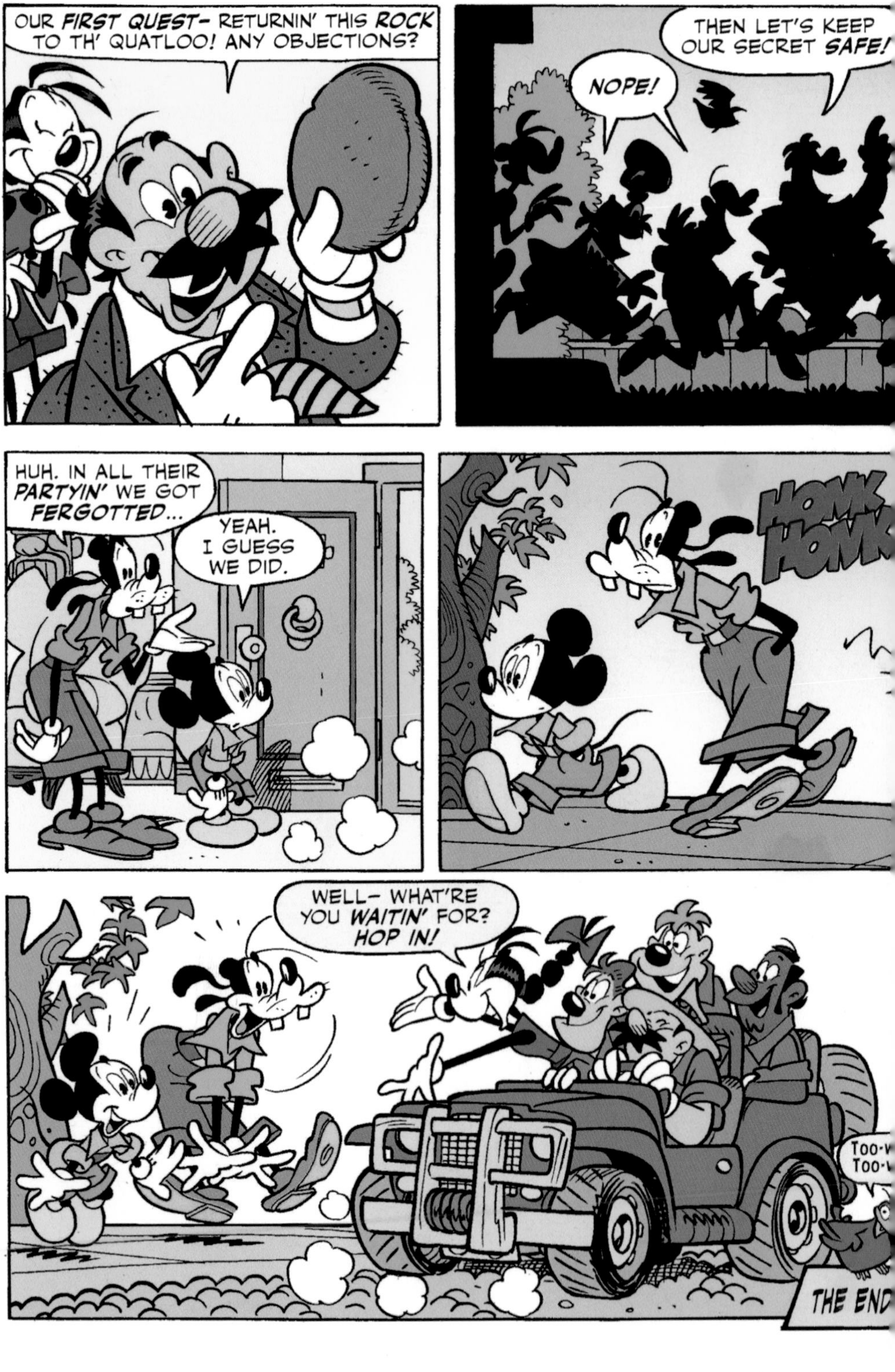
OUR FIRST QUEST– RETURNIN' THIS ROCK TO TH' QUATLOO! ANY OBJECTIONS?
NOPE!
THEN LET'S KEEP OUR SECRET SAFE!
HUH. IN ALL THEIR PARTYIN' WE GOT FERGOTTED...
YEAH. I GUESS WE DID.
WELL– WHAT'RE YOU WAITIN' FOR? HOP IN!
THE END

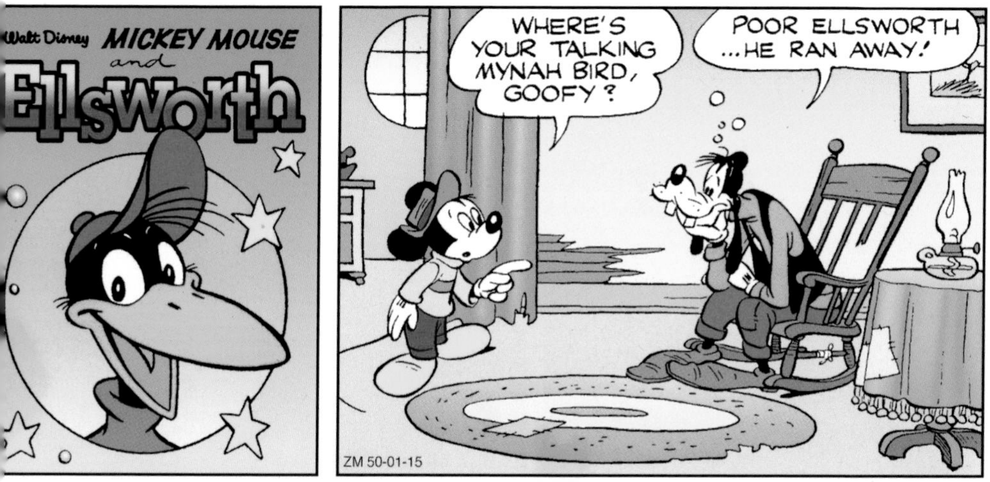
Walt Disney MICKEY MOUSE and Ellsworth
WHERE'S YOUR TALKING MYNAH BIRD, GOOFY?
POOR ELLSWORTH ...HE RAN AWAY!
ZM 50-01-15

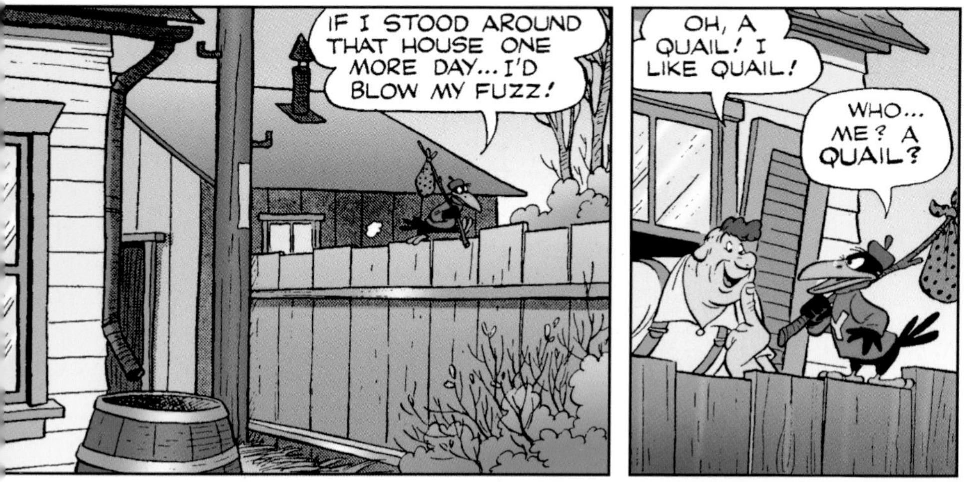
IF I STOOD AROUND THAT HOUSE ONE MORE DAY... I'D BLOW MY FUZZ!
OH, A QUAIL! I LIKE QUAIL!
WHO... ME? A QUAIL?

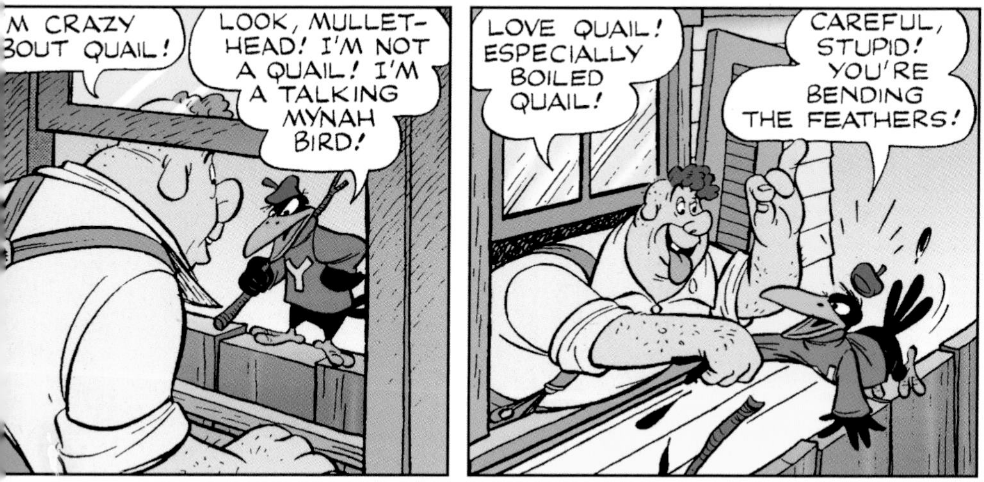
M CRAZY BOUT QUAIL!
LOOK, MULLET-HEAD! I'M NOT A QUAIL! I'M A TALKING MYNAH BIRD!
LOVE QUAIL! ESPECIALLY BOILED QUAIL!
CAREFUL, STUPID! YOU'RE BENDING THE FEATHERS!

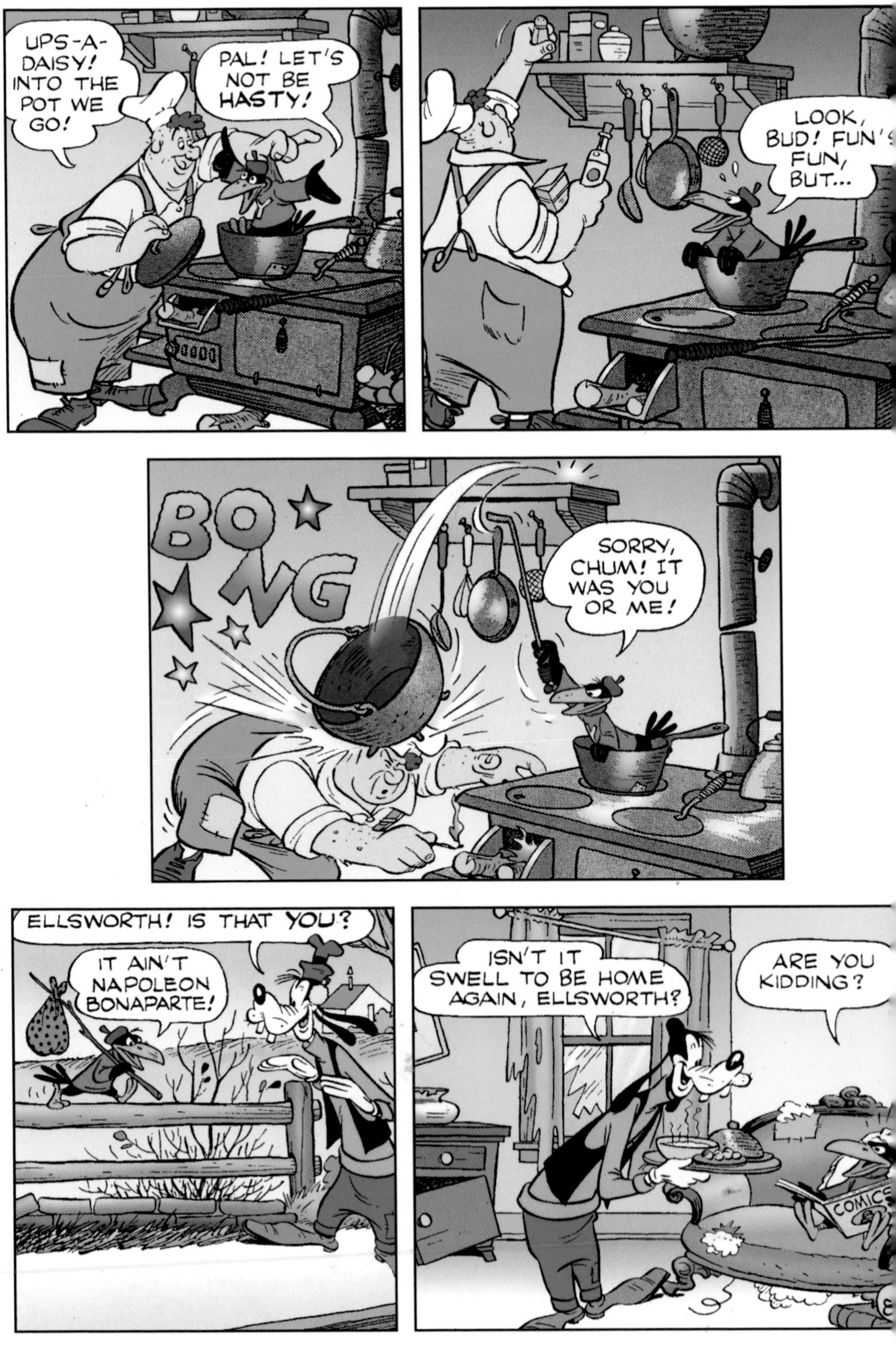

UPS-A-DAISY! INTO THE POT WE GO!
PAL! LET'S NOT BE HASTY!
LOOK, BUD! FUN'S FUN, BUT...
BONG
SORRY, CHUM! IT WAS YOU OR ME!
ELLSWORTH! IS THAT YOU?
IT AIN'T NAPOLEON BONAPARTE!
ISN'T IT SWELL TO BE HOME AGAIN, ELLSWORTH?
ARE YOU KIDDING?
COMICS

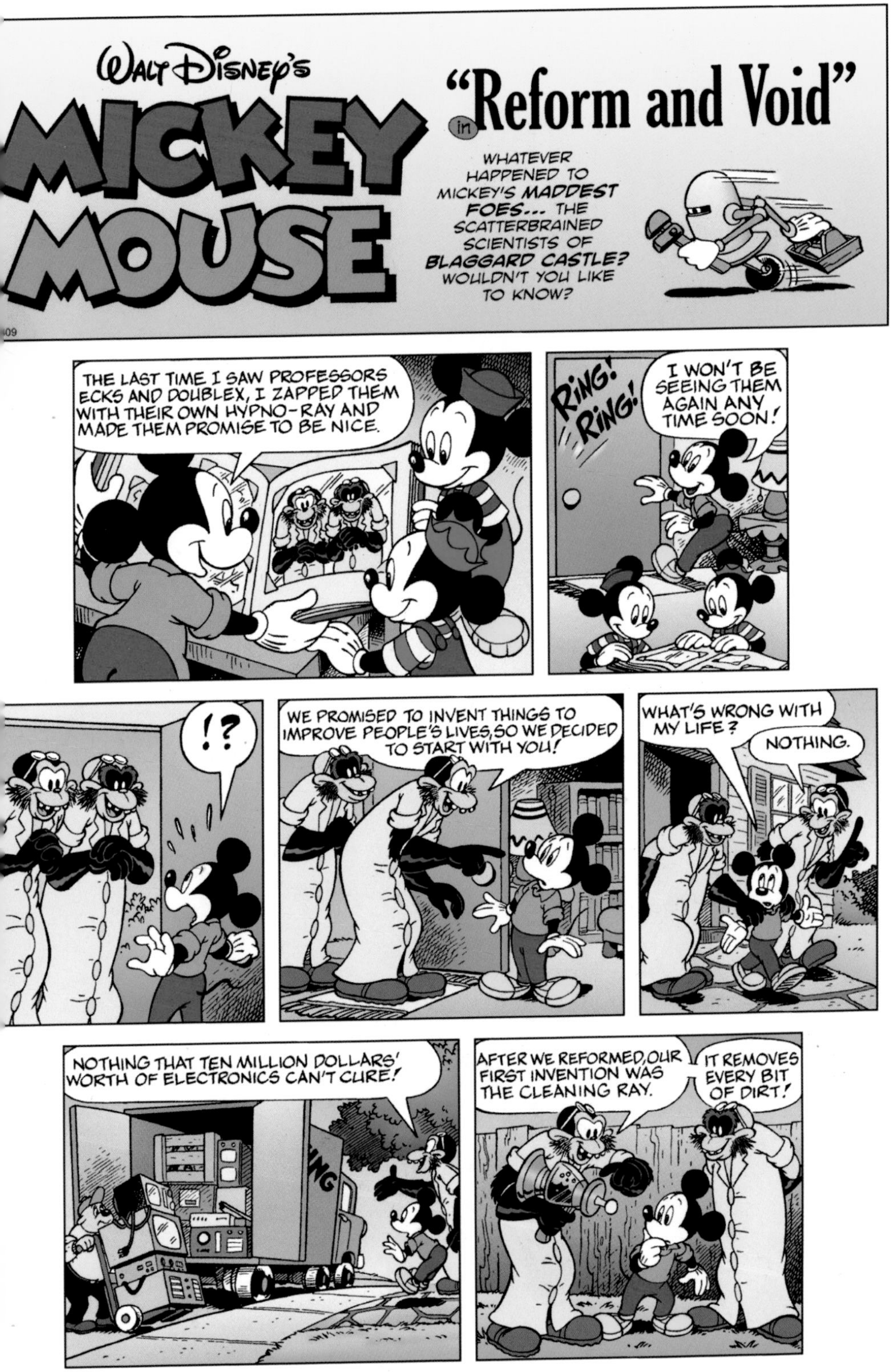
WALT DISNEY'S
MICKEY MOUSE
in "Reform and Void"
WHATEVER HAPPENED TO MICKEY'S MADDEST FOES... THE SCATTERBRAINED SCIENTISTS OF BLAGGARD CASTLE? WOULDN'T YOU LIKE TO KNOW?
THE LAST TIME I SAW PROFESSORS ECKS AND DOUBLEX, I ZAPPED THEM WITH THEIR OWN HYPNO-RAY AND MADE THEM PROMISE TO BE NICE.
RING! RING!
I WON'T BE SEEING THEM AGAIN ANY TIME SOON!
!?
WE PROMISED TO INVENT THINGS TO IMPROVE PEOPLE'S LIVES, SO WE DECIDED TO START WITH YOU!
WHAT'S WRONG WITH MY LIFE?
NOTHING.
NOTHING THAT TEN MILLION DOLLARS' WORTH OF ELECTRONICS CAN'T CURE!
AFTER WE REFORMED, OUR FIRST INVENTION WAS THE CLEANING RAY.
IT REMOVES EVERY BIT OF DIRT!

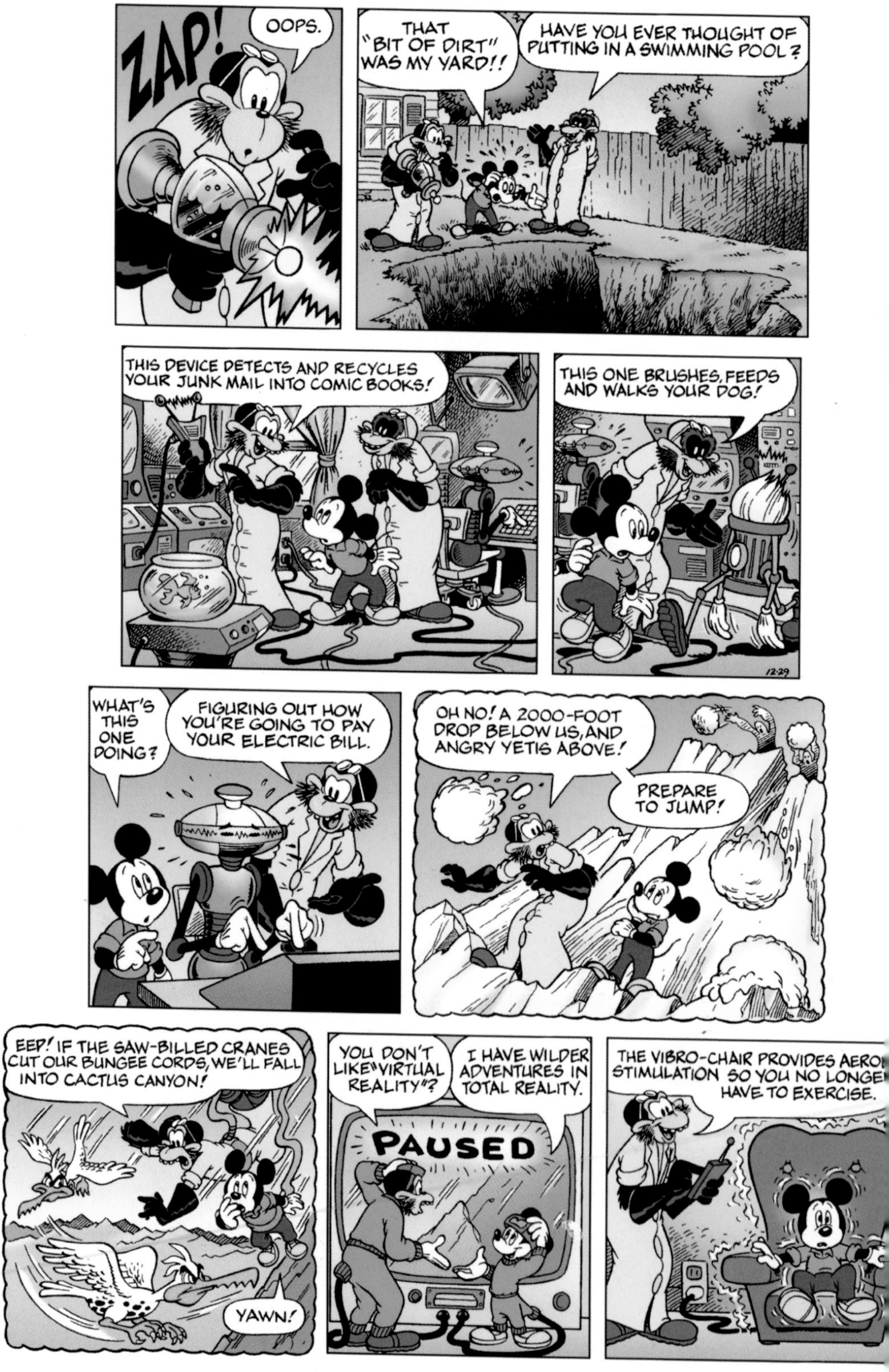
ZAP!
OOPS.
THAT "BIT OF DIRT" WAS MY YARD!!
HAVE YOU EVER THOUGHT OF PUTTING IN A SWIMMING POOL?
THIS DEVICE DETECTS AND RECYCLES YOUR JUNK MAIL INTO COMIC BOOKS!
THIS ONE BRUSHES, FEEDS AND WALKS YOUR DOG!
12·29
WHAT'S THIS ONE DOING?
FIGURING OUT HOW YOU'RE GOING TO PAY YOUR ELECTRIC BILL.
OH NO! A 2000-FOOT DROP BELOW US, AND ANGRY YETIS ABOVE!
PREPARE TO JUMP!
EEP! IF THE SAW-BILLED CRANES CUT OUR BUNGEE CORDS, WE'LL FALL INTO CACTUS CANYON!
YAWN!
YOU DON'T LIKE "VIRTUAL REALITY"?
I HAVE WILDER ADVENTURES IN TOTAL REALITY.
PAUSED
THE VIBRO-CHAIR PROVIDES AERO
STIMULATION SO YOU NO LONGE
HAVE TO EXERCISE.

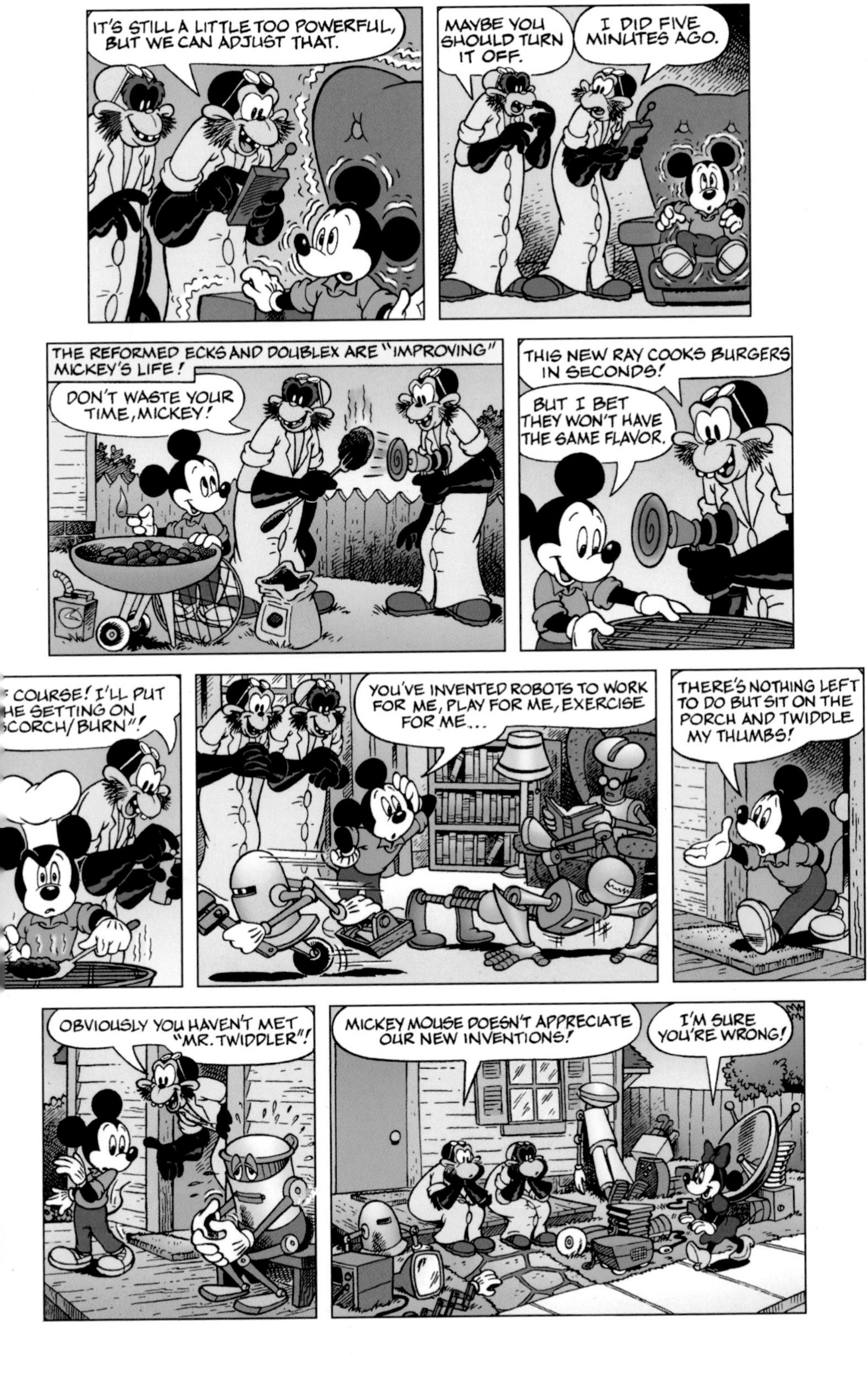
IT'S STILL A LITTLE TOO POWERFUL, BUT WE CAN ADJUST THAT.
MAYBE YOU SHOULD TURN IT OFF.
I DID FIVE MINUTES AGO.
THE REFORMED ECKS AND DOUBLEX ARE "IMPROVING" MICKEY'S LIFE!
DON'T WASTE YOUR TIME, MICKEY!
THIS NEW RAY COOKS BURGERS IN SECONDS!
BUT I BET THEY WON'T HAVE THE SAME FLAVOR.
COURSE! I'LL PUT HE SETTING ON SCORCH/BURN"!
YOU'VE INVENTED ROBOTS TO WORK FOR ME, PLAY FOR ME, EXERCISE FOR ME...
THERE'S NOTHING LEFT TO DO BUT SIT ON THE PORCH AND TWIDDLE MY THUMBS!
OBVIOUSLY YOU HAVEN'T MET "MR. TWIDDLER"!
MICKEY MOUSE DOESN'T APPRECIATE OUR NEW INVENTIONS!
I'M SURE YOU'RE WRONG!

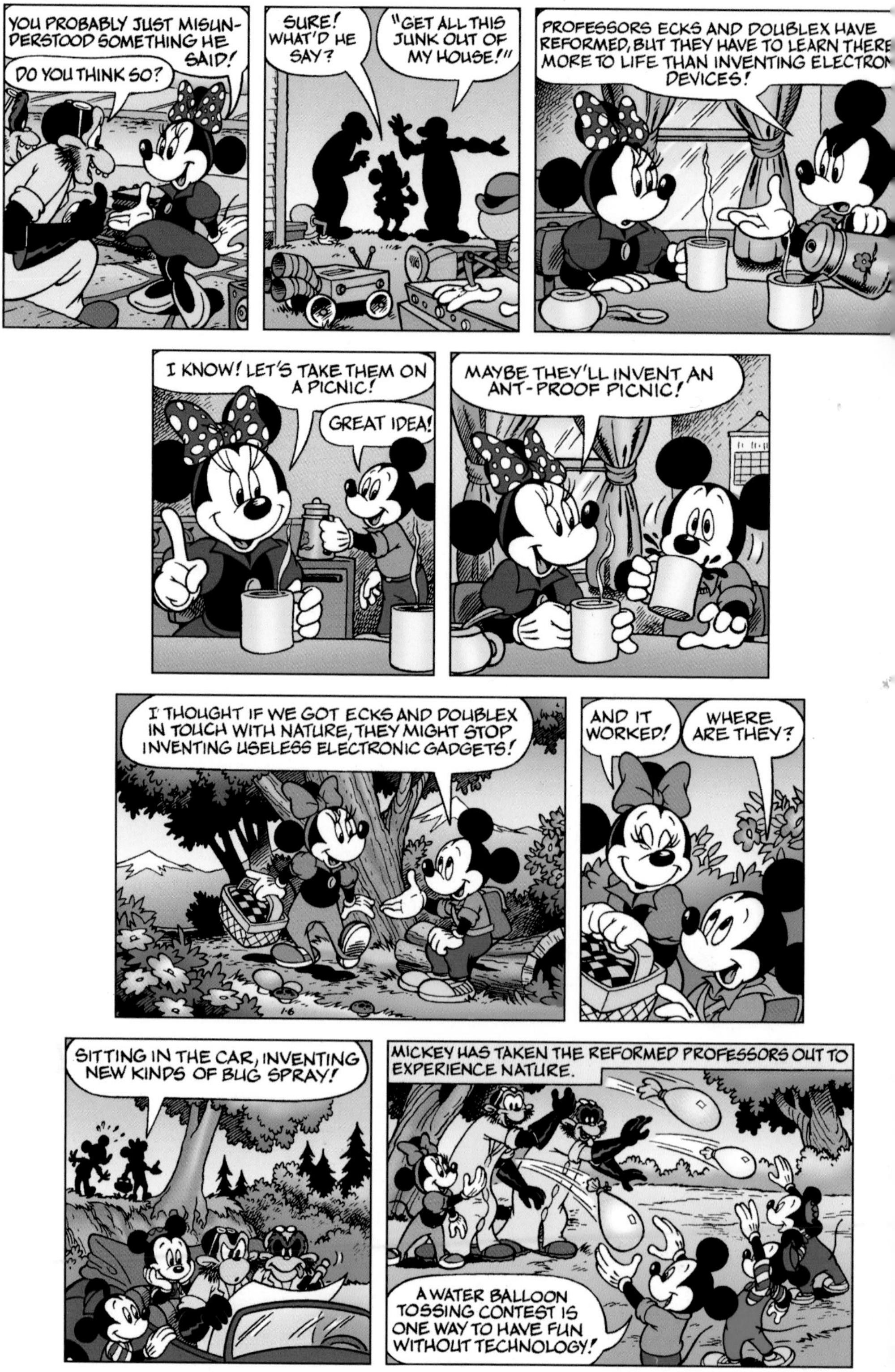
YOU PROBABLY JUST MISUNDERSTOOD SOMETHING HE SAID!
DO YOU THINK SO?
SURE! WHAT'D HE SAY?
"GET ALL THIS JUNK OUT OF MY HOUSE!"
PROFESSORS ECKS AND DOUBLEX HAVE REFORMED, BUT THEY HAVE TO LEARN THERE
MORE TO LIFE THAN INVENTING ELECTRO
DEVICES!
I KNOW! LET'S TAKE THEM ON A PICNIC!
GREAT IDEA!
MAYBE THEY'LL INVENT AN ANT-PROOF PICNIC!
I THOUGHT IF WE GOT ECKS AND DOUBLEX IN TOUCH WITH NATURE, THEY MIGHT STOP INVENTING USELESS ELECTRONIC GADGETS!
AND IT WORKED!
WHERE ARE THEY?
SITTING IN THE CAR, INVENTING NEW KINDS OF BUG SPRAY!
MICKEY HAS TAKEN THE REFORMED PROFESSORS OUT TO EXPERIENCE NATURE.
A WATER BALLOON TOSSING CONTEST IS ONE WAY TO HAVE FUN WITHOUT TECHNOLOGY!

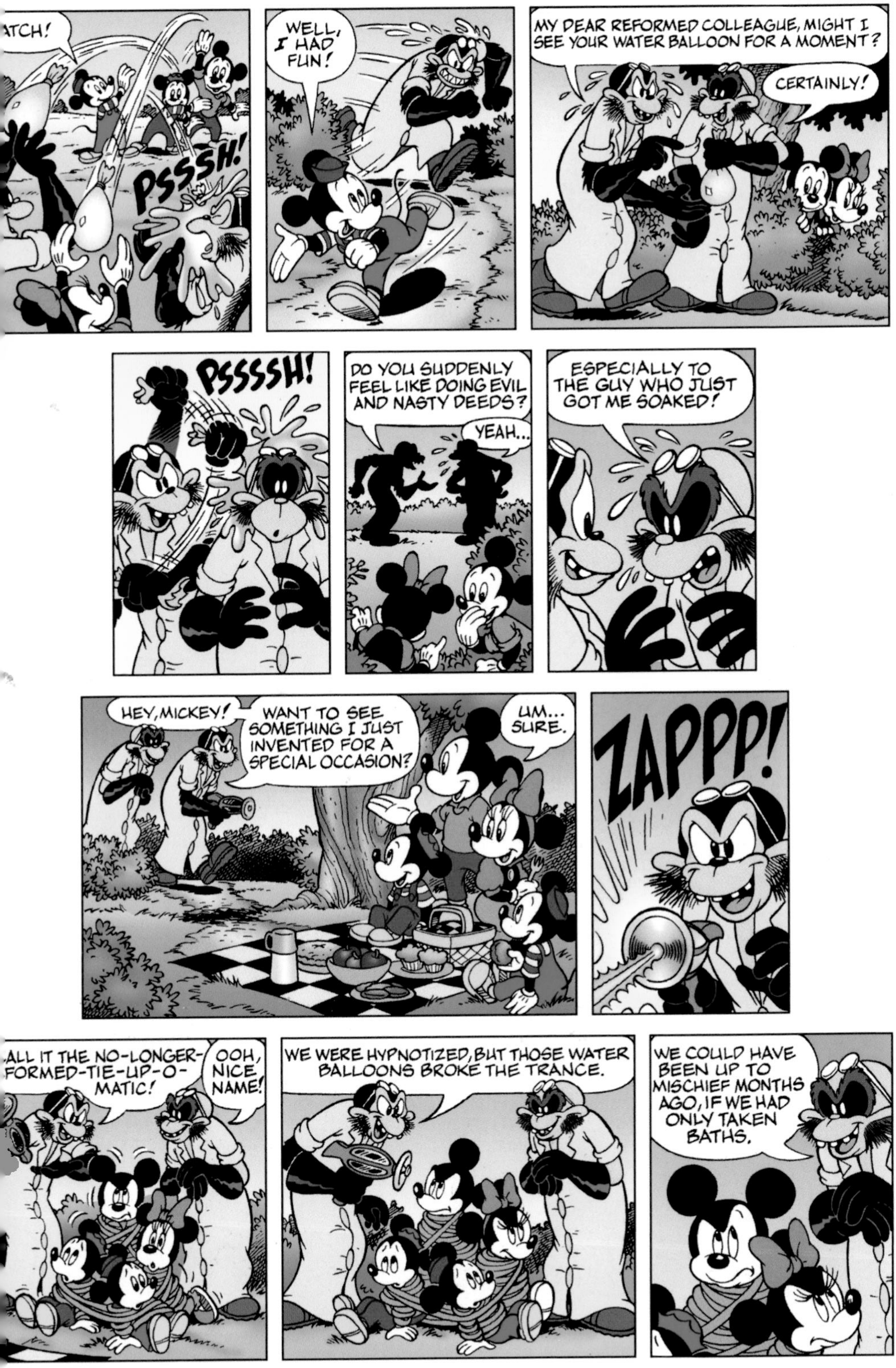

ATCH!
PSSSH!
WELL, I HAD FUN!
MY DEAR REFORMED COLLEAGUE, MIGHT I SEE YOUR WATER BALLOON FOR A MOMENT?
CERTAINLY!
PSSSSH!
DO YOU SUDDENLY FEEL LIKE DOING EVIL AND NASTY DEEDS?
YEAH...
ESPECIALLY TO THE GUY WHO JUST GOT ME SOAKED!
HEY, MICKEY!
WANT TO SEE SOMETHING I JUST INVENTED FOR A SPECIAL OCCASION?
UM... SURE.
ZAPPP!
ALL IT THE NO-LONGER-FORMED-TIE-UP-O-MATIC!
OOH, NICE NAME!
WE WERE HYPNOTIZED, BUT THOSE WATER BALLOONS BROKE THE TRANCE.
WE COULD HAVE BEEN UP TO MISCHIEF MONTHS AGO, IF WE HAD ONLY TAKEN BATHS.

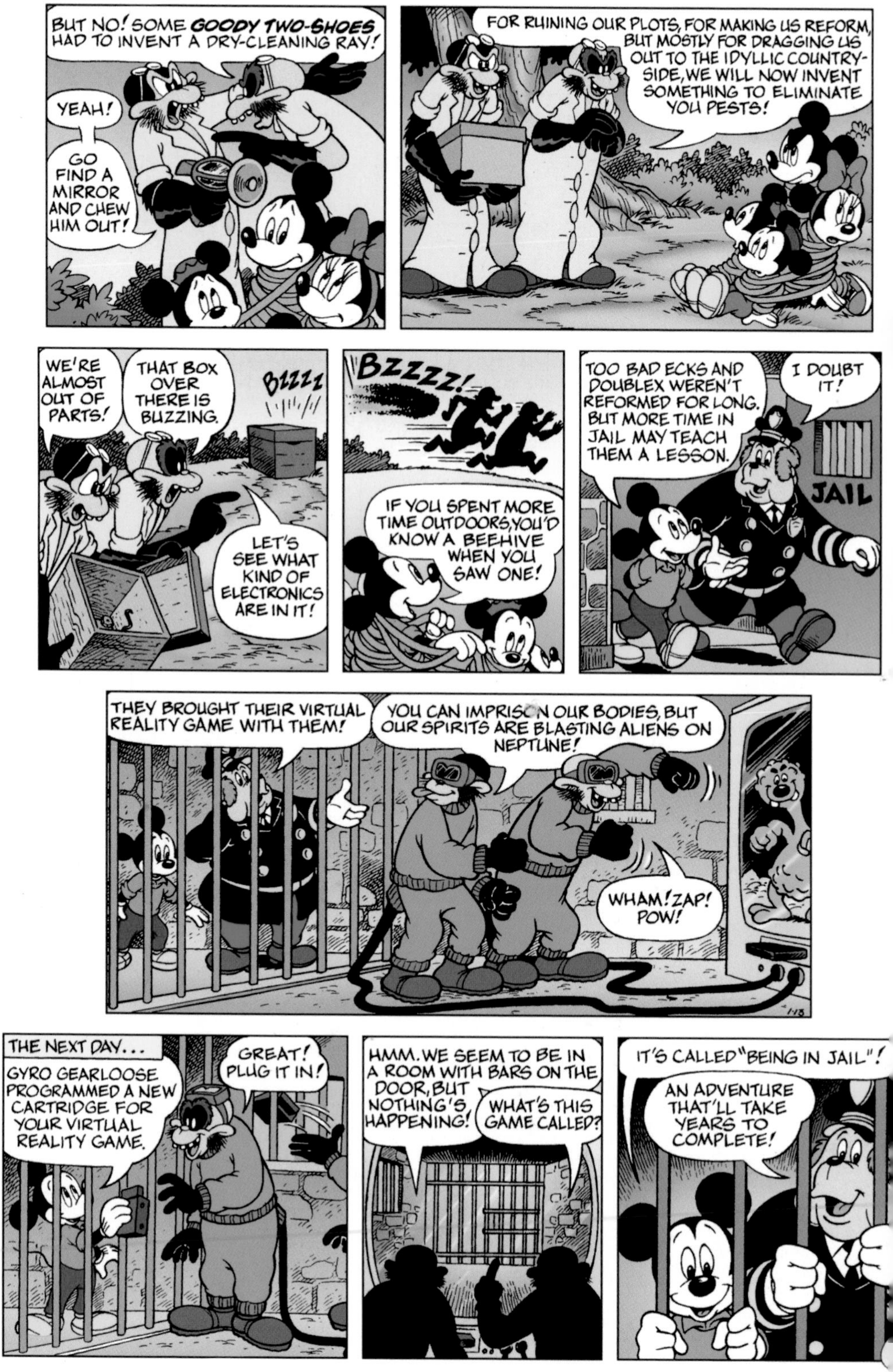
BUT NO! SOME GOODY TWO-SHOES HAD TO INVENT A DRY-CLEANING RAY!
YEAH!
GO FIND A MIRROR AND CHEW HIM OUT!
FOR RUINING OUR PLOTS, FOR MAKING US REFORM, BUT MOSTLY FOR DRAGGING US OUT TO THE IDYLLIC COUNTRY-SIDE, WE WILL NOW INVENT SOMETHING TO ELIMINATE YOU PESTS!
WE'RE ALMOST OUT OF PARTS!
THAT BOX OVER THERE IS BUZZING.
BZZZZ
LET'S SEE WHAT KIND OF ELECTRONICS ARE IN IT!
BZZZZZ!
IF YOU SPENT MORE TIME OUTDOORS, YOU'D KNOW A BEEHIVE WHEN YOU SAW ONE!
TOO BAD ECKS AND DOUBLEX WEREN'T REFORMED FOR LONG. BUT MORE TIME IN JAIL MAY TEACH THEM A LESSON.
I DOUBT IT!
JAIL
THEY BROUGHT THEIR VIRTUAL REALITY GAME WITH THEM!
YOU CAN IMPRISON OUR BODIES, BUT OUR SPIRITS ARE BLASTING ALIENS ON NEPTUNE!
WHAM! ZAP! POW!
THE NEXT DAY...
GYRO GEARLOOSE PROGRAMMED A NEW CARTRIDGE FOR YOUR VIRTUAL REALITY GAME.
GREAT! PLUG IT IN!
HMM. WE SEEM TO BE IN A ROOM WITH BARS ON THE DOOR, BUT NOTHING'S HAPPENING!
WHAT'S THIS GAME CALLED?
IT'S CALLED "BEING IN JAIL"!
AN ADVENTURE THAT'LL TAKE YEARS TO COMPLETE!

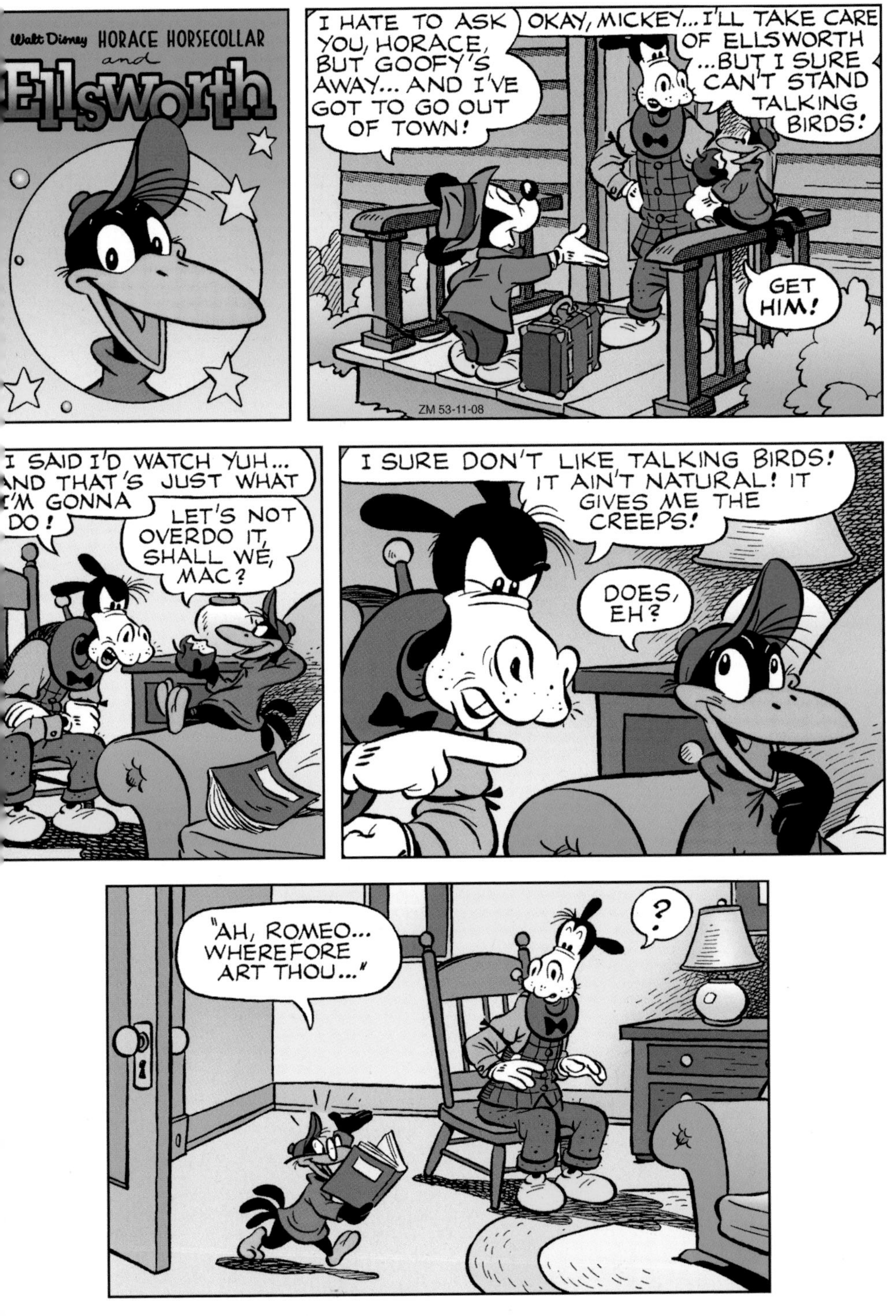
Walt Disney HORACE HORSECOLLAR and Ellsworth
I HATE TO ASK YOU, HORACE, BUT GOOFY'S AWAY... AND I'VE GOT TO GO OUT OF TOWN!
OKAY, MICKEY... I'LL TAKE CARE OF ELLSWORTH ...BUT I SURE CAN'T STAND TALKING BIRDS!
GET HIM!
ZM 53-11-08
I SAID I'D WATCH YUH... AND THAT'S JUST WHAT I'M GONNA DO!
LET'S NOT OVERDO IT, SHALL WE, MAC?
I SURE DON'T LIKE TALKING BIRDS! IT AIN'T NATURAL! IT GIVES ME THE CREEPS!
DOES, EH?
"AH, ROMEO... WHEREFORE ART THOU..."
?

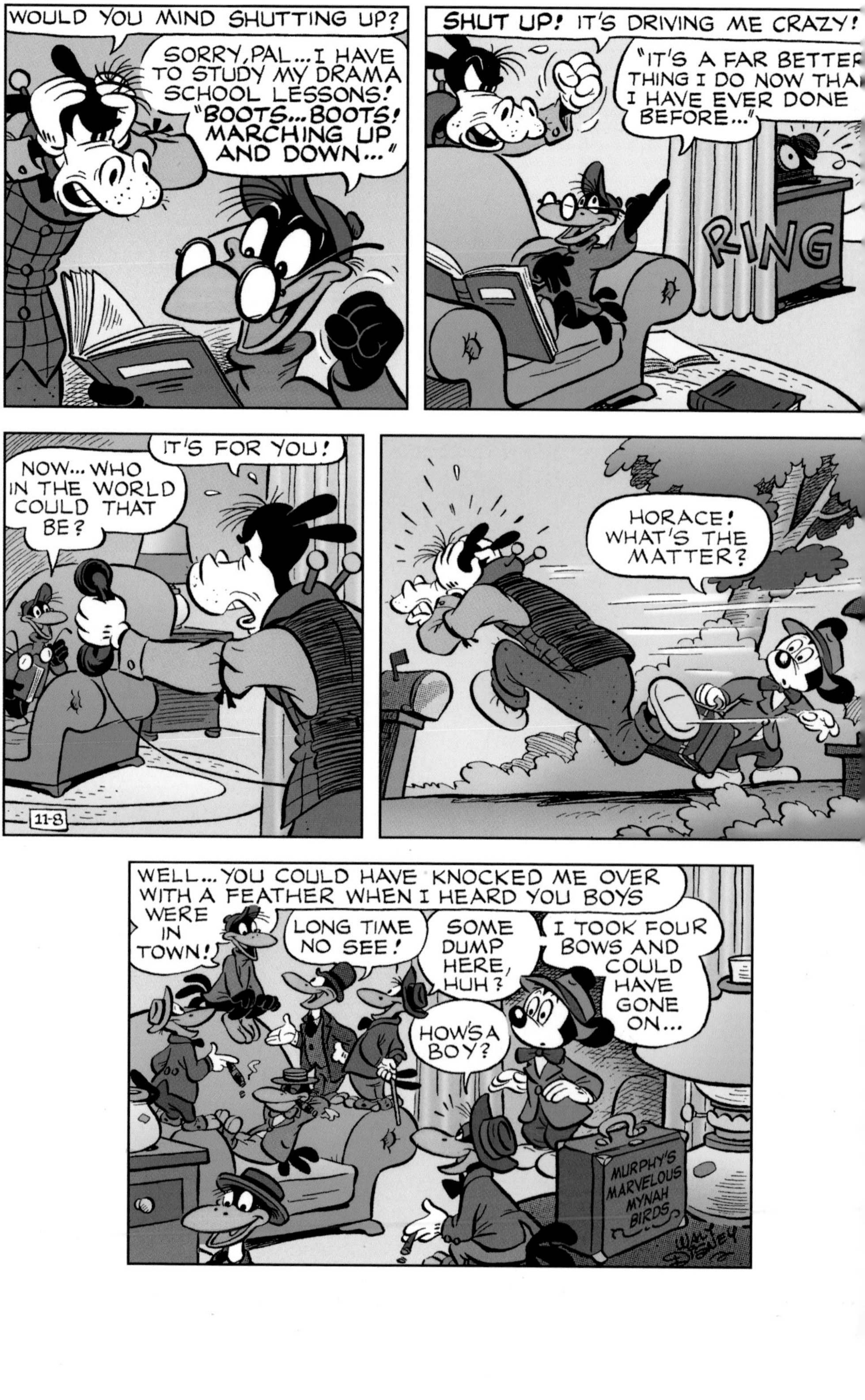

WOULD YOU MIND SHUTTING UP?
SORRY, PAL... I HAVE TO STUDY MY DRAMA SCHOOL LESSONS! "BOOTS... BOOTS! MARCHING UP AND DOWN..."
SHUT UP! IT'S DRIVING ME CRAZY!
"IT'S A FAR BETTE
THING I DO NOW THA
I HAVE EVER DONE BEFORE..."
RING
NOW... WHO IN THE WORLD COULD THAT BE?
IT'S FOR YOU!
11-8
HORACE! WHAT'S THE MATTER?
WELL... YOU COULD HAVE KNOCKED ME OVER WITH A FEATHER WHEN I HEARD YOU BOYS WERE IN TOWN!
LONG TIME NO SEE!
SOME DUMP HERE, HUH?
I TOOK FOUR BOWS AND COULD HAVE GONE ON...
HOW'S A BOY?
MURPHY'S MARVELOUS MYNAH BIRDS
WALT DISNEY

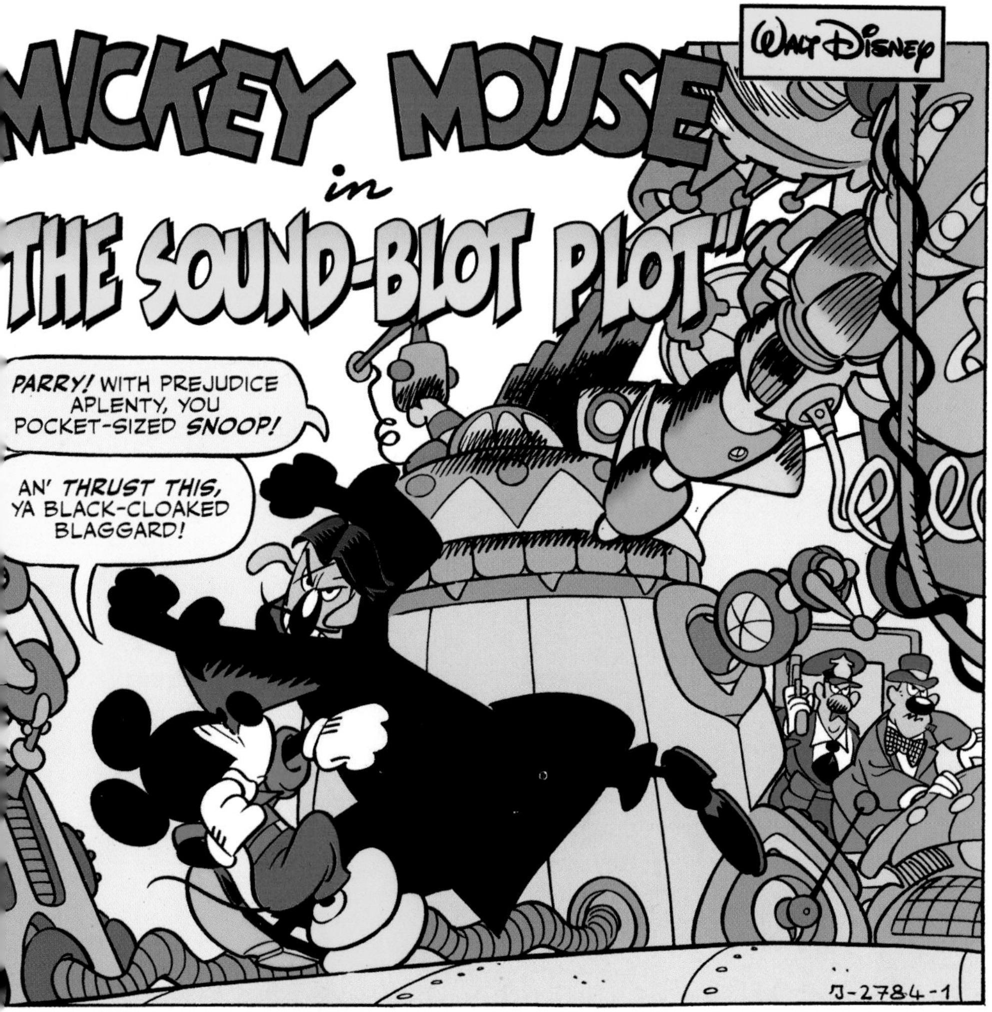
WALT DISNEY
MICKEY MOUSE
in
"THE SOUND-BLOT PLOT"
PARRY! WITH PREJUDICE APLENTY, YOU POCKET-SIZED SNOOP!
AN' THRUST THIS, YA BLACK-CLOAKED BLAGGARD!
J-2784-1

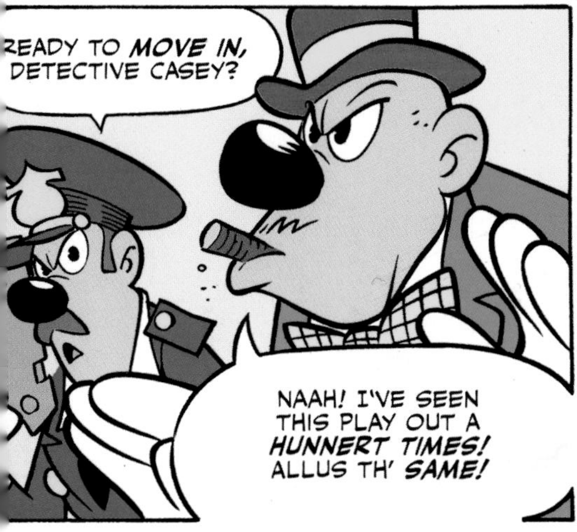
READY TO MOVE IN, DETECTIVE CASEY?
NAAH! I'VE SEEN THIS PLAY OUT A HUNNERT TIMES! ALLUS TH' SAME!

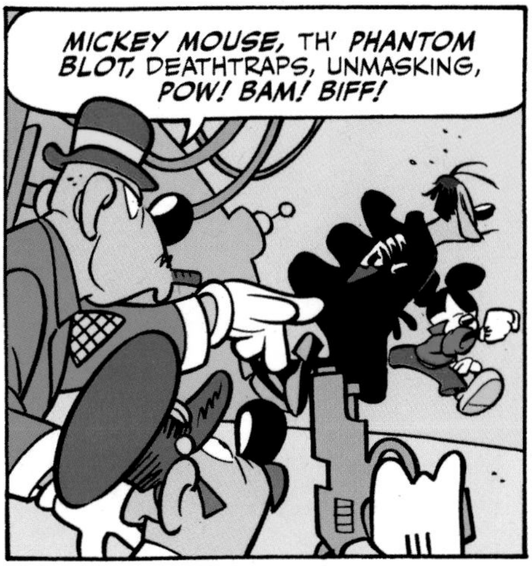
MICKEY MOUSE, TH' PHANTOM BLOT, DEATHTRAPS, UNMASKING, POW! BAM! BIFF!

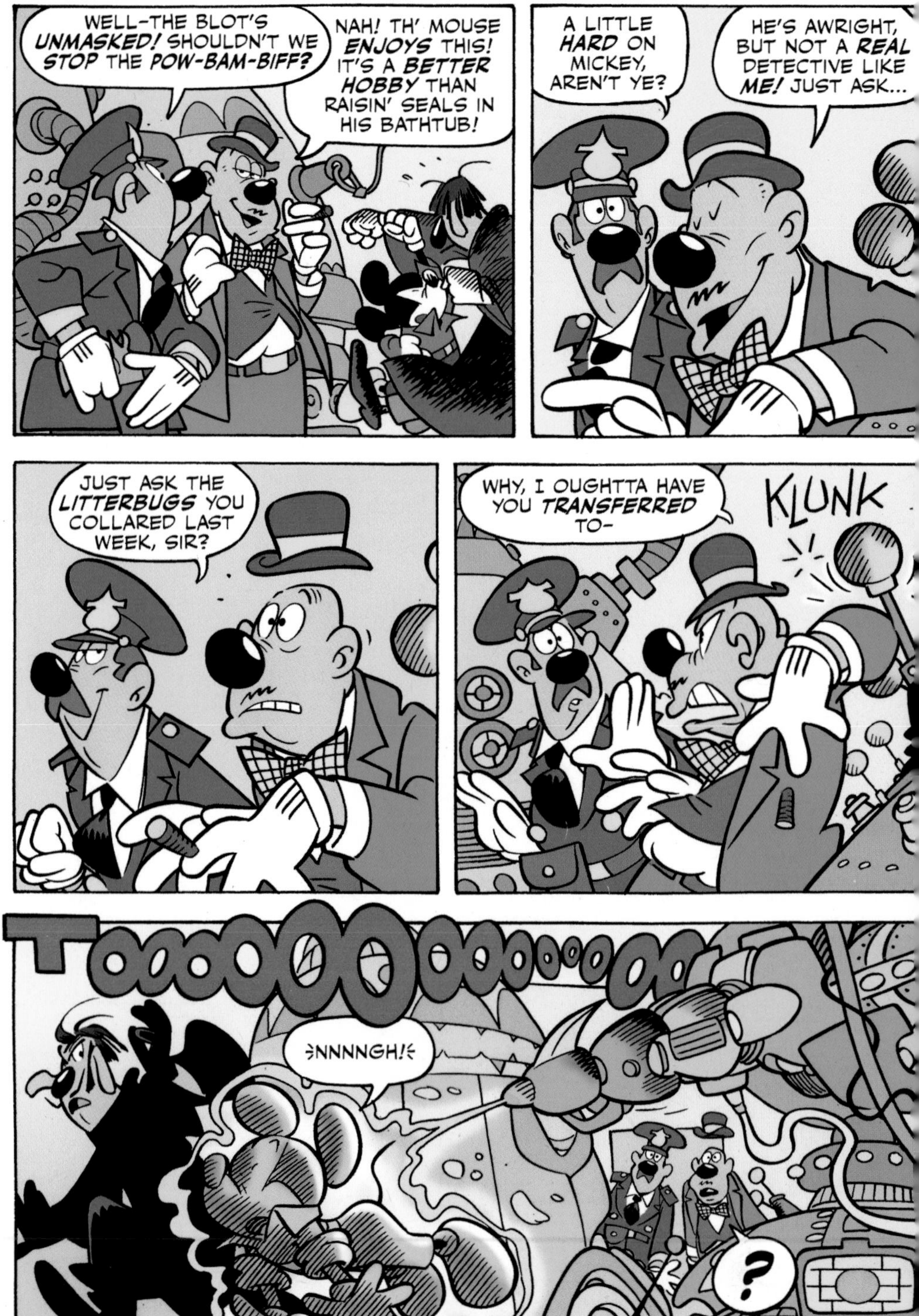
WELL–THE BLOT'S UNMASKED! SHOULDN'T WE STOP THE POW-BAM-BIFF?
NAH! TH' MOUSE ENJOYS THIS! IT'S A BETTER HOBBY THAN RAISIN' SEALS IN HIS BATHTUB!
A LITTLE HARD ON MICKEY, AREN'T YE?
HE'S AWRIGHT, BUT NOT A REAL DETECTIVE LIKE ME! JUST ASK...
JUST ASK THE LITTERBUGS YOU COLLARED LAST WEEK, SIR?
WHY, I OUGHTTA HAVE YOU TRANSFERRED TO–
KLUNK
TOOOOOOOOOOOOOOO
NNNNGH!
?

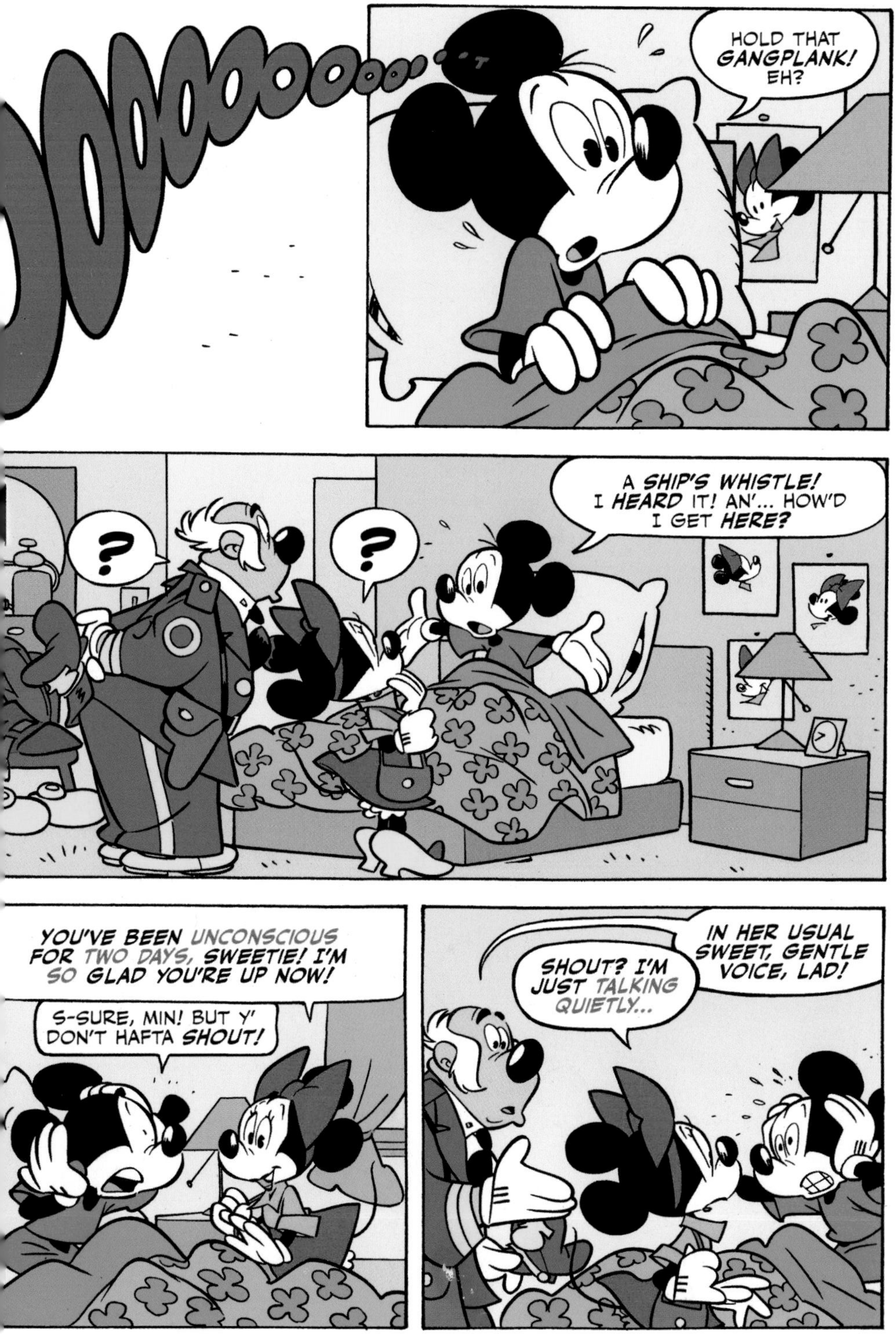
OOOOOOOOOOooo...
HOLD THAT GANGPLANK! EH?
A SHIP'S WHISTLE! I HEARD IT! AN'... HOW'D I GET HERE?
?
?
YOU'VE BEEN UNCONSCIOUS FOR TWO DAYS, SWEETIE! I'M SO GLAD YOU'RE UP NOW!
S-SURE, MIN! BUT Y' DON'T HAFTA SHOUT!
SHOUT? I'M JUST TALKING QUIETLY...
IN HER USUAL SWEET, GENTLE VOICE, LAD!

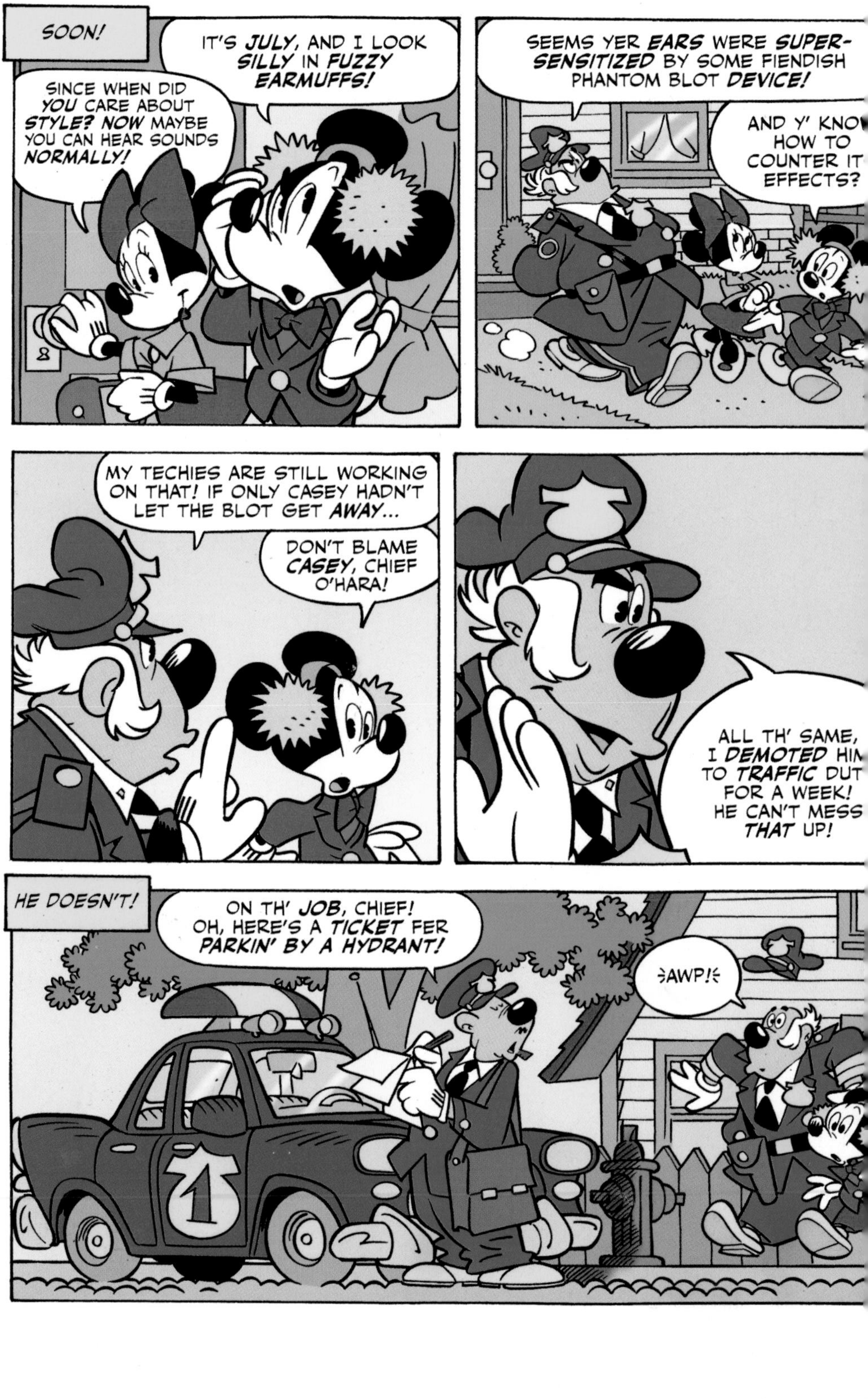
SOON!
IT'S JULY, AND I LOOK SILLY IN FUZZY EARMUFFS!
SINCE WHEN DID YOU CARE ABOUT STYLE? NOW MAYBE YOU CAN HEAR SOUNDS NORMALLY!
SEEMS YER EARS WERE SUPER-SENSITIZED BY SOME FIENDISH PHANTOM BLOT DEVICE!
AND Y' KNO HOW TO COUNTER IT EFFECTS?
MY TECHIES ARE STILL WORKING ON THAT! IF ONLY CASEY HADN'T LET THE BLOT GET AWAY...
DON'T BLAME CASEY, CHIEF O'HARA!
ALL TH' SAME, I DEMOTED HIM TO TRAFFIC DUT FOR A WEEK! HE CAN'T MESS THAT UP!
HE DOESN'T!
ON TH' JOB, CHIEF! OH, HERE'S A TICKET FER PARKIN' BY A HYDRANT!
AWP!

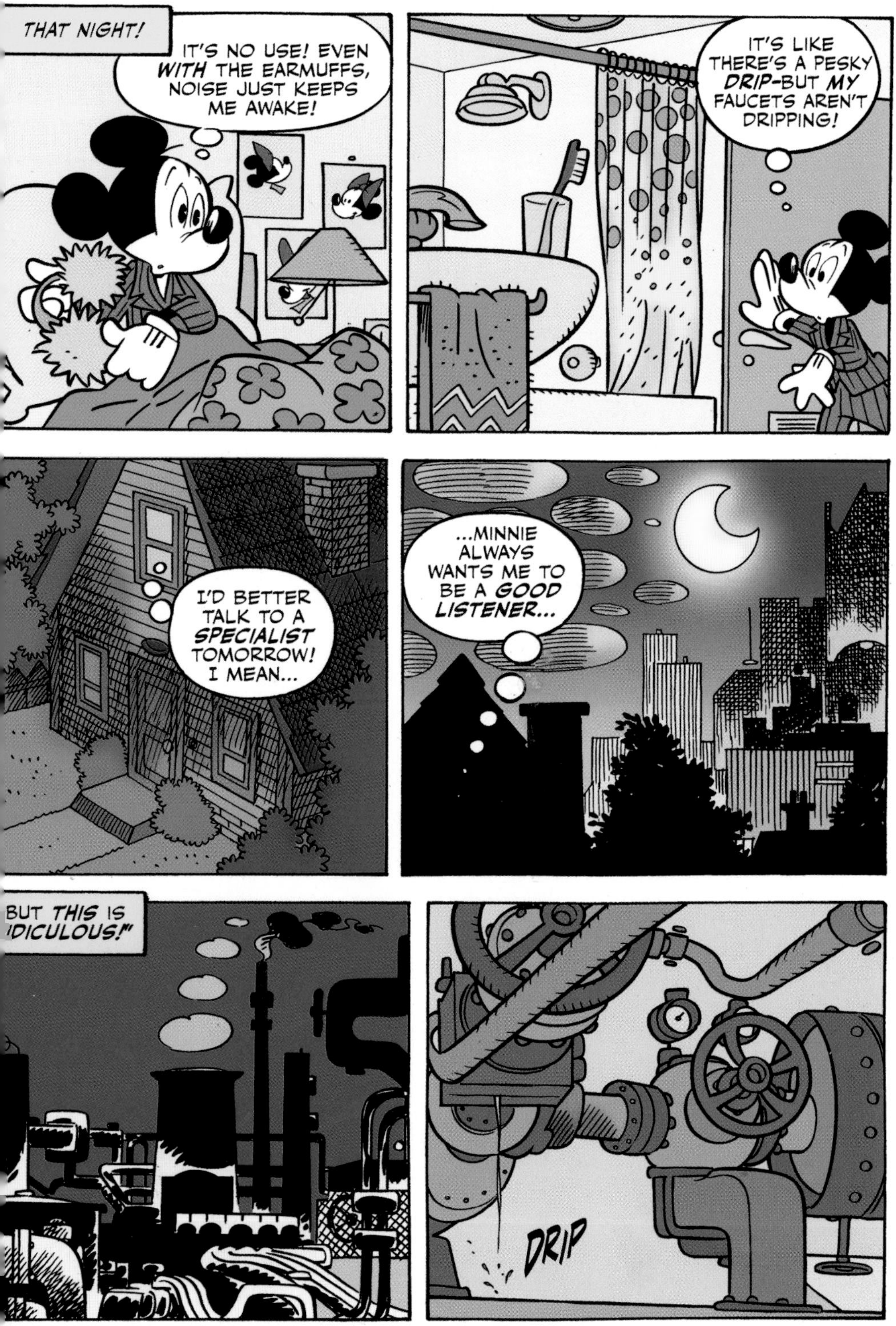
THAT NIGHT!
IT'S NO USE! EVEN WITH THE EARMUFFS, NOISE JUST KEEPS ME AWAKE!
IT'S LIKE THERE'S A PESKY DRIP-BUT MY FAUCETS AREN'T DRIPPING!
I'D BETTER TALK TO A SPECIALIST TOMORROW! I MEAN...
...MINNIE ALWAYS WANTS ME TO BE A GOOD LISTENER...
BUT THIS IS IDICULOUS!"
DRIP

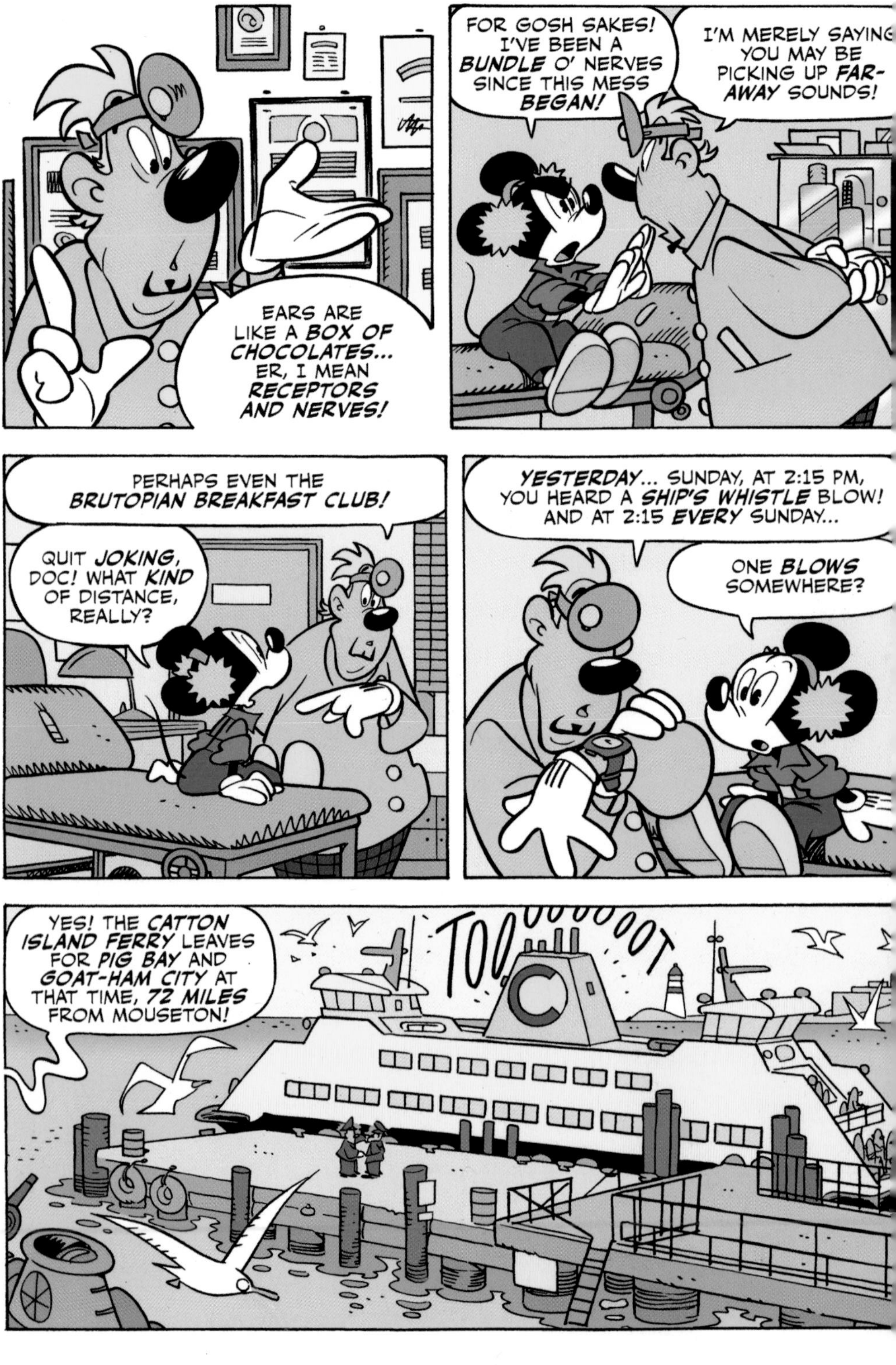
EARS ARE LIKE A BOX OF CHOCOLATES... ER, I MEAN RECEPTORS AND NERVES!
FOR GOSH SAKES! I'VE BEEN A BUNDLE O' NERVES SINCE THIS MESS BEGAN!
I'M MERELY SAYING YOU MAY BE PICKING UP FAR-AWAY SOUNDS!
PERHAPS EVEN THE BRUTOPIAN BREAKFAST CLUB!
QUIT JOKING, DOC! WHAT KIND OF DISTANCE, REALLY?
YESTERDAY... SUNDAY, AT 2:15 PM, YOU HEARD A SHIP'S WHISTLE BLOW! AND AT 2:15 EVERY SUNDAY...
ONE BLOWS SOMEWHERE?
YES! THE CATTON ISLAND FERRY LEAVES FOR PIG BAY AND GOAT-HAM CITY AT THAT TIME, 72 MILES FROM MOUSETON!
TOOOOOOOOOT

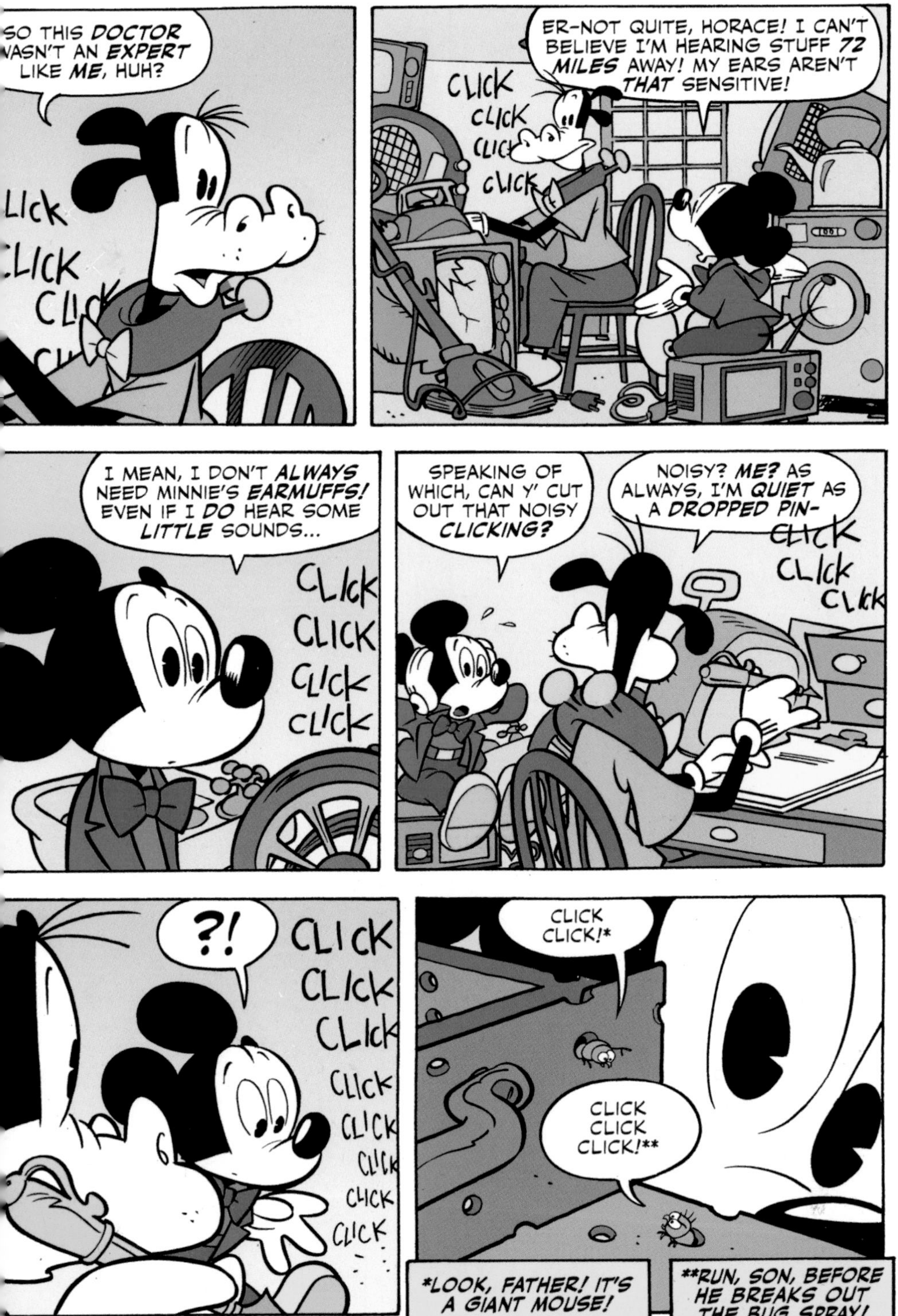
SO THIS DOCTOR WASN'T AN EXPERT LIKE ME, HUH?
CLICK
CLICK
CLICK
ER—NOT QUITE, HORACE! I CAN'T BELIEVE I'M HEARING STUFF 72 MILES AWAY! MY EARS AREN'T THAT SENSITIVE!
CLICK
CLICK
CLICK
CLICK
I MEAN, I DON'T ALWAYS NEED MINNIE'S EARMUFFS! EVEN IF I DO HEAR SOME LITTLE SOUNDS...
CLICK
CLICK
CLICK
CLICK
SPEAKING OF WHICH, CAN Y' CUT OUT THAT NOISY CLICKING?
NOISY? ME? AS ALWAYS, I'M QUIET AS A DROPPED PIN—
CLICK
CLICK
CLICK
?!
CLICK
CLICK
CLICK
CLICK
CLICK
CLICK
CLICK
CLICK
CLICK CLICK!*
CLICK CLICK CLICK!**
*LOOK, FATHER! IT'S A GIANT MOUSE!
**RUN, SON, BEFORE HE BREAKS OUT THE BUG SPRAY!

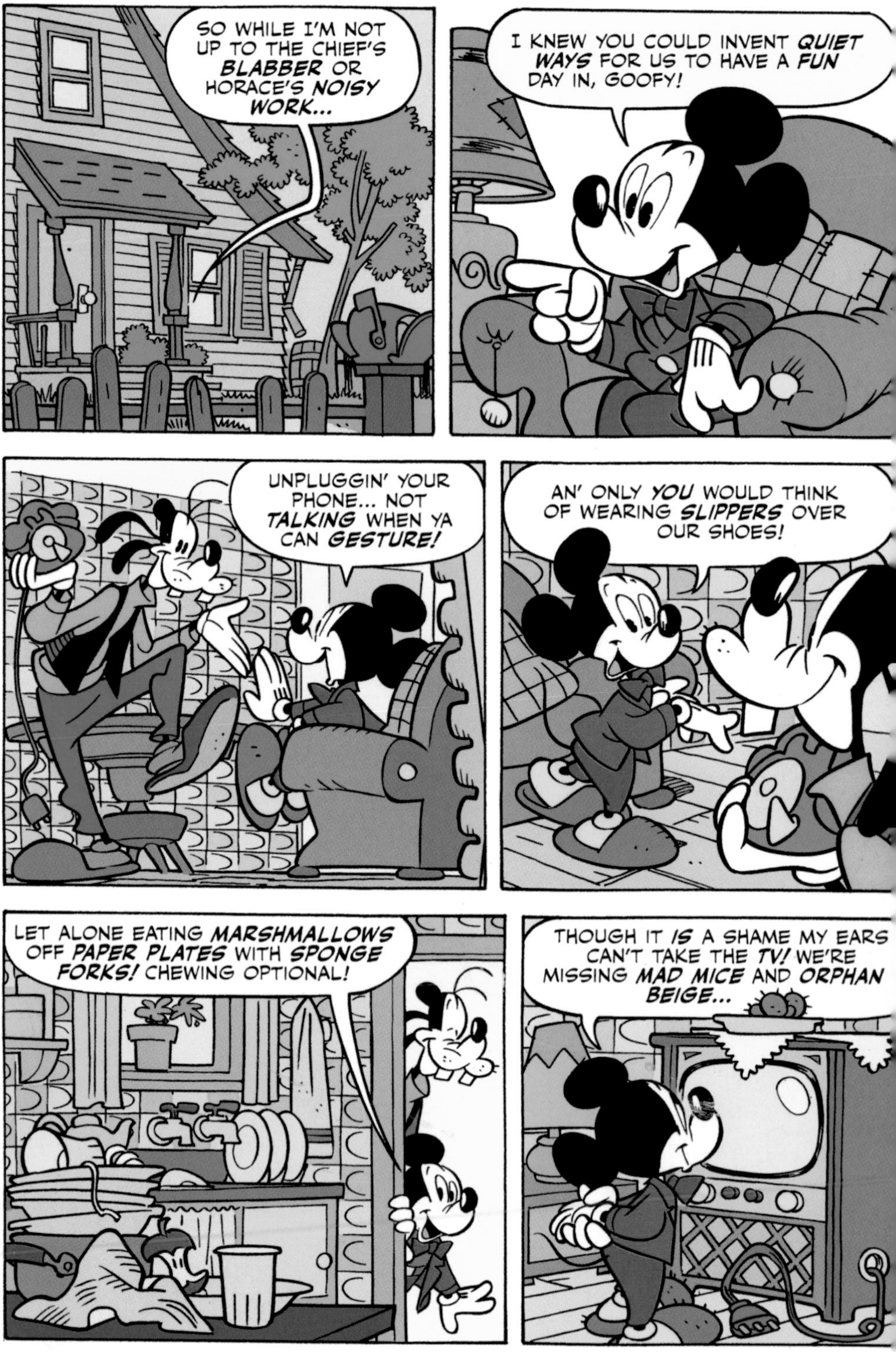
SO WHILE I'M NOT UP TO THE CHIEF'S BLABBER OR HORACE'S NOISY WORK...
I KNEW YOU COULD INVENT QUIET WAYS FOR US TO HAVE A FUN DAY IN, GOOFY!
UNPLUGGIN' YOUR PHONE... NOT TALKING WHEN YA CAN GESTURE!
AN' ONLY YOU WOULD THINK OF WEARING SLIPPERS OVER OUR SHOES!
LET ALONE EATING MARSHMALLOWS OFF PAPER PLATES WITH SPONGE FORKS! CHEWING OPTIONAL!
THOUGH IT IS A SHAME MY EARS CAN'T TAKE THE TV! WE'RE MISSING MAD MICE AND ORPHAN BEIGE...

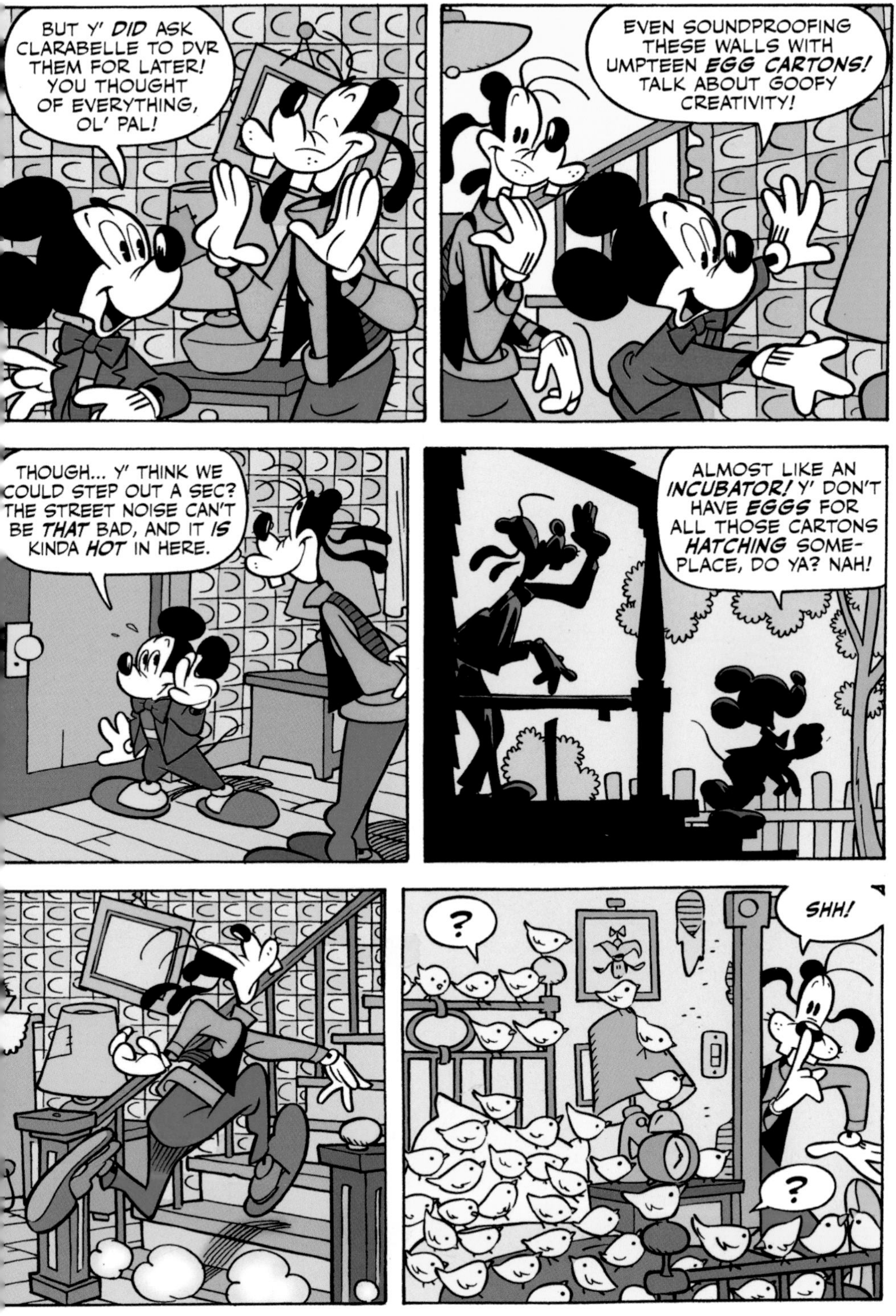
BUT Y' DID ASK CLARABELLE TO DVR THEM FOR LATER! YOU THOUGHT OF EVERYTHING, OL' PAL!
EVEN SOUNDPROOFING THESE WALLS WITH UMPTEEN EGG CARTONS! TALK ABOUT GOOFY CREATIVITY!
THOUGH... Y' THINK WE COULD STEP OUT A SEC? THE STREET NOISE CAN'T BE THAT BAD, AND IT IS KINDA HOT IN HERE.
ALMOST LIKE AN INCUBATOR! Y' DON'T HAVE EGGS FOR ALL THOSE CARTONS HATCHING SOMEPLACE, DO YA? NAH!
?
SHH!
?

A FEW DAYS LATER...

KLUD
KLUD

I'M *COMIN'!* I'M COMIN'! NO NEED TO BUST TH' DOOR DOWN!

ALLOW ME TO INTRODUCE MYSELF! I AM *DR. TIM TINNABULATION...* EAR EXPERT!

EH? DOOR-TO-DOOR *DOCTORS, NOW?*

I SPECIALIZE IN WAVES! ULTRASONIC, SUBSONIC, STEREOPHONIC! AND *ONE OTHER* VERY *SPECIAL* KIND OF WAVE!

WHAT *"WAVE"* WOULD THAT BE, I WONDER...

WHY, THE WAV *"HELLO!"* GLA TO SEE YA!

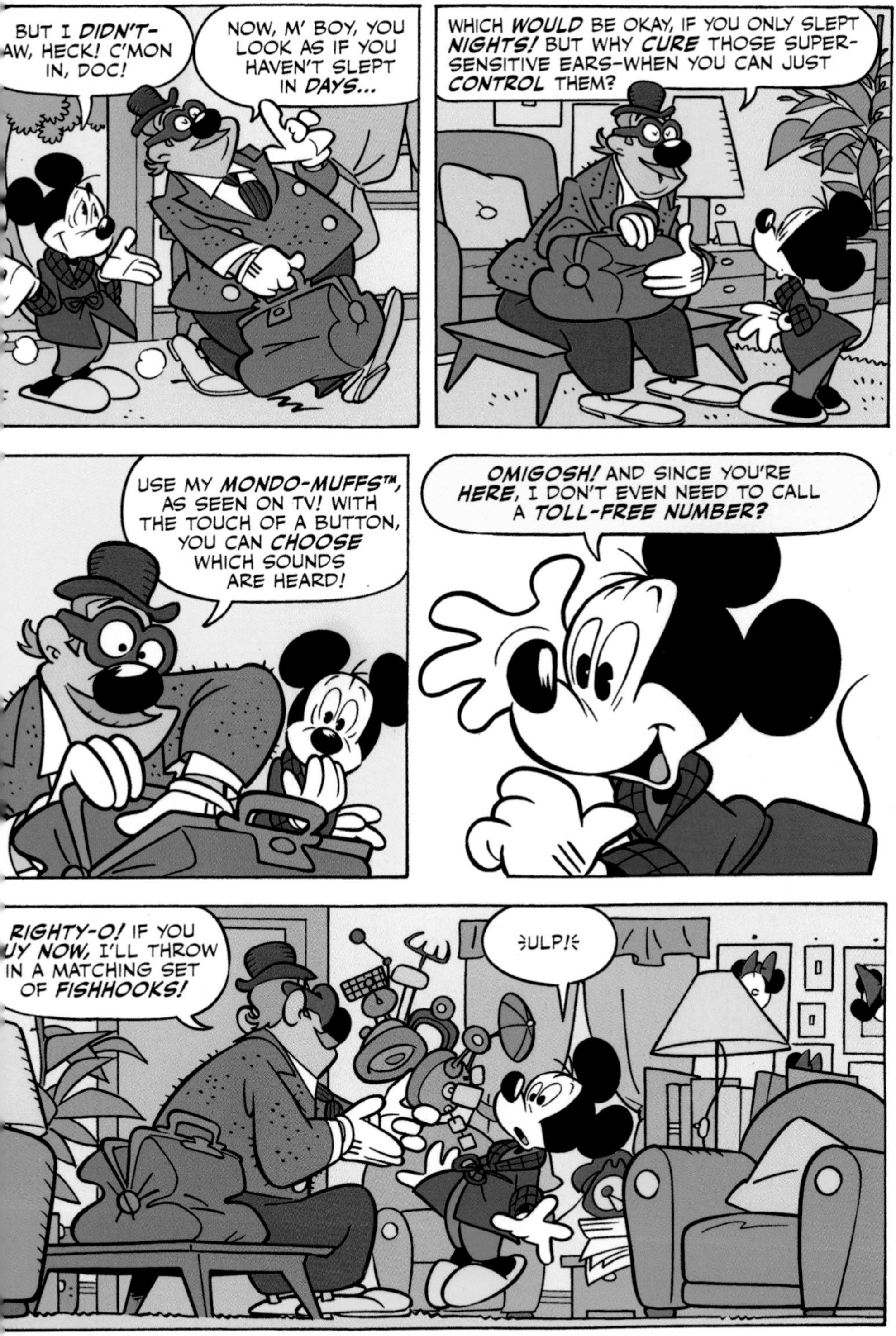
BUT I DIDN'T- AW, HECK! C'MON IN, DOC!
NOW, M' BOY, YOU LOOK AS IF YOU HAVEN'T SLEPT IN DAYS...
WHICH WOULD BE OKAY, IF YOU ONLY SLEPT NIGHTS! BUT WHY CURE THOSE SUPER-SENSITIVE EARS—WHEN YOU CAN JUST CONTROL THEM?
USE MY MONDO-MUFFS™, AS SEEN ON TV! WITH THE TOUCH OF A BUTTON, YOU CAN CHOOSE WHICH SOUNDS ARE HEARD!
OMIGOSH! AND SINCE YOU'RE HERE, I DON'T EVEN NEED TO CALL A TOLL-FREE NUMBER?
RIGHTY-O! IF YOU UY NOW, I'LL THROW IN A MATCHING SET OF FISHHOOKS!
ULP!

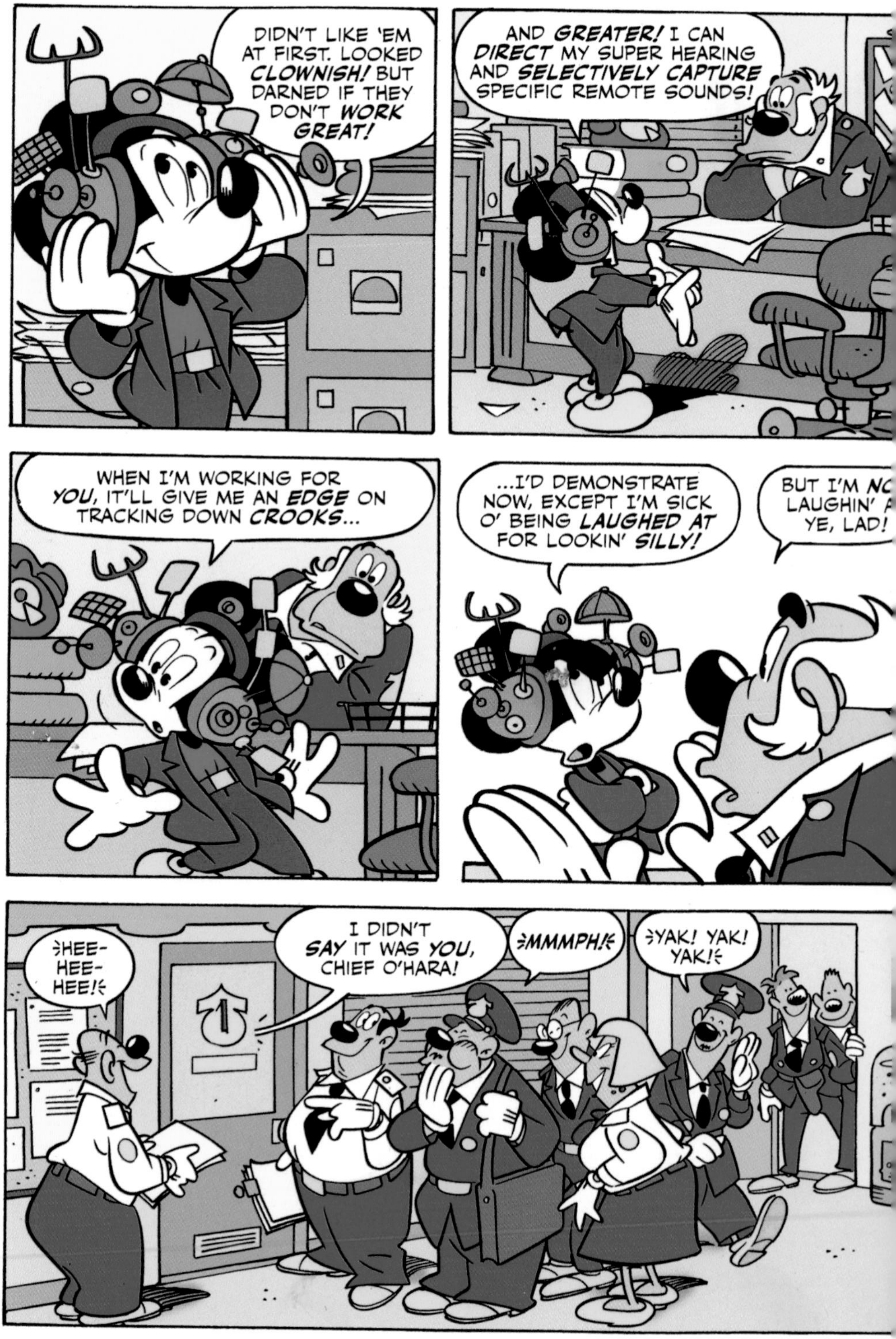

DIDN'T LIKE 'EM AT FIRST. LOOKED CLOWNISH! BUT DARNED IF THEY DON'T WORK GREAT!
AND GREATER! I CAN DIRECT MY SUPER HEARING AND SELECTIVELY CAPTURE SPECIFIC REMOTE SOUNDS!
WHEN I'M WORKING FOR YOU, IT'LL GIVE ME AN EDGE ON TRACKING DOWN CROOKS...
...I'D DEMONSTRATE NOW, EXCEPT I'M SICK O' BEING LAUGHED AT FOR LOOKIN' SILLY!
HEE-HEE-HEE!
I DIDN'T SAY IT WAS YOU, CHIEF O'HARA!
MMMPH!
YAK! YAK! YAK!

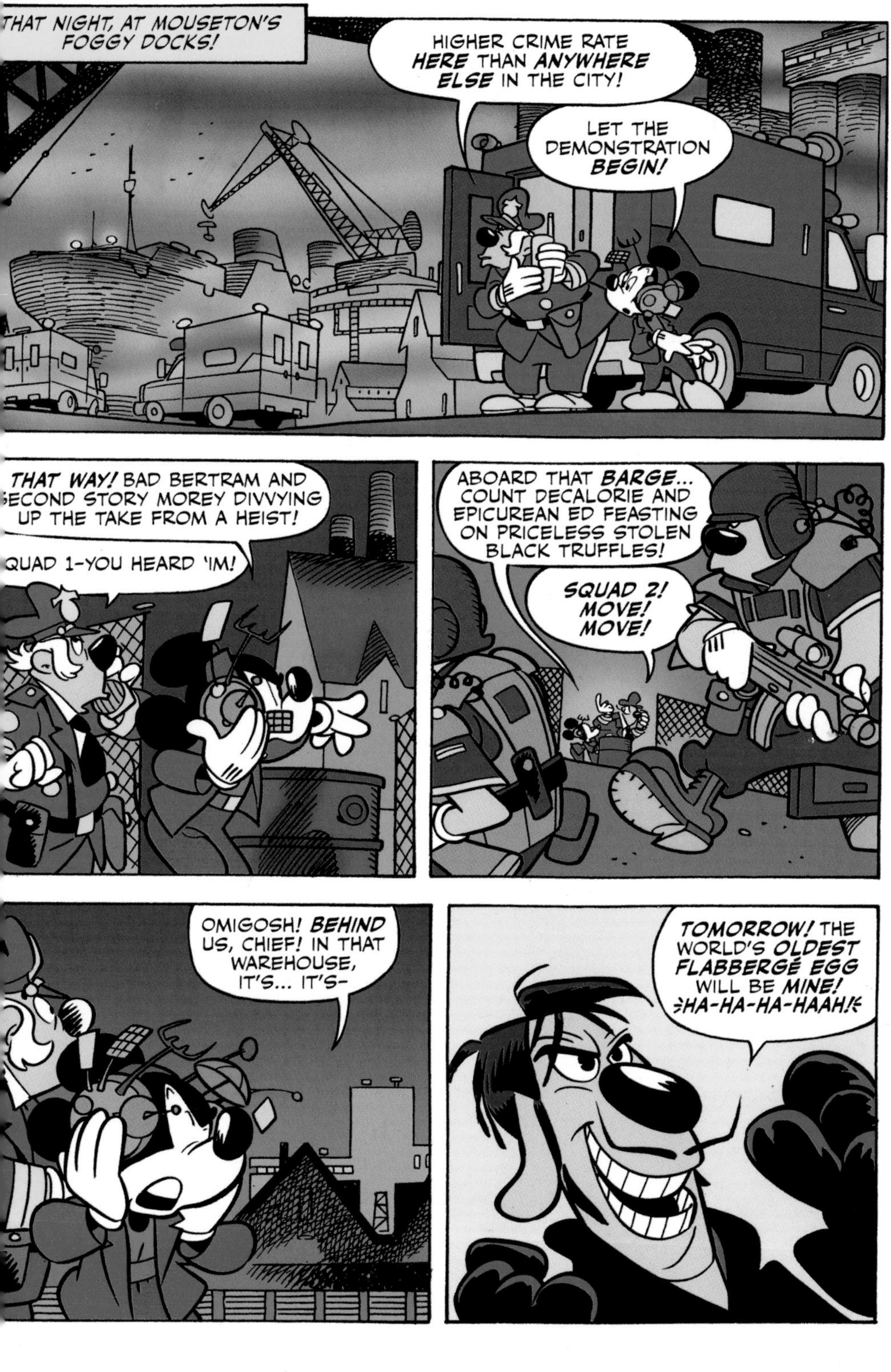
THAT NIGHT, AT MOUSETON'S FOGGY DOCKS!
HIGHER CRIME RATE HERE THAN ANYWHERE ELSE IN THE CITY!
LET THE DEMONSTRATION BEGIN!
THAT WAY! BAD BERTRAM AND SECOND STORY MOREY DIVVYING UP THE TAKE FROM A HEIST!
SQUAD 1–YOU HEARD 'IM!
ABOARD THAT BARGE... COUNT DECALORIE AND EPICUREAN ED FEASTING ON PRICELESS STOLEN BLACK TRUFFLES!
SQUAD 2! MOVE! MOVE!
OMIGOSH! BEHIND US, CHIEF! IN THAT WAREHOUSE, IT'S... IT'S–
TOMORROW! THE WORLD'S OLDEST FLABBERGÉ EGG WILL BE MINE! HA-HA-HA-HAAH!

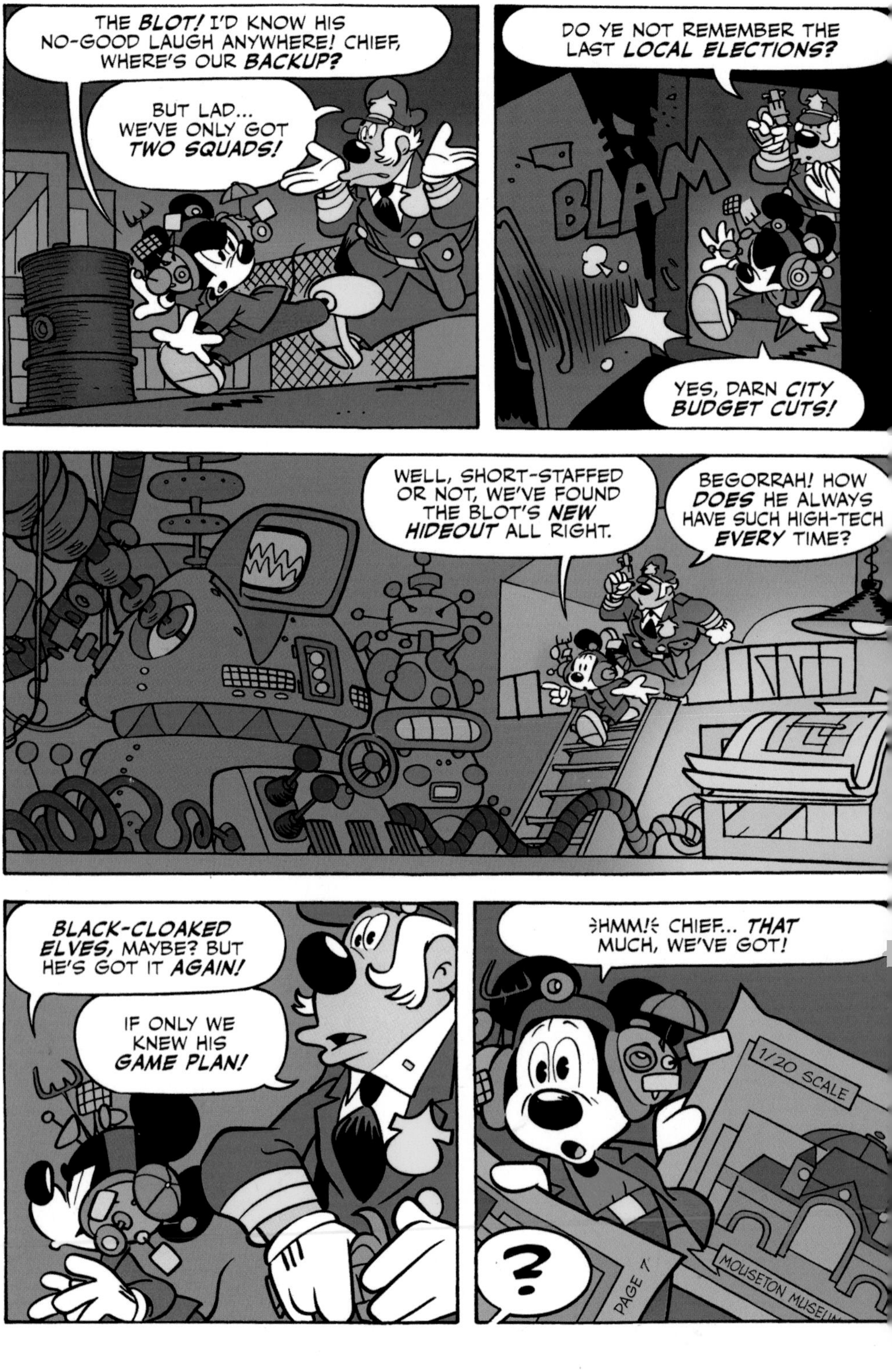

THE BLOT! I'D KNOW HIS NO-GOOD LAUGH ANYWHERE! CHIEF, WHERE'S OUR BACKUP?
BUT LAD... WE'VE ONLY GOT TWO SQUADS!
DO YE NOT REMEMBER THE LAST LOCAL ELECTIONS?
BLAM
YES, DARN CITY BUDGET CUTS!
WELL, SHORT-STAFFED OR NOT, WE'VE FOUND THE BLOT'S NEW HIDEOUT ALL RIGHT.
BEGORRAH! HOW DOES HE ALWAYS HAVE SUCH HIGH-TECH EVERY TIME?
BLACK-CLOAKED ELVES, MAYBE? BUT HE'S GOT IT AGAIN!
IF ONLY WE KNEW HIS GAME PLAN!
HMM! CHIEF... THAT MUCH, WE'VE GOT!
1/20 SCALE
MOUSETON MUSEU
PAGE 7
?

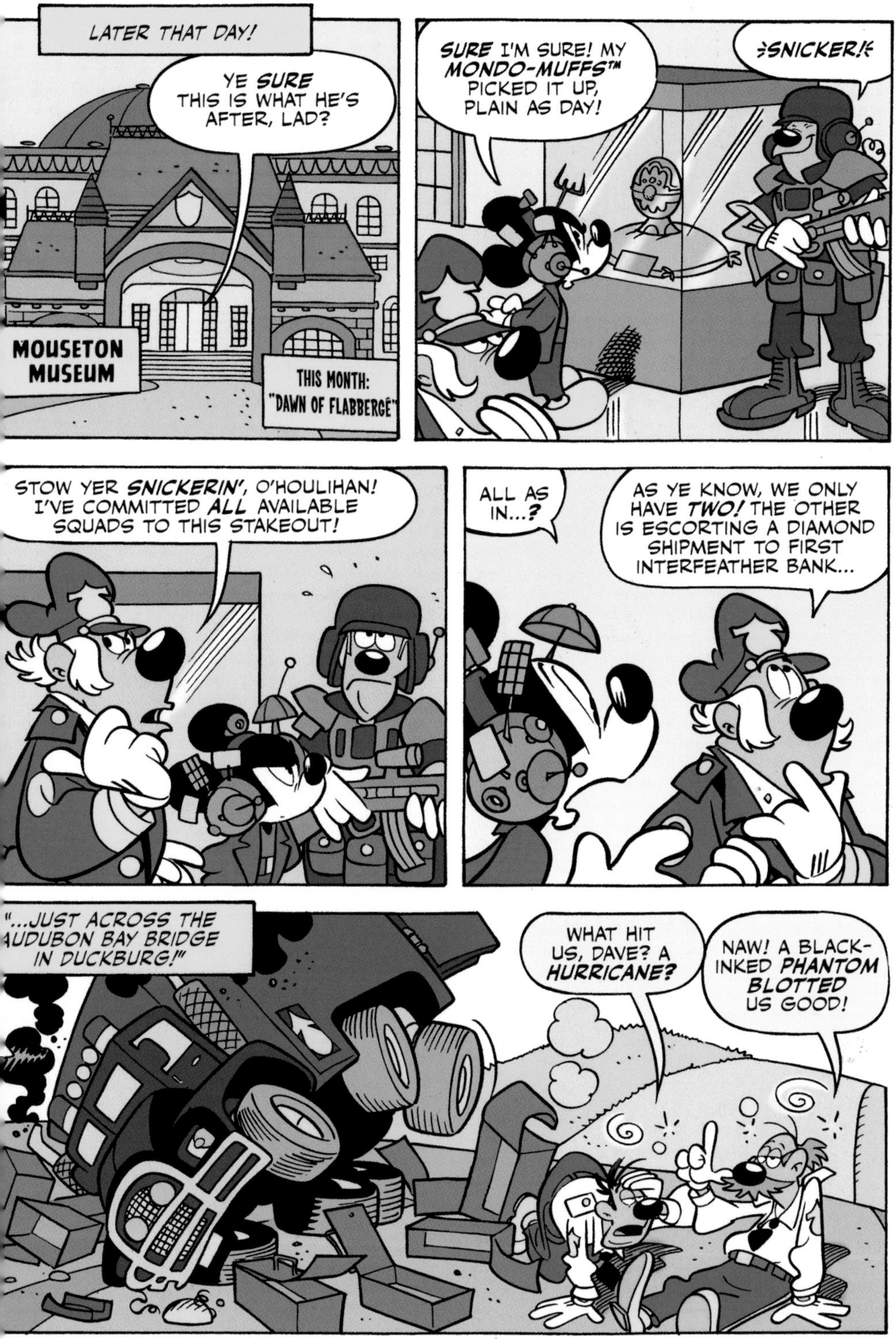
LATER THAT DAY!
YE SURE THIS IS WHAT HE'S AFTER, LAD?
MOUSETON MUSEUM
THIS MONTH: "DAWN OF FLABBERGÉ"
SURE I'M SURE! MY MONDO-MUFFS™ PICKED IT UP, PLAIN AS DAY!
SNICKER!
STOW YER SNICKERIN', O'HOULIHAN! I'VE COMMITTED ALL AVAILABLE SQUADS TO THIS STAKEOUT!
ALL AS IN...?
AS YE KNOW, WE ONLY HAVE TWO! THE OTHER IS ESCORTING A DIAMOND SHIPMENT TO FIRST INTERFEATHER BANK...
"...JUST ACROSS THE AUDUBON BAY BRIDGE IN DUCKBURG!"
WHAT HIT US, DAVE? A HURRICANE?
NAW! A BLACK-INKED PHANTOM BLOTTED US GOOD!

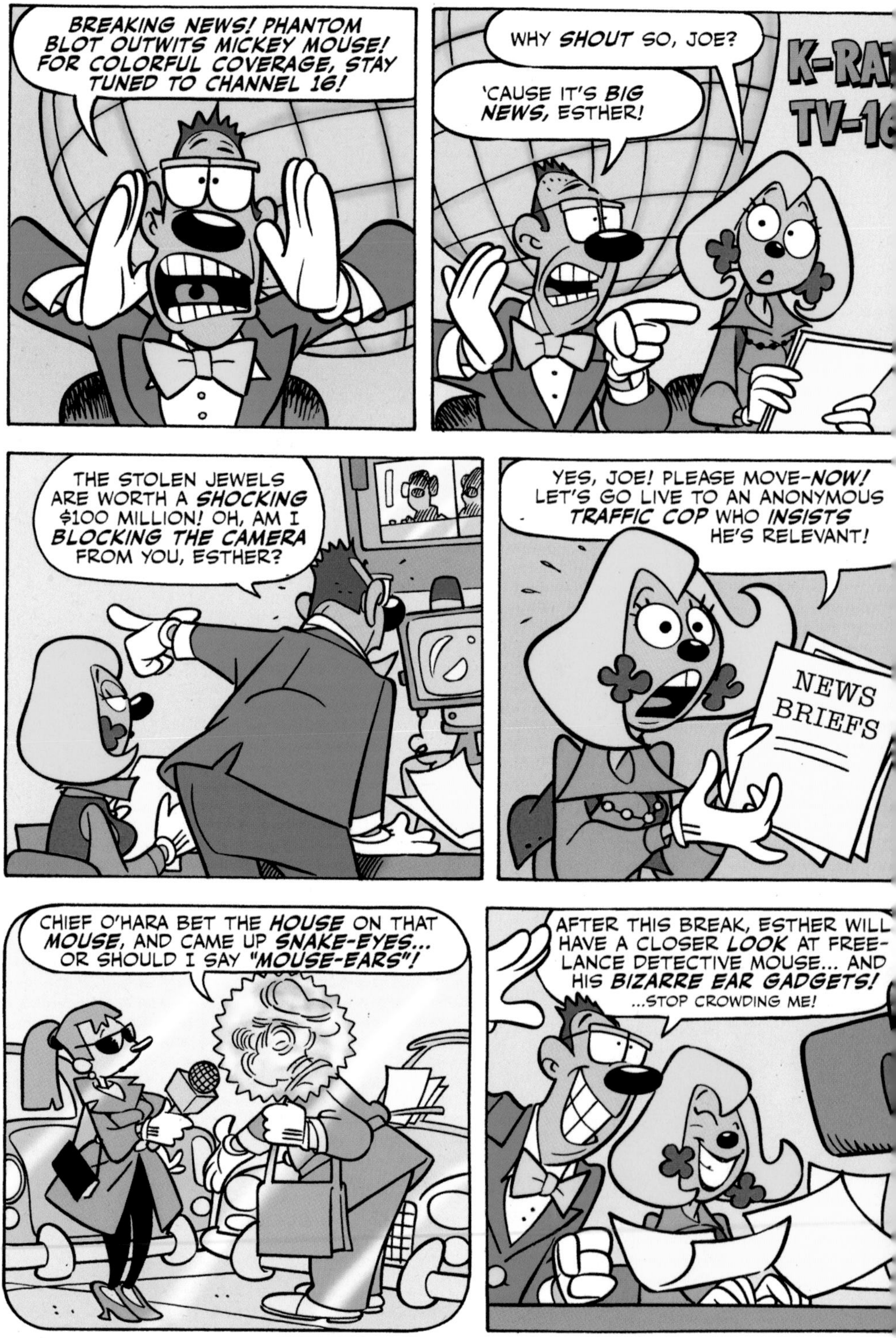

BREAKING NEWS! PHANTOM BLOT OUTWITS MICKEY MOUSE! FOR COLORFUL COVERAGE, STAY TUNED TO CHANNEL 16!
WHY SHOUT SO, JOE?
'CAUSE IT'S BIG NEWS, ESTHER!
K-RA
TV-16
THE STOLEN JEWELS ARE WORTH A SHOCKING $100 MILLION! OH, AM I BLOCKING THE CAMERA FROM YOU, ESTHER?
YES, JOE! PLEASE MOVE–NOW! LET'S GO LIVE TO AN ANONYMOUS TRAFFIC COP WHO INSISTS HE'S RELEVANT!
NEWS BRIEFS
CHIEF O'HARA BET THE HOUSE ON THAT MOUSE, AND CAME UP SNAKE-EYES... OR SHOULD I SAY "MOUSE-EARS"!
AFTER THIS BREAK, ESTHER WILL HAVE A CLOSER LOOK AT FREE-LANCE DETECTIVE MOUSE... AND HIS BIZARRE EAR GADGETS!
...STOP CROWDING ME!

SOON ENOUGH—
BACK AT THE STATION!

BUT I'M *NOT* THE COP WHO TALKED TO THAT NEWS CREW, I SWEAR!

P.D

P.D

NOT THAT THIS *FACE* AIN'T MADE FER TH' SCREEN, AND ALL...

IT'S NOT ABOUT *YOU*, CASEY!... "SURE I'M SURE," I SAID!

CHIEF O'HARA GOT EMBARRASSED *BAD*... AN' IT *REALLY IS MY FAULT.*

OH! WELL, MEBBE IT *WAS!*

NEXT TIME TH' MAYOR AN' TH' COMMISSIONER ASK TH' CHIEF ABOUT HIS *TOP SLEUTH,* HE'LL SAY—

GET ON THOSE *TRAFFIC TICKETS,* CASEY! I MAY SOON BE *JOININ'* YE!

?

?

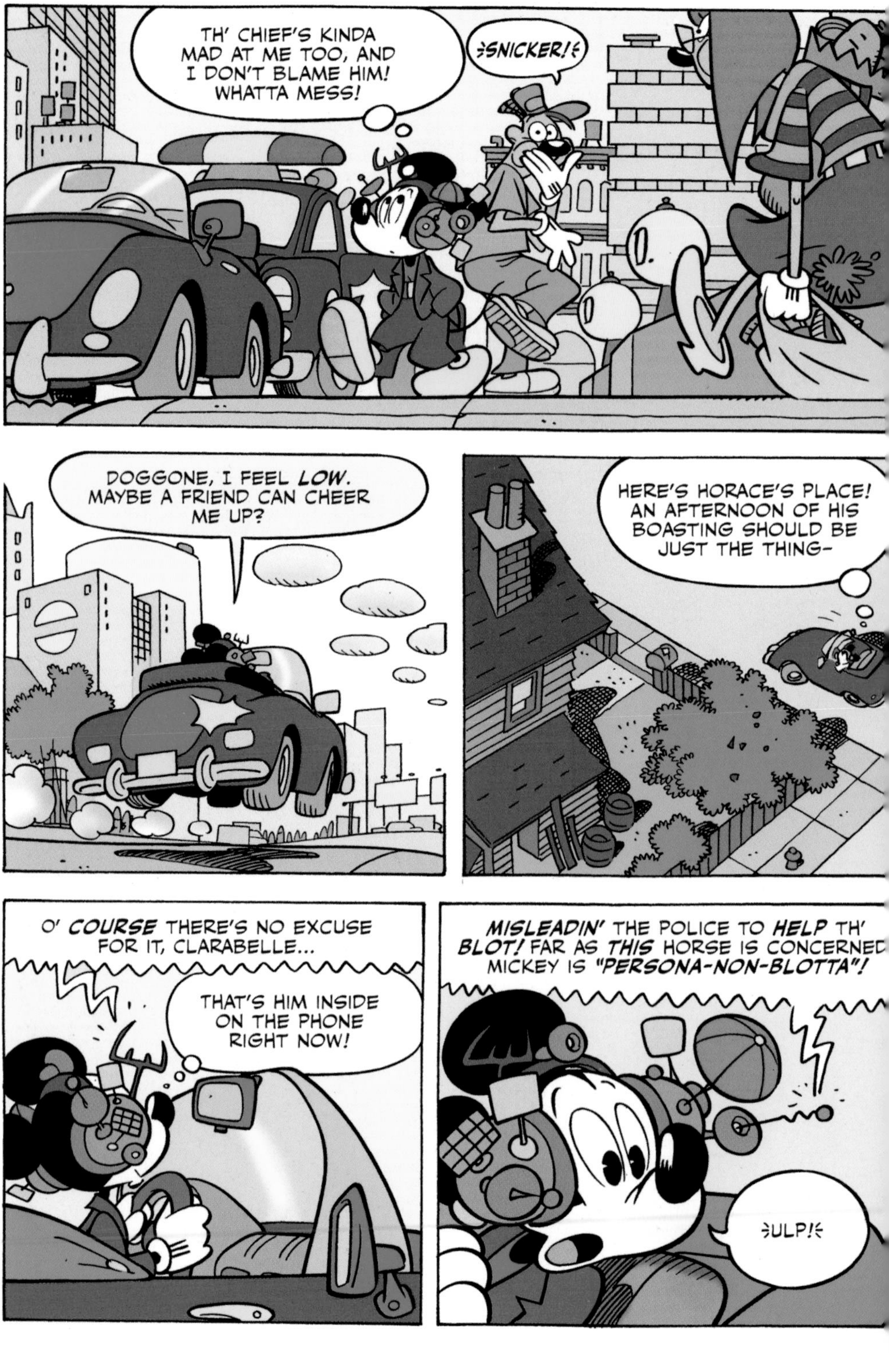
TH' CHIEF'S KINDA MAD AT ME TOO, AND I DON'T BLAME HIM! WHATTA MESS!
SNICKER!
DOGGONE, I FEEL LOW. MAYBE A FRIEND CAN CHEER ME UP?
HERE'S HORACE'S PLACE! AN AFTERNOON OF HIS BOASTING SHOULD BE JUST THE THING–
O' COURSE THERE'S NO EXCUSE FOR IT, CLARABELLE...
THAT'S HIM INSIDE ON THE PHONE RIGHT NOW!
MISLEADIN' THE POLICE TO HELP TH' BLOT! FAR AS THIS HORSE IS CONCERNED MICKEY IS "PERSONA-NON-BLOTTA"!
ULP!

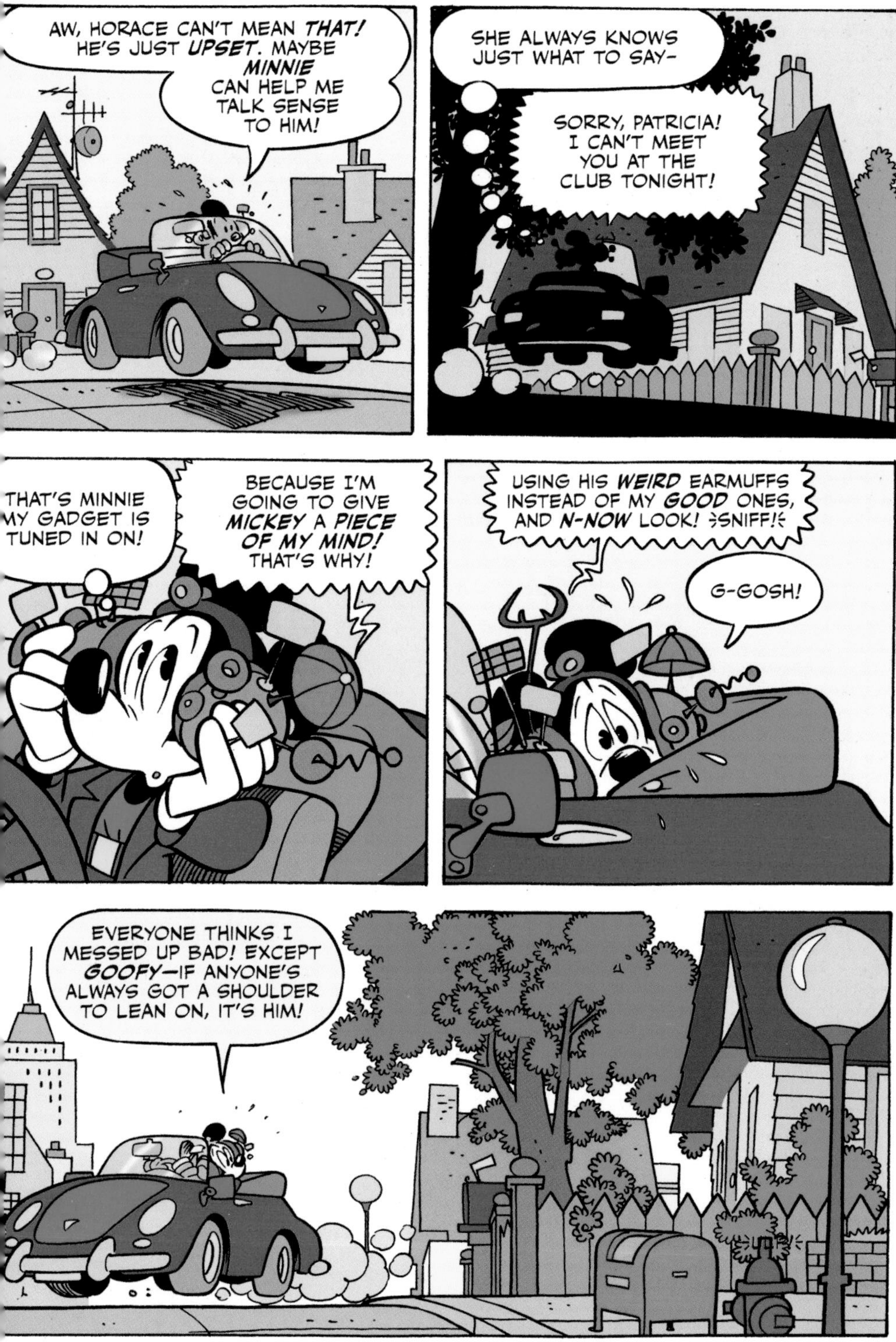
AW, HORACE CAN'T MEAN *THAT!* HE'S JUST *UPSET*. MAYBE *MINNIE* CAN HELP ME TALK SENSE TO HIM!
SHE ALWAYS KNOWS JUST WHAT TO SAY-
SORRY, PATRICIA! I CAN'T MEET YOU AT THE CLUB TONIGHT!
THAT'S MINNIE MY GADGET IS TUNED IN ON!
BECAUSE I'M GOING TO GIVE *MICKEY* A *PIECE OF MY MIND!* THAT'S WHY!
USING HIS *WEIRD* EARMUFFS INSTEAD OF MY *GOOD* ONES, AND *N-NOW* LOOK! *SNIFF!*
G-GOSH!
EVERYONE THINKS I MESSED UP BAD! EXCEPT *GOOFY*—IF ANYONE'S ALWAYS GOT A SHOULDER TO LEAN ON, IT'S HIM!

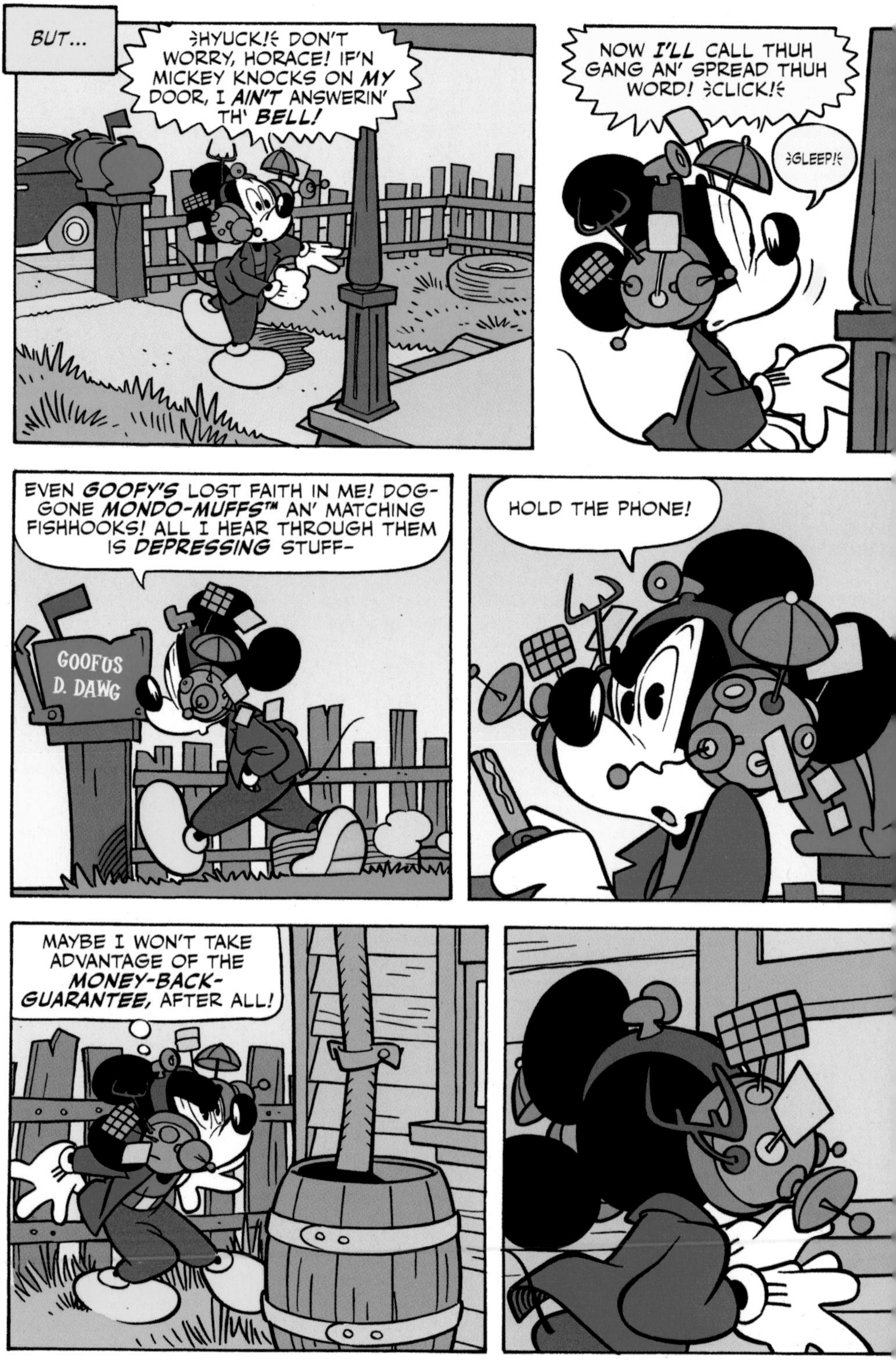
BUT...
HYUCK! DON'T WORRY, HORACE! IF'N MICKEY KNOCKS ON MY DOOR, I AIN'T ANSWERIN' TH' BELL!
NOW I'LL CALL THUH GANG AN' SPREAD THUH WORD! CLICK!
GLEEP!
EVEN GOOFY'S LOST FAITH IN ME! DOG-GONE MONDO-MUFFS™ AN' MATCHING FISHHOOKS! ALL I HEAR THROUGH THEM IS DEPRESSING STUFF–
GOOFUS D. DAWG
HOLD THE PHONE!
MAYBE I WON'T TAKE ADVANTAGE OF THE MONEY-BACK-GUARANTEE, AFTER ALL!

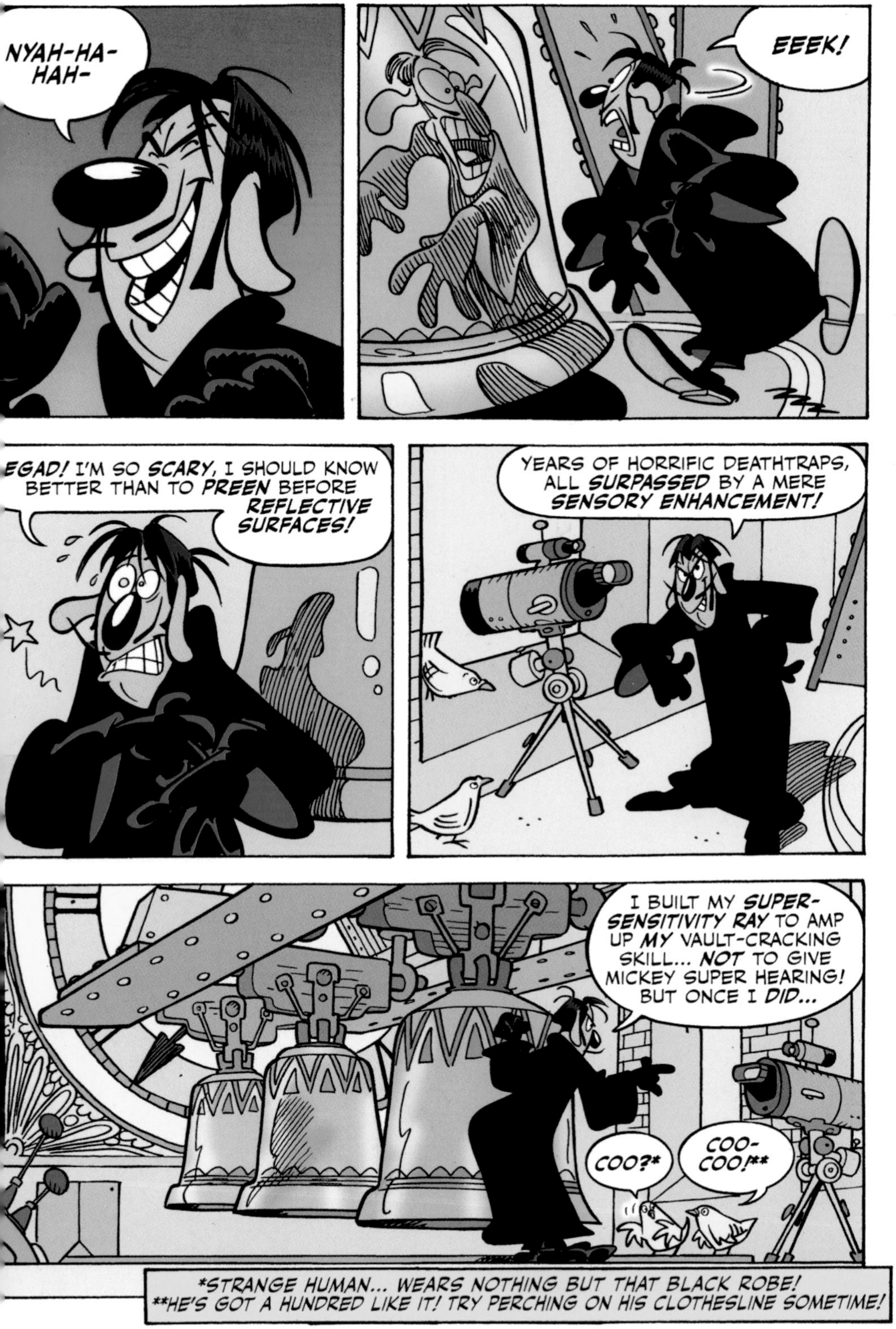
NYAH-HA-HAH-
EEEK!
EGAD! I'M SO SCARY, I SHOULD KNOW BETTER THAN TO PREEN BEFORE REFLECTIVE SURFACES!
YEARS OF HORRIFIC DEATHTRAPS, ALL SURPASSED BY A MERE SENSORY ENHANCEMENT!
I BUILT MY SUPER-SENSITIVITY RAY TO AMP UP MY VAULT-CRACKING SKILL... NOT TO GIVE MICKEY SUPER HEARING! BUT ONCE I DID...
COO?*
COO-COO!**
*STRANGE HUMAN... WEARS NOTHING BUT THAT BLACK ROBE!
**HE'S GOT A HUNDRED LIKE IT! TRY PERCHING ON HIS CLOTHESLINE SOMETIME!

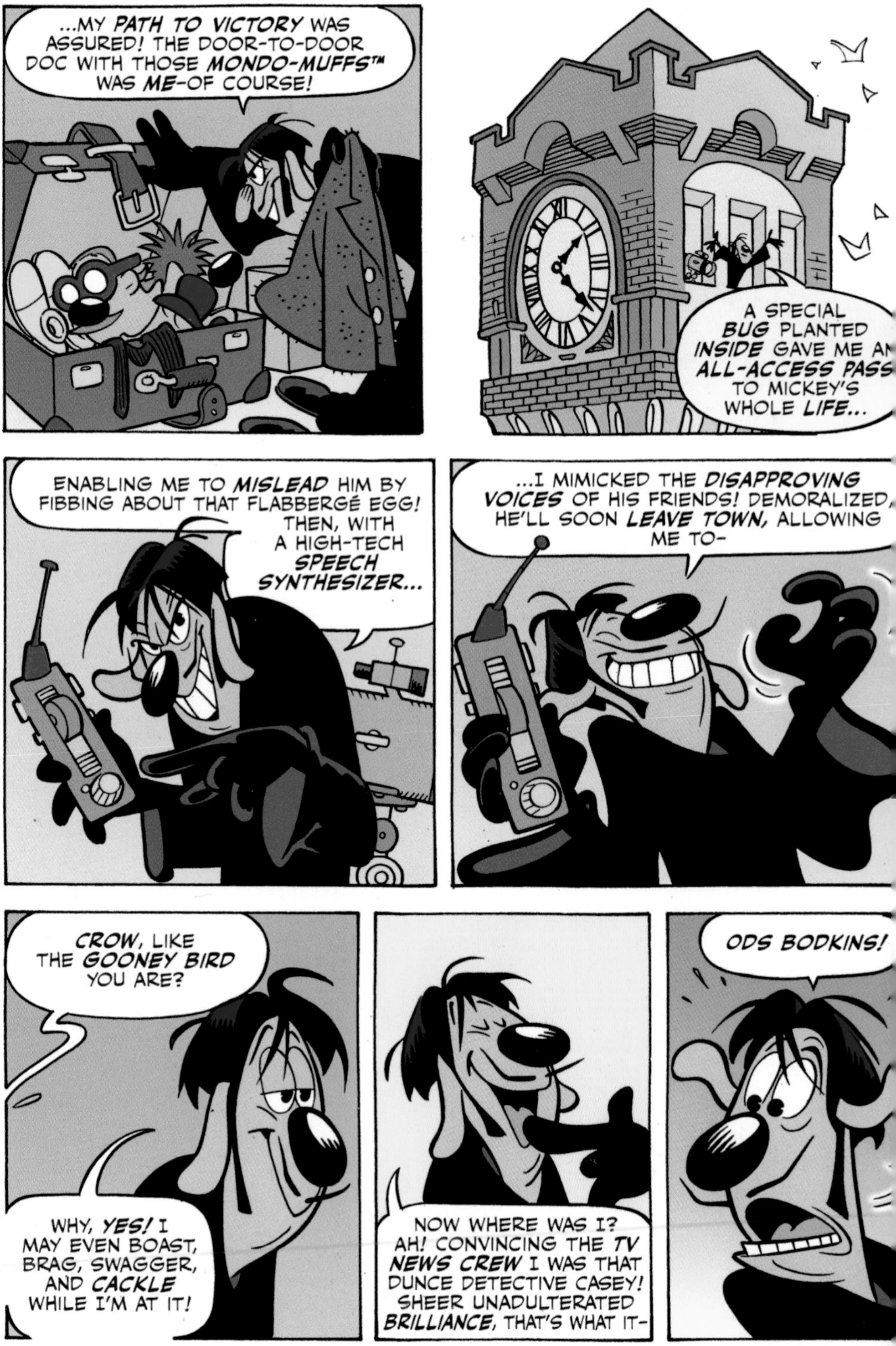
...MY PATH TO VICTORY WAS ASSURED! THE DOOR-TO-DOOR DOC WITH THOSE MONDO-MUFFS™ WAS ME-OF COURSE!
A SPECIAL BUG PLANTED INSIDE GAVE ME AN ALL-ACCESS PASS TO MICKEY'S WHOLE LIFE...
ENABLING ME TO MISLEAD HIM BY FIBBING ABOUT THAT FLABBERGÉ EGG!
THEN, WITH A HIGH-TECH SPEECH SYNTHESIZER...
...I MIMICKED THE DISAPPROVING VOICES OF HIS FRIENDS! DEMORALIZED, HE'LL SOON LEAVE TOWN, ALLOWING ME TO-
CROW, LIKE THE GOONEY BIRD YOU ARE?
WHY, YES! I MAY EVEN BOAST, BRAG, SWAGGER, AND CACKLE WHILE I'M AT IT!
NOW WHERE WAS I? AH! CONVINCING THE TV NEWS CREW I WAS THAT DUNCE DETECTIVE CASEY! SHEER UNADULTERATED BRILLIANCE, THAT'S WHAT IT-
ODS BODKINS!

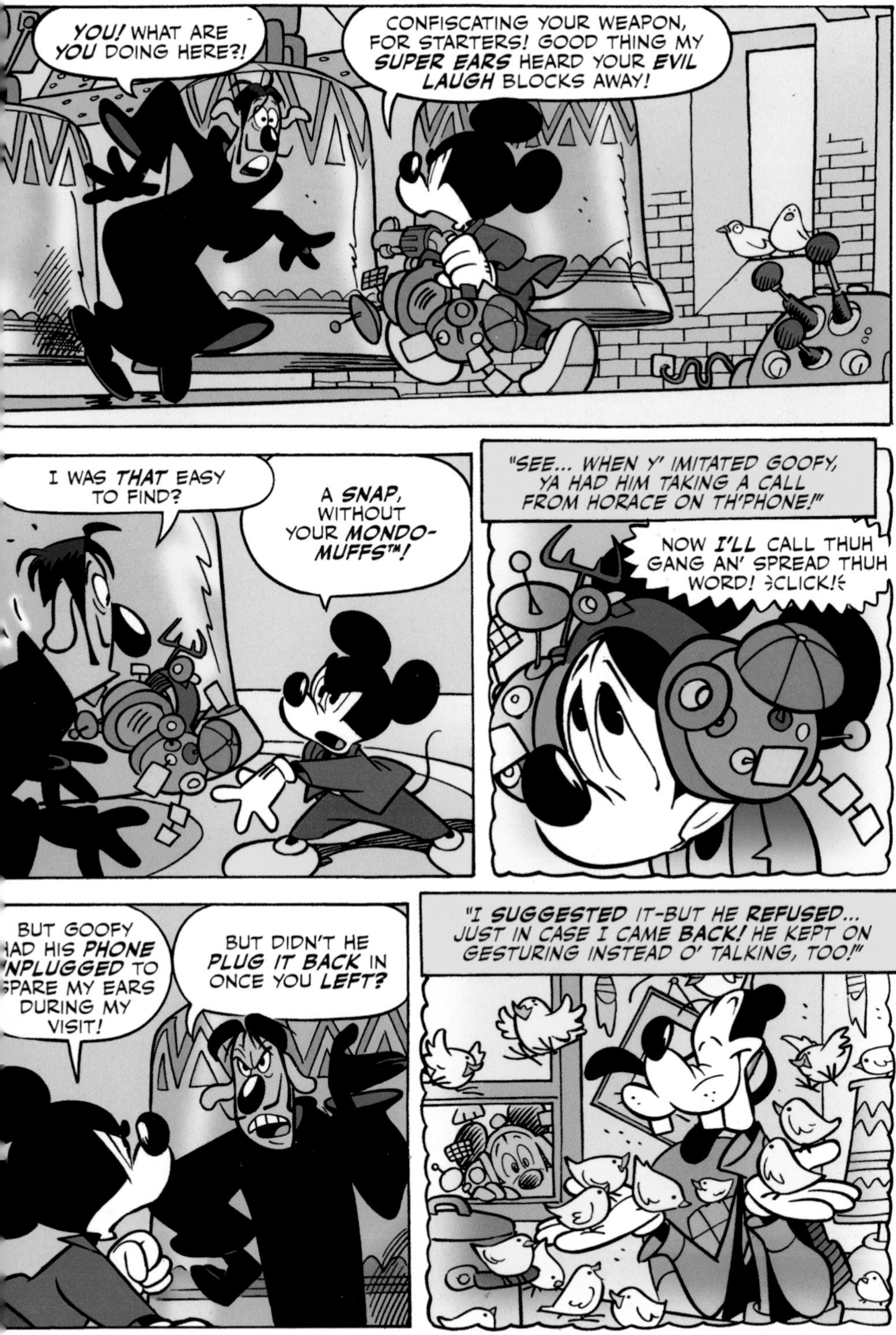

YOU! WHAT ARE YOU DOING HERE?!
CONFISCATING YOUR WEAPON, FOR STARTERS! GOOD THING MY SUPER EARS HEARD YOUR EVIL LAUGH BLOCKS AWAY!
I WAS THAT EASY TO FIND?
A SNAP, WITHOUT YOUR MONDO-MUFFS™!
"SEE... WHEN Y' IMITATED GOOFY, YA HAD HIM TAKING A CALL FROM HORACE ON TH'PHONE!"
NOW I'LL CALL THUH GANG AN' SPREAD THUH WORD! CLICK!
BUT GOOFY HAD HIS PHONE UNPLUGGED TO SPARE MY EARS DURING MY VISIT!
BUT DIDN'T HE PLUG IT BACK IN ONCE YOU LEFT?
"I SUGGESTED IT–BUT HE REFUSED... JUST IN CASE I CAME BACK! HE KEPT ON GESTURING INSTEAD O' TALKING, TOO!"

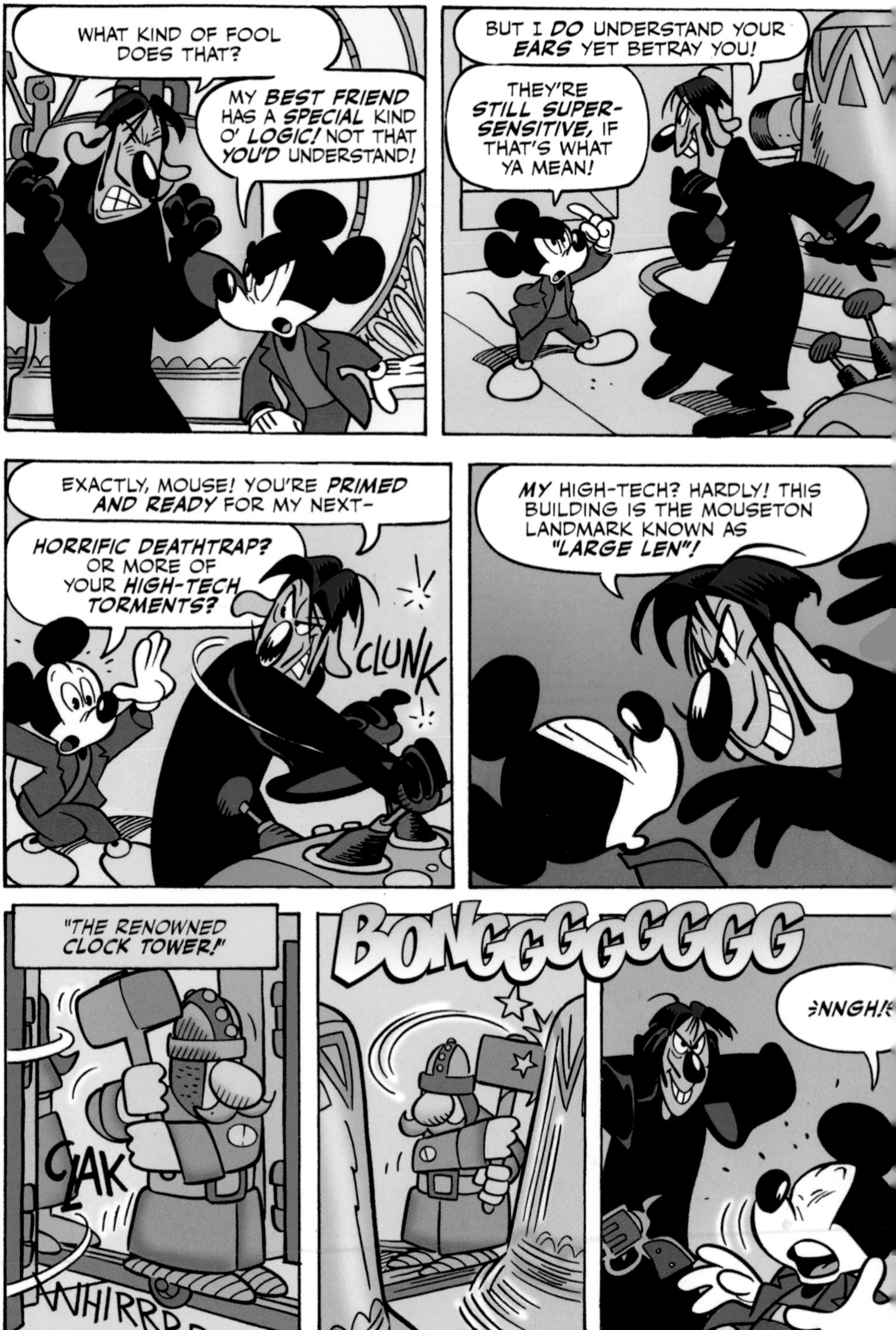

WHAT KIND OF FOOL DOES THAT?
MY BEST FRIEND HAS A SPECIAL KIND O' LOGIC! NOT THAT YOU'D UNDERSTAND!
BUT I DO UNDERSTAND YOUR EARS YET BETRAY YOU!
THEY'RE STILL SUPER-SENSITIVE, IF THAT'S WHAT YA MEAN!
EXACTLY, MOUSE! YOU'RE PRIMED AND READY FOR MY NEXT-
HORRIFIC DEATHTRAP? OR MORE OF YOUR HIGH-TECH TORMENTS?
CLUNK
MY HIGH-TECH? HARDLY! THIS BUILDING IS THE MOUSETON LANDMARK KNOWN AS "LARGE LEN"!
"THE RENOWNED CLOCK TOWER!"
CLAK
WHIRRRR
BONGGGGGGGG
NNGH!

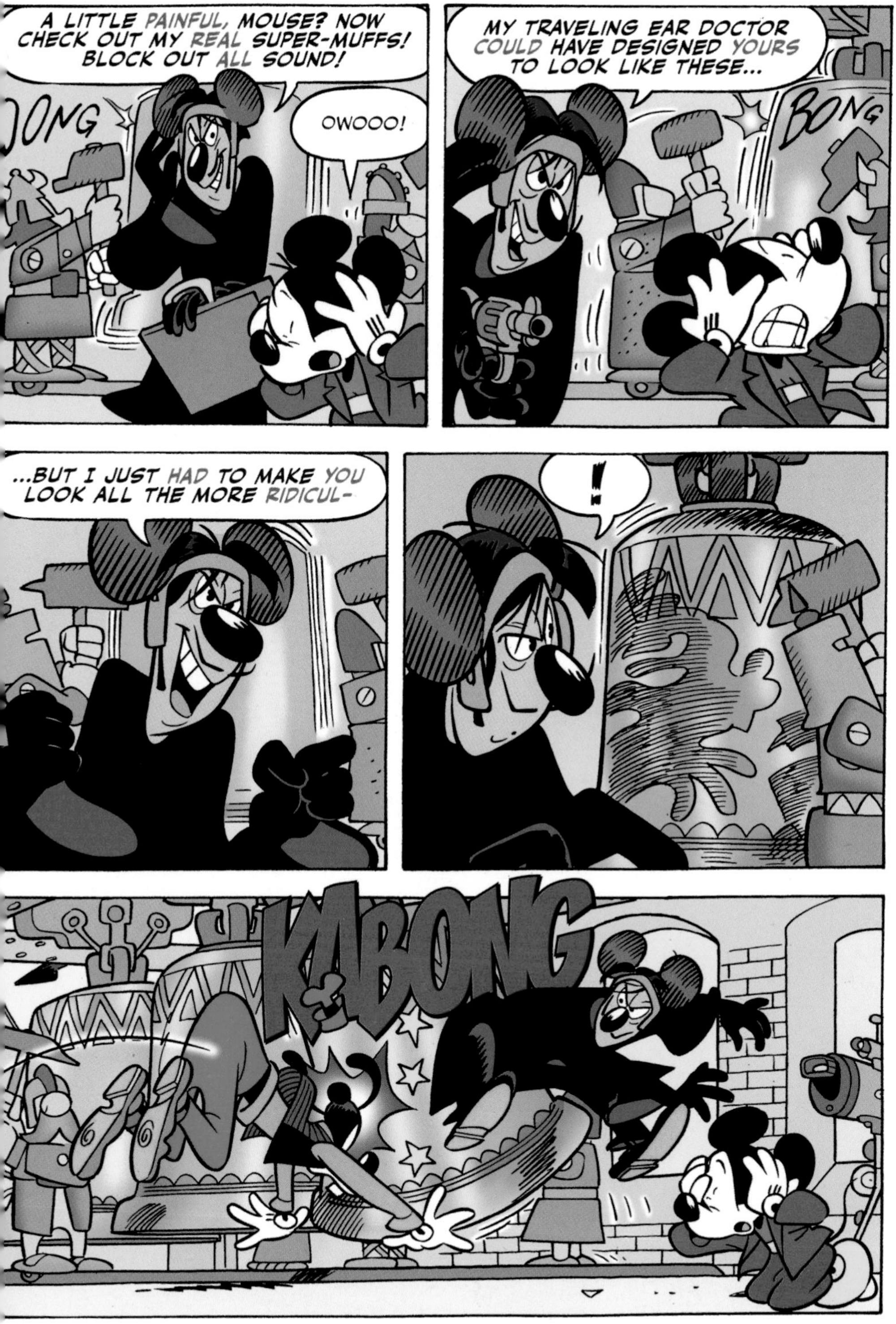
A LITTLE PAINFUL, MOUSE? NOW CHECK OUT MY REAL SUPER-MUFFS! BLOCK OUT ALL SOUND!
DONG
OWOOO!
MY TRAVELING EAR DOCTOR COULD HAVE DESIGNED YOURS TO LOOK LIKE THESE...
BONG
...BUT I JUST HAD TO MAKE YOU LOOK ALL THE MORE RIDICUL-
!
KABONG

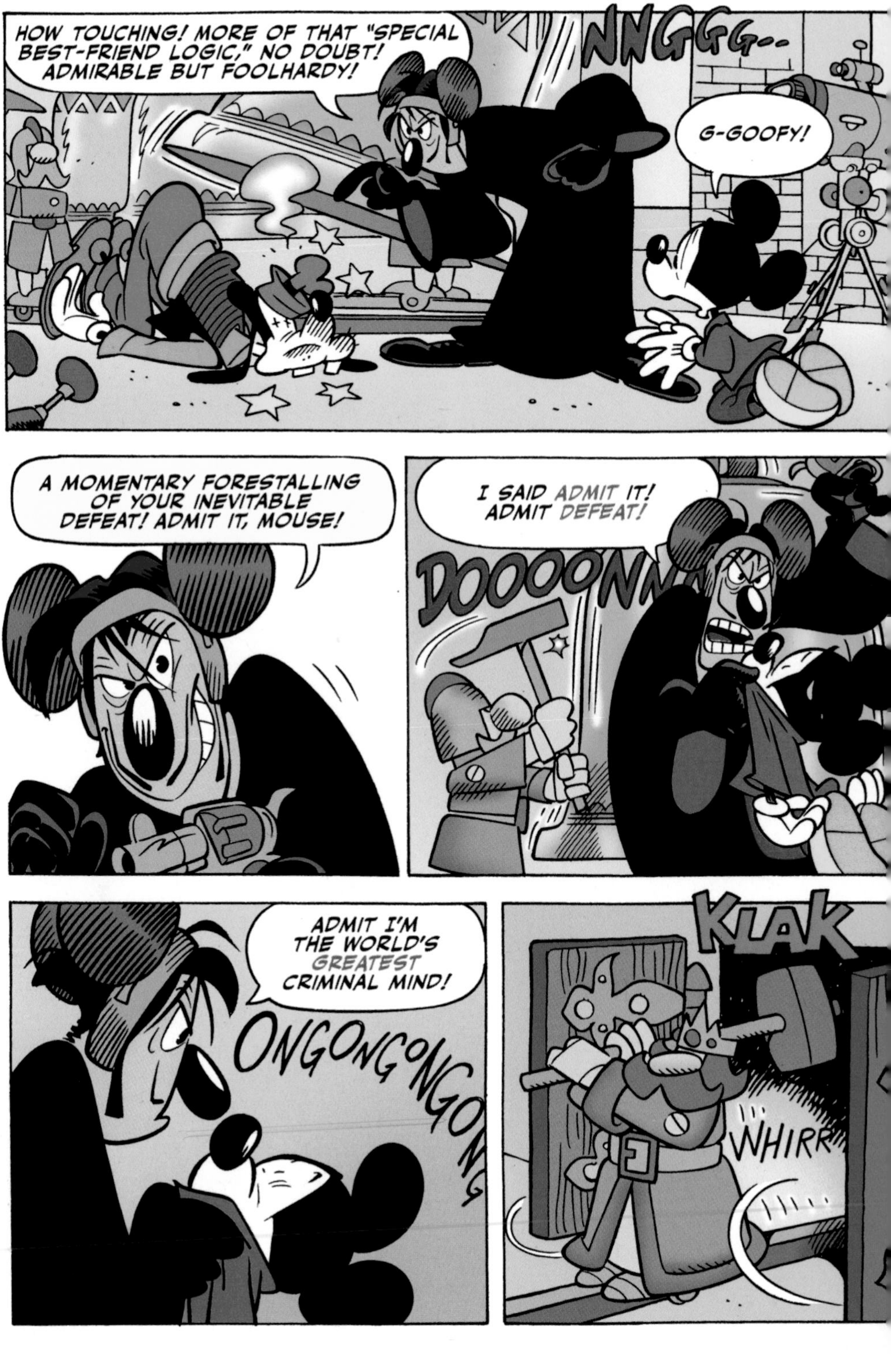
HOW TOUCHING! MORE OF THAT "SPECIAL BEST-FRIEND LOGIC," NO DOUBT! ADMIRABLE BUT FOOLHARDY!
NNGGGG..
G-GOOFY!
A MOMENTARY FORESTALLING OF YOUR INEVITABLE DEFEAT! ADMIT IT, MOUSE!
I SAID ADMIT IT! ADMIT DEFEAT!
DOOOONN
ADMIT I'M THE WORLD'S GREATEST CRIMINAL MIND!
ONGONGONGONGONG
KLAK
WHIRR

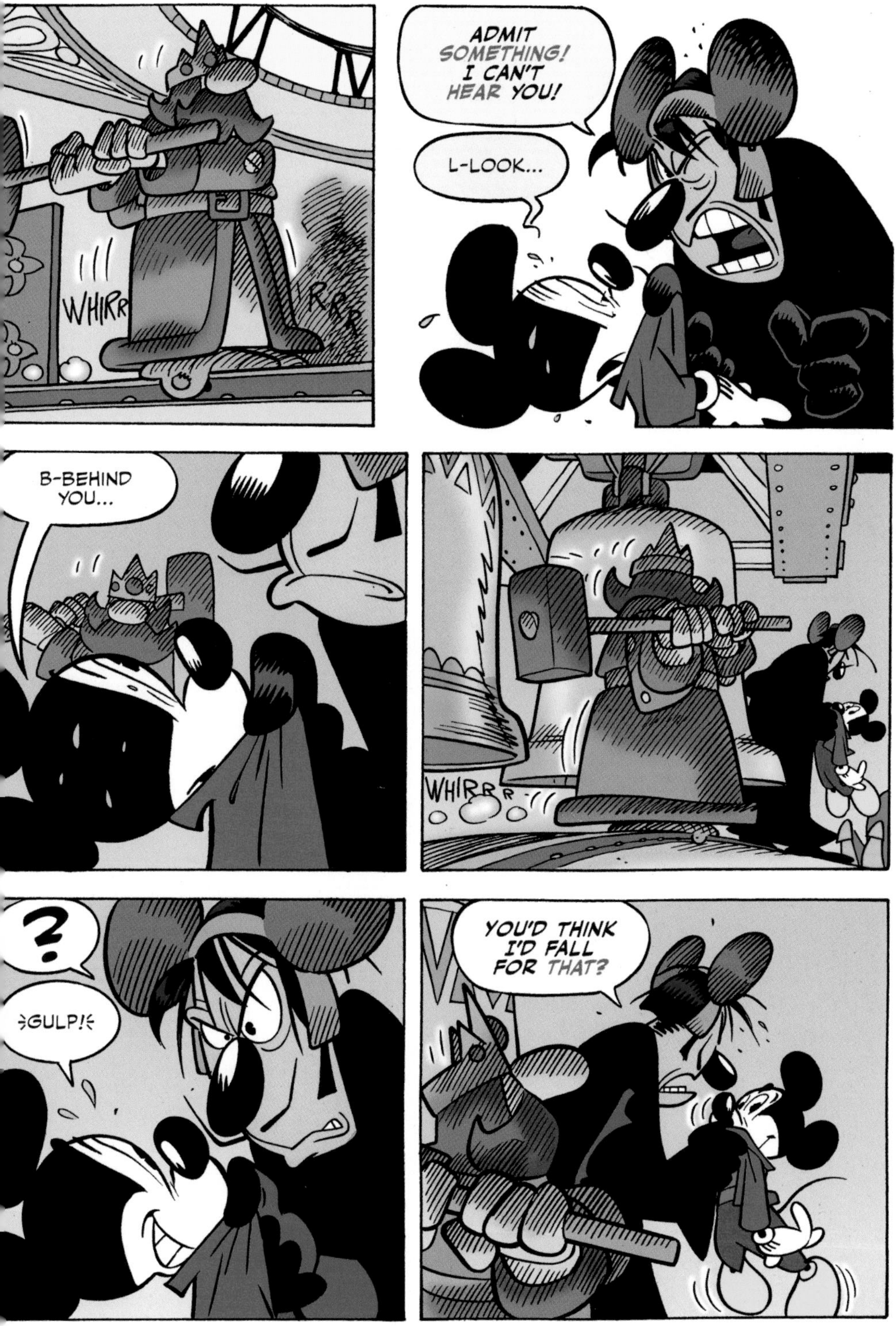
WHIRR
RRR
ADMIT SOMETHING! I CAN'T HEAR YOU!
L-LOOK...
B-BEHIND YOU...
WHIRRR
?
GULP!
YOU'D THINK I'D FALL FOR THAT?

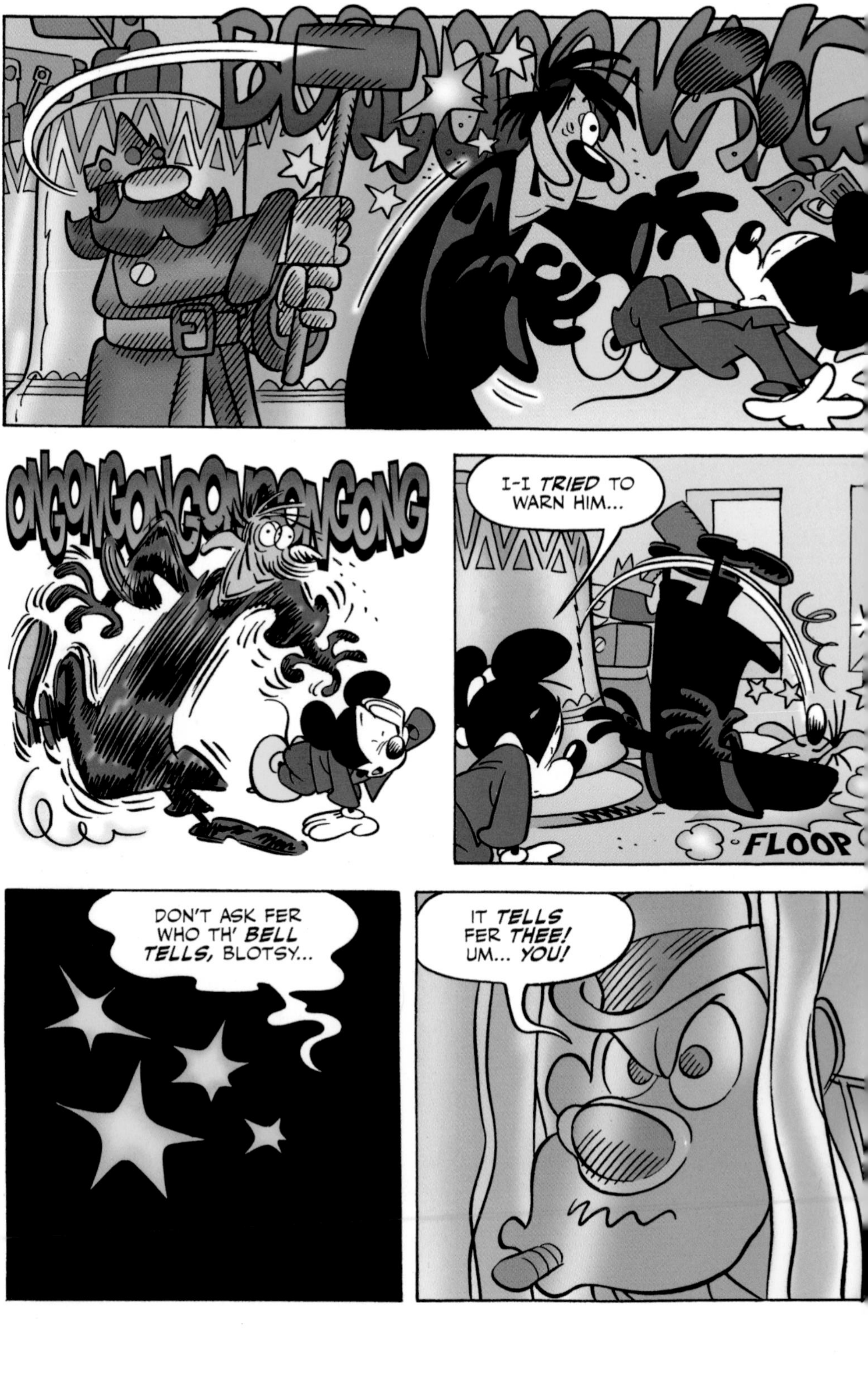

ONGONGONGONGONGONG
I-I TRIED TO WARN HIM...
FLOOP
DON'T ASK FER WHO TH' BELL TELLS, BLOTSY...
IT TELLS FER THEE! UM... YOU!

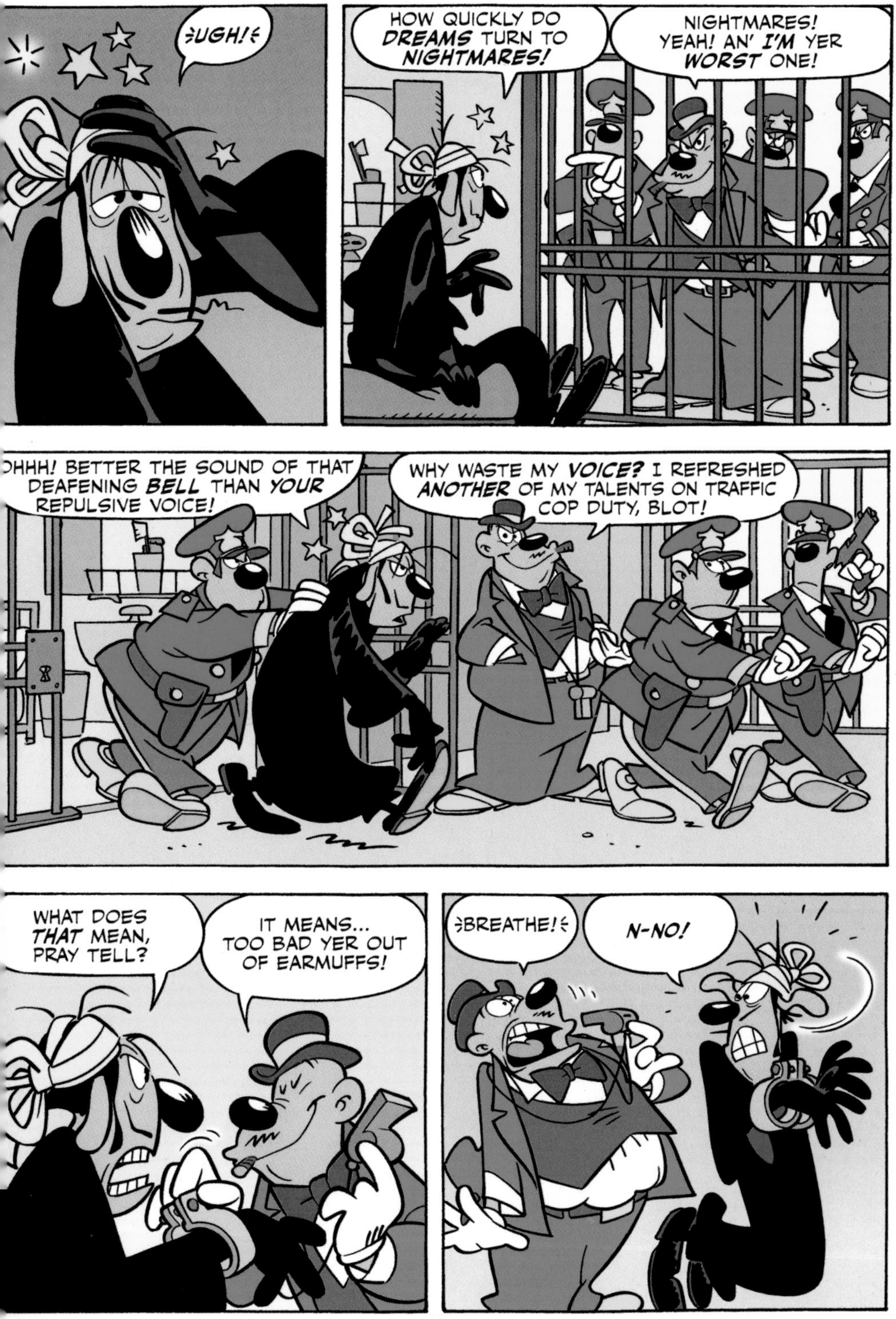

UGH!
HOW QUICKLY DO DREAMS TURN TO NIGHTMARES!
NIGHTMARES! YEAH! AN' I'M YER WORST ONE!
OHHH! BETTER THE SOUND OF THAT DEAFENING BELL THAN YOUR REPULSIVE VOICE!
WHY WASTE MY VOICE? I REFRESHED ANOTHER OF MY TALENTS ON TRAFFIC COP DUTY, BLOT!
WHAT DOES THAT MEAN, PRAY TELL?
IT MEANS... TOO BAD YER OUT OF EARMUFFS!
BREATHE!
N-NO!

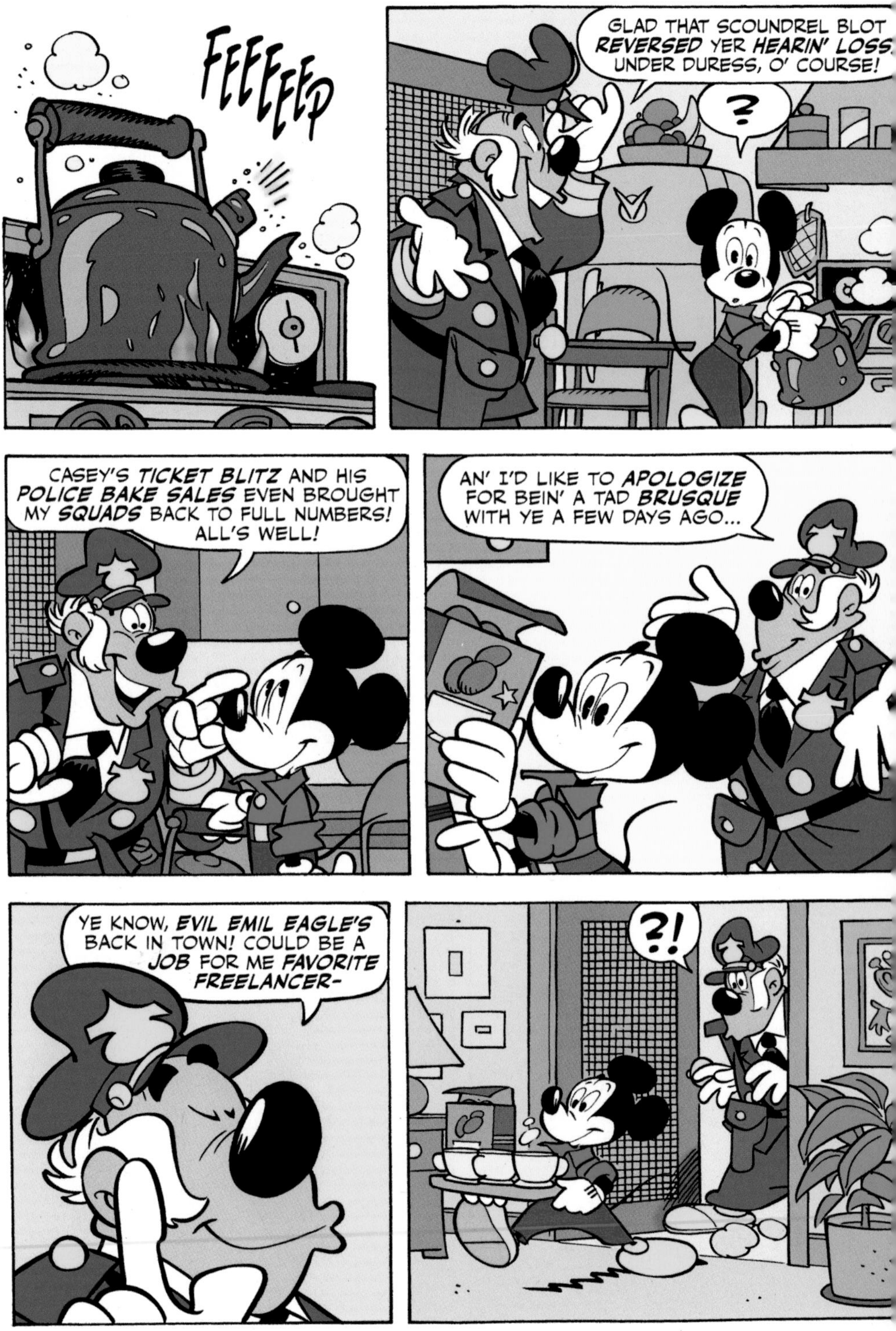

FEEEEEP
GLAD THAT SCOUNDREL BLOT REVERSED YER HEARIN' LOSS! UNDER DURESS, O' COURSE!
?
CASEY'S TICKET BLITZ AND HIS POLICE BAKE SALES EVEN BROUGHT MY SQUADS BACK TO FULL NUMBERS! ALL'S WELL!
AN' I'D LIKE TO APOLOGIZE FOR BEIN' A TAD BRUSQUE WITH YE A FEW DAYS AGO...
YE KNOW, EVIL EMIL EAGLE'S BACK IN TOWN! COULD BE A JOB FOR ME FAVORITE FREELANCER-
?!

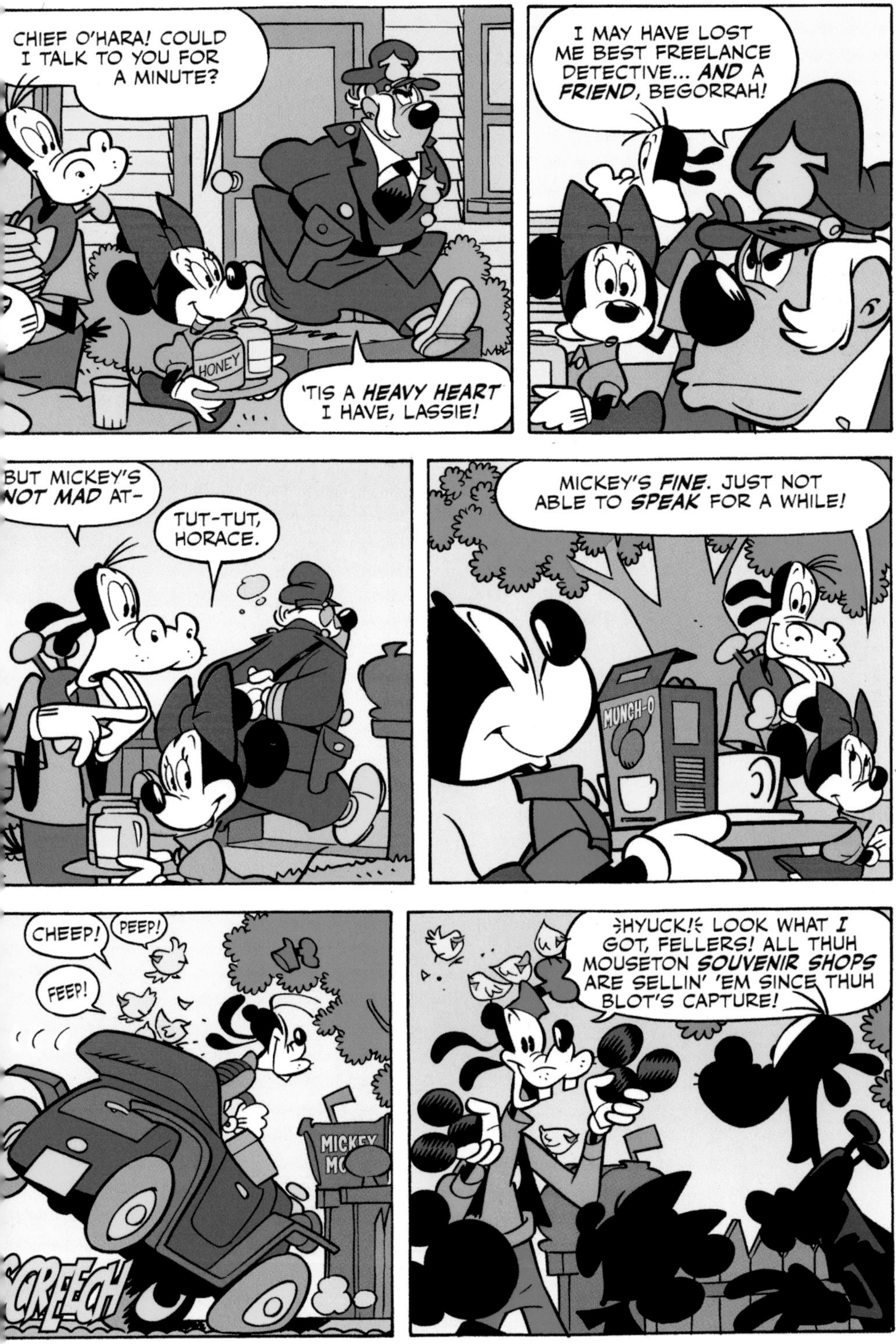
CHIEF O'HARA! COULD I TALK TO YOU FOR A MINUTE?
HONEY
'TIS A *HEAVY HEART* I HAVE, LASSIE!
I MAY HAVE LOST ME BEST FREELANCE DETECTIVE... *AND* A *FRIEND*, BEGORRAH!
BUT MICKEY'S *NOT MAD* AT-
TUT-TUT, HORACE.
MICKEY'S *FINE*. JUST NOT ABLE TO *SPEAK* FOR A WHILE!
MUNCH-O
CHEEP!
PEEP!
FEEP!
SCREECH
MICKEY MO
HYUCK! LOOK WHAT *I* GOT, FELLERS! ALL THUH MOUSETON *SOUVENIR SHOPS* ARE SELLIN' 'EM SINCE THUH BLOT'S CAPTURE!

SO MICK DOESN'T WANT THE CHIEF TO FEEL *RESPONSIBLE* FOR HIS CONDITION?

HE'S *NOT!* WHEN THE BLOT RESTORED MICKEY'S HEARING, A *SIDE EFFECT* WAS TEMPORARY *VOICE* LOSS!

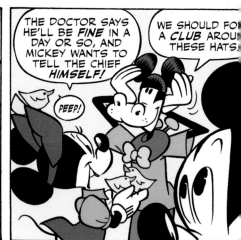

THE DOCTOR SAYS HE'LL BE *FINE* IN A DAY OR SO, AND MICKEY WANTS TO TELL THE CHIEF *HIMSELF!*

PEEP!

WE SHOULD FO A *CLUB* AROU THESE HATS.

OR HOW ABOUT THROWING A *PARTY?* WE'LL BE HAVING ONE ONCE HE'S WELL!

FEEP!

CHEEP!

PEEP!

THE BOYS HAVEN' ASKED HOW MINNI *KNOWS* ALL THIS WHEN I *CAN'T TALK*

PEEP!

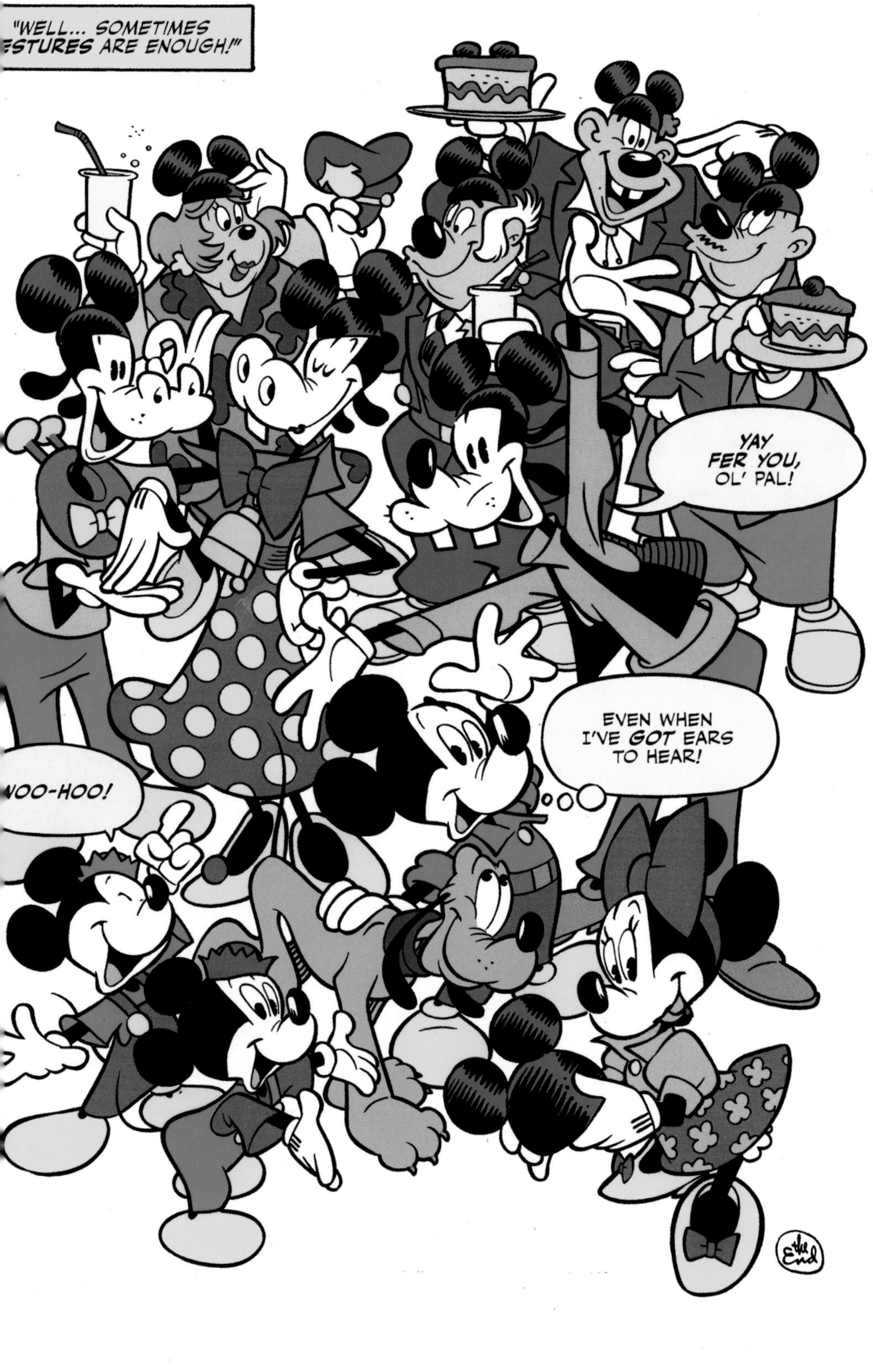
"WELL... SOMETIMES
ESTURES ARE ENOUGH!"
YAY
FER YOU,
OL' PAL!
EVEN WHEN
I'VE GOT EARS
TO HEAR!
WOO-HOO!
the End

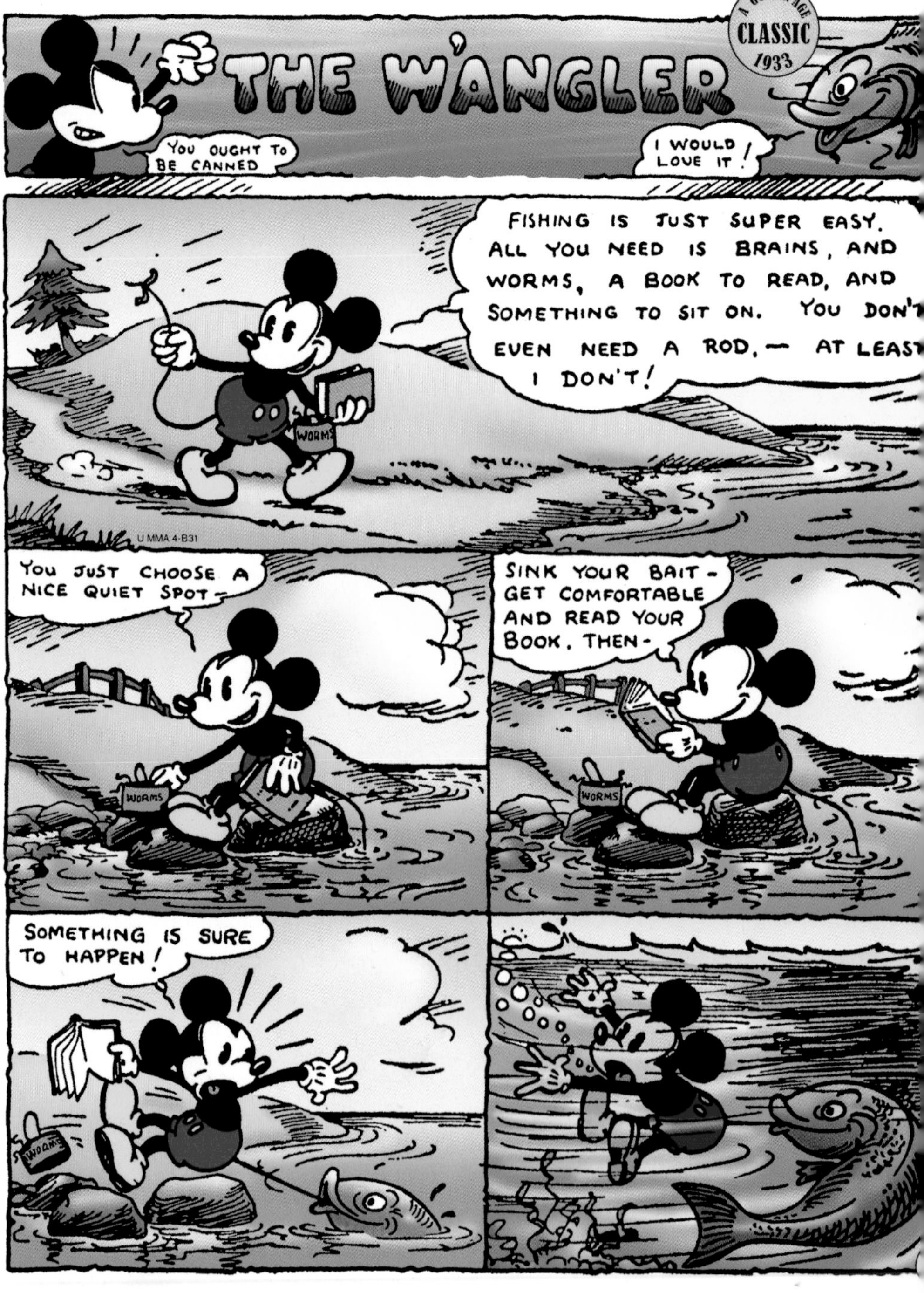
THE W'ANGLER
A GOLDEN AGE CLASSIC 1933
YOU OUGHT TO BE CANNED
I WOULD LOVE IT!
FISHING IS JUST SUPER EASY. ALL YOU NEED IS BRAINS, AND WORMS, A BOOK TO READ, AND SOMETHING TO SIT ON. YOU DON'T EVEN NEED A ROD, — AT LEAST I DON'T!
WORMS
U MMA 4-B31
YOU JUST CHOOSE A NICE QUIET SPOT —
WORMS
SINK YOUR BAIT — GET COMFORTABLE AND READ YOUR BOOK. THEN —
WORMS
SOMETHING IS SURE TO HAPPEN!
WORMS

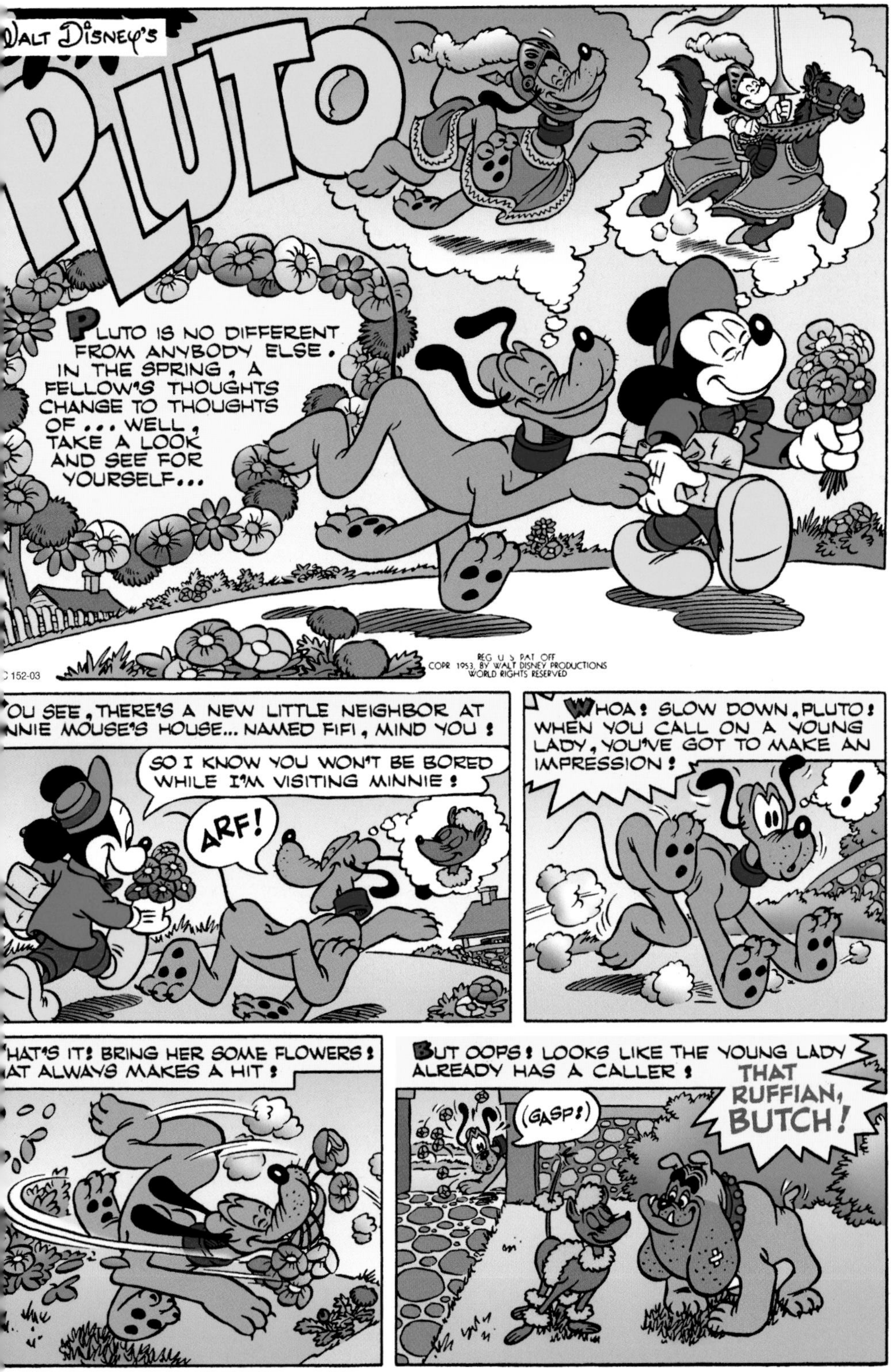

WALT DISNEY'S
PLUTO
PLUTO IS NO DIFFERENT FROM ANYBODY ELSE. IN THE SPRING, A FELLOW'S THOUGHTS CHANGE TO THOUGHTS OF... WELL, TAKE A LOOK AND SEE FOR YOURSELF...
C 152-03
REG. U. S. PAT. OFF. COPR. 1953, BY WALT DISNEY PRODUCTIONS WORLD RIGHTS RESERVED
OU SEE, THERE'S A NEW LITTLE NEIGHBOR AT NNIE MOUSE'S HOUSE... NAMED FIFI, MIND YOU!
SO I KNOW YOU WON'T BE BORED WHILE I'M VISITING MINNIE!
ARF!
WHOA! SLOW DOWN, PLUTO! WHEN YOU CALL ON A YOUNG LADY, YOU'VE GOT TO MAKE AN IMPRESSION!
!
HAT'S IT! BRING HER SOME FLOWERS! AT ALWAYS MAKES A HIT!
BUT OOPS! LOOKS LIKE THE YOUNG LADY ALREADY HAS A CALLER!
THAT RUFFIAN, BUTCH!
(GASP!)

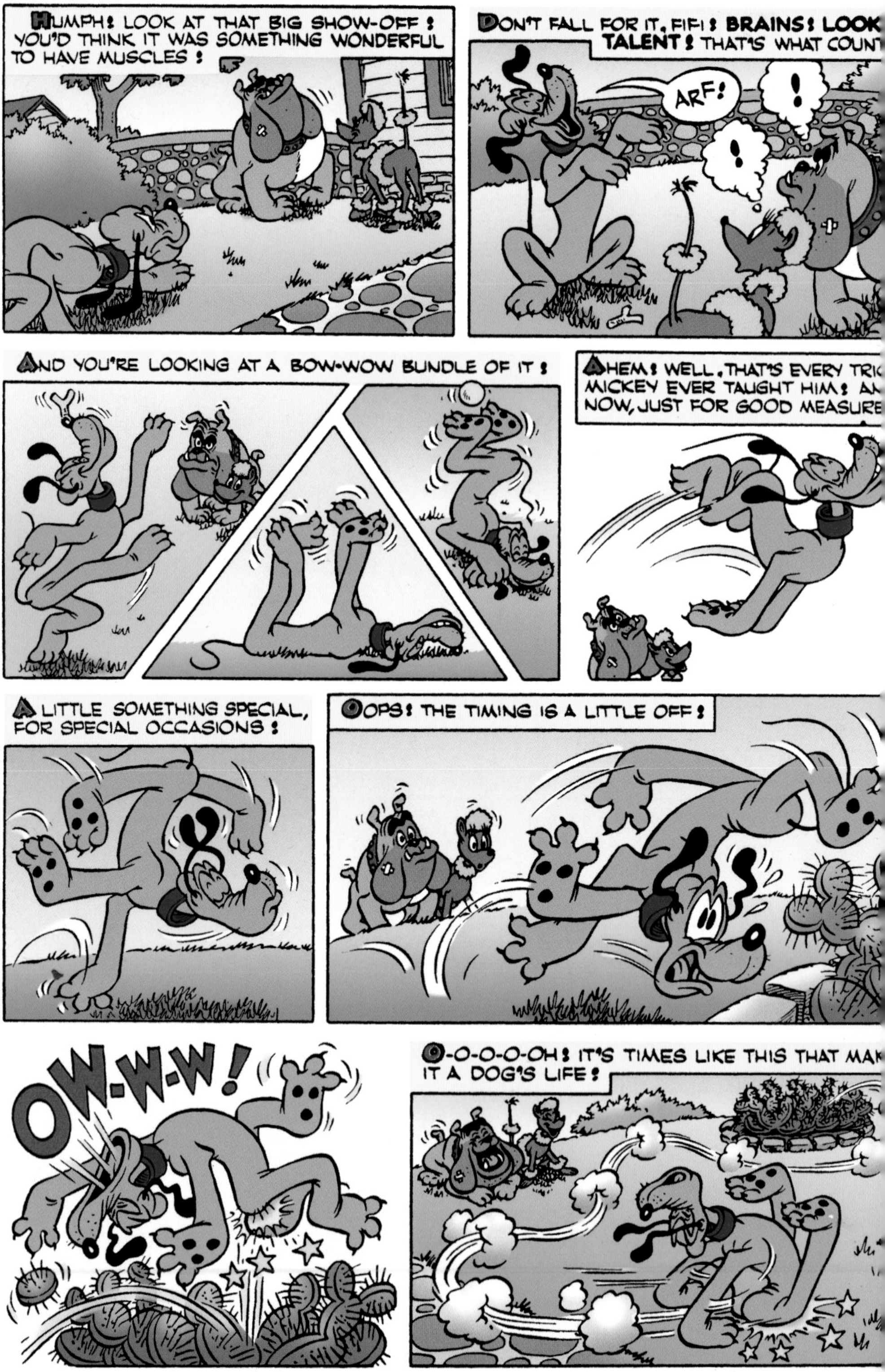

HUMPH! LOOK AT THAT BIG SHOW-OFF! YOU'D THINK IT WAS SOMETHING WONDERFUL TO HAVE MUSCLES!
DON'T FALL FOR IT, FIFI! BRAINS! LOOK
TALENT! THAT'S WHAT COUNT
ARF!
!
!
AND YOU'RE LOOKING AT A BOW-WOW BUNDLE OF IT!
AHEM! WELL, THAT'S EVERY TRI
MICKEY EVER TAUGHT HIM! A
NOW, JUST FOR GOOD MEASURE
A LITTLE SOMETHING SPECIAL, FOR SPECIAL OCCASIONS!
OOPS! THE TIMING IS A LITTLE OFF!
OW-W-W!
O-O-O-O-OH! IT'S TIMES LIKE THIS THAT MAK
IT A DOG'S LIFE!

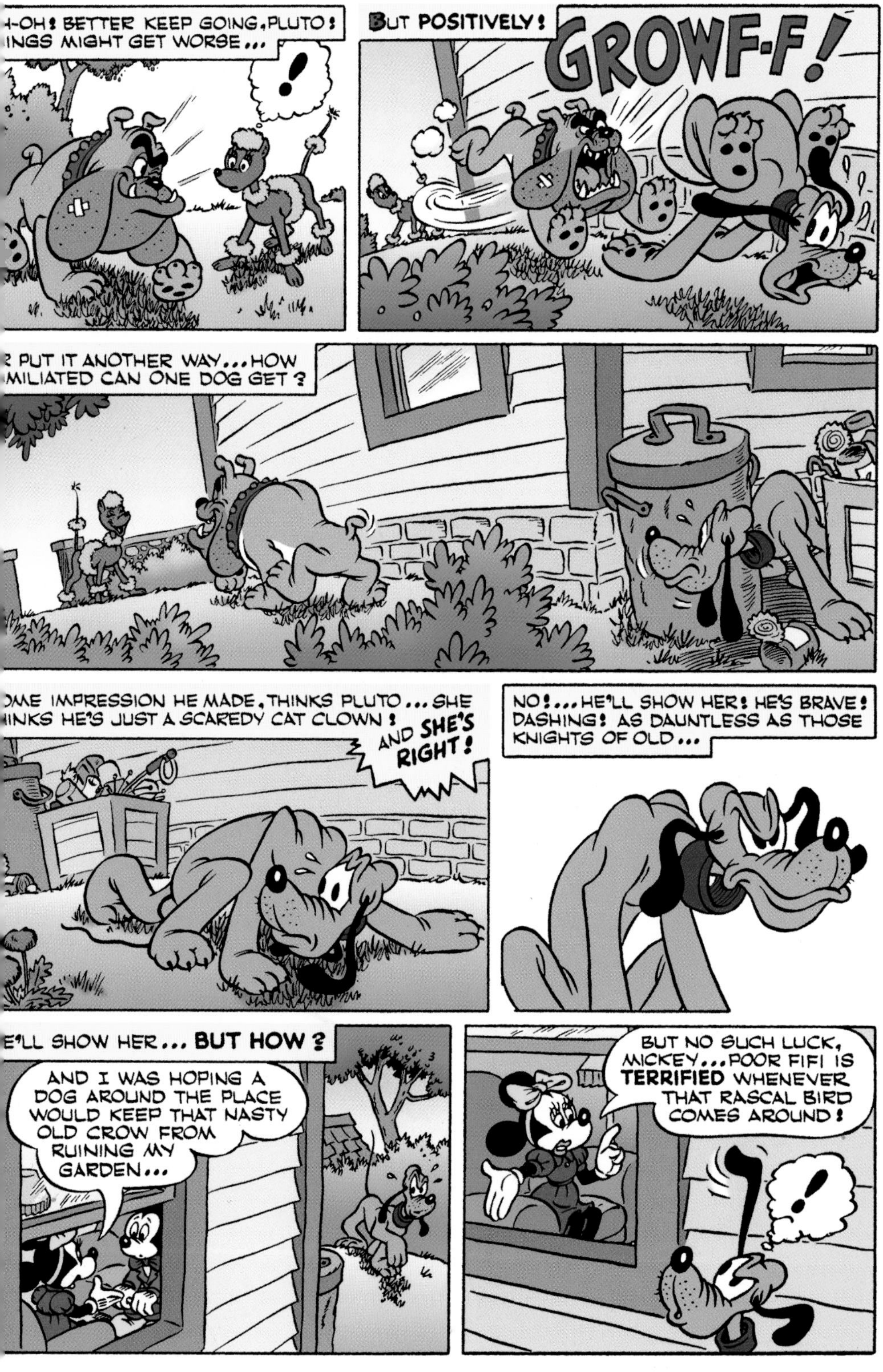
H-OH! BETTER KEEP GOING, PLUTO! INGS MIGHT GET WORSE...
!
BUT POSITIVELY!
GROWF-F!
R PUT IT ANOTHER WAY... HOW MILIATED CAN ONE DOG GET?
OME IMPRESSION HE MADE, THINKS PLUTO... SHE HINKS HE'S JUST A SCAREDY CAT CLOWN!
AND SHE'S RIGHT!
NO!... HE'LL SHOW HER! HE'S BRAVE! DASHING! AS DAUNTLESS AS THOSE KNIGHTS OF OLD...
E'LL SHOW HER... BUT HOW?
AND I WAS HOPING A DOG AROUND THE PLACE WOULD KEEP THAT NASTY OLD CROW FROM RUINING MY GARDEN...
BUT NO SUCH LUCK, MICKEY... POOR FIFI IS TERRIFIED WHENEVER THAT RASCAL BIRD COMES AROUND!
!

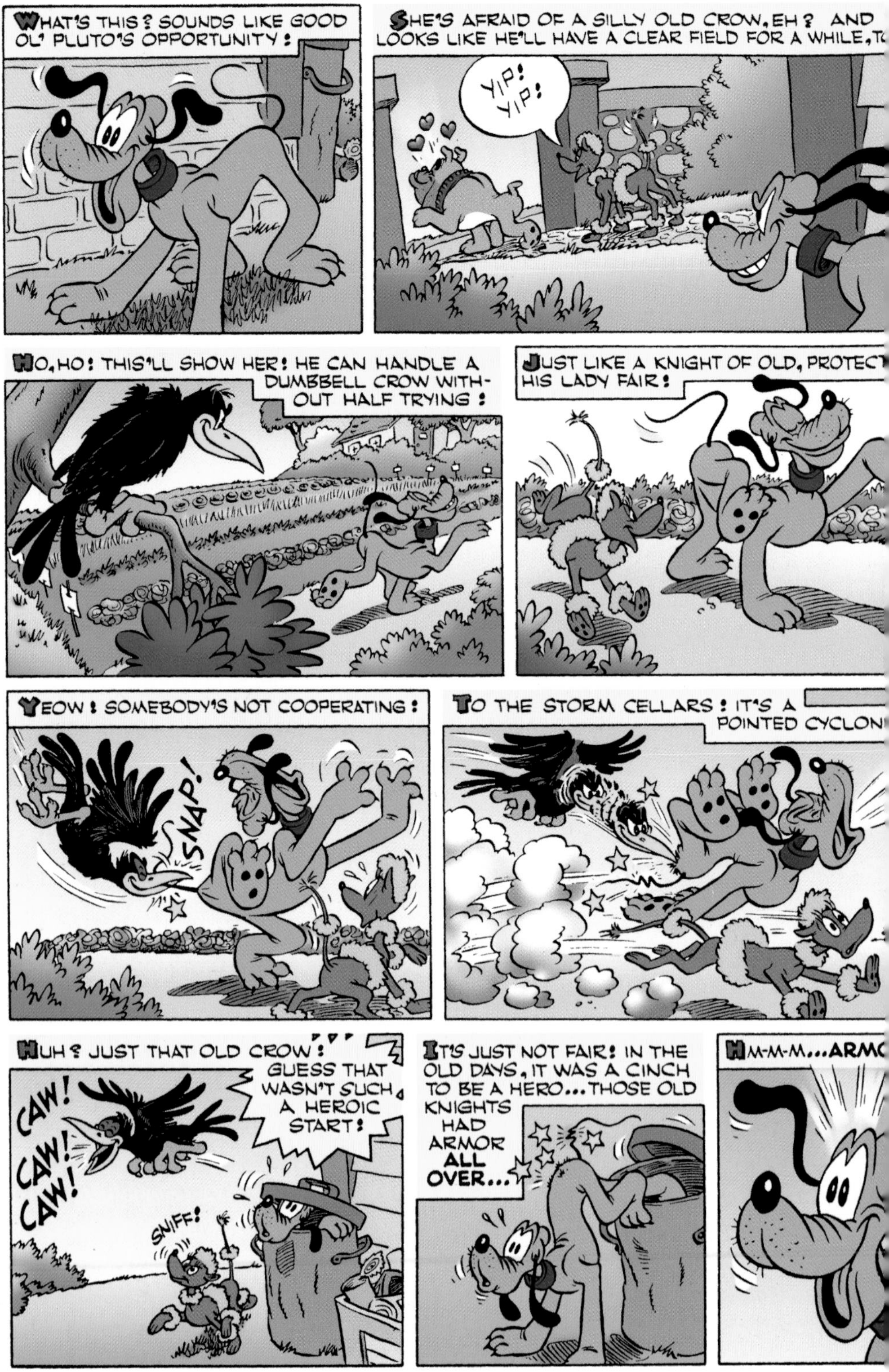

WHAT'S THIS? SOUNDS LIKE GOOD OL' PLUTO'S OPPORTUNITY!
SHE'S AFRAID OF A SILLY OLD CROW, EH? AND LOOKS LIKE HE'LL HAVE A CLEAR FIELD FOR A WHILE, T
YIP! YIP!
HO, HO! THIS'LL SHOW HER! HE CAN HANDLE A DUMBBELL CROW WITH-OUT HALF TRYING!
JUST LIKE A KNIGHT OF OLD, PROTECT HIS LADY FAIR!
YEOW! SOMEBODY'S NOT COOPERATING!
SNAP!
TO THE STORM CELLARS! IT'S A POINTED CYCLON
HUH? JUST THAT OLD CROW! GUESS THAT WASN'T SUCH A HEROIC START!
CAW! CAW! CAW!
SNIFF!
IT'S JUST NOT FAIR! IN THE OLD DAYS, IT WAS A CINCH TO BE A HERO... THOSE OLD KNIGHTS HAD ARMOR ALL OVER...
HM-M-M...ARMO

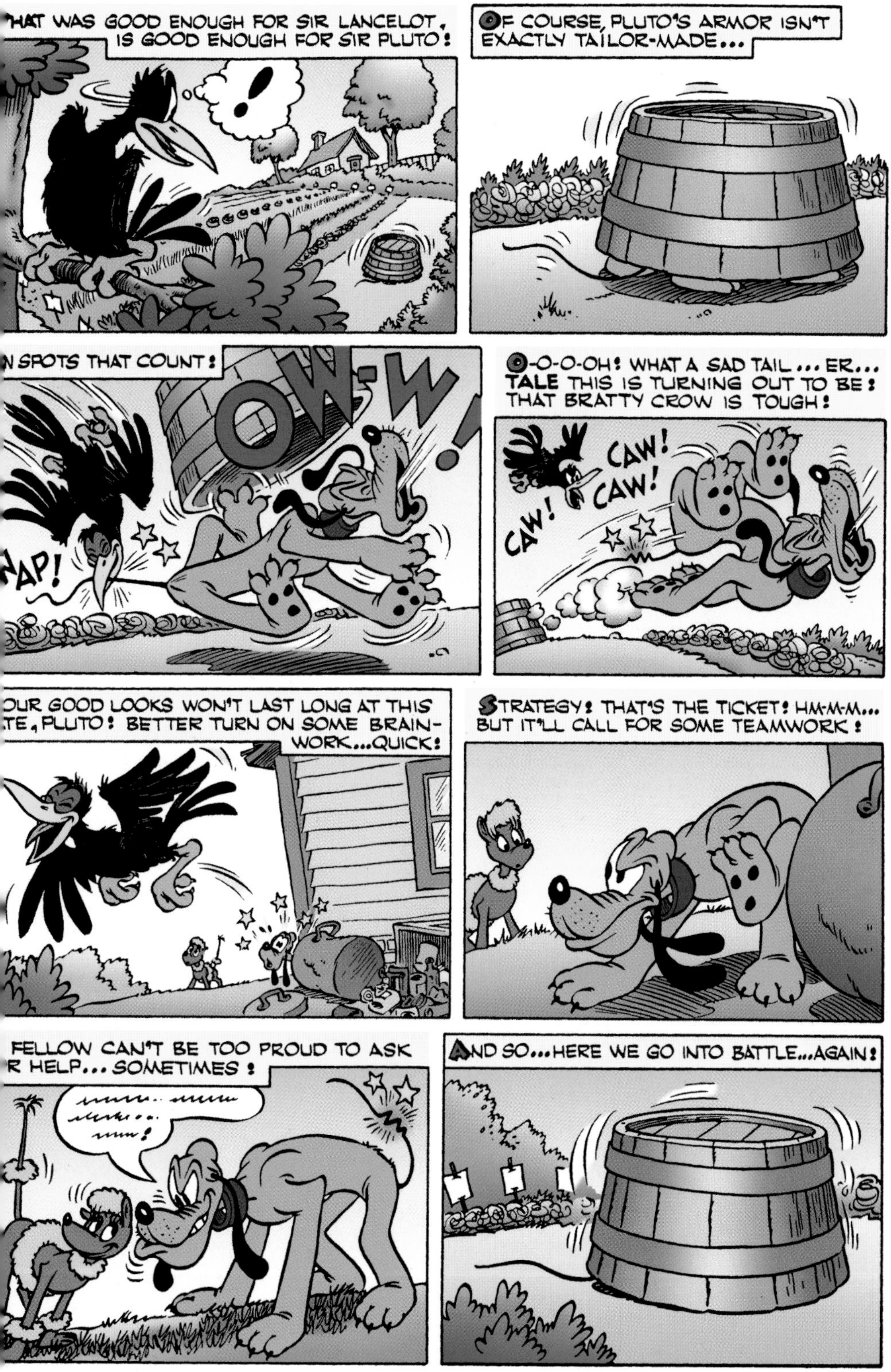
HAT WAS GOOD ENOUGH FOR SIR LANCELOT, IS GOOD ENOUGH FOR SIR PLUTO!
!
OF COURSE, PLUTO'S ARMOR ISN'T EXACTLY TAILOR-MADE...
N SPOTS THAT COUNT!
OW-W!
AP!
O-O-O-OH! WHAT A SAD TAIL... ER... TALE THIS IS TURNING OUT TO BE! THAT BRATTY CROW IS TOUGH!
CAW! CAW! CAW!
OUR GOOD LOOKS WON'T LAST LONG AT THIS TE, PLUTO! BETTER TURN ON SOME BRAIN-WORK...QUICK!
STRATEGY! THAT'S THE TICKET! HM-M-M... BUT IT'LL CALL FOR SOME TEAMWORK!
FELLOW CAN'T BE TOO PROUD TO ASK R HELP... SOMETIMES!
AND SO...HERE WE GO INTO BATTLE...AGAIN!

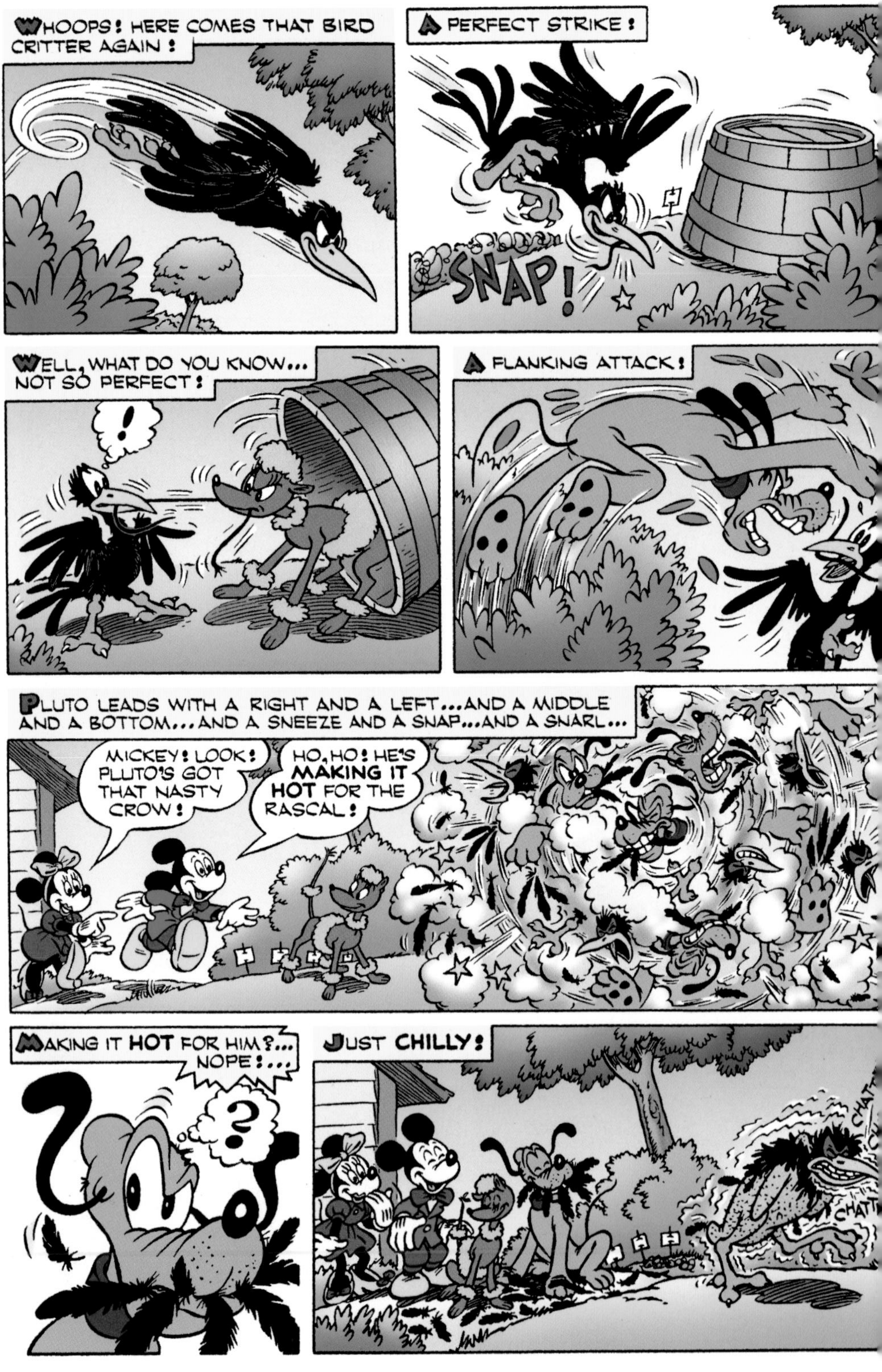

WHOOPS! HERE COMES THAT BIRD CRITTER AGAIN!
A PERFECT STRIKE!
SNAP!
WELL, WHAT DO YOU KNOW... NOT SO PERFECT!
!
A FLANKING ATTACK!
PLUTO LEADS WITH A RIGHT AND A LEFT...AND A MIDDLE AND A BOTTOM...AND A SNEEZE AND A SNAP...AND A SNARL...
MICKEY! LOOK! PLUTO'S GOT THAT NASTY CROW!
HO, HO! HE'S MAKING IT HOT FOR THE RASCAL!
MAKING IT HOT FOR HIM?... NOPE!...
?
JUST CHILLY!

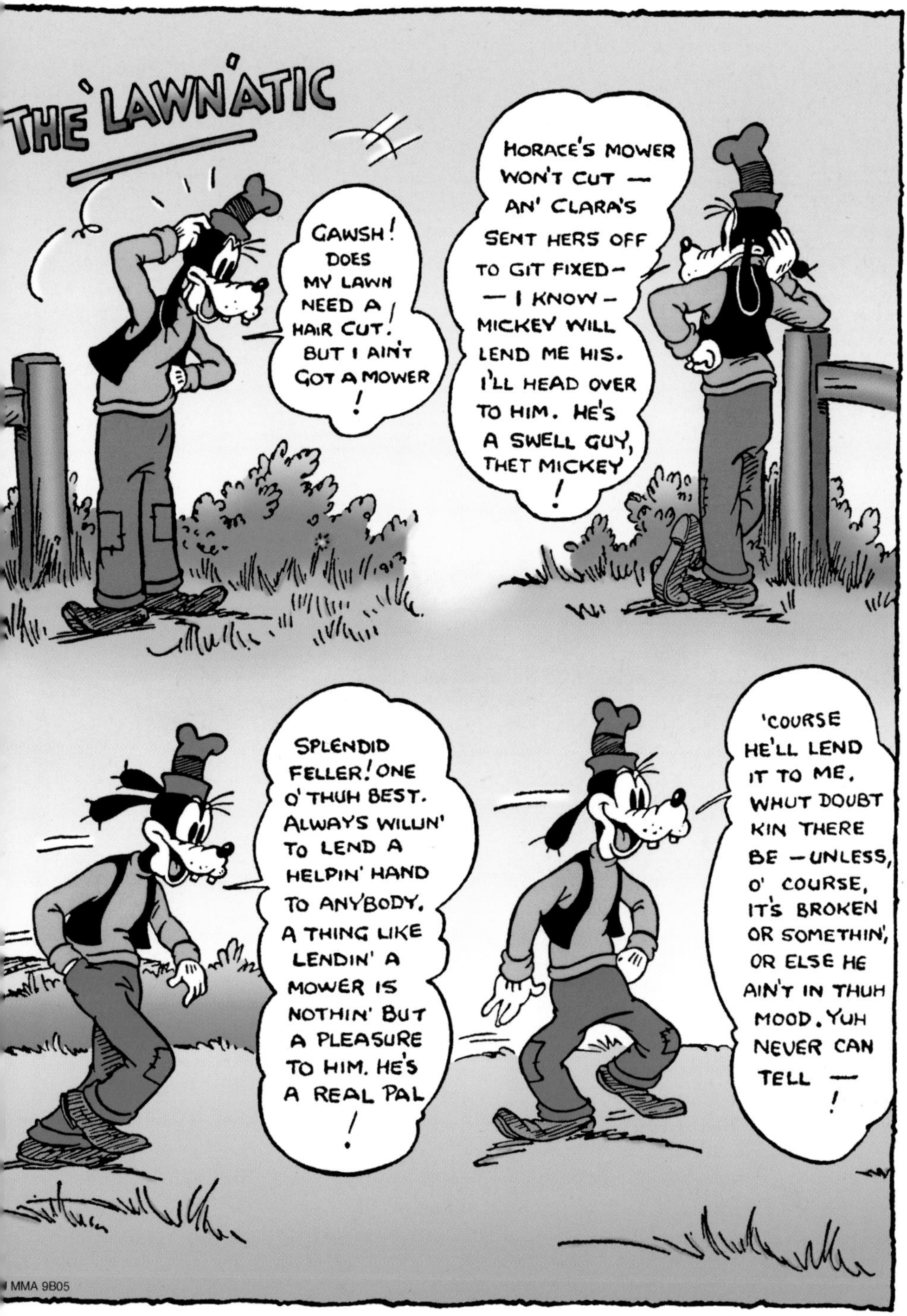
THE LAWNATIC
GAWSH! DOES MY LAWN NEED A HAIR CUT! BUT I AIN'T GOT A MOWER!
HORACE'S MOWER WON'T CUT — AN' CLARA'S SENT HERS OFF TO GIT FIXED— — I KNOW — MICKEY WILL LEND ME HIS. I'LL HEAD OVER TO HIM. HE'S A SWELL GUY, THET MICKEY!
SPLENDID FELLER! ONE O' THUH BEST. ALWAYS WILLIN' TO LEND A HELPIN' HAND TO ANYBODY. A THING LIKE LENDIN' A MOWER IS NOTHIN' BUT A PLEASURE TO HIM. HE'S A REAL PAL!
'COURSE HE'LL LEND IT TO ME. WHUT DOUBT KIN THERE BE — UNLESS, O' COURSE, IT'S BROKEN OR SOMETHIN', OR ELSE HE AIN'T IN THUH MOOD. YUH NEVER CAN TELL —!
MMA 9B05

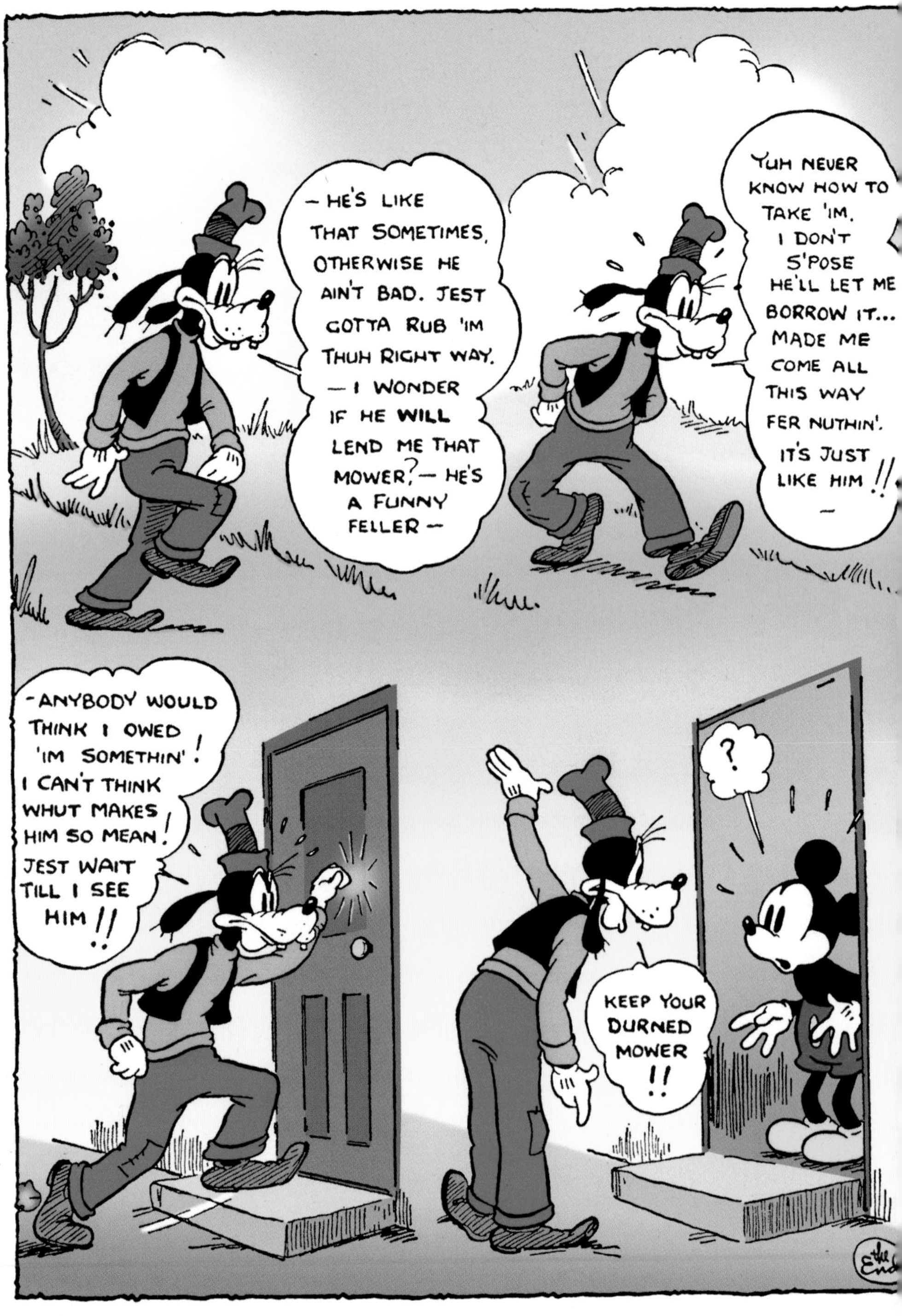

— HE'S LIKE THAT SOMETIMES, OTHERWISE HE AIN'T BAD. JEST GOTTA RUB 'IM THUH RIGHT WAY. — I WONDER IF HE WILL LEND ME THAT MOWER? — HE'S A FUNNY FELLER —
YUH NEVER KNOW HOW TO TAKE 'IM. I DON'T S'POSE HE'LL LET ME BORROW IT... MADE ME COME ALL THIS WAY FER NUTHIN'. IT'S JUST LIKE HIM !! —
- ANYBODY WOULD THINK I OWED 'IM SOMETHIN' ! I CAN'T THINK WHUT MAKES HIM SO MEAN ! JEST WAIT TILL I SEE HIM !!
?
KEEP YOUR DURNED MOWER !!
The End

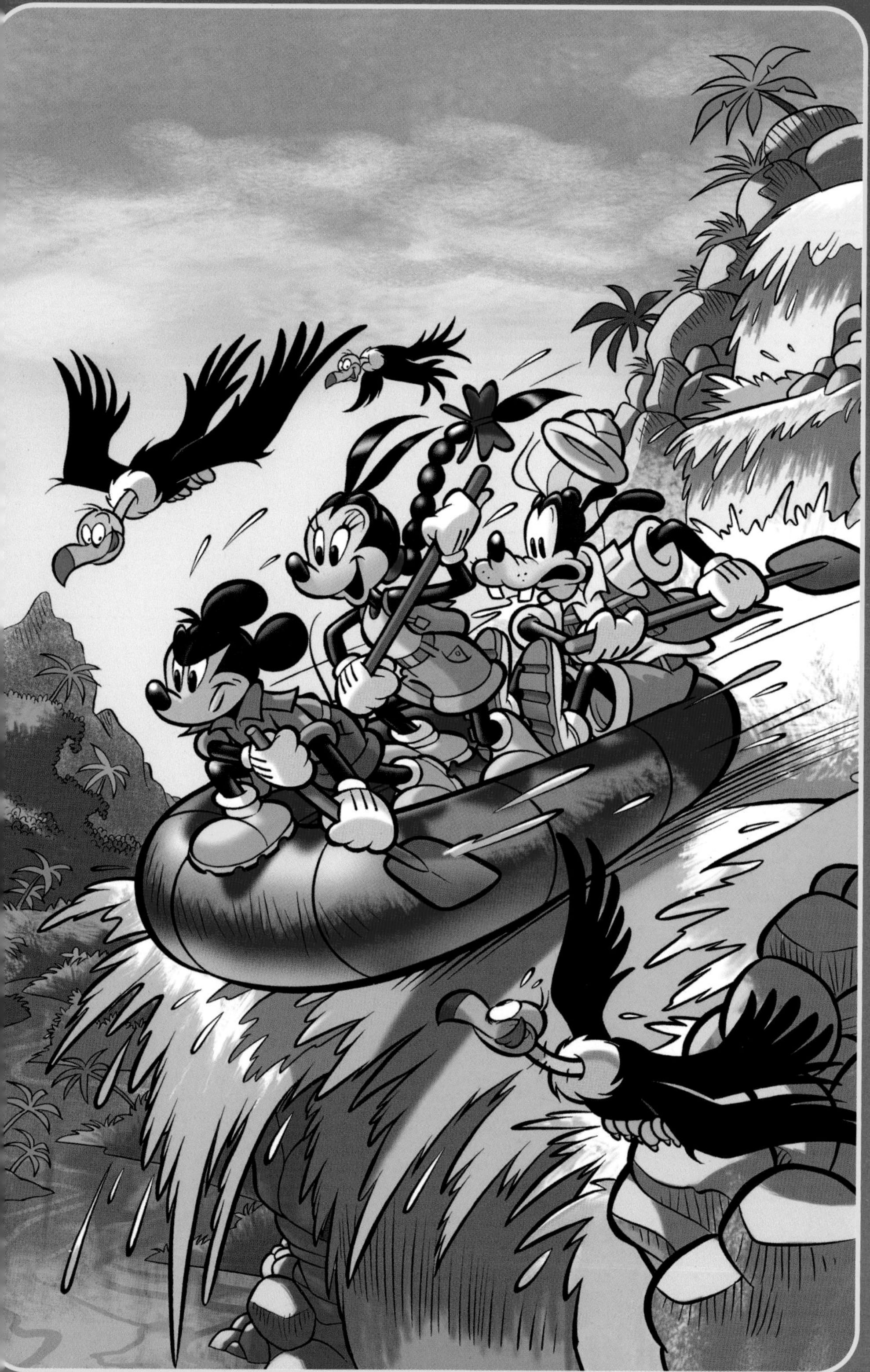

Art by Andrea "Casty" Castellan

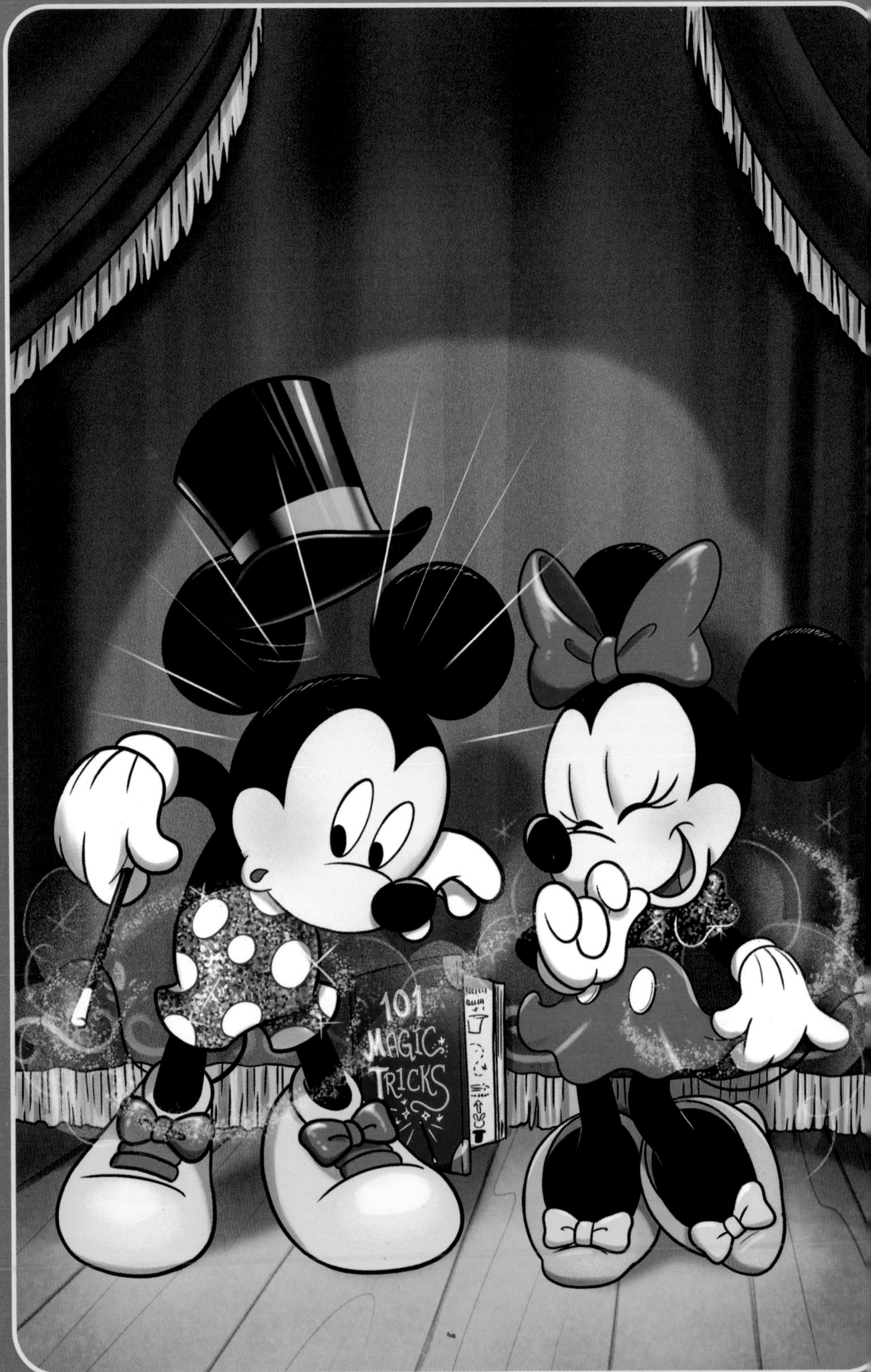
101
MAGIC
TRICKS

Art by Amy Mebberson

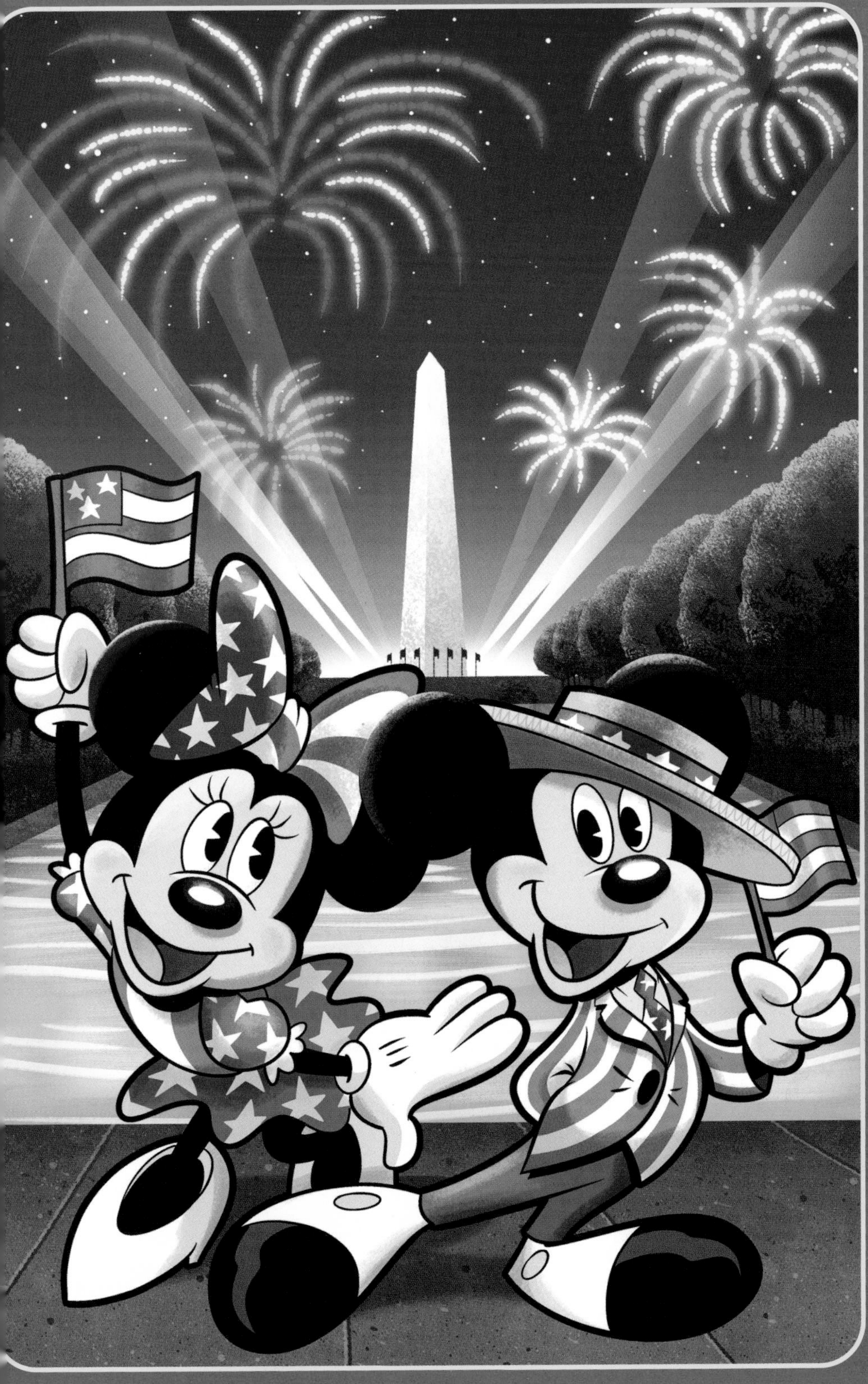

Art by Derek Charm

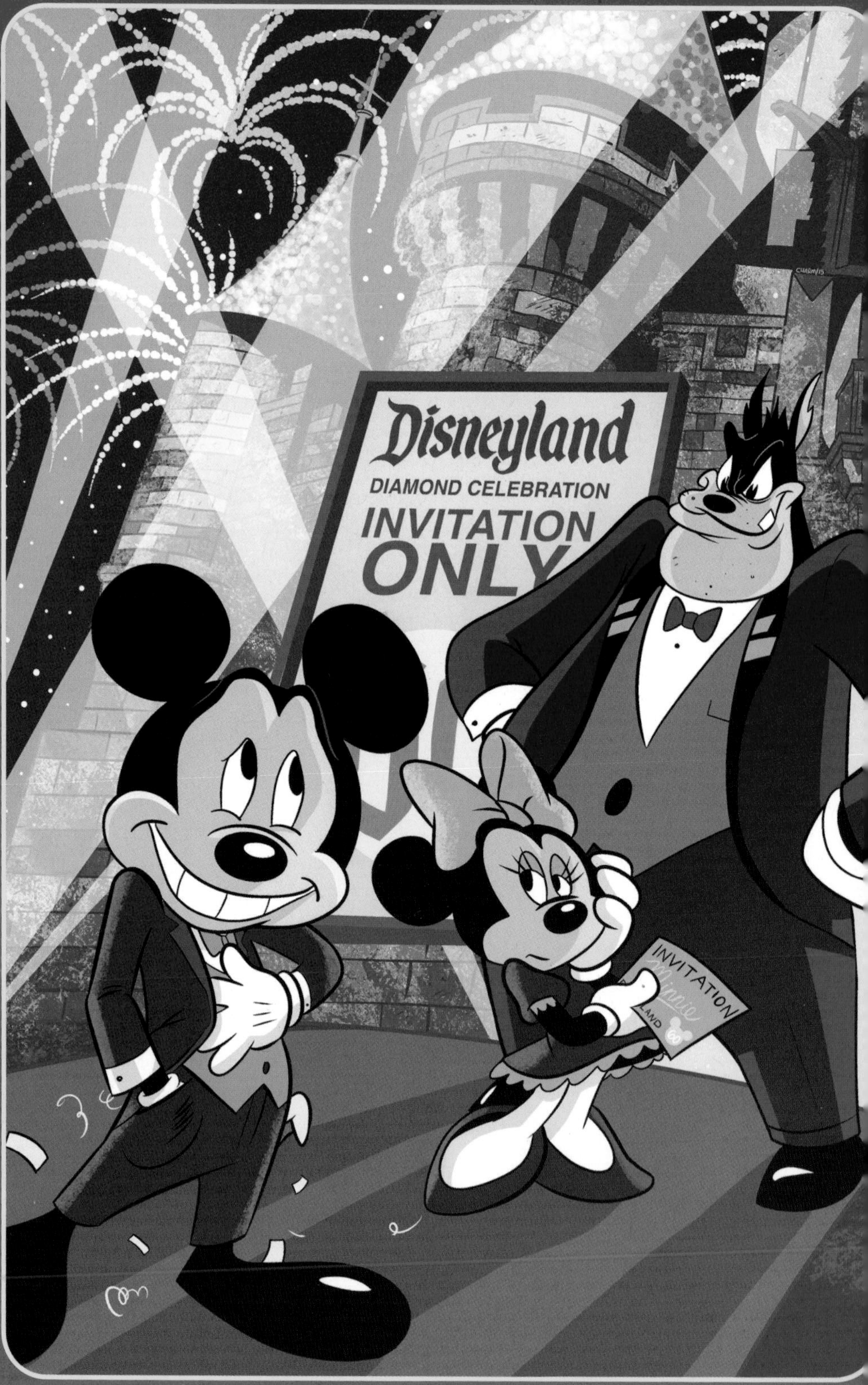
Disneyland
DIAMOND CELEBRATION
INVITATION
ONLY
INVITATION

Art by Derek Charm

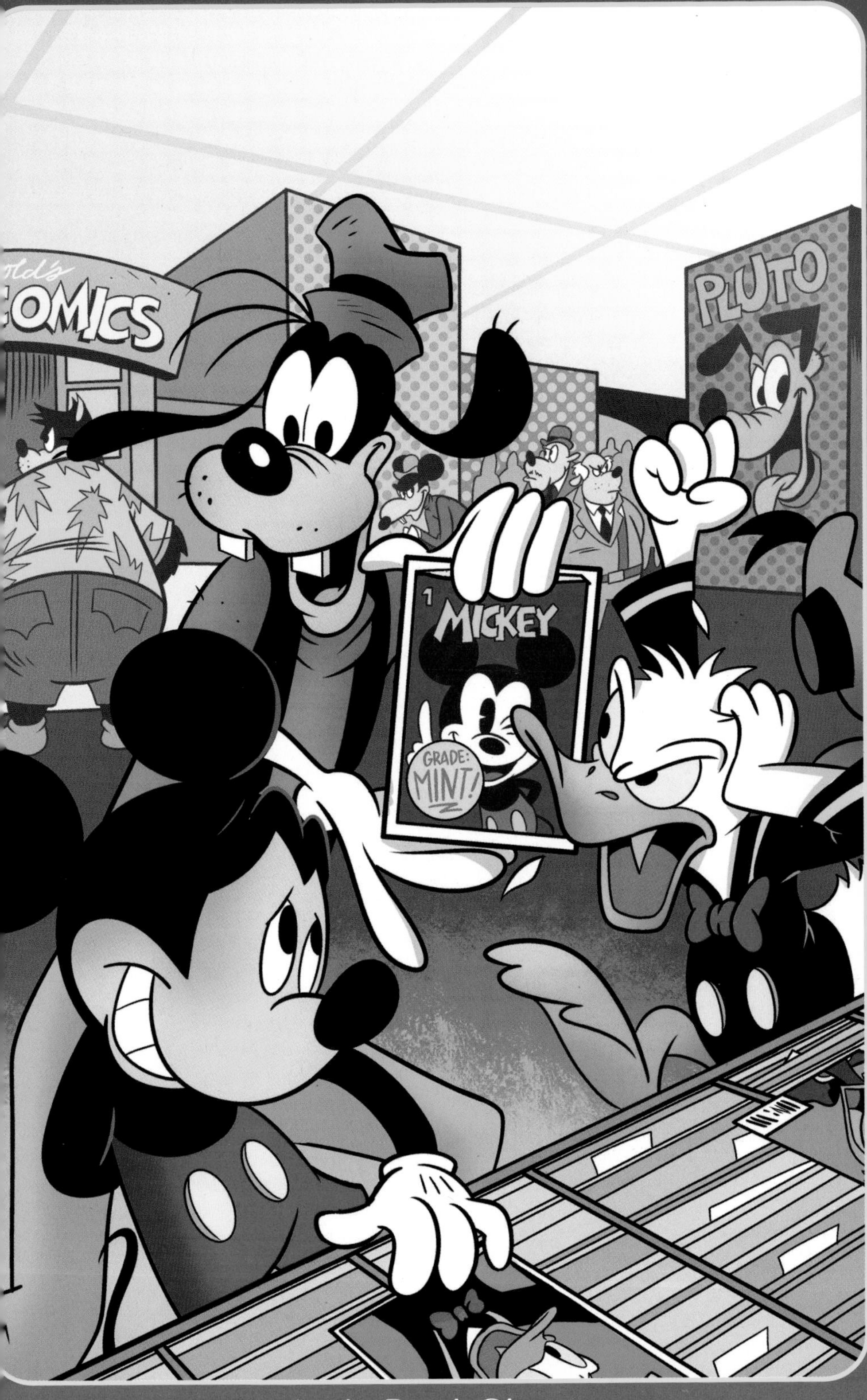
COMICS
PLUTO
1
MICKEY
GRADE:
MINT!

Art by Derek Charm

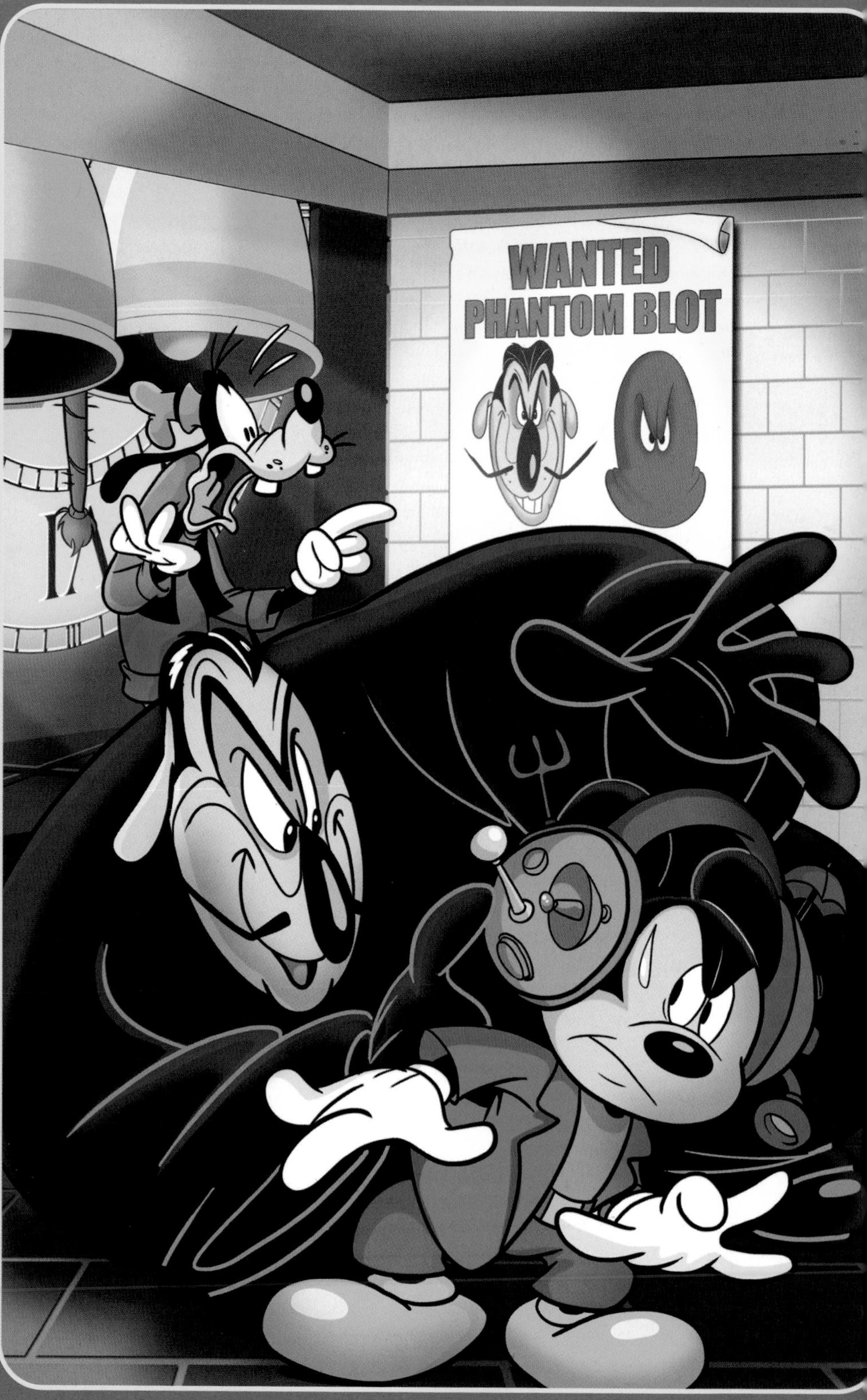
WANTED
PHANTOM BLOT

Art by Dave Alvarez

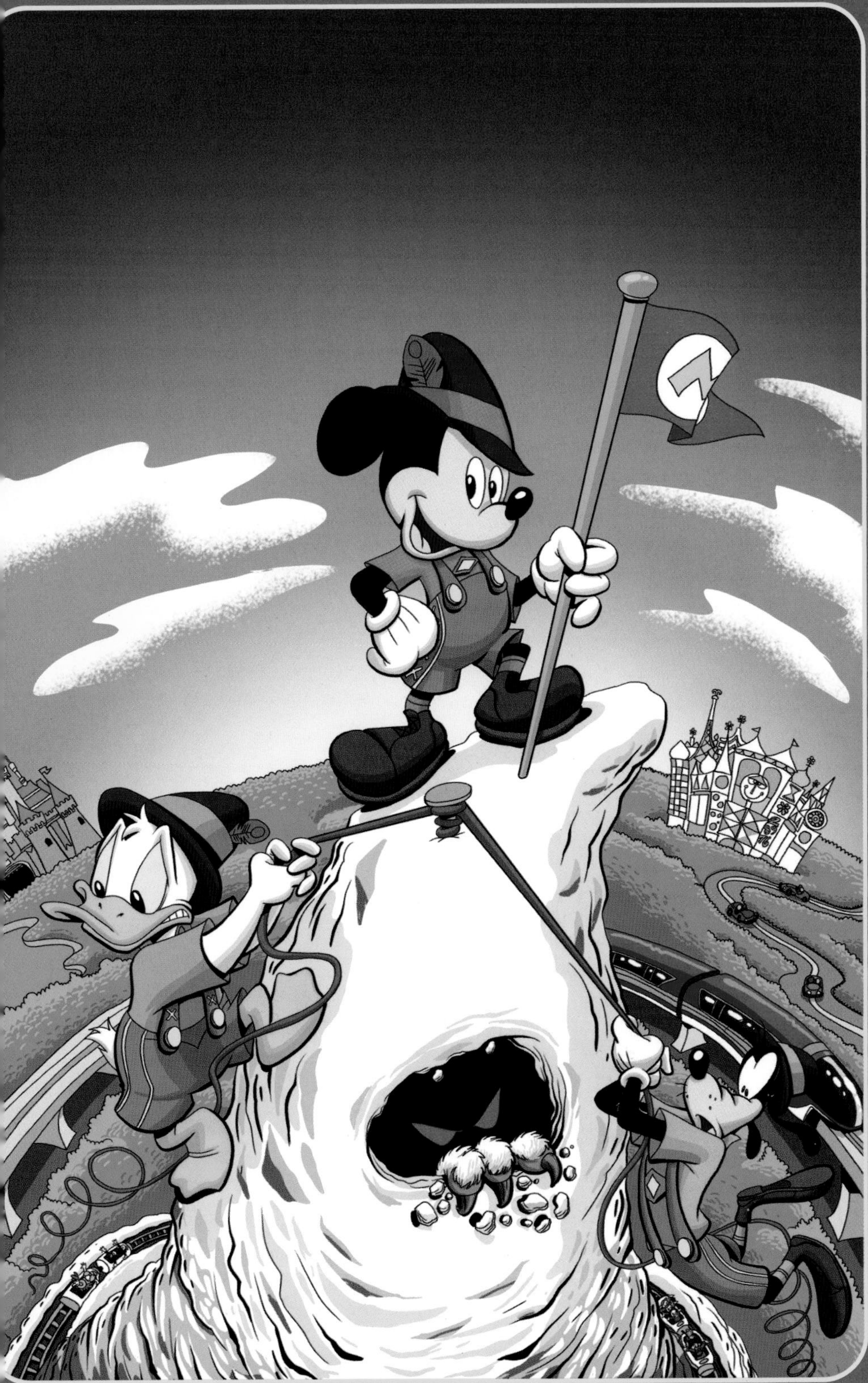

Art by James Silvani

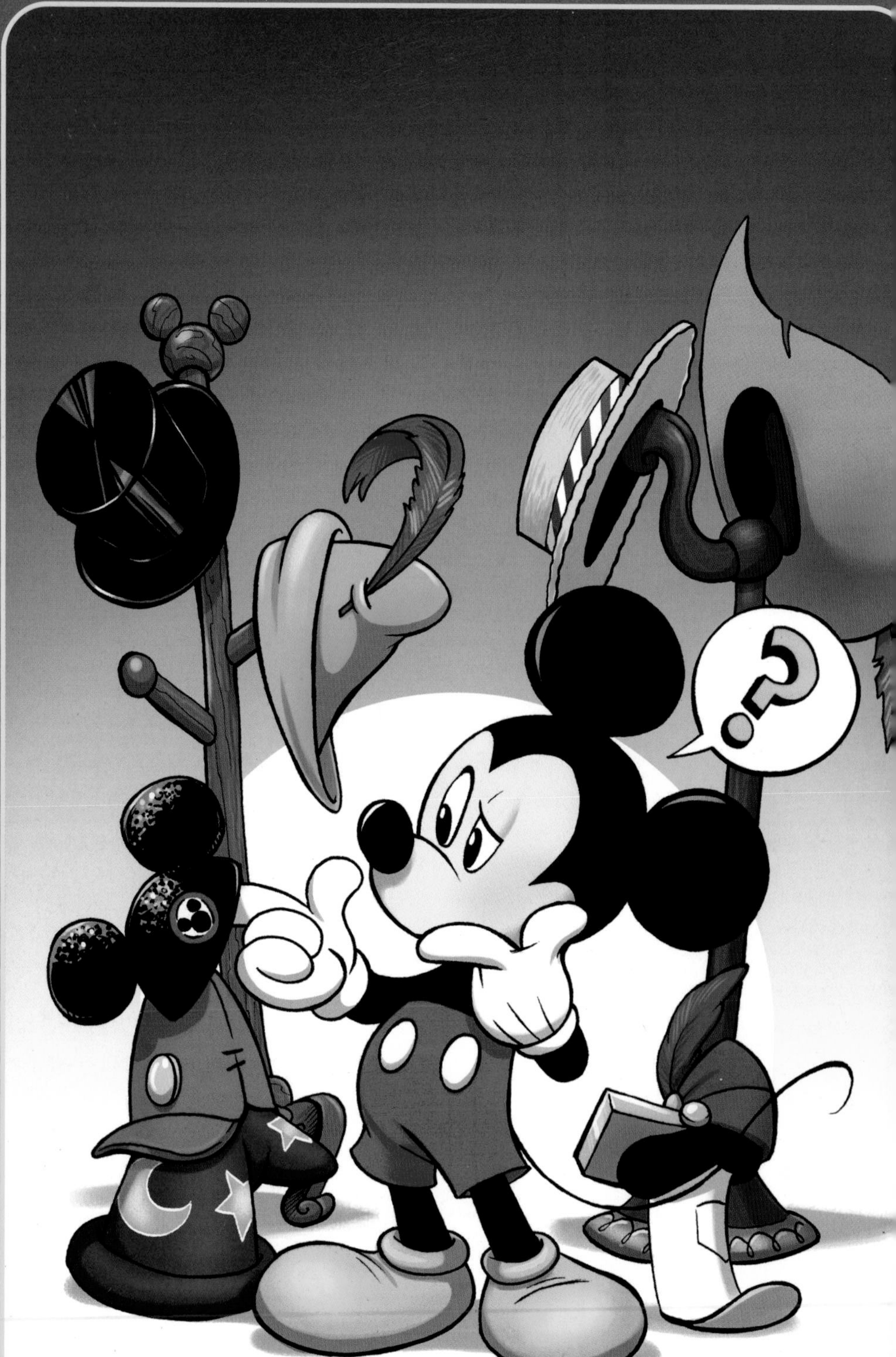
?

Art by Amy Mebberson

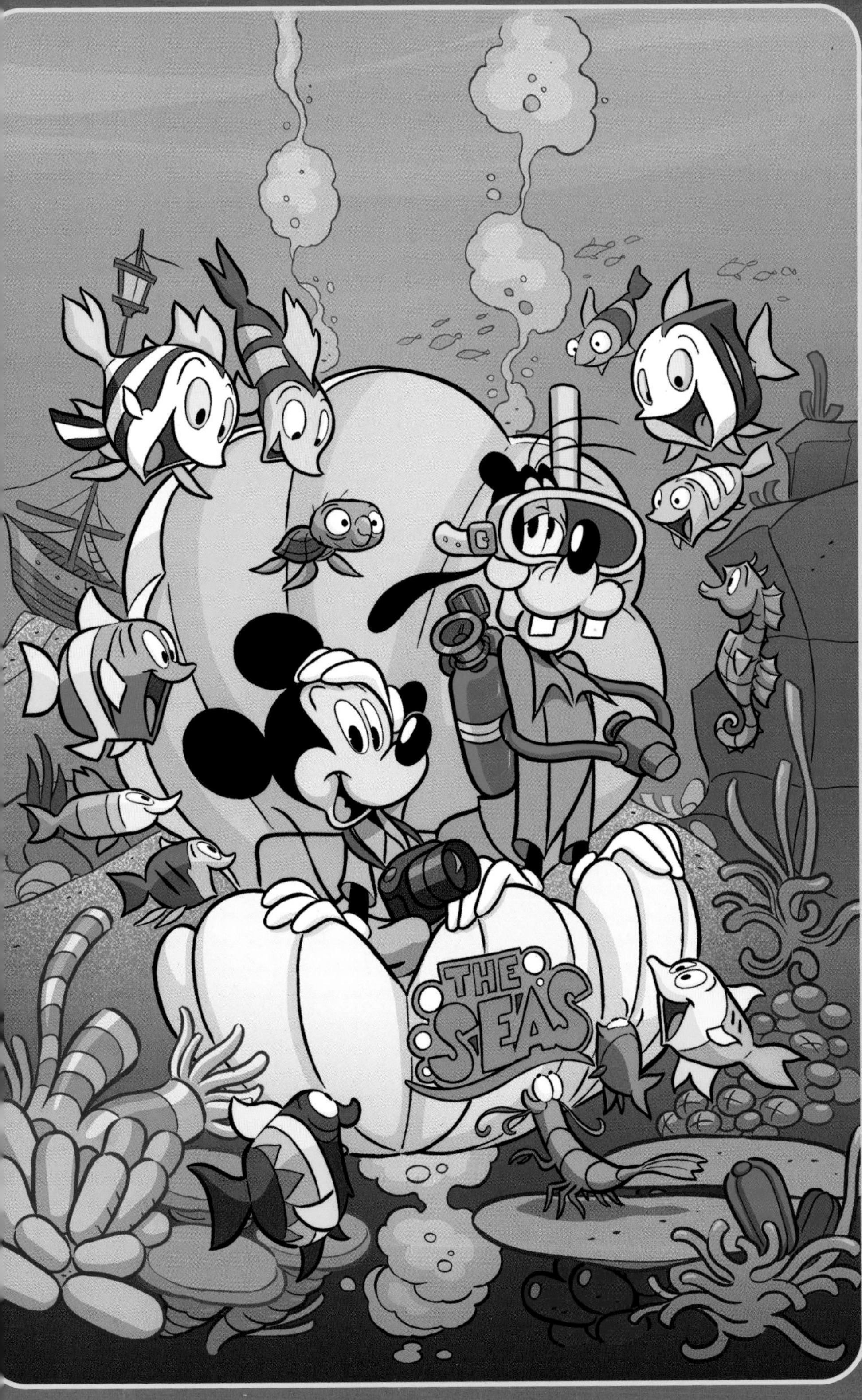
THE SEAS

Art by Andrea Freccero

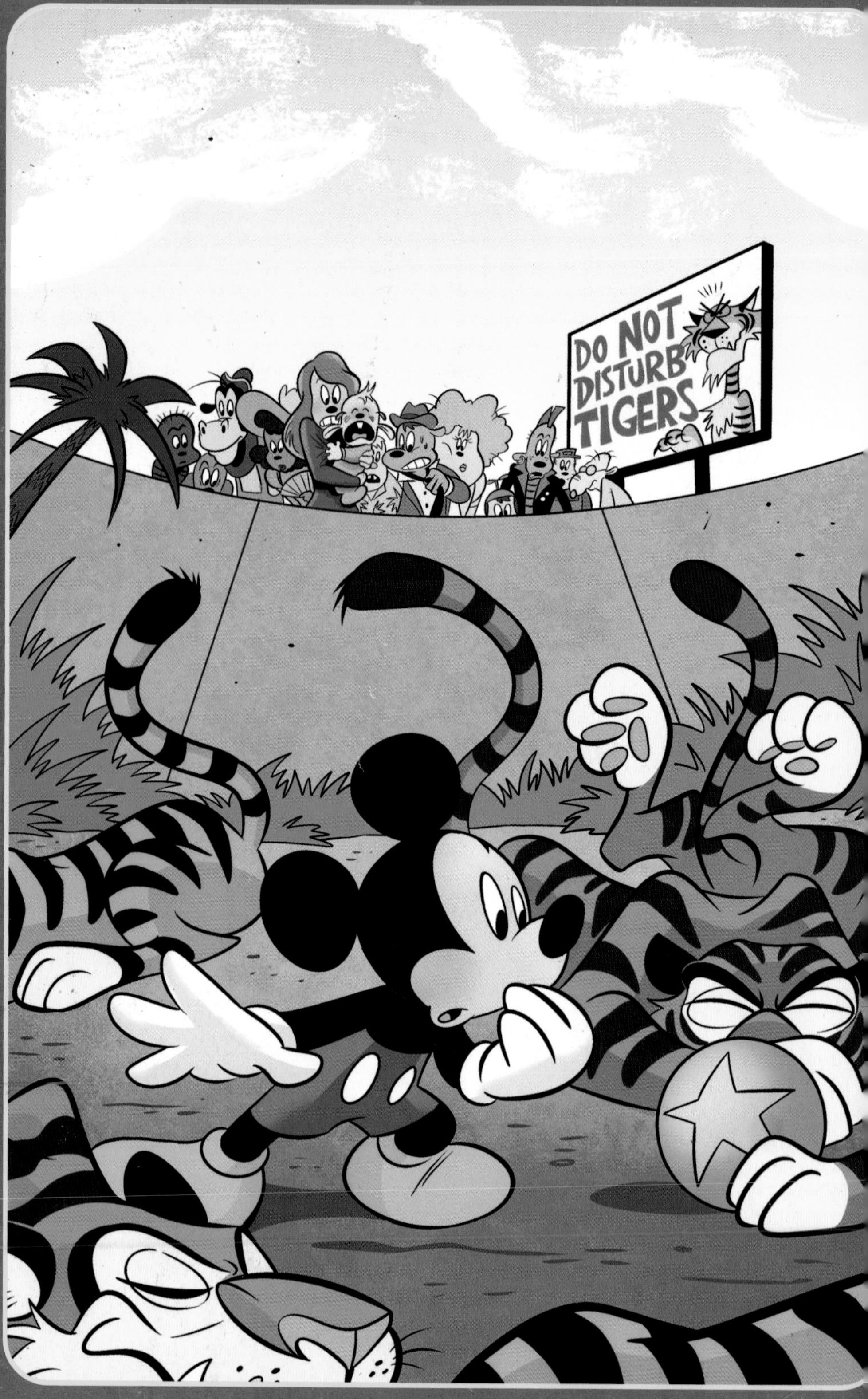
DO NOT
DISTURB
TIGERS
Art by Derek Charm